DEAD MERCENARY'S TRAIL

Jake Armitage Thriller Book 2

Simon W Clark

SWC Press

Dead Mercenary's Trail

Copyright © Simon W Clark 2023

All rights reserved

PAPERBACK ISBN: 978-0-6455536-3-5

E-PUB ISBN: 978-0-6455536-2-8

For Annalise,
despite all odds made the impossible a reality.

DEAD MERCENARY'S TRAIL

Chapter 1

THE MAN SHIELDED his eyes as the sun receded beyond the water's edge. To the west, Manila dazzled with silvers and gray. He checked his watch. Six-twenty P.M. Perfect. A yacht bobbed gently to the east. He squinted at the ship's deck through binoculars. No movement.

A second, taller man appeared. "Have we made visual?"

Confirmed the vessel. Target is hidden from sight." The first man relinquished the binoculars and fastened his wetsuit zip. All black.

The taller man remained silent.

"We'll move out at nineteen-hundred hours. Twenty minutes swim to the target's vessel," said the smaller man. He had led the team on the last three missions since leaving the U.S. army in his wake, each successful outcome cementing the reputation of the two-man team. Capable and reliable: a partnership forged in Afghanistan.

The retracted sail ends danced in a gentle breeze. The men made their preparations in silence. Guns and ammunition checked and loaded. Get in and get out. One target. Straight kill. Swim back.

He took the salt air in his lungs. A seagull navigated the rail with ease as the leader watched. The target was a trained contractor. This would be the most difficult assignment yet. If they could pull this off, the next jobs would be increased pay: demand double or triple rates. His heart beat elevated slightly with adrenaline.

"This one will take some slick maneuvers. Tricky." The

taller man concentrated on his pack as if reading the leader's mind.

He nodded in agreement. "We'll flank the vessel. Stick to the plan. No room for error."

Beads of water splashed the hull as the second man slipped into the waves. The water darkened, light fading with his descent. Blue, cold nature in all directions. He activated the lights in his hood and followed to the right of his leader, avoiding the water churn.

The current flowed across the leader's torso. To conserve energy, he kicked in small motions. He estimated the journey at eighteen minutes. Fish dashed across his vision and the lieutenant swam close behind.

At ten minutes, the smaller man slowed and waved. The second swimmer caught up, pulling alongside his peer. They kicked gently toward the destination. He always felt so calm and insignificant in the sea. Nothing mattered, including mankind, at this magnitude. Specks of sand in a vast desert.

A white shape glinted at fifty meters. The strike point came into view. A yacht hull. The leader pointed to the stern. Paths split, converging at the vessel from either side. He waited one minute, the white surface smooth to gloved hands.

He visualized the task at hand. The mission completed in measured steps.

Chapter 2

THE GLOOMY TERRAIN expanded in his vision. Gray path ran to an iron bridge hung over a river. Jake's legs pounded the ground. A female voice cried his name. He spun as the landscape shimmered.

Shopfronts looked like Europe. St Petersburg. Prague. He couldn't pinpoint his location.

"Jake." Katerina said. The voice surrounded him like stereo.

"Help me!" she cried out, high-pitched and loud.

He reached for his SIG. Nothing in the shoulder holster. Checked his lower back. He twisted and gripped the familiar steel. He went to take aim.

A figure flashed from an opening ahead. The same voice filled his ears. Katerina. Heart pounding, he backhanded his brow. One hundred feet. His arm straightened. The cross hairs on his sights blurred. He could not concentrate or sight the target.

"You don't want to miss." The man pressed a gun to her head. "I'll kill her."

They moved in a macabre dance, stepping left and right. Each tried to get the drop on the other. Jake aimed. The two men moved like synchronized swimmers. Dance of death. He avoided Katerina's eyes. His palm went clammy. The weapon threatened to slip.

I can't hold it.

The man grinned. "Too late, Jake."

Her face contorted to a silent scream.

A thin yellow streak broke the drape gap. Jake Armitage bolted upright, arms braced and palms flat on damp sheets. Blood pumped his temples. Dreaming. The sweatshirt stuck to his chest. He shrugged off the garment and pulled on a fresh one. The floor was solid.

Comforting. His jeans lay on the chair. He plunged each leg in and tugged on socks and shoes.

The laptop blinked on his desk. A pulsing red light caught his eye. The silent sensor alarm. Intruders. He analyzed the screen. Two hits on the deck rails. One on the stern, the other on the bow.

You were never lonely for long on the South China Sea.

To reduce visibility in the window, he dropped low and scurried to the drawer. He felt around and found the SIG Sauer. The magazine was loaded. He thumbed the safety.

Waited. Listened.

Pirates or a hit team?

Spine against the wall, he peered up the stairwell. The fourth step turned a sharp right-angle. Blind spot. He backed against the edge and put out a portable shaving mirror to check the view. The berth entry was closed. Moonlight shimmered behind the opaque glass.

Jake eased the door and extended into the main cabin. He strained to hear against the lapping water. Footfall light. Gentle rock. He crouched low, moved around the couches, and touched the tinted sliding doors. The intruders were close; his situation demanded perfect execution.

A shadow darkened the window. He eased the door latch. The outside figure stared at the glass. Jake waited in the eave. The door cracked. White fell over the boards. A weapon came first. He pulled the barrel down, caught the trigger finger and twisted. The butt of Jake's SIG cracked the intruder's forehead. A tall, bearded man with a slim build fell forward.

He swung the intruder's weapon, but the attacker managed to block the second blow.

Dazed but not down, the man in black partially recovered his stance. Impressive. He punched Jake's hand and his fingers loosened. The weapon clattered across the deck. They faced off in the center. A jab and elbow as each man countered blows and retaliated with equal speed.

4

The man reversed toward the south wall, sensing his defense faltering. Jake maintained the offense, driving his opponent to the corner. His attacker threw a high roundhouse kick, desperate to gain an advantage.

Jake dropped and threw a hard, low kick. His foot struck the calf sideways due to the proximity. Not ideal but did the trick. A snap filled the cabin. The intruder shuddered and fell to the good knee.

He lifted the SIG and shot the man in the chest, twice. The body collapsed.

A thud sounded from the upper deck. Jake stepped over the man and into the night air. He circled the perimeter, keeping out of sight. The first round ricocheted the rails.

"I'm over here," Jake said.

Sparks flew. The second intruder sprayed an outdoor lounge.

Jake sprinted inside, across the salon width, and hit the deck on his back. The momentum thrust him at the bow. Arms stretched, he hit fiberglass. The second intruder jumped to cover. Jake pumped the trigger. Bullets whizzed at the sky, passing harmlessly through the night.

Jake pushed to his feet. He hugged the wall, listening for footsteps. At the curve, a barrel pointed straight at his chest.

"Place the weapon on the deck slowly."

Jake squatted, his finger away from the trigger. The weapon thudded at his feet.

"Steer the ship northwest." The man gestured upward at the bridge.

Breathing deep, Jake's heartbeat gradually returned to normal speed. He gained his feet and climbed to the bridge. At the top, he trod across the short landing to the wheel. The turnkey sat in position. A throaty rumbling underfoot. The turbines fired to life. His captor outside a two-meter radius with the weapon trained at hip level.

"Stay on this path for three nautical miles."

The dark waters shimmered. Boat steady at fifteen knots, they charted a course parallel to the coastline. On his right, the silhouette of tree lines receded into the land. The mainland was far enough away to escape visual. Their destination had to be another vessel. His best guess was pirates. This no-go-zone worked for and against his survival tonight.

A beam lit up the shadows. Its blue focus trailed the ocean, resting on the hull. Jake squinted to compensate, riding at the outline.

"Slow to ten knots as we reach the ship."

Figures moved behind the light. The red-peeling iron flank indicated a large, aging dhow common to these parts. They flew under the radar as many poor fishermen still used them in the allowable zones.

He banked at the base. A voice yelled in another language. Tagalog. He knew it but could not understand. A rope ladder unraveled.

"Climb up to the boat."

Jake complied and avoided the obstacles. He emerged on the deck and waited. The intruder became impatient and thrust the gun at his spine. Jake climbed the rope steps. At the top, two pirates pointed weapons from a safe distance. A shorter Asian man with a moustache prodded him with the barrel. From the shadows, a younger pirate grinned, a semi-automatic in hand.

"Go down the stairs." The English was heavily accented with Tagalog.

He curved around the deck. A barrel of diesel fuel in the cabin. His arms dangled at his side, palms out to show there was no resistance. The assassin called out in Tagalog. A pirate swung a cable to attach to the yacht's stern. They planned to tow his boat and not let it go to waste. Engines fired as the iron beast came to life. He let them push and shove him without protest. If the pirates became more confident, they might relax, put down their guard slightly so he could find an edge.

An opening bent downward to semi-darkness. His mind raced on an exit strategy but the options were slim. A waft of fish drowned his senses. He stooped into the narrow passage, heading to the bowels of the vessel. A solid door with a glass pane in the center greeted them. Moisture on the walls and floor. The shorter one opened it and gestured.

"Your new home."

The other pirate laughed maniacally.

A metal seat positioned under a naked light. A disused storeroom that doubled for kidnap and interrogation. Hands shoved him at the chair. A fist to the solar plexus doubled him up as he sank to the seat. Hands bound from behind with a rope. An amateur's job. The door clanked shut.

The rhythm of the ship helped him lull into a meditative state. He ignored the chill as time crept away. His wrists turned, moving against the rope. The bonds loosened slowly.

A masked face at the glass. He straightened his spine. The assassin. A creak of protest as the latch released. The door fell ajar. He circled Jake.

"You killed my partner. For that alone I should shoot you right now." The man spoke English with a blended accent, part American, part European. He hit Jake with a jab.

"What are two mercenaries doing attacking a civilian's yacht in the middle of the night?"

"I will ask the questions. We both know you are not a civilian. Why are you out in these waters?"

"I like the solitude."

The assassin punched his face.

Jake relaxed his neck and moved with it. The man was holding back, getting warmed up for a session. He ignored the pain by separating his mind, going to a different place.

"We can keep going, if you like."

"I'm a sailor out on a cruise."

"In a no-go zone?" The assassin flexed his hand, getting ready for the next jab. It came from the left this time. Jake's cheek stung and burned.

The ropes had a slight give from his efforts. He guessed they had been moving for at least two hours. His energy was diminishing so he summoned his will power. The assassin bent and stared Jake in the face.

"Tell me why you're here."

Jake put his focus at the wall. He wondered what these guys wanted: if it was a straight contract kill.

Chapter 3

TWO MORE HITS to the jaw. Jake grinned at his captor, ignoring the sting. Sweat dripped on the man's hairline from the exertion. Jake smelled garlic on his breath. His head throbbed. The man's elbow telegraphed the next punch.

Jake tipped and swung his forehead at the incoming fist. It collided with his skull twenty centimeters earlier than his attacker had planned. The hardest bone in the body.

Hand bones cracked first. A scream followed. Jake rocked on his feet with the chair attached to his body. He turned one-eighty degrees and pivoted the chair legs at the crouched assassin. The impact made a sickening, wet noise. A gargled cry cut short. He rammed the fallen captor again. The thud sounded as the injured body collapsed to the floor.

He pulled and twisted his hands free from the rope. Nausea threatened to drop him. He stood over the prone attacker. A search of the pockets and he found a cell phone. Footsteps from the stairs. He made it to the front wall as a pirate ran into the room. Jake clotheslined the man's throat.

The pirate managed to fire as he fell on his backside. A shot whizzed past Jake's moving torso, ricocheting the wall. In proximity, he grappled and forced the pistol from the intruder's grasp. The weapon skidded away.

He scooped the gun and shot the pirate. The man slumped to the floor. He shot the second assassin in the chest and head. No point leaving these guys alive. The door slammed as Jake ran out into the corridor. Bolting up the stairs, blood pounded in his ears. A crew of pirates surely awaited him. He slipped onto the landing with the weapon cocked, eyes peeled to the shadows for danger.

The first attacker ran from his left and copped a bullet in the throat. Jake rammed the body and used it as a shield. Daylight hadn't broken. He swung toward portside as a figure launched from the west. A weapon blasted into the dead body. Jake fired at the pirate as he dropped the body shield. He hugged the edge. The cabin wall gave him cover and he retraced his steps.

A pirate jumped into his path. He wrestled the man and punched him in the face. Jake followed with a right elbow and smashed his nose. The man staggered on his feet like a drunk. A shot at close range and the pirate's head bounced on the deck. He took the fallen man's pistol and ran at the spot he had entered.

The attacker came from the side. Too close to fire. Jake ducked and did a backward sweep. The man's leg folded.

He looked over the rail. His yacht bobbed on the ocean. The vessel was connected by a nylon rope line. He shoved the pistol into his belt. Random noise close behind. He shrugged off his jacket and swung it over the nylon. It passed a sturdy test. He perched on the edge and shimmied down to the yacht. At the end, his foot found purchase on the stanchion. He saddled the bow quickly, cognizant of his vulnerable position. On deck, he launched at the connection point and tugged at the hawser. The nylon had been secured in haste. Stiff fingers made the work painful. Mid-way he turned and fired at the dhow's deck to keep the enemy wary. He pulled and twisted the clasp. The messenger line slackened, fell away into the waves.

Silence from the dhow made him suspicious. He kept sights on the ship as he jogged the length. A moving target was harder to hit. A face at the rail above. Jake aimed and pulled the trigger. The man fell away. He stumbled to the bridge and started the engines. The ocean bubbled beneath the yacht. He concentrated on the controls.

His surprise escape bought him one or two minutes to exit. He spun the bow with the steering. The yacht turned from the larger ship. He pushed the throttle gradually higher. Bullets flew from the pirates, most going wide and plopping the water in Jake's wake. Noise and shouts echoed over the sea. The pirates were not giving up, but still cautious after their fallen comrades. Water churned as he increased speed. Two hundred meters from the enemy's ship and he could see the pirates were not pursuing. He had the advantage in a faster vessel.

The odometer read eighteen knots. Jake clenched his teeth to fight weariness. He sat on the speed and waited until the pirate vessel was out of visual. A canopy of stars twinkled overhead. The display showed they had travelled southwest on the dhow. A major port would be his best bet. He set the coordinates past his original position. His jaw ached and he touched it tenderly. No bruises yet. Lucky the interrogator had not progressed to the serious punishment. The shoreline became visible as he charted a course to Manila.

He set the autopilot to clear his head. The body might still be on the floor. He descended the hatch and checked the lounge. His first attacker was missing. They must have taken the body.

Moonlight lit up a channel of ocean. He rotated to the salon and flicked the switch. Light flooded the furniture. The couch sunk under his weight. He checked the cell phone he took from the second assassin. No passcode. Jake swiped the settings. No apps besides the basics. Two calls from the same number. He scrolled through the media. No other content.

Who were they and what did they want? A robbery seemed unlikely now he'd seen their gear. *Professionals with military skills. But why were they with the pirates?*

He switched the cell phone from silent. If someone knew of this location, there could be more ambushes. It might pay to keep it on for now to intercept any comms. He returned to the bridge and took the wheel. The autopilot clicked to manual. Water churned, producing white foam in the vessel's wake. The boat geared up, slicing through the sea, a white foamy trail weaving in its wake. The ocean always calmed him faster than land.

An adjustment set the dials and instruments to the harbor. Manila was the closest and best port to start. He needed to think this setback through. A lump weighed his left side. He rummaged in his trouser pocket and tossed the cell phone on the dashboard.

The attack was a slick military job and he had no real cargo worth their time. Cash in the safe, a few valuables. These guys were after him. Either a straight hit or a kidnap. Jake guessed the latter.

The reason why they had the backup vessel sitting within a five-hundred-meter radius.

He contemplated the miniature city skyline. The enemy needed the tech and intel to find him here as well. *An enemy from the past or a new one?* No doubt Saint Petersburg had left many power brokers searching for him. The narrow escape he made five months ago had left many adversaries. A corrupt colonel and an oligarch were the main ones. He'd thwarted an arms deal which included uranium, a major payoff for these individuals and funding a political coup. Jake and Katerina had exposed corruption to the highest level of government and a conspiracy that reached American political shores. An ex-special forces captain, who worked for the oligarch, had been killed along with a veteran CIA operative.

The city blinked as he steered the vessel. Katerina entered his mind for the first time since waking. The dream had been similar for weeks. Ever since she flew to Syria last month, she'd been on his mind. Her exit from Russia five months ago and relocation to Prague, where he'd found her, had precipitated his decision to leave the NSA. They'd bought the yacht and been sailing the oceans since. Recently he'd decided to be open to the possibility of contractor work should it arise. She'd agreed in principle, but it may require further discussion.

He ramped up to twenty knots. A gust of wind swept him from the rear. The Syria opportunity had come up and Katerina was keen to close off this chapter of her past. Her former partner had been killed during the Russian occupation. A suspected torture of the journalist.

The buzzing drew his attention. He glanced down as the assassin's burner shook. Blue emanated as he turned the screen. A message:

If the job is done, come to the Diamond Tea, Manila. Zero eight hundred.

Engines rumbled to the twinkling lights as bleakness shed and the sky lowered around him. He would hit land in two hours. This allowed time to dock and perform surveillance on the Diamond Tea House.

Chapter 4

A COOL SALT breeze battered his face. One hand on the controls, Jake logged onto a device and did a search on Diamond Tea. Three hits in the city, narrowed down to the most likely. A rundown tea house near the main jetty in Manila. Street view showed luxury cars fanning out from rows of concrete shopfronts. Worn signs sat below a bank of grubby tinted windows bookended by a lender and a commerce bank. Charming establishment.

He memorized the source number of the dead intruder's text message and uploaded it into tracking software. If the burner number led nowhere, he'd try a triangulation, get a position before he threw the cell away. An online platform allowed him to book a position on the jetty. He preferred to use cash on all transactions, to avoid a trail, but used a payment gateway under a fake name for emergencies. The map displayed a ten-minute walk at most to the tea house from the dock position.

Early morning light splinters cut through the shoreline haze. Drab gray structures with fading flickers of yellow danced in the semi-darkness.

It struck Jake that he should keep the phone until the meet. If thrown overboard, his enemies could track it. Offline status was suspicious. He replied:

Assignment complete. See you at the Diamond.

The vessel slowed on arrival, he scanned for the right slot. Zero six-ten hours. Jake took two-thousand PHP Singapore dollars from a locked drawer and hid the key. The yacht touched the rubber fenders. He secured it to the cleats and crossed the cracked timber landing. Early morning traders were shouting orders. Workers in waterproof gear passed bundles and boxes of goods from boats to waiting trucks.

He cut through the melee to an intersection and turned right.

More workers waited at bus stops. He scanned a row of colonial style frontage. The next block gave way to glass high rises towering over street level older bunkers. He spotted the Diamond Tea House over the next block. A taxi with tinted windows slowed to the curb edge and the window came down. The driver indicated to Jake.

Perfect.

He nodded and jumped in the rear.

"Where to boss?" an Asian man in his thirties with glasses smiled.

"Drive around the block a few times please. I'm looking for good cafes and a hotel for later."

The tint provided perfect cover for surveillance without being seen.

"I'm a tour guide sometimes so can show the sights!" the driver bobbing his head at the rearview. "I'll charge a flat rate."

"Sounds good. Let's drive for twenty minutes and see how we go."

The morning fog lifted gradually revealing the hustle and bustle, the commuters increased numbers. Above the haze the Marina Bay Sands Hotel watched over the city. The driver pointed at a landmark and explained in broken but understandable English that their city was the greenest in the world. Technology being used here to recycle and rejuvenate was cutting edge and lowered the footprint and harm to the environment. They passed the Diamond twice, on the second Jake noticed an American smoking discreetly near the door.

"Pull up over here." Jake pointed to bay opposite the entry.

"Sure boss."

A double entrance provided an expansive angle of the patrons and exquisite lighting framed the main zone. The front tables had patrons in both working class and corporate attire. He scanned the rear and stopped at Caucasian sitting with his back to the wall. Jake's heart leaped. The man had half a head of gray hair, twenty extra pounds and wore civilian clothes. But he recognized him straight away. McCallister.

He sunk back in the seat. Jake hadn't seen General McCallister since Afghanistan. Rumored to have moved from military to intelligence. NSA operations.

"You ok boss?" the driver said.

Jake emerged from his thoughts. He focused on the dashboard.

"I'm fine. Let's sit here for two minutes and I'll get out. How much do I owe you?"

"Two hundred Singapore dollars will be good. I give you discount."

"Thanks." He handed the notes and exited onto the sidewalk.

Cars passed in the single lanes. He waited in the chill. At seven-thirty-eight A.M. the sun fought the gray mist producing a trademark Manila haze. McCallister's presence was an early morning surprise he could do without. A lethal attack on the yacht and now a dubious figure from the past materialized like a ghost. He avoided the main window of the Teahouse and walked to the next shopfront with a visual in the glass. McCallister calmly drank a tea, oblivious to his surroundings.

Taking a concealed weapon elicited much risk from local law enforcement, but he had no choice. Threats were too numerous. He waited until the Caucasian smoker turned and slipped into the establishment behind two men of equal height. The layout gave way for an L-shaped alcove at the front. He sat on the edge facing the entrance and ordered a green tea.

The beverage came quick and hot. Delivered by a young woman who smiled sweetly. Jake switched off the burner and placed it in his pocket. The morning crowd thickened, adding more layers to his hidden position. Out front the bodyguard paced the sidewalk. A portable signal jammer would come in handy but he'd have to compromise. He planned to replace the burner soon in case they tried to match the signal but McCallister might not be expecting him either and caught unprepared. This situation gave him a stomach churn, instincts going haywire.

At five to eight A.M., he stood and pushed through the patrons to McCallister's table. The general caught his eye.

"Jake Armitage. I'll be dammed." McCallister rose slowly and held up his arms, palms out. "I'm not carrying."

If McCallister was surprised he certainly didn't show it.

"General McCallister. What are the chances."

"Retired general. Please sit."

"You don't seem surprised to see me." Jake moved around the table and lowered into an adjacent booth. The serving counter sat opposite, his back against the wall. Front window on his right.

"That's better." Jake said.

McCallister nodded and shifted to his left. "Still keep the old habits I see."

"Safety first. Especially after my midnight visit from your friends."

The general settled in, and placed his hands on the table surface. "I won't ask if you're carrying."

"Wise choice. Why did you send the assassins and who are the pirates? I was captured and roughed up for nothing."

"Collateral damage. They begged for the job. I knew those mercs couldn't take you out. A win-win for me. The pirates were from a previous contract. Because you were so hard to locate, the mercenaries used their knowledge of the area to get a fix on you."

"What a mess..." Jake signaled for another tea. "Funny way of getting in touch."

"I had to bring in help, who in turn needed more help."

"That was intentional, McCallister. I'm retired from the NSA. I saw your boy out front. Not too conspicuous."

McCallister shifted in his chair. "I'm working on their skills.

Good men are hard to find: point in case, Jake. I heard you've left, but open to some contracting?"

A server placed Jake's drink on the table. He blew on the steam and waited.

"I'll get to the point. I am running operations in Europe. NSA. We have difficult operators that need a bit of specialization to take down."

Jake took his fresh tea and sipped. "As in me?"

"Yes, that was the idea."

"Why me?"

"You're one of the best NSA agents." McCallister paused and lowered his head. "I saw you take out that group of insurgents in the Korengal Valley back in 2015. Single handedly."

"The Valley of Death." Jake fought the image back, concentrating on the present. Bodies blown to bits, arms and legs lying in the dirt. The wailing and screaming of innocent peasants echoing in the mountains. Noise offset only by the constant ringing in his ears from improvised explosive devices. IEDs. Immense bloodshed in the name of the Taliban. "That's in the past, McCallister." He took a deep breath.

McCallister nodded. "Also the target is the oligarch you dealt with in Russia," McCallister observed. "You know his moves better than most. Because of your actions, he fled Russia, but we cannot have him setting down roots in Europe. Especially Paris, where the extremist movement are gaining followers almost exponentially."

A knot formed in Jake's stomach. "That Russian assignment is classified."

"I've got clearance."

"You'll understand, with your latest stunt, why I have trust issues."

The background noise took over as the two men sat in silence.

McCallister had a checkered history in Afghanistan. Civilians were shot under a cloud of suspicion. A military hearing later

19

exonerated McCallister but did not convince many that he was innocent.

"What's the oligarch up to?"

"Arms shipments. Mainly to extremists and terror organizations: Taliban, Jihad, ISIS. Not to mention African and Asian warlords, mercenaries, private armies, and so on. Anywhere there's conflict, up pops the oligarch. We suspect he's dabbling in uranium again. Half-life and anything that can be weaponized."

A woman in an apron stopped at Jake's elbow, hands on hips. "Would you like food?"

McCallister shook his head, followed by Jake. He handed her money for the tea. She smiled and left.

"The pay day is huge on this one. 500,000 US dollars. You name your bank. I'll give a deposit of half on acceptance to show our good faith."

The smell of noodles and eggs wafted from the kitchen. Katerina filled Jake's head as he sat silently reviewing the proposition. She wouldn't get back for a week but could definitely help with IT and logistics. The oligarch knew her connection to him and may take revenge in the future. Neither of them was safe. This money could set them up for longer and get rid of the oligarch. Trusting McCallister was still an issue. "What outcome are you expecting?"

"I'm realistic. Confirmed kill would be the ultimate solution, but stopping his trades indefinitely is a good start. That's phase one. If his suppliers and clients lose trust and we shut down a major network, you can keep the deposit for this." He watched McCallister and waited. "Phase two: capture and put him in a black ops site. We can get intel on more major players. That would be ideal. Or confirmed kill."

"That sounds more like the CIA."

"Joint operations work if it benefits the same goal."

"If I agree, there are a few conditions. I'll work out a more effective way of communication. You'll hear from me when necessary:

no tracking. No other contractors." He pulled the attacker's burner cell from his pocket and shoved it across the table. "Any mercenaries or interference and I walk, and keep the money. Understood?"

McCallister rubbed his chin, an intense expression forming. "I can green light all that."

A sweeper pushed a broom over the floor. Jake picked up a card from the café and wrote down his account number. He pushed it across the table. "Transfer the deposit into this account straight away. Fast clearance. Once it lands, I'll get moving."

"Sure thing." McCallister slipped the card into a pocket.

"I'll be in touch, McCallister. Remember the rules."

McCallister waved his right hand.

The door hinges squeaked, a salt wind swiped Jake's cheek. His day had ramped up another notch.

Chapter 5

PEDESTRIANS HAD GATHERED since his chat at the Diamond Teahouse. Jake ignored McCallister's grim guard dog, pacing the concrete in a cloud of smoke. Motorists crawled through the brightening day. He circled the next block at a leisurely pace to shake any possible trackers, NSA or otherwise. Loose stones flicked off his boots and McCallister's offer took hold. He didn't trust the arrangement but wanted to take out the oligarch once and for all. The free world wouldn't be safe until the oligarch was eradicated. Getting paid provided an unexpected bonus and keeping Katerina safe gave the ultimate incentive.

The yacht bobbed as he scrambled on board and descended the stairs. From a lock-up box under the bed, he took out a fake passport. He preferred the sea or trains for travel, due to anonymity, but time was a factor. The weapon slid into a slot and he locked it with the key. Contacts in Paris would fence a pistol.

In the shower stall, he kept the water cool to shrug his weariness. He toweled off fast and opened the vanity. The razor blade took off a three-day growth. Soap suds disappeared in the sink and he placed the dirty clothes in the laundry. He shrugged on a fresh sweatshirt and jeans. A small amount of deodorant stick under the armpits. Almost felt human. He shoved a blue and white baseball cap over his head, great for obscuring his face on CCTV monitoring. A casual but neat tourist in his early thirties stared back at him.

The cockpit windshield reflected the bay, heating the smooth timber wheel. He relocated the vessel to a separate, more private section of the harbor and paid using a different card. One month's payment in advance should be enough time to cover any unexpected delays. Travelling light, he stuffed the fake travel document into a carry bag. George Perry was his latest alias. Three months old from his counterfeit contact in Spain. A change of clothes and basic toiletry followed.

Under the desk, a concealed drawer held currency. He reached for a bundle of euro notes: 10,000 in worn fifties and hundreds. The plane ticket he'd pay for in cash at the airport, checked price online. He loaded the tablet to the Windows screen and checked flights. 2,556 USD. He gathered the American notes and separated the bundle into the carry bag so the total cash wouldn't be suspicious at the airport. No questions or potential issues. Bringing this quantity of money undeclared is an offense, and a red flag if he got caught.

He logged into his offshore account. McCallister's deposit had cleared.

The burner Katerina used went straight to message bank. He left a message for her to get in touch. Her safety in Syria, plus the connection to him, increased the risk factor, recent events amplifying the danger. McCallister's attempted hit during the night had not given him extra peace of mind.

To add another layer of security, he covered the facing boat flank with a tarpaulin. It might also deflect possible scrutiny from visual tracking. The vessel had been found once by McCallister and he wanted to avoid detection again. For an extra fee, a rent-a-cop would pass by every day and monitor his docking station. He'd paid that cost for a fail safe.

Cooking odors and city noise greeted Jake as he climbed onto the jetty. The morning brought warmer weather, so he bought a cheap pair of knock-off Ray Bans from a stall. He headed west, weaving to the denser parts of Manila. A taxi rank sat in a haze of diesel fumes. He took the first one and gave him the destination. The Nino Aquino airport had a moderate number of commuters. The sound of luggage bag wheels mixed with overhead announcements in soft female voices.

The next flight to Paris departed at three P.M. that afternoon. Just over nineteen hours. One stop. He bought a business class discounted fare with Emirates for a last-minute deal in cash. The Middle-East airline had great service and was harder to hack from American agencies. Best of both worlds.

"Do you have check-in luggage, sir?"

"Not this time, thanks."

"Have a good flight, Mister Perry." She pushed his passport across the counter.

"Thank you."

Tarmac rumbled with planes taking off and landing. Jake settled into his seat. A flight attendant placed an orange juice on his table. Business class layout provided more privacy. Fatigue hit him hard; he battled to stay awake for takeoff. Grit the teeth. Trucks and planes moved over the tarmac as he stared out the window.

Engines kicked in and wheels lifted. As they hit 30,000 feet, he fell into a doze.

A jolt woke Jake from his slumber. He stretched to the monitor and pressed the flight information. They had been flying for over four hours. He requested a light meal of salmon and vegetables, and eased into the cushion.

The food came and he mused over the Paris locality the oligarch had chosen. A hotel in the north-west appeared to be his common base. Close to terror recruitment and high crime areas. The oligarch had a private army of thugs and collateral damage was never an issue. He chewed a bite of fish and perused the map.

A hunch formed that the area was a pitstop for the Russian to a bigger design and plan. Dealing small-time arms seemed beneath the oligarch. There had to be a bigger payoff.

The attendant gathered his tray. He folded the table, left the TV running, and slept for the remainder of the leg.

Jake connected at Dubai and arrived at Charles de Gaulle at just past seven A.M. A young attendant examined the photo and details, compared it to his face through the transparent shield. He smiled. Bar-code machine beeped and he was on his way. The George Perry document made it through Paris passport control without incident. Quality work again from his contact in Barcelona.

Fragrance and souvenir shops stacked in a line, surrounding the exit path. A global exchange kiosk lit up white. He placed 2,000 USD on the counter.

"All in euro, please. Fifties and twenties."

"As you wish." The man with slicked back hair stacked the euro.

He bought a navy-blue cap from a vendor, France World Cup embossed on the front.

"Oui, monsieur, if you're short of clothes, we have these quality garments on sale." The sales attendant pointed at a rack of sweatshirts. Blues and dark grays blended into the environment and were not too bold. He picked one of each color and paid for the lot in cash.

An escalator took him to the subway, a station landing on the B-line. He purchased an all-day pass and studied the map. The Directorate-General of External Security was based in the outer region of Paris in arrondissement twenty. France's foreign intelligence agency should have extensive information on the oligarch's operations. His contact would set him up with a weapon and basic intel.

If all goes to plan.

The phone rang five times before his contact answered. "Lavigne."

"*Bonjour*. It's Sphinx." An old codename Jake hadn't used since his last assignment in Europe.

The silence lasted ten seconds. "How long has it been?" Lavigne paused to sharpen his memory. "Must be at least four years. Are you using a burner?"

"Always. Can we meet ASAP?' I'm in twenty now, near the office."

"Let's do Lou Pascalou, the bar on Rue des Panoyaux. I'll leave now."

"See you there in ten minutes."

He clicked off and checked his map.

Lou Pascalou sat near a corner, seating and tables spilling to the open air. The relaxed atmosphere attracted all types, at all times of the day and night. He entered the Art Nouveau entrance, passed by the eclectic fittings, and ordered a spritzer.

The DGSE agent stood hunched at a table in the corner, blending into the back wall décor. He placed the bottle on the table surface.

"Drinking the light stuff, I see." Lavigne peered at him with an intense gaze. "Are you here on your own passport?"

"Don't ask, don't tell." He took a swig and balanced on the stool. "It's been a long night. Came here as a last-minute design."

Lavigne's brow knitted. "Lucky I know you're reliable. You look under the pump. Not here under duress?"

"Depends on your definition really." Jake raised an eyebrow, trained on the patrons at the bar.

"I see. What do you need?"

"Co-operation on intel for start. This has to do with Paris safety as well. Highest level."

"Go on."

"What do you know about an oligarch named Tellav Ivanov?"

"Name rings a bell. Something came up with a wiretap we were doing a few months ago. A group nearby in Trappe I think. Need to refresh my memory."

Jake sipped the sparkling and leaned over. "He's bad news. Fled Russia six months ago under a raft of serious charges. Involvement with arms, coercion, murder, political influence; you name it.'"

"Now he's set up base in Paris like many of his comrades."

"Correct."

"Is this official NSA business?"

"As far as anyone is concerned, yes. They approached me in a very unorthodox way and asked me to come onboard. I won't bore you with the intimate details, but my semi-retirement has been put on hold."

"Prior dealings with this oligarch, huh?" Lavigne scanned a group of younger men in their twenties as they pushed to order a round of beers. The leader was waving his hand as if intoxicated.

Jake nodded and slugged his drink.

"Well, I'm glad it's you they sent and not one of those younger ones."

"He's got a lot of money and resources."

"The oligarch or the NSA?" Lavigne gave a deadpan expression.

"Both." Jake smiled. The Frenchman hadn't lost his sense of humor.

"Business as usual here."

"Maybe bigger. Uranium and warheads. Sophisticated military technology as well. I have some leads on a hotel out this way."

"I'll check what intel we have in the system as current. Then we can dig deeper and plan a strategy We've got budget cuts on manpower and limited resources, but I'll definitely help you," Lavigne said.

"Can you set me up with a weapon and body armor? A SIG, any P, with boxes and a vest will do."

Lavigne nodded. "Let's meet tomorrow and I'll bring that gear. I've got a safehouse where we can transact without surveillance. I'll text you the address and let you know the time." The Frenchman opened a map on his cell and angled it to Jake. "We had the oligarch around this area in the nineteenth. I believe he's living in a local hotel there."

The atmosphere in the bar had increased in tempo. Groups of young students crammed the tables, ordering rounds of pints.

"Thanks, Lavigne, appreciate your help." He rose from the stool and weaved to the door.

The air outside smelt sweeter: floral mixed with hot pastries from a nearby bakery. Jake found the nearest station and descended the stairs. A hotel he had noticed earlier would be the ideal location to stake out the oligarch.

Chapter 6

SHARDS OF YELLOW pierced the threadbare drapes, obscuring Katerina's view of her laptop. She tilted the base and rubbed her eyes. The clock radio shone red digits from the side table. Eight-thirty-seven A.M. Another all-nighter. An air-con wall unit chugged, battling to keep the room cool.

A dusty trademark cloud hovered knee high in the streets. Damascus markets were setting up in the presence of soldiers. Children ran between stooped parents. The peace could be disturbed at any moment, an outburst or threat imminent. She stretched and yawned, drained a water bottle on a pile of papers.

The inbox highlighted four unread emails landed in the last hour. She scanned the subject lines of each to see which was most urgent.

Chekov the journalist, her friend and colleague, had sent an email detailing the leak of classified information. One he could not go public with under fear of incarceration or death. Politics were still tumultuous under the current dictatorship, in fact worse than six months ago. Sources indicated the Russian President was allegedly planning an attack on a neighbor. He hated the Soviet dissolution implemented by Gorbachev, having referred to it on multiple occasions as the biggest atrocity of the twentieth century. Of course, he wanted to regain control of more resources and power.

Katerina read between the lines on this conspiracy. Chekov would believe it's either Ukraine or Belarus. The evidence did strongly point to either of these countries, she had to admit. With Jake and her narrowly escaping Saint Petersburg six months ago, no action surprised her regarding Russian politics. She replied to Chekov:

Hi, hope things are well. Please be careful as you've risked your life for many worthy causes. I'm in Syria investigating my ex-partners' murder and will see Jake soon. Stay in touch.

K.

Her attention returned to the current assignment. She had managed to find a witness that saw a Russian reporter taken away with another journalist. A local Syrian. This occurred on the same day he went missing on August 12, 2015. She compared her notes. A video came, followed by torture. In eight days, the execution.

The burner sat on the table. She extended over the furniture to check her calls. The battery had nearly gone dead. She swiveled toward the charger, plugged the device into the power source. It beeped with a message. Stale smoke wafted in the window crack so she eased it closed. In the dim light, the menu lit blue. She scrolled to missed calls. Jake's latest number.

The robotic answering service attendant sounded. "You have one new message."

Password entered and she hit one to listen:

"Hi, Katerina it's me. I have an issue. If you could call me back for explanation, that would be great. Don't stress too much in the meantime. I'm on a plane and landing in Paris at seven A.M. Tuesday."

A plane... What happened to the yacht?

She checked Paris time: five-ten A.M. Two hours behind Damascus. Too early to call as he'd be in the air. An empty jar balanced on the tiny kitchenette counter. She was out of caffeine, her most essential food. The fridge was bare and not enough milk to make a short black.

The hotel key lay on the table. She scooped it in a pocket and wrapped a hijab over her hair. It was easier to blend in. Shades to cover her eyes also helped.

An odor of food and flora carried in the breeze. She descended to the worn carpet in the foyer and stepped onto the loose gravel sidewalk. Particles in the air brushed her cheek. She pulled the fabric over her mouth. Motorbikes revved past from both directions, commuters navigating the shops. The yellow particles settled in the midst. Gray mountains domineered the skyline.

She hurried over to a smallgoods vendor and pushed into the tight entrance. Coffee jars were stacked along a shelf in the middle aisle. She took a carton of milk from the fridge and picked a long loaf of local bread. Thicker than most flatbreads and chewy on the inside, it had a smoky flavor from the seeds. In the next aisle, she grabbed a packet of rice, and a tray of meat from the fridge.

The female shop attendant nodded, avoiding direct eye contact. Katerina stacked the food on the counter. She noticed a small smile as the woman packed the goods into a small bag.

"Thank you," Katerina said and gathered up the shopping. A windy gust accumulated from the east; she kept the sunglasses covering her eyes. Thoughts of Jake crossed her mind. He was flying to Paris suddenly, and not knowing the reason made her uneasy. Her heartbeat rose and she battled to calm her nerves. Car horns beeped randomly, as if a unique language. Voices traded in the wind. She mounted the makeshift curb, avoiding aggressive pedestrians.

She had to wrap the investigation up fast and get out of this city. Her phone read nine-twenty A.M. Still a few minutes to kill. A fruit grocer had quality produce sometimes, so she stopped and checked. Pomegranates were fresh. She moved to the apples, put two in a bag, paid and exited the shop.

Troops patrolled the growing heat, assessing each person as they conducted duties. A checkpoint glistened one-hundred feet away; the boom gate rose and fell, pendulum-like. Cars banked up to the horizon, vanishing at a bend. Pollution and despair.

She walked to the hotel room, took the stairs, and put the milk and meat in the fridge. The other groceries went in the cupboard, but she left the coffee jar on the counter. She shrugged off the head scarf. Palms out flat on the table, she took a deep breath. Relax. In-and-out. She took the remote and flicked on the aircon. It rumbled to life for another marathon stint. The heat was already starting to sap her motivation. She made a coffee and sat at the desk.

The screen blinked at her in the half-lit room. Her gaze focused on the letters, lost in Jake's mysterious message again. She rubbed her eyes and forced herself to open her inbox. An unread reply from the brother of the reporter that was imprisoned with her partner. It had taken months to track him down. A sip of instant coffee. Strong flavor. He'd been overseas and a little lost since his brother's passing.

She checked the clock display: ten-thirty-six A.M. Time to call Jake.

Chapter 7

THE TEXT FROM Lavigne beeped. Jake had a quick glance at the safehouse address. A small one-bedder apartment in the nineteenth, ten minutes from the current location. He corrected his bearings at the nearest corner and checked the landscape. The lunchtime crowd spilled from the restaurant outside the hotel. He pulled on his cap, filed into the revolving door, and headed to the main reception.

A young woman in a smart maroon uniform was poised at a computer on an aged marble surface. This made the four-star-rated place slightly upmarket, but not overly pretentious. Its proximity to the oligarch's base was the main advantage, and multiple exit points gave strategic advantage.

Jake's shirt and jeans gave off a business vibe with the hint of a wide range of corporate occupations from sales to IT. Only politicians and real estate agents wore a suit and tie these days. Dressed to push an agenda. A man wearing a two-piece suit and tie would be remembered and many people became guarded, sus of the wearer's intention. Guarded meant memorable.

Blend into the environment; do not stick out.

He reached the line and waited to be served. In addition to his attire, most corporate meetings were conducted online via Hangouts, Zoom, or a similar platform, thanks to the COVID pandemic. Casual was the new business norm, a trend started decades ago by pioneer Steve Jobs and his trainers. Jake had business cards made up under the Perry name, just in case. The elderly customer finished up, took their belongings and walked slowly away. He stepped up to the marble edge.

The woman smiled. "*Bonjour*. How can I be of assistance today?"

"*Bonjour*. I'm booked in under Perry, thanks."

"I'll check now for your details." She typed and read. "Can I have your identification please?"

He pushed the passport over the marble surface.

"Thank you." She glimpsed the document. "Room 120. It's on the first floor, as you requested. Four nights." The woman stretched to a cabinet and slid an electronic card. "Here's your key."

"Cheers." He adjusted the bag strap and took the plastic card.

"Do you have any large luggage you'd like help with?"

"No, thanks. Just travelling light with the one carry bag and a laptop. I'll find my own way up." He met her eyes. "If I need to extend the same room, will that be possible? Not sure how my meetings will go."

"Yes, that's fine. Please ring the desk if you need anything. The lifts are down to your right. Hope you have a nice stay."

He walked off, satisfied he'd engaged the right amount of small talk. Not too much, not too little. Dropped lines for the 'in town for business' impression. A pair of plants bookended the lifts. He pressed up for level one. A nice countryside painting hung above the buttons. The doors pinged and came apart. He stepped out at level one and located his room six doors down. An exit stairwell sat at the end of the corridor.

The room had modern décor and plenty of light from a large living room window. A bench and small sink wrapped around the corner. The blinds clicked open: a clear view of the street. A lower level was preferable for quick access and escape. In an emergency, he required speed and minimum travel time.

He lay the main carry bag on the queen-size bed.

His burner vibrated and rang. He clicked the answer button. "Hello."

"Hey, it's me." She avoided saying her name over the phone.

He placed the laptop bag on the desk and straddled the edge of the bed. "Hey, you. How's it going over there?"

"Not bad. I've been worried about your message though.

What's this about Paris?"

"I didn't want to alarm you. Had a visit last night from two strangers. Out in the South China Sea." He paused and touched the bed quilt. "They didn't come for a friendly chat."

"O bozhe!" She exhaled and her tone lowered. "Sorry, a little strung out. I'm relieved to hear your voice. Does it have anything to do with Russia?"

He sighed. "Sort of. An old colleague of mine decided to drop a line. I'm fine but cannot say the same for my two visitors."

She stayed silent.

"I tracked them back to Manila via a burner message. Located their employer who happens to be an old contact from my days in Afghanistan. Not a coincidence, of course. Seems he wanted to make me a proposal."

"What a story. Funny way of doing it."

"That's what I thought. The contact wanted me for an assignment. To eliminate a dangerous individual at large in Paris."

"Who?"

He opened the slider and stared out the balcony onto the sidewalk. "Our old friend the oligarch."

"Damn. I thought we got rid of him. Let me guess: all the usual black-market transactions?"

"Pretty much. Except now he's in a new playing field with a refreshed database. Europe. Some new suppliers, I believe, and a bigger portfolio on offer: diversity and quality. All for the highest bidding psychopaths."

"And you're going after him?" She sounded out of breath.

"My old employers made me an offer too good to refuse. Plus I don't like him lurking out there seeking revenge. It's a loose end we could do without."

"That's true," she said quietly.

He could feel her worrying. The line fell quiet for thirty seconds.

Jake spoke first. "How's your research investigation going?"

"I've uncovered more detail, but it's grinding to a halt. Soon I'll speak with the brother of the man captured with my ex-partner. Might be a dead end. Excuse the pun."

"That's a shame."

"Nearly at the point of letting it rest. They didn't want Russia here, but had no choice, and my ex became collateral damage."

"I heard. I hope you achieve some closure."

"Thanks. So do I."

"Can you help me remotely with data searches, please?"

"Of course. I'll be here for another three days at the maximum. Maybe less. But I can always help remotely. What do you need?"

"Nothing yet, thanks. I'll let you know. Good luck with the search."

"Bye. Stay safe."

The line went dead.

A modern-shaped square faucet aligned with the shower head. He pulled the handle and dunked his head under the warm flow, massaged his scalp. Until he got set up with gear, it would be too risky hitting the street. Water streamed over his face in a soothing rhythm, soap suds mixed in the drain between his toes. He fought the drowsiness.

The oligarch's suspected hotel was four to five blocks east. If he bought a small kitchen knife, concealed in his pants, that would tide him over.

He toweled and dressed on the bathroom tiles. The branded polo sweatshirt went well with trendy cargo pants and Puma joggers. On the event of being made, he'd break into a casual jog; the outfit allowed for this adjustment. A dark stubble from the twenty-eight hours since his Manila transit would add believability. He pulled on the blue World Cup cap he'd bought on the way from the airport.

Chapter 8

THE GPS LED him to Laguiole Cutlery, a nicely lit, upper-end store with a wide range of kitchenware. In the entrance, an attendant welcomed him with upturned palms. If only they knew what sort of knife-customer he was. He perused the second aisle for the fancy steak blades with flat handles. LED lights were mounted above all product displays. He scanned the vast array of variety; each shelf contained a dozen models. A quality blade had a chunky handle. Not suitable for his requirements.

He picked a three-inch model topped with a thin dark handle. The blade was light in his hand. It would conceal well in his cargo waistband or even a side pocket. He took it to the countertop, placed it on the glass.

A tall woman, with a healthy dose of make-up, nodded in approval. "Very reliable blade. Are you paying with card or cash?"

"Cash. You recommend it for kitchen cutting all vegetables and meat?"

"Absolutely and we have a twelve-month guarantee. Full refund if you're not happy." She tapped on the register to process the sale. "Would you like that gift-wrapped?"

"No, thanks." Jake smiled. "I'll take it with a small bag."

Dark clouds lowered over Paris, blocking the sun and threatening to deliver a downpour. Jake took the plastic off the blade and deposited the packaging into a trash can. He sought cover in a park with thick tree trunks and low foliage. Away from prying eyes and witnesses, he put the blade inside his waist band, fit perfectly concealed. It would do until he met up with Lavigne for more weapons.

The walk to the suspect hotel brought no shadows he detected. He doubled-back three times and reached a corner two blocks from the oligarch's suspected base. It sat nestled in a residential pocket. A small cluster of trees and a park gave way to a cobbled slope. The residents varied in appearance. Groups of middle to lower socio-economic younger people milled aimlessly. Houses would still be a reasonable price and were mixed with older, high-density apartments. The African influence in the area he found apparent as he passed a small supermarket dedicated to the culture.

A block away from the oligarch's hotel, Jake circled the nearby buildings to get a lay of the landscape. He scanned a bank of windows leading to an embankment. Cars were parked parallel to the sidewalk. A spattering of patrons sat in a traditional corner French café. The hotel entrance lay 300 yards down a smaller avenue. Shop fronts punctuated medium high-rise residential apartment towers. An old area yet to be gentrified, like many in the outer parts of north-west Paris.

The oligarch must be slumming it compared to his majestic properties back in Russia. Jake didn't want to get any closer and risk being seen by the target or any cohorts that may recognize him.

He walked back past the café, but took the opposite side of the road. A vibration in his pocket. He pulled out the burner. "Hello."

"It's me," said Lavigne.

"How's it going?" Jake turned the corner and sat on a seat.

"I can meet you later today in the safe house."

"Good. I'm a little light. It's nearly twelve now."

Lavigne clucked his tongue as if making a calculation. Probably a nervous tic that evolved to a habit. "What about two-thirty? That's the earliest I can do."

"See you then." He clicked off and gained his feet. A small bird dived from a tree bough and took off towards some friends.

Perfect timing. He felt vulnerable with just the knife, although his close, hand-to-hand combat skills with a blade were lethal. If a hidden sniper took him out, the weapon was useless. With a gun, he'd have at least a chance at return fire.

He descended to an underground station and caught the subway again. The carriage had a smattering of passengers, mostly gaps, which suited him fine. He checked the nearest faces first, detecting unusual patterns or interest. An elderly woman sat alone in a booth in front. Two children clapped and played around a weary-eyed mother.

The oligarch would have some kind of routine. Jake would need to locate him first, coax him into a public place without being made himself. Doing business on this covert scale with certain locales here would require discretion and privacy. His strike point would need minimal CCTV security so the oligarch could not be detected, biometric or otherwise, and possibly captured.

Train brakes screeched to a halt. He stood and clicked the button to open the door. Fumes overtook his senses as he alighted. The tiled, deco, curved tunnels were all similar. He browsed shop windows to catch reflections. Most people kept to themselves, absorbed with their own thoughts. At a café, he bought a chicken salad wrap.

He started on the meal on the walk back. At the hotel, a different attendant sat at the reception desk. The man smiled and greeted him with *"Bonjour."*

The fire exit stairwell was empty as he checked the layout. Hard concrete with LED lights overhead, minimal windows. Standard level for modern hotels. He went up to the second story to explore options. The corridor wrapped the same direction as one with equal size gaps between rooms. He descended back through the same route: didn't want to show up too long on the CCTV on the wrong floor.

He studied a map of the area to pinpoint other possible hotels. The area was still foreign without walking more streets. Once he got a feel for the atmosphere, he could peg the zones.

Two P.M. He shrugged on a hoodie for Lavigne's meeting and went through the lobby. A light drizzle pattered on the glass. Gray clouds hung low, giving the old stucco buildings a gloomy cast. He pulled the hood over the cap and jogged to the main junction. Smokers hugged the walls, gathered in pockets under the eaves. The GPS had Lavigne's apartment as a fifteen-minute walk, so he took the long way. Windy avenues pushed leaves to blanket the ground. The cultural diversity of the area led to introspection and everyone kept to themselves.

I hope the Frenchman has more intel on the oligarch.

Chapter 9

LAVIGNE'S SAFEHOUSE LAY hidden in a warren of centuries-old brick towers. Jake stepped on a concrete apron that preceded the block to ascertain which entrance to take. Clothes fluttered on a rack from a balcony above. The click of an elderly resident's walking frame mixed with a dog bark. He noticed a street number marked on the flank after his second lap. Entering a breezy foyer, he climbed an old wooden stairwell that had seen better days.

On the second knock, a shadow passed over the keyhole. He positioned himself within sight. A chain rattled, followed by the scraping sound of a heavy metal latch. Lavigne cracked the reinforced door. A gun barrel glinted in the gloomy corridor. Jake met his gaze. Lavigne lowered the weapon and tilted his head. An average timber door from the outside, from the inside it transformed to a reinforced bank vault.

He followed Lavigne into the kitchen. A cardboard delivery box and a tablet sat on the table.

"There you go, as requested." The Frenchman stepped away and leaned against the countertop.

"Cheers." Jake sat at the table.

The box contained a SIG with a spare magazine, a SAPI vest, two boxes of rounds. The side of the cardboard had a courier sticker. He pulled the gun slide and checked the chamber. P226. Short barrel: good for close quarter combat. Stainless steel and compact for greater accuracy and less mishaps. He slid the SIG in the small of his back. The jeans belt kept it snug enough. He closed the box and pushed the flaps' one-in one-out pattern.

"Thanks for getting the equipment."

"If you kill him, you're doing me a favor too. But don't make a mess. I want it clean and as efficient as possible. Minimal collateral damage." Lavigne opened the fridge and balanced two Stella Artois bottles. He placed them on the table and pulled off the caps.

"Got it. Anymore intel? That hotel I watched today is not his likely residence."

Lavigne nodded and pushed the beer toward him. "We've picked up another wiretap on the oligarch. One day ago. I've got him pegged in this area." Lavigne took a long swig from his Stella. He opened the tablet and pointed at a GPS display. "Not sure of the exact location, but talking shop with known associates of a Nigerian warlord. Among others."

"What lovely wholesome company he maintains." Jake took note of the geographic pinpoints on his burner. A definite pattern, and Katerina might be able to aid in narrowing down the target's location.

"I guarantee this warlord transaction is just for entrée," Lavigne said.

"Petty cash to bolster his depleted resources. Fleeing Russia without your last and biggest payday has consequences. Need to flush the oligarch out in the open and get to the bigger picture, and fast." Jake sipped from the bottle. It was chilled and felt good as it passed down his throat.

He leaned back in the chair and examined the old-world charm of the kitchen. Flower pattern drapes, ageless little grooved sink, worn surfaces and homely tiles, as if your kindly grandmother had lived in it for years. A warm sensation gathered in Jake's chest.

"Agreed." The Frenchman pointed to a red dot on the tablet. "This café in Chateau Rogue has a lot of activity. We're picking up significant conversations around some key players and code words. Ones that match our Russian man."

Jake scrutinized the icons and bookmarked it in his burner. "All possible hotspots to zone in."

"We can meet here in the future, but refer to it as the downtown bar when on air."

"Thanks for the beer." Jake drained the bottle and got to his feet.

"Sure thing."

"Stay in touch."

Outside the clouds had lightened and lifted slightly, sidewalk semi-slick from the rain. He took the quick route straight to the hotel room to offload the equipment. A medium level of afternoon commuters made checking his back take longer.

Katerina stared at her laptop and weighed up the chat she had with the captive's brother. His recollection and information aligned with hers in almost every aspect. One point he'd made about the execution revealed a conflicting date: the man claimed her ex-partner was killed a day later than she thought. She rubbed her eyes and stretched. A group of kids played near her window, kicked up dust in the heat. The orange disc burned on the horizon. She moved about the cramped living zone, wishing she received answers at a quicker pace.

The phone rang, pulling her from pacing the worn carpet. She fished for it under loose papers on the desk.

"Hello," she said as it clicked.

"Hi there. How's things?" Jake's voice sounded faint as a whisper, despite the lack of noise interference in the room. Her heartbeat rose, glad to be pulled away from the onerous exploration.

"Getting there slowly. You know how these things are."

"For sure. I wanted to ask if you could please narrow down the location of our friend."

"I'll try. What do you have?"

"Emailed you a screengrab of the map. He's been calling in this area in the last two weeks. Conversations with buyers. We're trying to triangulate."

"We?" Katerina swigged water. She put her feet up and pushed back toward the aircon unit.

"DGSE; I have a contact there."

Her inbox chirped. "OK, I can see it and I'll check other

sources for him as well. May help us."

"Thanks."

"Just finishing this work and I'll get straight on to it."

"Talk soon. Bye."

She perused the map. The red icons were clustered in the nineteenth and it twigged something in her memory. Open media sources could have the answers. She loaded news archives from the last six to twelve months. Keywords were inputted and she scanned the subject lines. It came up on the tenth line and she clicked it open. A Russian named Ivan Lenkov had been arrested plotting an attack with a known terrorist. They had a warehouse that contained crates of weapons. The profile came up on the guy: ex-military living in France, current status serving time on a string of charges.

A connection to the oligarch started to form. She shifted her position. Drank and read. An associate had been arrested with Lenkov but had escaped conviction. The second man's name was documented as Alexei Gusev. It came with an arrest photo but scant background to be found on record. She searched Russian law enforcement but came up with nothing more. A further data dive into government databases through a backdoor and she came up with a cell number for Gusev. Could be old, but worth a try.

She typed a summary and attached the profiles of the two men to an encrypted email. The associate might still be working for the oligarch and still in Paris. He could ID the second thug when he's casing the oligarch's location. DSGE might be able to get a fix on him. She pressed the send button to Jake over a VPN connection.

The aircon chugged and rattled. She gazed at the kitchen. A slab of bottled water lay half empty in a cupboard. She bent and took a fresh one from the plastic. Afternoon trade slowed in the heat. Shoppers were thinning as older cars crawled past the canvas canopies. She wondered how much different the city would be without interference.

She shed her clothes as she stepped into the bathroom. Water ran cool in the small shower cubicle. She shut the curtain. Her study into the victim's brother would take two to three more hours. She sighed and rubbed soap into her face.

Chapter 10

THE EMAIL CAME as Jake returned to the table. He scanned the first line of the message. Two Russian suspects working in Paris. Connected to the oligarch. One in jail, the other at large. Katerina came through already. He marveled at her efficiency.

He clicked one of the photos. The second guy's face loaded in color. Olive complexion with brown eyes. Could pass for French. No distinguishing marks other than a few nicks and small scars, possibly from brawls. He texted Lavigne the name Alexei Gusev, basic physical description, and the number to do a check. The cell number rang out without a voicemail. A solid location lead was required to take this to the next level. He held off on an update to McCallister until an associate to the target had been confirmed.

The reply came from Lavigne:

I'll run a check and get back to you ASAP.

He fed the spare magazine for the SIG with rounds and stored it in a pocket. A basic check on the weapon showed it to be in good order. He pulled it apart and cleaned the parts. It went back together smooth. The SAPI vest and remaining box of bullets he placed in a bag and shoved under the bed. He pulled a different cap over his hair.

The cluster map Katerina sent narrowed the activity to a smaller area. He could start on that this afternoon, save any more specific intel. His burner went off. Lavigne had located a bar that Gusev, the second thug, had frequented in the last seven days. An undercover reported that meetings occurred usually late afternoon between traders involving Gusev and other persons of interest to the Directorate-General. The laptop closed with a click. He straightened, grabbed the card key from the wall holder, and headed down to the entry.

A guest shuffled by as he shut the door. The middle-aged woman was well-to-do in heavy jewelry and a brand-name dress. A memory of his Russian neighbor in St Petersburg came to mind. She gave a pensive expression as the elevator doors rumbled shut.

On the breezy sidewalk, the clouds remained bunched and gray. The bar café address Lavigne sent displayed as a twelve-minute walk. Slopes and hills marked the terrain. He kept to open areas to watch the window reflections. He evaluated the passing faces; most were average citizens going about their day. No stalkers at this stage.

A subway entrance loomed on the blacktop. Beyond this point, tertiary students spilled from a nearby university into brasseries for mid-week sessions of socializing and revelry.

Bookended by a grocer and a laundromat, the bar in question spread over a double frontage. A discreet walk through to the toilets. No men with Gusev's features were present.

He entered a café, paid for a juice, and sat at the glass window. The reflection would hide his face as he monitored the bar. Patrons came and went for afternoon drinks and snacks. Young people made up less than half, older African men in small groups the majority. Jake swallowed his drink and studied the burner occasionally to avoid scrutiny from the café staff.

At five-twenty-six P.M. two men entered. One matched the height and description of Gusev. He left casually and entered the bar. The men were seated in a back wall booth. A selection of four beers were the most popular. He chose a French one and took a table six feet away, facing the door. This gave good mobility for action and view of the exit.

Gusev acted a little twitchy, but soon relaxed after two double whiskies in rapid succession. Perhaps he had a bowel irritation or his diet lacked the right nutrients. The patron noise, mixed with background music, made eavesdropping a challenge. He could only pick up a word here and there. They spoke in French, which made it more difficult to ascertain. The plan, as he saw it, would be to follow once Gusev left, either on foot or in a cab.

Gusev's companion had a much darker complexion and could

be one of the warlord's lieutenants. The second man wore a cap and looked fit, even under loose attire. He didn't drink alcohol and sat on a water. Both men could be carrying, concealed in several positions.

The atmosphere became competitive as patrons swelled to the bar. A young guy stumbled, bumped him as he shifted in his chair. He tipped his cap as the man veered to his group. Shouts and cheers became louder and more frequent as the lager flowed.

He checked the time: seven-fifty P.M. The African stood, Gusev shook hands, and they parted. He waited. The Russian drained his drink, moved around a rowdy table of partygoers, and exited the bar. Jake slipped out onto the street, catching a glimpse of Gusev as he disappeared on a bend.

Outside, the temperature had dropped five degrees. He zipped the hooded jacket, pushed his hands into his pockets. Gusev headed east toward a cluster of trees on a wider avenue. The map indicated a small four-star hotel sat five minutes away on the hill. If he knew the location of Gusev's residence, that would strengthen the chance of finding the oligarch. He stuck to the edges and bends, out of visibility.

The target climbed the verge onto an embankment. He held back from the strong streetlights that hovered over the traffic. People milled in small groups around a ground floor restaurant. A takeout window for Chinese food attracted a line of customers. He stayed at the bend. A horn beeped as the Russian jaywalked into oncoming traffic.

Gusev entered the hotel. *La Belle Ville*. Green vines crawled around the windows and balconies. His heartbeat rose. An entrance sided by a bank of glass walls. He retreated to a grass strip with a bench obscured by trees. Further surveillance on the hotel and he'd narrow down Gusev's involvement.

He waved a cab and returned to the hotel to pick up equipment. A short-range Wi-Fi scanner on his laptop would pick up signals within a two-hundred-feet radius. He ascended the stairwell and packed his computer in a carry bag. The lightweight armor slipped on under his sweatshirt.

A light drizzle danced in the moonlight, reflecting the faded deco molds. The cab pulled up on the first signal.

"*Bonjour*. Café opposite the *La Belle Ville*."

The driver took off from the shoulder. They eased up to the curbside eatery in five minutes. He paid ten euros and told the driver to keep the change.

"*Merci*."

A steady stream of customers came from both directions in the restaurant below. Jake studied the hotel entrance and noted a lobby with single armchairs. One camera fixed at the sliding glass. He tucked the cap, bolted over the road. Absorbed on his cell phone, he entered the automatic doors and sat in the lobby against the back wall. He flipped the lid and loaded the main page. If Gusev used the hotel Wi-Fi, he'd be able to track the signal quickly.

The counter staff did not notice him. A man in his twenties serviced an elderly couple, another four people waiting in line. The scan showed four connections in French; the screens could be individually scrutinized. None were likely to be the target.

He broadened the range toward the upper floors and picked up three more terminals. A cooking show and YouTube clips were displayed on the first two. Google searches for fashion outlets and the famous cemetery *Pere Lachaise*. Tourist attractions. Not the target's choice.

Chatter from the reception got louder. He glanced over and saw less people waiting in the queue. The top floors gave him two new connections. An inbox displayed the subject lines in Russian.

Got him. He registered the terminal ID for future reference.

The program copied the email content. He waited for the download. An attachment contained specs for warheads. Measurements and impacts were listed. He held his breath. This shipment couldn't be trading to the warlords and local extremists.

He hacked the terminal audio and plugged his headphone jack. The platform enabled the recording function. He activated the process.

The hotel reception line reduced to the last two people. In raised voices, a pair of young men were booking a room. No doubt irritated by the long wait. *This might work in my favor: prolong the distraction long enough to get eavesdrop on Gusev.*

A conversation between two men had commenced in Gusev's room. The heavy Russian dialog, bounced to the second, could be the oligarch. Words were spoken fast; the audio faded with interference. He strained to understand the conversation: 'Shipping container... Netherlands tomorrow.' Static or outside interference. He caught '... bound for Japan.'

The second man suggested a meeting. A plaza food court called *Boom Boom Villette*. Tomorrow at ten-thirty A.M.

Silence. Jake stopped the recording and quit the connection. The laptop closed with a click. He took off the headphones and strolled to the doors. As the glass panels slid apart, he scrutinized his phone, head down and away from the CCTV.

Night security at the hotel consisted of one young man. He smiled and continued to the bay, got into the apartment without any further contact. The audio file sounded clearer with a bit of tweaking. He sent it to Lavigne for analysis. Gusev was a low-level thug. He'd need to move up the food chain to get to the oligarch. This meeting could be the one.

Boom Boom Villette sat nestled by water on the edge of the nineteenth arrondissement. He heated a bowl of rice in the microwave and took a spoon from the drawer. The clock read eleven-ten P.M. He studied the center layout. A food court in the center had a variety of fast food from McDonalds to Chinese takeout. Surveillance and IDs in the morning would be the most effective approach. He'd take the SIG in case a situation arose. The public toilets were situated in the west corner. They could be an opportunity.

The rice became dry at the bottom, so he threw the remainder in the bin. He set the alarm for six A.M.. The SIG went under the bed within arm's reach.

Chapter 11

A THIN WHITE line formed on the windowsill. Jake opened an eye at a clunk sounding somewhere in the hotel. Five-sixteen A.M. The basin filled with water, he splashed his face, surprised that he did not remember the dream. For the last six days, the same sequence. A chase with a gun. Katerina held at gunpoint. His skills evaporated and rendered useless.

On the living room floor, he stretched and meditated. Sat still, legs crossed.

"I'm energized and fully protected."

He did one hundred pushups. His chest expanded with each repetitive movement, heart pumping blood faster. A quick shower with hot water relaxed the tension in his muscles. He swiped the condensation on the mirror, stared into the reflection. The lack of sleep had begun to show.

The kitchen tiles were cold underfoot. He tipped muesli into a bowl, added milk from the fridge, and settled at the table. The computer booted quickly. A map of *Boom Boom Villette* shopping plaza flickered in 3D. He memorized the exits, staff corridors, elevators and lifts, and fire stairwells. He knew every meter of the structure. It may not be necessary, but better to know and not need it, than to need it and not know.

Lavigne had sent a message. The second man from Gusev's meeting last night worked for a criminal syndicate from the Congo. Small-arms dealer using the underground network in Paris. The Frenchman's agency had been tracking their movements for six months.

At the sink, he rinsed the bowl, dried with a towel and placed it in the single cupboard. He brushed his teeth twice a day for personal hygiene, but also to avoid being memorable. If your breath had an odor, people tend to recall. All these factors must be covered in order to blend into the crowd.

The weapon sat on the table. He'd left it in the bathroom while having a shower and now placed it in the small of his back. A second, hooded, dark gray jacket fastened up to the neck, a rugby cap pulled over his hair. In the carry bag, he took a micro-tracker. If the second guy proved more important than Gusev, he'd track him to the next destination.

The stairwell was empty. Cold morning air circulated the sidewalk, shards of light breaking through gaps in the clouds. Pedestrians increased in numbers as they marched to work in both directions.

He hailed a cab. In two minutes, one eased over and the passenger window buzzed open.

"*Bonjour, monsieur.* Where too?"

"*Bonjour.* Take me to a hire car place. One near the hotel please." He crouched at the window.

"No problem."

The driver took off in a northerly direction, weaving into the dregs of peak-hour traffic. The GPS guided them to a car rental agency on Gambetta Avenue in the twentieth. He got out at the gate and walked across the lot. The vehicles were all new models, the office in a large, stand-up booth. Peugeots were the most numerous.

"I'd like to hire a rental for three days. A model economical with gas, but some power too." He hired a late model, navy-blue Peugeot, one of the most common and best-selling models in Paris. Windows with maximum smoke tint. Engine upgrade to 1.5 liter for extra grunt. Perfect for blending in when following a target.

The GPS had been upgraded, according to the sales attendant. He inputted *Boom Boom Villette*, turned onto the *Boulevards des Marechaux* and drove north. Parklands loomed on the left, hidden behind rows of red and green tree foliage. In gaps, he could see the Eiffel tower jutting into the pale blue sky. The bridge took him over *La Villette* which ran west into the canal, *La Bassin* and met the Seine. On summer days, swimmers enjoyed the three open-air pools, surrounding banks dotted with umbrellas and lounge chairs.

A barrier surrounded the red structure, the building like a prop from the original nineteen-sixties *Star Trek* with Shatner and Nimoy. Shoppers gathered in numbers on the concrete and grass, the canal waters glinting in the background. He spotted a parking area a few streets away, walked the rest of the way to the front.

The interior gave way to silver monuments and gleaming escalators. Shop fronts flowed in an orderly and tasteful fashion. He grabbed a takeout coffee and roamed the perimeter of the food court. Surveillance cameras were limited in number and most were static positions. A shoe shop that sold active footwear provided an idea. Tacked to shelves and walls, dozens of options were available. He tried on a medium pair of black trainers, spare pairs always needed.

A shopkeeper placed them in a branded, reusable bag with the receipt. The carry bag gave a layer of authenticity: a shopper in the food court with purchase.

Gusev sat in a booth opposite McDonalds kiosk. His companion, sitting at a right-angle to Gusev, held a cell phone. The second man, heavyset and taller, sucked on soft drink and leaned in to talk. Fairer brown hair than Gusev and probably late twenties, He could pass for Russian or French.

He held back, keeping a distance of thirty feet from the targets. They'd both be ultra-paranoid, ready to act at the slightest concern. Shopping centers were difficult to stake targets, regardless of the cover. At quarter-to-eleven, the lunch buyers were still a good hour away. Jake chose a seat between the escalator and the public bathrooms.

A play with the burner, sip the coffee, check the shop signs; he alternated between activities. Gusev chatted, looking casual.

On the next table, a mother juggled three boys to their seats. The youngest—must have been five years—screamed and cried, refusing to settle. She shook her finger, telling him off.

He returned focus to the men. At eleven-ten A.M., the second man walked off toward the escalator. Jake waited until the target made it out of the general sphere. He grasped his bag and followed, leaving a fifty feet gap. Talking on his cell phone, the man sidestepped slower shoppers, aiming at the exit to the parking lot.

Jake needed to get ahead to avoid suspicion, or being made if he showed too much interest in the plates. As they got closer to the exterior, he leveled with the target, but opposite sides of the corridor. Plants and sculptures separated them, people veering in and out. A kiosk with a neon telco sign blinked, staff waving to grab attention. He changed course, broke to a jog, and pushed through a door.

The target stopped at the threshold. Jake had to keep the momentum going or be caught. He ducked behind a truck. The target pulled a cell phone from his pocket, staring across the sea of cars. In his other hand, a key fob; the chirp was close. Coming around the truck's cabin, Jake dawdled near the sound, sunglasses covering his eyes. He spotted the man's ride.

A green sedan—Renault Megane: last year's model. He edged toward the vehicle, coming up from the rear. Diagonal, and from the right, the target advanced. Jake memorized the license plate: DA 625 VT. At the next row, he kept walking, bobbing his head in the direction of the other side of the parking lot as if trying to find his car.

The Renault door slammed, the engine fired. This must be Gusev's next level of management. At medium pace, he backtracked to the hire car—not too fast, not to slow—texting the plates to Lavigne while he walked.

Chapter 12

BY THE TIME Jake sat behind the wheel, Lavigne had replied. The plates from Gusev's friend came up as a company vehicle registered to a trading name and postal drop box located near the docks. It had few other assets or employees. This led to a law office that acted as proxy, shuffling paperwork and administration, hidden behind a confidentially clause. A wall of shelf companies and limited liability that led nowhere.

The second guy's name was Boris Morozov, a middleman who specialized in introductions, took a commission on every deal. Never served jail time in Europe. Always a go-between, didn't care to know his client's intent or motivation.

Jake used an old backdoor into the NSA database and ran checks on the addresses and names. In the first data dives, nothing new surfaced. He sent an email to Lavigne requesting a cell number and to place a wiretap on Boris.

Birds squawked from the canal, cutting into the high trees, taking flight before the rain. The oligarch had to be nearby, holed up in luxury. He drove south to a hill in a park and hid in a secluded area. Window down, he watched over the treetops. He spotted a sheltered rest area with seating. Water in hand, he slung the computer strap over his shoulder and sat in the shaded area near the car.

An AI program crawled through past transactions and bank reporting. It connected the little information he discovered and resourced remote links in the data. Offshore records that went nowhere again, dead ends at every turn.

He stared at the landscape, a northerly wind scattering leaves over the grass. The afternoon brought little change to the overcast. Intermittent rays failed to brighten the gray horizon.

The primary company was suspiciously blank, deliberately cleaned, and left with the basics to satisfy tax obligations or prying eyes and investigators. There had to be something tangible. The mouse cursor spun. He figured the program must be finishing and covering off the last bits of data. He placed the laptop to the side and eased back on the bench.

As the software wound up, an alert flashed. A match. He squinted at the numbers, hoping for a tangible lead. A payment was made to a company last year from one of the connected accounts. A quick check on the account name: Ivanov. The oligarch.

His burner rang, pulled him out of thought.

"Thanks to those plates and description you sent, I've got something on Boris Morozov. His number and a few associations. We intercepted a few suspects in connection with ongoing enquiries, so he's mixed up with the arms trade here. How much we are yet to verify." Lavigne paused; paper rustled in the background. "Also calls made to a French citizen. An entrepreneur with wide business interests. Her name is Eloise Dupont. Made her money in manufacturing and art. Not sure if this is directly related to the oligarch."

"Interesting." Jake closed the computer lid.

A teenager with a dog walked by.

"Boris' number and last known address is being sent to you. We will keep an eye out, and on the air waves, and let you know any developments as they arise. Remember I have limited manpower too."

"Hundred percent, as millennials say. I'll keep you posted."

The phone cut out.

He drove out of the gravel parking lot and headed south-west. The road merged with *Avenue de Flandre* to follow the canal toward the Seine. A shop sold baguettes, so he pulled into the road shoulder and went inside. The smell made him hungry. He bought a double-turkey baguette, added lettuce, cheese and pickles. It came with a rich French sauce. He took an apple juice from the fridge, paid and left.

The GPS icon flickered over the address for Boris Morozov. A small house in the eleventh arrondissement behind a retail strip. He pressed the DIRECTIONS button and lowered the sunglasses over his face.

Entering a narrow avenue, past two bars and up a lane with a gym, young people sat al fresco in groups, laughing and enjoying the limited sunshine. A cobbled slope brought him to a sharp right behind a glitzy but faded brasserie that had seen better days.

The former stable cum storeroom had been converted to a bedsit tacked onto the bar on first-level stilts. He reversed to the front, left the car parallel parked, and walked to the rear section of dirt, the Renault out of place, tucked between two rickety posts and a lean-to.

The stairs creaked and shifted under his weight. Reaching the landing, he sidled by the window. A fridge against the wall, scuffed countertop with a sink. Boris sat at a rustic timber table staring at a pile of white powder. Tweaker. Beer bottle in hand, another man stood with his back facing Jake. A TV on mute played in the corner. Don't get high on your own supply; they didn't get the memo. The oligarch must be using up these local expendables.

He retreated down the stairs and fixed a micro-tracker under the Renault fender. Covered by shrubs, the lane didn't attract visitors. A flimsy mailbox marked the entrance, framed by the fence, the only evidence of the rear address. He climbed the unmade path, crossed the road, and bought a bottle of water. Stools lined the window. He sat and watched. He couldn't see cameras or surveillance on the bar exterior. Boris probably didn't bother, thinking his connections and reputation were security enough.

In the car, he switched the handheld console on. It connected to the tracker and flickered to life. He waited for the icon to appear on the map grid. The Renault sat stationary in the same spot. Time and patience would reveal the usefulness of the night club junkie cum middleman.

He started the engine, pulled into the lane, and drove to the main avenue. A web of small streets curved into the twentieth. The GPS took him north, along *Boulevard de Menilmontant* and a straight run past the pillared gates of *Pere Lachaise*. He imagined the dead souls it contained, many famous names such as Jim Morrison and Oscar Wilde laid in eternal rest, no longer concerned about the world's issues.

Over the junction, he came to a strip of shops and parked. A Chinese restaurant had nasi goreng and a chicken rice combination on the menu. The order took ten minutes. A waiter carried a steaming bag with three containers. He paid for the food and got back into the traffic.

The monitor showed no movement from Boris. Near six P.M., he braked in a side street near his hotel. He grabbed the food and the tracking console, placed it in his bag, and headed inside.

An increased interest in the specials meant the hotel lobby declared capacity. The chatter and small talk of hungry people always seems to be loud. It required many 'excusez moi' and 'pardon et moi.'

He closed the door and sank into the couch. The dust danced in the air. He propped the tracker monitor on a table, the weapon within grasp. The meal went down with swigs from the beer bottle.

A text came from Lavigne. The Frenchman had been scanning the towers but no hits on the oligarch or any of his associates.

Jake replied:

Went to address, located Boris. Tracker on car. Awaiting further action. May need backup. Let you know. Update soon.

The transmitter console beeped. Boris was on the move.

Chapter 13

THE RED DOT blinked on the grid, moving southwest at the city. Jake watched the console, the car's path weaving through a web of streets. He threw the bag of rubbish in the trash compartment.

Microwave digits glowed: seven-twenty P.M. He checked the equipment spread over the table. The weapon cleaned and ready, he studied the tracker monitor display. It could be a long night if the icon ended at a far place. The best strategy would be drive out early in the same direction, be in proximity when Boris lands.

Daylight receded behind the horizon, city lights lacing the edge of the Seine in golds, greens and reds like Christmas. He shoved the tracker device in the carry bag and grabbed his cap. The SIG returned to the small of his back.

The fire stairwell echoed with his footsteps. A side exit meant he avoided most of the dinner rush. He tossed the bag onto the passenger side and fired up his ride. A light patter of rain hit the windshield as his hire car joined the traffic flow, a sea of red taillights snaking into the turn.

He watched the monitor. The icon neared the Seine where a side street met the main avenue. The route didn't make sense. He examined the median. A straight line of trees ran parallel up the middle. Paris loves its flora.

A right turn. The icon slowed. He waited for pedestrians.

The tracked car stopped at a cluster of prestigious town houses: stylish, expensively maintained century-old features. Cabled and shuttered balconies loomed over cobblestone laneways. One needed lots of money to live in a nineteenth-century mansion in the first arrondissement. Jake swapped lanes, checked both side mirrors, and kept on thirty mph. No familiar cars. Five minutes away against the traffic flow, maximum seven.

A light hung over the entrance, and Boris' car setback from the curb. He ran the address. It came up under a woman's name.

At nine-forty P.M., two figures stood backlit at the entrance. The first a man. Boris. Followed by a female, shorter, and petite in dress and coat. She slipped a key in the lock. A gust kicked up her coat tail. The pair walk to the road bend, took a left at the fork.

The street curled at a right angle under a streetlight. Jake followed from thirty feet. Ahead on a roof awning, neon letters in red and blue over double-glass. Music pumping onto the street. He kept visual, but right back from a corner shop. A doorman nodded at the female and they vanished inside.

He moved in behind a group of attractive young clubbers. The staff unhooked the fancy rope, too busy flirting with the women to give a guy in a cap much notice. He took in the layout. Fifty to sixty feet deep to the rear wall. The targets were ordering drinks. He hung back, scoping from the edge.

Overlapping conversations. The DJ was taking a break, a trance mix playing on the speakers. A bar wrapped the far east side. He kept his head low, moved through the patrons. Young women in cocktail dresses, men more casual: some in caps and similar attire.

Boris and the woman took their conversation to a booth. Jake shouldered into bodies, aimed at the bar. A young woman took his order and slid the beer bottle into his hand. The atmosphere livened as more people flowed onto the dance floor. He parted with fifteen euro and did a lap of the perimeter.

In the corner, he sent Lavigne a text with the woman's address and description. He sat two tables away from the pair, waiting for the reply. The beep came in ten minutes.

Sophia Laurent. She is an entrepreneur in primary manufacturing textile. Non-executive chair on three boards. Shareholder in a major fashion brand. There's a vague connection to the oligarch two months ago. We're investigating.

The music changed to drum and bass. *Why would a successful businessperson be associated with a low-level middleman and trafficker?* Different lights strafed the dance floor. The DJ clambered behind the booth and raised his hands. Arms went up in response. Boris waved at a waitress who leaned in to hear the order.

Nine-fifty P.M. Jake stretched his spine and stood, careful not to be in their visual. Sophia sat on a spirit glass. Boris smiled and chatted, drinking his alcohol twice as fast.

Jake passed the dance floor and ducked out into the night air. Circling back to her townhouse, he pulled up the maps app. A laneway cut behind the buildings. No motion cameras or sensors. Unusual. The cobblestones were slick from recent rain. A six-foot paling fence marked the boundary of her property. He took gloves from his pocket, squeezed them onto each hand, and pulled himself to the top. A flower bed cushioned his dtop.

The brick-paved area had an outdoor metal setting, two chairs and a table. Vine creepers covered a garage on the west side. He crept to the iron security door. An older style with a solid but basic latch. He poked the tension wrench in the hole. Each pin gave way in turn with applied pressure. He cracked open the teak door, slipped inside and shut it behind him.

A renovated kitchen with pendant lights glinted in the dark. Stainless steel appliances recessed under a circular stone countertop. High end set-up. The kitchen had nothing of note. He started with the living room, searching drawers, but kept it neat. The stairs curved to a first-floor landing. A bathroom set in marble. Opposite, a good size bedroom with a queen bed. He didn't expect to find incriminating evidence lying around. A large robe had a good collection of gowns and dresses. There was a small pistol in the side table. Three bullets, one in the chamber. Interesting.

He checked the top floor, found another two small bedrooms and a bathroom. These were guest bedrooms: less furniture and basic bed linen. He took the corkscrew stairs to ground level and contemplated the kitchen to work out what to do next.

Chapter 14

SOPHIA PERCHED ON the curb. Headlight beams blinded her. She averted her eyes. Boris gave a sharp horn blast and revved into the turn. She bristled. A person in his position should not be drawing attention to himself—and her. Discretion is preferred: always keep a low profile.

She sighed and squinted at her keys under the sparse streetlight. Nausea swept over her, as though she'd drunk much more than two vodkas. Her companion had consumed five glasses of the spirit, some suspected double strength top-ups. Maybe the years were catching up.

A creak sounded from the rear. The neighbor's dog barked: his usual greeting. She placed her coat on the rack. The deadlock firmly in place, keys were placed in a drawer below the sideboard.

She made it to the connecting archway roped in shadows. Flicked the light switch. She suppressed a gasp and her hand went to her mouth. A man with a cap and COVID face mask sat at the table. Her initial instinct was to scream. Having thought better of it, she opted to wait for the stranger to speak.

"Hi, Sophia. Please do sit down." Jake smiled and pointed at the table. The gun rested on his knee. "The safety is on. I mean you no harm if we can talk amicably."

"Who are you?"

"I'd just like to ask you a few questions." He sat back from the edge to maintain enough distance between them.

She nodded and lowered into a seat opposite, gaze locked with his.

"I'm seeking a Russian last seen here in Paris. Ivanov."

Her confidence rose. "So you break into my home. What does this have to do with me?"

"You keep some questionable company. I saw the meeting with

Boris."

"I'm a businessperson and am permitted to have meetings."

He shifted his feet and watched her. "These are people of interest to law enforcement. That makes your practises come under question."

"Do you mind if I make a coffee?" she said, refocusing on the appliances.

"Sure, but no sudden moves."

Laurent slouched to the bench and grasped the coffee maker. A spark and a hiss as the gas stove fired. She opened a packet of European grounds and heaped a spoonful into the percolator[zf1]. Every action slow and deliberate, cool under the pressure of an armed stranger in her house.

"I need Ivanov's location from you."

"Why should I help you? My involvement is circumstantial at most."

"You're complicit, to say the least, with two crime figures. I have evidence of your meeting, and wiretaps with Boris. Do you really need the heat of being followed and tapped more closely?"

The device on the stove whistled. She took it off and poured the contents into a mug. "Would you like one?"

"No, thanks."

"I'm in a compromised position here. These people are not to be trifled with. More danger than you understand."

"It will be worse if you continue to do business with them. The visits will become more formal, and from local government institutions. They will take this matter much further. Your reputation would not recover from a major investigation, much less prosecution."

He let the words sit for a minute as she sipped her coffee. The cogs were working overtime in her mind. She stared at the darkness out the window.

Finally, she tilted her head as if returning to the room. "There are other partners and board members of my companies. It's a complex arrangement."

"So I am aware. Is textiles and fashion taking a battering now? I know you run some legit businesses, so unsure of the need for such dubious associations."

Laurent ignored that comment and sighed. "If I give you this information, what then? You cannot guarantee there will be no retribution."

"I won't bother you anymore if the intel is correct. Immunity cannot be given, but I can put in a word with certain people that you cooperated. No promises. Perhaps you could beef up your security. But you might be advised to cease transactions with the likes of Boris. You would not want to be caught in the middle and come up on other radars with Interpol or law enforcement."

Laurent said, "Wait here, please. I'm going to the next room."

He nodded and shifted the chair for a better view.

Lights flooded the living room. A high-end chaise lounge faced a wall-mounted TV. He could see a walnut side table near a fireplace. She bent down at an antique desk drawer and shuffled the contents. Papers rustled. He straightened his back and extended his right leg outward.

The light clicked off as she waited in the archway.

"He moves every week or so and changes his number constantly. The current location is *Roi de Sicile* on Rivoli, his room in the deluxe apartments at the smaller side. He has covert personnel on both entrances."

Jake nodded. "No doubt. Anything else you can tell me?"

She pressed her phone and went through the menu. "Here's a burner number he used a few days ago. As far as I know, it has not changed yet. He's had this one a bit longer. Not sure why."

"Got it." He gained his feet. "Mind if I use the front door this time?"

"Be my guest."

Laurent led into the dimly lit foyer and flipped the switch, heels clicking on the hardwood.

"I hope this will be the end of the matter," she said over her shoulder. "Remember I can get to you too."

She closed the door after him. The temperature had dropped another two degrees. He turned right in the cold breeze and circled back to the car in case someone was watching.

He drove out of the lane, Laurent's words echoing in his mind. Her networks would be bigger with each new contact. At the next intersection, he checked his mirrors. Headlight beams shone behind him. He was sure the car was the same color as the one when he left: a late model red Audi. The traffic signal went green. He pulled a hard right without the blinker at the last second, pressing the accelerator.

The Audi tires squealed as the vehicle tracked the same path. Jake hammered down the avenue, hunting for a getaway. Traffic thickened at the juncture ahead. A green light flickered into amber. He ramped up over the limit, punching over the white lines on a red signal.

Tires screeched and a horn beeped. The needle sat on one hundred kilometers per hour. He fishtailed at a laneway. The GPS showed a right angle, car slid into a slot in an overhang. Jake got out and crept toward the opening, hugged the brick wall. He pulled the SIG and flicked off the safety.

The Audi braked at the mouth. Door slammed. A shadow fell over the concrete. The swish of clothing indicated a possible weapon draw.

Jake knelt at a stack of cardboard waste. A large man peered into the gap. Jake held the weapon ready to point and shoot.

The man called out in French, words beyond Jake's rudimentary understanding of the language. He could not see a weapon but that did not mean the assailant was not armed. Vehicles slid past on the road beyond, beams bobbed on the man's position. A second stream of French which ended with the word 'Laurent.' The guy would be wary of potential witnesses.

A standoff as both men waited in silence.

Footsteps receded. The engine purred. Tires crunched on asphalt and stone; the Audi turned away.

After a quick outer check for trackers, Jake sunk behind the wheel and exited by the other side.

Chapter 15

LATE AFTERNOON SUN beamed on Katerina's shawl. Dust stirred in her wake, commuters coming home from work. She'd walked close to one mile, from one side of the city to the other. A quick break to catch her breath and she paused to drink water. She backhanded sweat beads away. The shades and headdress were still not enough to protect from the heat.

A rickety gate and small fence separated the home. She knocked on the blue-painted door, waited for someone to answer. A second tap echoed into the house. She heard footsteps on a solid floor.

The door cracked and a young man answered. "Can I help you?"

"Is Amin home, please?"

He nodded and retreated into the house. The hushed voices of two males.

Amin came to the doorway. He seemed to glide, hover off the ground. Rather than comment, he watched her and smiled.

"Hi. I am Katerina. I came to speak to you about the kidnap."

The captive's brother tipped his head toward her. "I don't want this conversation to go to the wrong outlet. I have a family to protect."

"I understand. Please know that I will not publish this information. Only want to investigate what happened to my ex-partner and why. If you could please spare me some time to speak briefly, that would be appreciated."

He angled past her to peer at the dusty road. An old car drove by, followed by a cyclist going the other way. Amin waved her inside and shut the door.

"You must stay out of sight. We can both be in danger being seen in public by the wrong person."

She followed him into a side entrance to a larger room. The

drapes were drawn, an old couch against the wall.

"Please sit."

"I need to know did their deaths have to do with the Taliban? It wasn't just a kidnap and ransom, was it?"

The man's face turned to stone, his eyes hazy. For a minute, they sat in a silence like an eternity.

"Nothing is simple in Syria. We have been in conflict for hundreds of years. On some occasions with ourselves." Grief touched his face, pity mixed with love for the hopeless situation in his country. His raisin eyes sought her gaze. "Because your partner was Russian, he was worth more to them as a hostage. A political statement."

"Or defiance."

"Yes, that could be it too. One day I hope we can have peace here in our country."

She nodded "So do I."

He shifted position and stared out the crack in the window. "I don't think this will be achieved in my lifetime."

"Is there anything else you can recall?"

"I am sorry, but this is the extent of my knowledge on the matter. My brother crosses my thoughts every day and is always in my daily prayers. The tragedy is ongoing for all of us unfortunately."

Katerina rose. "Thank you so much for inviting me into your home."

He showed her to the blue door.

"Take care." She placed the shades on her face and made sure the shawl was secure.

The heat was still beating down, but a gentle breeze provided some relief. She swallowed water, preparing for the journey. A group of teenagers talked loudly outside a neighbor's house. Car tires crunched on the gravel. She began her long walk back to the other side of the city.

Colors of surrounding structures reflected over the hotel as Jake pulled up to the curb. He killed the engine and checked the entrance. The odd window flickered with life, but most were dark, bedded down for the evening. He left the face mask in the console and took the fire stairwell two steps at a time.

He walked the empty corridor, secured the door, and activated the power with his key card. The time read one-ten A.M. Bag shrugged off, dumped on the table, he shed the day's clothes in a pile in the bathroom. The pair of shorts he had in the bedroom.

In a pair of shorts, he rotated through various positions, pumping out sets of fifty push-ups with two-minute breaks between. At the end, he did hovers and other core exercises until sweat formed on his brow. Two discs of electrolyte dissolved in a glass of water. He drained the contents and turned the shower on.

The water ran over his face, comforting after the hectic night. He didn't trust Sophia Laurent and suspected she was hiding information about the extent of her association with the oligarch.

Boris had served well enough. If the oligarch surfaced and he neutralized the threat, it would be job done. He cut the water and straightened the bathmat. Hot water had relieved some of the aches and pains. Fresh underwear, a sweatshirt and sweatpants lay out on the bed. He shrugged them on and sat in front of the TV.

He sent Katerina an email including the details of Sophia Laurent and asked for a background check. She would connect with different sources to Lavigne and might come up with valuable intel on the wider operation. Any deeper insight into the oligarch's international network of companies held the most mystery, how far this had spread.

The first update to McCallister would be brief and to the point. If scanners or tracking were about, the window consisted of three minutes.

McCallister's phone rang five times before he picked up.

"Hello."

"It's Sphinx."

Silence as McCallister processed the handle. "How are you?"

"Close to the target. I've located his hotel and working out the next move."

"Nice one, son. It's tricky locating these guys but I knew we could rely on you. Let me know when it's done."

"I'll be in touch."

Jake placed the burner down. The phone went black, battery low. A USB cable connected it to power. He poured water into a glass. Canal lights glittered like heaped dragon treasure, spanning for miles in the darkness.

A bird fluttered on the rail and took off toward the trees. The upmarket section of the oligarch's hotel would be his next move. His bodyguard had already been made, watching on the street. There would be more inside. He finished the water, considered a possible balcony he could go to if he could identify the room number and position. On exit, a sniper angle might be possible, depending on the neighboring structures. Hardware upgrade required. Penetrating the hotel and getting out would be too risky. Surveillance at dawn. Wait until the oligarch left the building; scope the terrain, calculate the opportunity and risks.

He sent a text to Lavigne.

I'm getting closer. Dawn? Chance or a rifle, full kit? 90 meters. Total deniability. Let me know.

He lay down in bed, meditated on a mantra to clear his head. The exercise made him tired, helped with shutting down the mind and body.

Sounds of the city faded as he drifted off into sleep.

Chapter 16

JAKE OPENED AN eyelid. Blood throbbed in his temples. He rolled out of the sheet, placed feet on the floor. Katerina's talk about the ghosts of the past came to mind.

Five A.M. He used the bathroom and padded to the lounge. First sign of dawn broke in shards, piercing the living room in elongated knives. The burner flickered to life. Lavigne. He took it off the charger.

Delivery. Door knock in five.

Cereal tumbled into a bowl. Knock on the door. He cracked it. Carry bag, full kit. Corridor empty.

He chewed cereal and finalized the dawn task requirements, checking Google maps. The oligarch's hotel had a mix of commercial and residential buildings. High and low-rise buildings in *Le Marais*. For surveillance, a block down from the private entrance would be a good start. The hotel sat two back from the corner. If the oligarch had a driver pick-up scenario, an opening in the gap might be an opportunity. Perfect timing and execution.

Five thirty-three. He brushed his teeth, pulled on jeans and a fresh black hoodie, alternated caps to dark gray, backpack loaded: pair of gloves, tracker monitor, rifle scope for long vision, a blue cap and a spare magazine. Two flash grenades tucked in the bottom. The weapon slotted to the small of his back.

He jogged down the stairwell. The smell of eggs, pastries and meat as the hotel restaurant fired up the breakfast menu to start at six-thirty. He slung into the rental and pulled out into traffic. Dew glistened on the grass, sidewalks dry with little rainfall last night. He moved lanes, sticking to the limit. Not many cars this time of morning.

Did a lap to check mirrors for shadows, noted any familiar drivers and vehicles, pedestrians in fixed positions near the hotel. Appeared to be clear. Harder to stalk with minimal commuters on the road. He arrived at the rear entrance in fifteen minutes.

The shop fronts were closed except for a laundromat a few doors down across the other side of the road. A forty-something, bulky, man in a dark suit paced the sidewalk opposite. Ex-military or career bodyguard. Tall, with an upright stance, hair short top and sides, he talked on a cell phone.

With his burner, Jake sent a photo of the man's profile to Lavigne to check for a match.

Pedestrians swarmed the sidewalk as morning peak rolled into action. Jake swigged from a water bottle, shifted in the seat. He opened the door and hovered on the curb. The stretch went through his hamstrings, straightened his spine. A click in his back. Swiveled his neck in each direction. More clicks.

A quick lap past the shop fronts, he maintained visual on the hotel exit. Gray clouds hung low, promising rainfall at any moment. The commuters were dressed as genuine workers; scarves and long coats to combat the weather. The attire could hide potential danger.

Jake returned to the car and passed the scope crosshairs over the oligarch's thug. The bodyguard hung back at the corner, trying to be discreet. He scanned the hotel exit with a distinct squint. A dip of the chin indicated a lapel mike. If the oligarch left the hotel, they would radio this gorilla first. That would preempt departure, give off a signal, hopefully in enough time to act, Jake reasoned.

Eleven A.M. The henchman dipped his chin. Lips moved. Jake sat upright and pointed the scope. The man walked to the curb and examined the pedestrians that passed.

Had to be the oligarch's exit. Jake screwed a suppressor on the SIG barrel, placed the firearm on his front under the jacket. It would still produce a bang but reduce the volume.

He put the mask on, casually opened the car via the passenger side, and slipped onto the sidewalk. The traffic and movement gave his position sufficient cover. He walked casually to the pedestrian lights. The crossing ticker clicked faster and the green light flashed. The crowd of walkers hid him from sight, moving with the cluster over the intersection.

A trash bin sat on the corner, green metal mesh with a silver cap. He stood next to it and fumbled in his pocket as if retrieving a lost personal item. His fingers found the flash grenade and he pulled the pin, dumping it into the trash can. The hotel door swung outward, facing toward his position. A burly man in a suit came first, sunglasses on despite the overcast. Following close came a loafer-covered foot: the oligarch.

The burly guy came to a stop, not concerned about the flow of people. Reconnaissance left, right, and left again. He waved at the guy opposite with the universal sign.

All clear.

A countdown from five. Slow and steady. The oligarch's party turned and strolled toward Jake's position. He kept his head lowered, cap visor obscuring his face. In forty seconds, the oligarch would pass his position and turn right, or take the lights straight ahead.

He moved around the bin. The group reached a window ten feet away from his position. A couple walked between him and the first bodyguard. No collateral damage. Head down, he passed the group, circled until he had a clear scope of the target's back.

The lights went green. Diagonally across the street, the first thug tailed the pair. A bang echoed like fireworks or a discharge. The bodyguard screamed in Russian. People ran in every direction, not sure of the source or damage. Jake pulled the pin on a second flash grenade.

A woman yelled. Jake threw the second flash grenade. It rolled behind the bodyguard and exploded. The chaos unfolded as if in slow motion. Jake pulled the weapon and fired at the oligarch's exposed back: one in the head, second in the back. A double tap. The SIG went back under his zip as he walked off diagonally across the sidewalk.

Sirens sounded in the distance. Passers-by jogged to join the people gathered at the body. He reached the car, clicked the alarm fob, and sank into the driver's seat. No one paid attention or glanced his way. Deep breaths. He started the touch ignition, checked both mirrors.

The blinker ticked as he joined the lane and cruised by the huddle on the road. A light patter began. He steered off the avenue and took a right, headed north toward the base.

Chapter 17

A STRIP OF cafes and restaurants in a tree-lined street. He continued through a banked-up section of traffic and out to a main avenue.

The establishment media would converge quickly on the murder scene. He needed to create as much distance as possible from the event. Lavigne would find out, if he hadn't already. The oligarch's network appeared larger than initially estimated. It felt like McCallister was hiding something and may rope him into more work now the Russian was dead.

He turned at a fork in the road, checking his lane for recurring cars. Up and coming mobsters and dealers were lining up to take Ivanov's place. The oligarch's death may be minor in the larger network. He took the highway heading toward the hotel.

Twelve-twenty P.M. His phone chimed. Katerina. He pulled over and picked up the call.

"Hey there."

"Hi, stranger." Her voice sounded sweet but weary.

"How's things? I miss you."

"Me too." She closed her eyes. "I've hit a dead end here and I'm packing up to go."

"Did you find what you wanted?"

"I think so. As much as I ever will."

"Good. I'm proud of you for trying." He caught his breath. "The oligarch's dead."

"That is news. Finally we are rid of him."

"A long time coming."

"I read your email. Laurent is connected to a chain of international shelf companies situated in Europe. I discovered the trail this morning, but I'm still researching. Assets in Netherlands and the United Kingdom. The oligarch has made payments and schedules for shipments from a warehouse address that showed up as Netherlands. Rotterdam ports."

"Interesting. It has to be connected to this syndicate."

"It sure must. I can go from here and travel to the Netherlands. Journalist contacts there with established media that will help and give me intel."

"We need to be careful poking around. There's a fortune behind this activity and ruthless people will do anything to protect it. I had someone follow me last night. Don't know who or why yet. The oligarch is a minor pawn in the larger network."

"I am always careful. It's a high-risk venture, but you know I'm up to it."

Jake smiled. He knew how resilient she could be. "Let me know when you land. And thanks for helping out."

"We're a team now, Jake. Miss you."

"Bye."

He continued to the hotel to offload the gear and regroup. The roads became busier, lunch hour, as he located a parking position. He locked the car, entered the lobby with a group of tourists. Fellow Americans who chatted and unfolded a large map. He boarded the elevator, swiped the card, and placed the backpack on the table.

His burner buzzed again.

"Hello."

"Nice work today. Those flash grenades come in handy."

"Thanks. Could not have done it without your supplies."

"Works out well as my department gets rid of another undesirable foreigner but we avoid the political issues. Deniability is the key." Lavigne paused. "Where to from here? Local?"

"Not sure. The arms connection with the oligarch is a lot larger than I initially estimated."

"We've suspected this for a long time, but don't have enough evidence yet. Happy to aid our allies, especially when it's mutually beneficially."

"I'll let my team know and be in touch about your equipment."

"Talk soon."

He laid the phone on the table, the next call foremost in his mind. Mission completed. He inputted McCallister's number and waited.

"Is it confirmed in Paris?"

"I've completed the contract and witnessed the body. He's gone," Jake reported.

Silence as the words settled.

"That's great. A major player in this race is gone. Someone else will step up soon."

"For sure." He waited for a response.

"I'll transfer the other half straight away."

"Appreciate that."

"Our intel shows an international network. One of the recent transactions the oligarch was involved in needs to be shut down." McCallister cupped the microphone as the noise muffled. "Will you roll into a new contract for five hundred thousand?"

"Are you vying for a promotion, McCallister?"

"Son, I'm protecting the interests of the free world. This threat could be global. The buyers are top level terrorists with unlimited budget. All threats of this magnitude need to be eliminated. You are closest to the scene and one of our best."

"That's what you said last time." Jake arched his spine and gained his feet. "What are the parameters?"

"Continue the investigation and find out where the last shipment was going, and most importantly, to whom. I've got a bad feeling the oligarch was setting up a really big one. That African warlord crate was pocket money in comparison."

"That's all I have to do? No further obligations?" Jake stared beyond the balcony at the rain pattering on the park. Birds had taken cover, windshield wipers at full speed on the traffic as tires sloshed in puddles. With Katerina heading over to Netherlands, he could see this contract to closure and they would both be back on the yacht in a week, at the most two.

"Once we know what country, the players and motives, I can make a decision from there."

"I'll begin this contract once the pay clears for the oligarch. Same rules: no tracking me or other contactors. Need to finish up here and move forward then."

"Sounds good. I will transfer the balance owed and add fifty percent for the next one as a show of good faith."

Jake terminated the call, logged onto his computer, and signed into the encrypted inbox. He checked his security protocols were still airtight. The assignment could not allow hacking or interception by the enemy. Katerina had sent the international transactions and some shipping container sizes. Her data sheets linked the oligarch's accounts consistently to these trades. The regular shipments had left Rotterdam regularly for six months. He opened the fridge, took a beer bottle, and cracked the top. The chilled drink tumbled down his throat and relaxation washed over his body.

A text came from Lavigne:

Meet you at safehouse seven P.M. Prob want to get out fast? No description perp yet. Law calling it ghost. True for most.

The last comments brought a chuckle. His ghost status to the wider community had become so intrinsic to his lifestyle. Often he forgot his own status when immersed in the process.

Laptop lapsed into screensaver mode. He paced the carpet, caught up on the bigger picture. If the arms buy for a terror attack was not executed in Paris, where would it be? With the oligarch gone, the network may only suffer a slight setback, if at all. The mystery arms buyer and their intentions forced his further intervention.

He drained the beer bottle. The rain battered against the glass. He felt like dozing. A meditation session would be healthier, but he wasn't in the mood. He rubbed his temples, focused on the clock: four-fifty-two P.M. Katerina's flight was scheduled to land in Rotterdam in five hours.

The carry bag sat on the countertop. He placed the weapon, scope, vest, spare magazine and rounds inside. In the bathroom, he brushed his teeth and freshened up with a shave. A clean, button shirt and jacket changed his appearance. He crumpled the hoodie and jeans in a bag.

The dinner crowd had swelled again, bringing plenty of cabs to the curb. A light sleet fell on an angle. Water trickled down the gutters. A block from the safehouse, he donated the clothes to a homeless man. The man muttered something unintelligible. He took it as a thank you.

Rain streaked the foyer entrance. He took the old timber steps two at a time. At the door, he knocked twice. Lavigne released the deadlock and they sat at the kitchen table.

He dumped the bag on the surface.

"Thanks for helping."

Lavigne shook his head. "Likewise. Our counterterrorism unit are doing cartwheels." He shifted the carry bag. "You want a beer?"

Jake smiled. "No. I'm good."

"Till next time."

"Sounds like a plan." He rose and shook the Frenchman's hand.

The rain continued relentlessly into the night, trees drooped, creatures retreated to warmer places. A single streetlight shed yellow over the cracked sidewalk. The residential blocks were gloomier in the wet. He read the dashboard, pulled on the demister switch.

The dark roads indifferent to the banished evil, the load was lighter without the gear. He knew McCallister had pushed his sensibilities but came in with a financial offer too good to refuse.

He strummed the steering wheel, the city glittering from the south, an eternal mirage of beauty. Sentimentality seemed to penetrate at the weirdest moments.

Katerina was the only thing that felt real. All else an illusion, a game, or a test.

Chapter 18

THE PLANE WHEELS screamed on the tarmac. Katerina roused from her semi-dream state after falling asleep upright. An announcement had been made in preparation for descent to Rotterdam twenty minutes prior.

She waited for the signal to disembark. Tomorrow morning, she would meet a journalist to discuss operations at the ports. A complex web of ownership within companies existed in the major exporters.

She collected her overhead bag, climbed the ramp into Rotterdam airport and made her way to the luggage collection belts. A digital board glowed twenty to ten P.M. People walked in both directions as she pushed a trolley into Customs. She passed her belongings on the x-ray scans and hailed a cab in the chilly breeze.

The three-star hotel sat on the verge of the industrial zone. This provided quick access to the area to investigate. She checked in at reception, unlocked the door and jumped in the shower. Fluffy towels were stacked on a rail shelf and she used one to dry her body. She slipped into sleepwear and sat in front of the computer.

A scan of her emails proved none were urgent. The journalist Mia Johnston had a British background. She'd moved to Netherlands three years ago after a one-year stint in Saint Petersburg, where they'd become colleagues and stayed in touch. An email confirmed their meeting at a nearby coffee shop at nine A.M.

Try as she may, Katerina could not hold back the yawns. She lay under the thick comforter And sleep came straight away, her body suffering from jetlag and the fifteen-hour flight.

She woke up with the limited dawn light through the window. The time digits glowed at ten minutes past seven. She pulled on a wool jumper over her top to beat the low temperature. It never warmed up north in the Netherlands. Laptop strap over her shoulder, she walked briskly, navigating the streets to the small shop in an industrial area. Seagulls squawked nearby, swarming for throwaways. The smell of salt water carried on the wind.

Mia Johnston sat by the window opposite the serving counter. She had a mug to her lips when Katerina glimpsed her.

"Hi, Katerina. How have you been?"

Katerina gave her a hug and they both sat down.

"What's been going on? You've been busy by the sound of it." Mia said.

"Yes, it's been very turbulent in Saint Petersburg recently, as you probably heard." She paused and ordered a cappuccino from the young waitress. "I've been travelling with a friend for the past six months."

"A friend...very intriguing." Mia winked and tipped her cup to her mouth. "Do tell me more."

Katerina felt herself blush. "It's a long story. I met someone and we left soon after. I needed a break: you know how it goes."

"Lucky thing. I don't know how that couple thing goes these days. Have been at the grind so much lately, no time for social life. One article after another, travelling around Europe to cover stories. Back-to-back. Late nights typing on the computer."

"That's the life of journalist."

"True. What brings you to Rotterdam?"

"I have been investigating a series of shelf companies in Paris. Transactions via persons of interest. Wondered if you could please help out?"

"Have you had breakfast?" Mia waved to the waitress.

"No, I'm famished."

The same waitress came over.

"Can I please have the eggs benedict with an orange juice?" Mia handed the menu.

"I'll have the same, thanks, but with grapefruit juice."

Katerina explained to Mia about the corruption, the oligarch and arms dealing. She gave an overall summary, and of the murder, without talking about Jake's involvement. Other people were complicit, including Laurent, in a broader network. The transactions led her to Netherlands where she hoped to learn about the company's dealings and buyers.

The waitress brought out their meals and put them on the table. They tucked into their food.

After five minutes, Mia wiped her mouth and spoke. "This could be dangerous."

"I don't want to put you at risk, Mia."

"Are you kidding? I'm a journalist; this is my job." She took a bite of food off the fork. "Of course I will help you. There could be something for me to expose here too. Under the right circumstances. First thing is I'll check the archives and databases on these addresses, and the names. We can meet or talk after that initial search."

"Thanks, Mia, really appreciate it."

"Think nothing of it."

They finished up their meals and settled the bill. Katerina trailed Mia outside. Shards of sunlight were breaking through the considerable cloud coverage.

"I'll give you a call later in the afternoon."

"Bye, Mia."

The sidewalks teemed with workers from the docks. Yellow and orange hi-vis vests flashed along the streets. At the hotel, she setup the laptop on the table and loaded the main menu. Searches on Sophia Laurent's various businesses came up with nothing new. The entrepreneur did a great job of keeping out of the public eye and established media. Even open sources and online presence proved minimal on the topic.

She rubbed her neck to relieve cramps. To get some exercise, she shoved her laptop in a bag and walked along the main drag. She bought a takeout carton of fries topped with meat from a food van. A path took her to a bench where she finished the meal and discarded the tray in a trash can. The street weaved past the Euromast, a TV tower with a restaurant and luxury rooms for rent.

She saw a juice bar and took a booth against the wall. Her computer loaded up and she did a round of antivirus scans. A waitress interrupted her, lost in her thoughts.

"Would you like to order?"

A quick scan of the drinks and she said, "A blueberry mint smoothie, please."

Chapter 19

A RESTLESS FEW hours of sleep took Jake into the early hours of the morning. Four-twenty. He threw off the sheets and padded across the carpet. Moonlight seeped into the living room as he swallowed medication for his headache. He flicked on the shower and stood under the hottest water he could bear. His troubles lifted with the steam.

The attire he chose gave the original casual business vibe of his initial stay: button shirt, dark jacket, casual trousers. A new red and blue cap. He pulled on the new pair of white New Balance sneakers.

He took in some cereal with the last of the milk, went to the bathroom, packed his luggage. Laptop bag swung over his shoulder, he pulled his luggage to reception and checked out. The usual breakfast smells were absent at this hour. A chilly mist hovered over the streets, supplemented by light rain. He locked in the car rental address and made his way to the main avenue. The weekday peak traffic had not accumulated yet, an hour away from full potential.

A train out of the city would be the best option. Zurich HB was five hours away. The quick fix to assess his position. He could stay in a hotel and wait for Katerina to find more information. It would be too risky to join her in the Netherlands straight away. Enemies might be watching.

He passed a gas station three miles from the depot, turned into the drive, refilled the tank to full, and paid at the counter.

The hire rental business had only three cars on the lot. He slotted it into a spot against the boundary fence. A young woman sat behind the booth. She refunded his deposit and called him a cab.

A first-class train ticket to Zurich cost two-hundred-and-fifty euro. Only twenty-five euro more than second-class. A no-brainer. He handed over cash, went into the turnstiles and onto the platform. The train arrived on time at nine. He boarded and took a window seat.

Other passengers sat in the carriage, but none were out of place or fit a watcher's profile.

An elderly woman took a seat near him. She fumbled with her purse as the train departed. A young couple crossed arms, kissed, and whispered in each other's ear. He thought of Katerina and hoped she would arrive safely at her destination.

The landscape became more rural as the train sped away from the city. Trees, cattle, and grass dominated the scene. Drowsiness took over from the lack of sleep, the rocking of the train lulling him to doze in an irregular pattern.

An inspector came and asked for his passport. He showed the George Perry document, the man nodded and continued. The train moved seamlessly in the rural environment. He rose, used the restroom, splashed water on his face. In the dining car, ordered a late brunch: club sandwich with chicken added, and a pint of light beer. The barman poured the beer from a tap. He waited until the meal came and searched for a spot. Passengers packed around the limited tables, but he managed to find a slot with a stool.

He stared out the window. Tension from the job yesterday slowly dissipated, French countryside left in his wake. The bigger picture regarding these large international trades made him apprehensive as to the nature of the scale and how much he wanted to get involved. The international trades had to be serious hardware, not small time like the oligarch's pocket money with the African warlord. That meant full-on, expert security and round-the-clock protection.

He finished the meal, returned the plate to a passing waiter, and strolled through the carriages to his seat. McCallister dragged him deeper with every contract. He had to work out an exit strategy soon, draw a line in the sand.

Commuters moved in the aisles, anxious to get to their destination. At just past two-thirty. Jake disembarked onto Zurich HB station. He walked two blocks to a currency exchange. Euro worked here as well, but he converted two thousand into CHf, the Swiss currency. He found a three-star hotel near the station on Google maps, checked in to a level one room, and paid in cash.

Fake plants lined the white-washed walls of the corridor. Clinical to the point of sterile. He ran the keycard in the slot. Uncomfortable furniture was scattered over the light-filled living area. A fridge and sink came with the standard room. The basics were what he wanted this time and helped being invisible.

He dumped the bags, lowered to the floor and crossed his legs. Thumb and index finger, touched together, joined in a circle, hands balanced on knees.

"I am energized and fully protected." He repeated the mantra, eyes open, cleared his mind of the stress and danger, regulated his breathing, heartbeat lowered, body at peace. Relaxed and refreshed, eyes on the furniture, he wound down with various stretches. The clock confirmed ten minutes of semi-conscious meditation. Body loose and limbs devoid of tension, It was as if he'd had an hour of deep tissue massage. He rose and sat on the couch, which sank with his weight.

The TV remote lay on a glass coffee table. He picked it up and surfed. First news, then sports. Late afternoon updates from around the world. He tuned the entertainment channels but they were broadcast in Swiss and other European languages showing foreign language soap dramas and movies.

A lap around the room and he checked the window. Bleak clouds, no rainfall yet.

He flipped open the computer and entered a digital backdoor on the NSA database. A dive into searches on the Netherland addresses showed a complex owner structure as per Katerina's comments. It churned over on remote links, but they were long shots at this stage. The oligarch's trades led to other account numbers and locations, but not enough detail.

The local news media mentioned the oligarch's murder. No reliable witnesses. No description of the offender or offenders. The flash grenades had served their purpose well. A clean getaway. Untraceable and no witnesses or footage.

Katerina. Tinged with a slight degree of guilt, Jake worked over the issue. She could be in a great deal of danger in Rotterdam. Poking into matters of powerful individuals that they wanted left alone. He replied email to Katerina, telling her to please be careful.

He scrutinized the detail, shook his head. She would not have it any other way. At least he let her know his feelings. He signed into his bank account and checked the balance. The full amount from McCallister had cleared for the last job and half the new one.

At three-thirty, Jake pulled on his cap, locked the room, and walked to the restaurant bar area in the east section of the lobby. He needed some more down time to release, wait for her next call. Zurich and Rotterdam shared the same time zone. No doubt she would be investigating the latest lead with her contacts.

The ice-cold tap beer, a European brand he could not pronounce, went down his throat easily. Drinkers shuffled past, all ages, many deep in conversations about various compelling topics. The barman worked his customers strategically, detecting the pace and catering the right number of refills. No one suspicious. He drank the beer and basked in the reprieve, a warm sensation as the alcohol hit his system.

A beep from his burner. Katerina asked him to call her. She's discovered something already. He drained the glass, settled in on the bar and surveyed the establishment. The area started to fill with late afternoon patrons. Chatter volume rose, people ordered drinks, and decisions were made. Dinner menu became available at six. The atmosphere made him feel like a regular guy for a fleeting moment.

He replied, stating he would call her in ten minutes from the hotel room.

Chapter 20

THE LAPTOP WENT black. Katerina straightened her back, a little frustrated with the data. She raised her hand to order another smoothie as the cell phone came to life. Mia's name flashed on the display.

"Hey. I have pored through our domestic and international database. It's so complex, it took me hours to get a basic framework. There's a chain of warehouses and containers owned by a consortium. I use that word loosely. These match your addresses. The relationship is a front for individuals attempting to understate their revenue." She hesitated. "That activity type usually indicates money laundering."

"Great. Thanks. What goods are they trading?"

"That is a strange one. I see textiles and agricultural machinery, but the numbers don't add up. That is where the laundering comes in. There's big international commerce here which is getting overlooked by the authorities. Might be bribes with customs. They could trade in arms, for all we know. This number and frequency of containers would not stand up to a proper audit."

"Where are they going?"

"Asia mainly: Hong Kong, Singapore, Beijing, and Paris. The most regular shipment is Japan. Four containers to Tokyo every month for six months."

"Any names yet?"

"Not one hundred percent, but I am drilling down. That Japan destination is a red flag."

"For sure." Katerina exhaled and squared her shoulders. This detail got them closer to the source. Suddenly she glanced around the juice bar, scanning the faces, a wave of paranoia sweeping over her. Jake had warned her to be careful of watchers, but there were none.

She lowered her voice. "This information is gold, Mia. I'll chat with my partner soon and get back to you."

"I will keep digging and let you know if anything new comes to light."

She closed her laptop and paid for the drink. Japan made her think. Outside, the gusty winds intensified.

Cabs lined the curb on the next block. She took one back to the hotel and didn't make eye contact until she made it to her room. Housekeeping had tidied up in her absence. The room looked like a hospital. She dialed Jake's number and waited.

"Hey, you." Katerina watched the gray landscape in the glass.

"Hi to you too. How's Rotterdam?"

"Weather could be better. Will not complain though. Caught up with an old friend today, which was lovely."

"How did it go?"

"She has searched her side thoroughly. We have uncovered a connection between the complex web of trading names. Unless hiding something, the scenario does not make sense. The quantity of cargo is more than what's on their books. Not a simple tax avoidance scheme either: too sophisticated."

"Money laundering and undeclared illicit goods for starters."

"Yes, we suspected as much too. A large, regular shipment of unknown goods to Japan raises an alert. Mia is exploring it further to find names at the top." She shifted in her seat.

"Japan is very interesting. That takes the spotlight off Europe. These transactions may have been bigger than the oligarch could fulfil after losing his Russian network."

"Let's keep uncovering." She cleared her throat. "I got your email. Thanks for caring, but you know I can take care of myself. Comes with the territory."

"Sorry. I sent it in a vulnerable moment."

"It's sweet. Miss you and talk soon."

"Ditto. Bye."

For an hour, Jake searched Japanese ports in the databases. All containers in the past six months and affiliations with Rotterdam, the oligarch, Russia, and Paris. Bribes had to be top-level government officials to avoid inspections. Almost all the way up the ladder. He separated the oligarch for the purposes of testing the data. A connection with Laurent or an unknown party might reveal a hidden link. The figures glowed as evening set in. He raked fingers through his hair. A break may help relieve the tension.

Tokyo was the next target. He walked the floor. The time read six-ten P.M. He picked the key card from the wall mount, closed the door, and took the stairwell to the lobby.

The hotel restaurant had a typical Swiss menu. He ordered a steak with fries and a garlic sauce on the side. A pint of a pale ale came chilled, his second for the evening. He took it slow, waiting for the food. If an emergency popped up, he didn't like to be impaired by alcohol, even slightly. The meal came and he cut into the steak. The garlic sauce became too much of good thing. He left the beer half finished, and went up to his room.

An evening of TV on the couch, watching a foreign movie, killed two hours. Something about a woman who falls for a drug dealer in Paris only to flee after an accidental overdose of one of their friends. His attention waned halfway into it, musing on the identity of his newest enemy. The show finished and he clicked it off with the remote. The heating turned to high as the night dropped to zero degrees Celsius.

A seagull hovered near the window edge, took off in flight toward the sea. He wore sweatpants to bed to combat the chill. On the bedside table, the burner cell charging, the knife he'd bought in Paris sheathed under the mattress. Can never be too careful. Without a firearm handy, he felt exposed.

He stared at the ceiling in the dim light, images of Katerina in Rotterdam flashing in his mind. He'd standby in Zurich for twenty-fours at the most. They were on the verge of a solid lead, ready to move on it straight away.

His thoughts dissolved as sleep overcame him.

Chapter 21

THE NEARBY PORT commotion belted out into the night, workers and heavy machinery, coordinated loads and unloads, always in constant motion. Mia flicked the living room switch. Yellow flooded the settee. She moved away from the night and sat at the table.

A city that never shuts down.

She continued her searches on the maritime trading from Rotterdam. Centered on activity in the past twelve months, narrowed down to the suspected limited liability companies and their partners, a volley of international names streamed, some known, others not.

An idea came to mind. Property transfers on warehouses, sheds and containers may reveal the true owners. She data-matched the vendors and buyers: company names with the directors, background checks and foreign investors. She captured all the information possible. A recent transaction caught her eye. The business had multiple property sites in Rotterdam, Amsterdam, and international assets. A global presence. She downloaded a sale of property in Netherlands. The cursor twirled.

The Erasmus Bridge lit up, a jeweled harp which loomed over the black waters like a lighthouse. Even at this late hour, ships for both business and pleasure glided underneath.

She worked a kink in her neck with her left hand, typed with the right. Her eyes weakened a touch with ten hours of staring at digital devices. On the cusp on wearing reading glasses, in the esteemed opinion of her optometrist, a digital detox was required at the very least. She sighed: not likely in this job.

The transfer document lit up. She scanned the first page. A Rotterdam warehouse complex that faced west, less than a mile from her apartment, had been bought out by a foreign interest. Six months ago. The time coincided with her enquiries. She pulled up the public website and read the spiels. It came with shipping contracts; the most lucrative were routes to Japan. She knew these were valuable resources to a large shipping company. High yield and very attractive. The major shareholder was listed as a private equity company owned by a French entrepreneur named Sophia Laurent.

Her heart jumped up her throat. Paydirt. The Japanese importing company had a PO box, but she found a company number and other basic details.

She emailed Katerina. The summary she typed included the details on the complex, the involvement of Laurent as an executive director, and background on the routes.

Blinds snapped shut. She moved about her apartment, paused at the stone island bench to rearrange a fruit bowl. The computer flickered blue. Her head throbbed faintly behind her eyes, a possible migraine: right arm propped her body weight on the countertop. She stirred cocao in milk and made a hot chocolate in the microwave.

The scent of confectionery relaxed her mind. She moved over the tiled floor and curled up on the couch. Late night news ran the latest stories. Nothing new. The heater pushed warm air over the living room. She sank into the cushions, eyes losing focus on the TV.

Rain hammered the glass as the wind intensified. Katerina rubbed her eyes. She walked the carpet to stay awake. The oligarch was more like a pawn on a chess board. An unknown enemy emerged from the Russian's death that revealed how minor the man's influence had been in this global threat.

The stress rose from her stomach, unsure of what powerful influence might be at play if the oligarch no longer exerted power. She contemplated a glass of wine to calm her nerves. A menu sat on the table. She scanned the options, moved to the red wines. Two Pinot Noir bottles but she did not feel like sweet. Shiraz too strong for the occasion. Cabernet Sauvignon would be perfect.

She picked up the handset and dialed.

"Hello, Miss Katerina. How can we be of service?"

"Can I please have a glass of your mid-range Cabernet Sauvignon?"

"Yes, or course. We will bring up it straight away. Please allow five to ten minutes."

"Thank you." The screen fell into standby. She waited at the glass wall, facing south, the night blurred in the diagonal rain streaks.

This global legacy of war at any cost always scared her. Profit and power driven with no regard for human life. As a journalist, she strived to expose these instances of evil, no matter the personal cost.

The doorbell rang. She squinted through the peephole. Room attendant. She cracked the door. A tall, pale young man in a red vest held a tray.

"Your wine, Miss Katerina."

"Thanks." She took the glass and closed the door. On first sip, the vino had flavor, aged well. She listened to the hotel sounds. The wine gave her a warm feeling.

Eyes fatigued and red, she left the computer and circled the furniture. She inhaled a breath and held it in her chest for five seconds. Relax. Exhale slow, five seconds. Diaphragm full, she repeated the exercise. With the canal nearby and water lapping, Rotterdam reminded her of Saint Petersburg. She took comfort in the familiar, and in helping Jake to thwart these enemies.

Her inbox chimed an alert. She leaned across and read the subject line. Mia had sourced the owners of the shell companies.

A breakthrough at last.

Katerina read the summary.

She shook her head, took a sip of wine. Her burner lay on the coffee table. She reached for it and typed a message to Jake:

Solid leads targets in Rotterdam. Tokyo. I'll stay, continue enquiries. Call back when you get a chance.

Chapter 22

KATERINA'S TEXT HAD Jake jump online to check prices and times for flights to Tokyo. With one medium-sized, check-in suitcase and one carry bag, packing would not take long. He checked his emails and closed the computer.

Tokyo had to be a strategic hub for this setup. The amount of finance funneled there was astounding. He wanted to know why this quantity of hardware ended up in the Japanese capital.

Bags sorted, he checked out, paid the extras in cash, and hailed a cab out front, the windshield wipers going full strength against the rain.

"The airport, thanks."

"No problem." The driver said, silver hair combed back.

Dark covered the early morning landscape, a gray sky lowering as they entered the freeway. Same weather as Paris.

At the airport, Jake purchased a business class ticket for the next flight departing at ten-thirty.

The first ten hours went by uneventfully. He caught up on sleep and ate bigger meals than he had in weeks. The plane landed and he connected at the next terminal. Fifteen hours since departing Zurich, they landed in Tokyo.

A money exchange kiosk offered good exchange rates. He converted four thousand euro into yen And took a cab.

"East side of Tokyo, thanks. Can you recommend a four-star hotel in that region?"

"Yes. It's called The Gate Kaminarimon." The driver turned right at a major intersection and nodded in the rearview. "It's by Hulic Group, so very nice."

Jake did a search and read the hotel profile. He checked the photos and position. Modern high-rise on a corner, it had multiple exit points. Strategic point to start.

"Let's go there."

Billboards flashed messages everywhere. He eased back into the seat. Overhead neon signs with major brands glowed at all heights. The cab weaved, trees swayed in the wind, and the city teemed with activity. They pulled up onto the curb in front of a young man in a vest.

"Thanks again." He paid the driver and backed out onto the curb.

The foyer had a fountain and a long, marble counter. He checked into a level one room and paid in cash.

He put his belongings in the living room and took a quick shower to freshen up. A two-day shadow had formed. He backhanded the steam on the mirror, left the stubble, and combed back his hair. A fresh sweatshirt with a clean pair of jeans. He shrugged on a light hoodie and sneakers. His uniform. The baseball cap went over his head. faux business cards in his back pocket.

Downlights lit up modern paintings of tranquil scenes with bonsai and cheery trees. He opened the stairwell door, took the steps two at a time. The lobby had a calm and upmarket vibe. Surveillance cameras were less prominent for a hotel of this status.

Asakusa had traditional and historical structures. Visitors flooded the area, which provided effective camouflage. He could get lost in the traditional craft shops and street-food stalls.

Nine-ten A.M. He had done his calculations on the plane: Tokyo was eight hours ahead of Zurich. Two laps of the block; he checked for watchers. Restaurants mixed with a temple and two high-rises. The sidewalk weaved through pedestrian lights and into a park section. Large bronze statues of historical figures bookended the entrance. He sat down on an outdoor seat and checked his surroundings. The spot was secluded. Ginkgo trees rose behind him, forming a barrier from the open space and path.

He put McCallister's number in the burner.

"Hello."

He didn't know which part of Europe McCallister was in, but he always sounded fresh.

"Sphinx." Jake cleared his throat. "I'm in Tokyo."

"You sure get around, kid."

"Wherever the business takes me. I need a local guide. Someone with the usual supplies and necessities."

"Got it. Hang on."

Jake waited and gazed at the busy streetscape. Commuters converged from all directions. Muffled sounds came through the speaker.

"Here we go. Try Akira Tanaka." McCallister read out a mobile number. "This guy will set you up with the basics."

"Appreciate it."

"Any updates?"

"Intel points to Tokyo. Not sure what the scope or motives are, or the strike point. But it's definitely bigger than previously thought. Much bigger."

"Positive. Keep me posted."

"Will do."

Punching Tanaka's number into the burner, he paced the grass.

"Tanaka."

"Hi, Tanaka. McCallister gave me your number. I'm in Tokyo requiring some basic supplies. Name is Perry."

A pause as the man assessed his reply. "Where are you now?"

"I'm near Nakamise Street."

"Meet me outside the Buddhist temple front of Hozomon Gate at noon today." Tanaka cut the call.

He had an hour to kill. The streets were busy no matter the

time. At a sushi bar, he ordered a meal pack with rice and salmon. Alfresco dining in the morning sunlight. He took a fork and napkins and sat at a table.

In the shade of the umbrella, he munched the food and assessed the ethnic mix of commuters. Many were Japanese corporate employees in formal wear, old and young. Some had cell phones or cameras. At least fifteen to twenty percent were Caucasian, European and African. Binoculars and cameras were very common. Tour guides in walking groups shuffled regularly by, pointing and chatting. Sightseers disembarked from buses, which made it even easier to blend. He took a forkful of salmon and rice. His presence on this side of town wouldn't be noticed.

At eleven-thirty, he threw the leftover food package in a trash bin, walked north up Kannondoori, past the souvenir stalls, and hit a T-junction. To his right, the two buddhas rose over the houses. It marked a traditional older section that remained intact, a historical tribute to imperial Japan.

A quick lap around the old perimeter. A dark SUV with full tint windows ran circuits around nearby streets. It had to be a government unit scouting for threats. He memorized the plates, entered a Seven-Eleven convenience store and walked the aisles. This allowed him to check for shadows and tails in the windows without making them. No walkers he recognized came past the glass. Another tourist bus stopped for refreshments. He took the opportunity to exit. Slipping behind the bus, he backtracked to the gates.

He entered the monument filled zone, and around the Boshi Jizo, another cultural landmark. The 'Mother and Child Jizo' sculpture represented Japanese that had died escaping China at the end of World War Two. He turned left, Hozomon Gate looming solid over the landscape.

Three lanterns and giant guardians marked the entrance. He read that the original gate had been constructed one thousand years ago. Vacationers mingled in large groups, chatting and pointing at the structure. Hanging back, he checked the single men that fit Tanaka's profile.

At five past two, crowds had come and gone. He spotted an

Asian man at the far side leaning against a timber post. Jake hustled around a cluster of sightseers. He caught the gaze of the man, who nodded and pointed at a corner.

"Perry?" Tanaka stepped closer.

"Yes. Good to meet you."

"Let's walk and chat. I know the way around here."

They circled the historical grounds for two minutes in silence. Tanaka pointed a few times, playing the harmless holidaymaker card well. Both men had dark sunglasses. Jake pulled the baseball cap lower. No surveillance cameras. Unusual. The government did not want to damage the fragile structures. Cameras were probably mounted on the exterior of the more modern buildings.

Finally Tanaka said, "What do you need?"

"A gun. Something reliable and smallish. I prefer a Sig. Level three or four body armor. Other tactical gear: a headlamp, binoculars and infra-red night vision."

"That's all?"

"Flash grenades if you have them. Maybe some intel as I get going."

"Mind telling me more about what threat we're uncovering?" Tanaka stopped at the sacred gingko tree.

"Not sure yet. Could be terrorism but I'm thinking it's a larger network. Profit driven. If so, it's a rough and rocky road for answers."

"Story of my life." Tanaka tipped his head at the tree. "It's eight-hundred years old. Burnt in the middle from bombing end of the Second World War."

Jake nodded. The stroll took them around to another gate.

"Are you secret service, Tanaka?"

"More like a permanent contractor." Tanaka regarded him through sunglasses. "I'll let you know when I have the gear. Less than five hours. Meeting place will be indoors next time."

He watched as Tanaka strolled off, disappeared behind a

cluster of people. The morning sun picked up pace, beating on his shoulders.

Chapter 23

A SLITHER OF dawn broke the blinds. Katerina roused and rolled the other way. Sounds of the port had been humming for hours. She opened an eye to check the time: eight-ten A.M. Researching until one A.M. with two glasses of wine had left her drowsy. She swung her legs off, steadying herself on the bedside table.

The burner contained two text messages from Mia. She read the first.

Call me when you get up.

The second was time-stamped thirty minutes ago:

Come on, Kat, get up and call me!

She smiled, fired off a reply, and padded to the bathroom:

Just woke. Will call you soon xx.

Hot water ran over her face. Liquid ecstasy. Palms flat on the tiles, she let the anxiety dissipate, dried herself, and opened her suitcase for fresh clothes.

Head sharper, she entered the living space and thought about food for the first time since waking. The café down the road had a good menu, but first she wanted to call Mia.

"Hey, sleepy head." Press noise in the background.

"Hi there, Mia. On the laptop till one this morning determining the veracity of those leads." She shifted her legs. "All good now though."

"Have you had caffeine?"

"Not yet." Katerina sighed. "I am definitely deficient in that department."

"Let's meet at the cafe near your hotel in twenty minutes."

"See you there."

In the kitchen, she drank a glass of water to try and rehydrate. She took a jacket and headed out.

The morning rush in full swing, a cold breeze hit her cheeks as she exited.

Mia waited, armed with two large, black cups, steam curling from the surface.

Katerina trod past customers and sunk to the table. "Thanks, you're a lifesaver."

"Don't mention it." Mia leaned forward. "I've been working on this case of yours. Trying to find these buyers. Mystified by which terrorists are pinpointing Japan. Very high risk if they get detected in customs."

"Their motive has got me puzzled too." Katerina blew on her hot beverage and put it to her lips. "In Japan there are many political factions and religious groups that are opposed. Take the assassination of the ex–prime minister last year. He claimed a grudge regarding the Unification Church and his mother's bankruptcy as the reason."

"Yes, crazy what some people will claim as an excuse. My next step is understanding and identifying the event they might be targeting." Mia gazed at the customer line, keeping her voice low.

"Agreed. Then we can reverse engineer back to the motives. Always a great plan."

"Where do you think we start?"

"On the motivation for Japan. Come with me to the office today and we can do some digging."

The street-food stalls were busy at one P.M., lines crammed back into the sidewalks. Jake sat at a table. Past the different heights of flora, he could see the public roads beyond the grounds. A loading bay Katerina had tagged might be risky to visit unarmed. He searched databases and located an executive employee named Riku that lived near the office. According to sources, this guy liked to drink in the local bars with clients during the day. A good target if he could meet him, as if by chance, and start up a conversation.

A Google map aerial view showed the warehouse layout. Tucked in the industrial section of the waterfront, away from the upmarket eateries and festivals. In his estimate, the space could hold a dozen shipping containers plus it had extra capacity. Away from the public eye for privacy and illicit activity. The delivery zone.

He angled the screen away from the sun to reduce the glare. Katerina and Mia were working on more specific intel regarding the location and owners. Something of this scale made it a difficult operation to hide. A reconnaissance of the outside area may give rise to additional answers. At the very least, a better feel for the terrain and security level.

The map calculated the walk to be ten minutes to the harbor. The craft and souvenir stalls on Nakamise-dori Street were overrun with shoppers, bustling to buy a piece of Japan to take home.

A left turn flowed to a wide road with confectionery and convenience stores. He headed east as the glistening reflection of Sumida River came into sight. On the north-east bank, the warehouse could be seen from the other side of the river.

Over the Azuma Bridge, he wandered the streets. Watching Lape's office, he waited in a café opposite the local bar below Asahi headquarters. He rang the main number and asked for Riku. A female receptionist said Riku was in the office, but on a call. Jake told her he was a large supplier of Lape, he would be in the Asahi bar in the next hour, And it would be advantageous for Riku to touch base with him.

He hung up and went to the bar, ordered a Japanese beer and sat al fresco near a large table directly opposite the Lape warehouse boundary to see the roller door.

If any patrons suspected him of watching the property, he was an average punter taking in a brew and enjoying the view. Shades on and cap visor pointed down to obscure his features as a fixed camera pointed out from the bar to the floor, the range limited to three square meters at the most. He doubted it had advanced biometric capability or gait recognition.

A double road-train truck entered the rear drive of Lape and the hydraulic brakes hissed to a stop. Over thirty-six meters long. Two stocky men came out of the hold. They were not convincing as workers. Too much bling and brand name clothing and accessories. Organized crime. Over the other side, a forklift hummed into action. Pallets were taken one by one. He shifted to get better visual. Plastic wrap covered the load, the shipment transported inside.

He drank the beverage, the rays giving a little afternoon warmth. Young couples strolled past and giggled at their private jokes. Music morphed from house into a drum and bass set. A backward lean gave Jake a casual vibe. He aimed to be invisible, just another guy in the scene.

A block of toilets was located on the right opposite the bar. He did a lap and noticed a few Japanese guys walking in. At the end, a younger guy took off his sunglasses and stepped into the main room. Riku.

The bathroom had an upscale layout: mosaic tile pattern, wall vines, and floating silver basins. Sensor flush activation over the toilets. He washed his hands and returned to the bar.

The young guy tilted his head; he returned the greeting.

"Riku, right?" Jake said and held up two fingers at the barman. He pointed at the Super Dry can.

"That's me." Riku offered a hand and they shook. "Do you speak much Japanese?"

"Only a little bit. Is English ok?"

The barman placed two fresh cans in front, ice cold. Jake handed over a large yen note and pushed the can with his index finger. The Lape executive wrapped his hand over it.

"Sure is. I am fluent with English. Perry, isn't it? You visiting Tokyo or here permanently?"

"Just in for a few weeks. Contracting," Jake said. "But I am looking to make it longer this time."

"Good you contacted the office. It's a great city to live in. Always an event happening. What can I help you with?"

"Cyber security. Consulting a minor government department. I won't bore you with the details. Can always do with another contract when this one ends. Had a look at Lape's site and noticed you could tighten the security."

"Actually, you're not wrong. Issues lately with a DDos attack put the system down for hours. Once we fix one problem, another comes."

"Securing your architecture to make sure this does not happen again is what I specialize in."

Riku nodded. "Sure. I can introduce you to the team so you can pitch this."

"Fantastic." Jake slipped his hand in a back pocket and held out a card. "Here's my number. Let's arrange a meeting, perhaps on a social level first might be best. Like over a beer."

"Large operation and diverse logistics. I may be able to fast track you." Riku raised his glass.

Jake followed. "Cheers."

Both men drained their cans, enjoyed the ambience.

Riku checked his watch. "I have a late work meeting, but great to meet you. Here is my card."

"Great meeting you, Riku. Let's do this again."

"Thanks for the shout. Let me return the favor. Talk soon."

He set aside the can and walked out into the parking lot. At four thirty-two. the sun had receded, but maintained a pleasant strolling atmosphere. He took the Azuma Bridge, taking note of any watchers. Commuters came and went, none he flagged.

The front of Lape Industries contained a glass wall and a reception desk. Whitewash walls hung with standard prints: white leather armchairs. A middle-aged Japanese woman sat behind a beige marble counter. Basic setup from the exterior. He strolled along from the opposite curb, not lingering longer than three minutes. To avoid being flagged by exterior cameras or seen and remembered, he departed the vicinity quickly. He needed to gain access to check inner layers of security.

Daylight receded fast. He circled south by the traditional section. The temples hung in the shadows like the ancient spirits of samurai evoked after dark, locked in eternal penance to haunt their battle fields. A superstition he guessed was shared by many people.

Chapter 24

MIA'S OFFICE WAS in a modest three-story squat in downtown Rotterdam. She used her electronic pass at reception and led them up the stairwell.

"It's quicker this way." They ascended concrete steps and into an alcove entrance.

"Welcome to the Rotterdam Times." Mia waved in the air.

Katerina followed her into a corridor of cubicles. LED tubes shone overhead, worn carpet below. A much calmer environment than her old office in Saint Petersburg. Mia stopped at an L-shaped desk and relinquished her bag and laptop case on the surface. Hands on hips, she scanned the work spaces, pointed at a nook with a terminal and chairs. She pulled up a second seat in front of a desktop computer.

"This is me. Please sit down. Make yourself at home."

"Thanks." Katerina shifted her knees under the desk.

"You can use this terminal and I have the laptop." She logged in and entered her password. The page loaded and a database prompt flashed. "I'm going to input the parameters for you." Mia clicked on the keyboard and navigated the apps. "Ready to go. That database is comprehensive and user friendly." Mia grinned and opened her laptop.

A search bar hovered; results flickered below. Katerina went for the open sources first. She read reports and articles in the publishing group archives.

The address she'd sent Jake fronted as Lape Industries. It had a board of executive directors based in multiple countries across Asia and Europe. A contemporary and slick website provided generic photos against solid backgrounds. Subliminal colors. Effective gloss.

She scrolled into the first tab, the 'About' section with impressive twenty-first century corporate buzz words. It might hook even a hardened business investor. The shipping contracts and storage held the most profit for these operators.

An effective shield to hide the truth. Add legitimacy and build a brand. The question of the prime activities glared at her from the sterile blue light. Logistics encompassed the core nature of the business. But was that all? A private company status indicated they were not beholden to shareholders. Smart move considering the cargo coming into their possession.

A dispute occurred eight months prior between a worker and a member of the public. The matter was dealt with out of court and no charges were laid against either party. It did not seem relevant.

She flagged the URL and important parts, and threw a wider net to the immediate suppliers. Connections were added and discovered, and she typed in everything she could muster. Each digital trail she followed hit a dead end. She took a deep breath and covered a yawn with her hand.

"How's it going there?" Mia interrupted her train of thought.

"Not bad, but not that good either. Have not uncovered new evidence so far." She stretched and stood.

"Let me show you the coffee machine," Mia said.

An archway at the end of a short passageway opened into a kitchen. Three people sat around a table chatting, a fridge in the corner next to a microwave.

"Cups are up in this cupboard." Mia placed two cups in the large device and pressed the labelled buttons. "Milk in the fridge. It's self-explanatory and I'm sure you've used one before."

They took the beverages back to the desk. Katerina slouched in her chair. She drank and searched the wider web for any further information. Lape kept a tight lid on their affairs. Minimal industrial disputes and followed all the local regulations. They even contributed to a community charity. Tax deduction and improved the public image.

The frustration grew the more she drilled into the databases. She took her cup to the kitchen and washed it in the sink. Across the corridor, she entered the female bathroom. A quick refresher and a lap of the level made her feel lighter. She saw the pier through the glass floor-to-ceiling wall. There had to be a flaw or a way in to bypass this organization's façade.

She returned and sat staring at the cubicle divider. Pins stuck in pamphlets and brochures covered the entire wall. An attractive young reporter stumbled by in a short dress and high heels, stalked by a cameraman in ripped jeans. She hurried him along, pointing and gesturing. They bickered like an old couple as she aimed at the stairwell. The two colleagues finally vanished with a clang of the exit.

The saver flashed as she mused on the challenge. They were dealing with a powerful entity. She worried how close Jake had gotten to these people and the danger. The stakes were getting higher. She slowed down her breathing, settled into her chair.

Big inhale, hold, and long, slow exhale.

At eleven-thirty, Mia gazed over at her. "I might have stumbled onto a connection: a non-executive board member of the parent company linked to an act of terrorism. Two years ago, they conceived a plan to bomb a major water plant in Tokyo. It is out of our time-range so we missed it in previous searches. The board member had been exonerated from the charges after a lengthy court battle, but the connection was noted by the Japanese counterterrorism unit. Interpol also flagged all associates and kept it on record."

Mia clicked her mouse and a photo loaded. A Japanese man in his later thirties to early forties. Salt and pepper hair. "Haruto Suzuki."

"That's a solid link." Katerina pushed back from the desk and angled at the screen. She scanned the contents, confirming the person had a position on the board. "Why would they allow this individual to remain after such controversy?"

"Must be money or influence."

"And the not guilty verdict." Katerina shook her head.

"He's non-executive but wields much sway on the board. Also knows all the company strategies moving forward." She minimized the photo. "I will forward this to you now so you can pass it on to Jake."

"Thanks, Mia."

Katerina waited for the beep. She forwarded the email to Jake with a summary of her own, Suzuki's photo, profile and background legal case included.

Chapter 25

THE EMAIL FROM Katerina came just before eleven P.M. Jake read the contents and opened the photo. A Japanese guy in his forties. Great work. He wrote she had been a great help and asked if she could thank Mia on his behalf.

He flexed his legs, regarded the Tokyo nightscape. Lape were accessories in the receipt of illicit contraband. If only because of Suzuki's influence, he suspected the company were nonetheless beholden and complicit.

Colors caught his peripheral vision. A neon jungle shone, vertical boards with the illusion of an infinite number of colors. Singapore was the only equal to Tokyo's extensive use of neon boards.

A company pie chart flickered in split colors. The profit distribution indicated clues for their motives.

In the NSA databases, he used a backdoor he had setup prior, and entered anonymously. Suzuki's criminal file went back a decade. He loaded the main documents. A list of known associates popped up, some legit and others not. The businessman had been flagged by the DoD and Interpol. His current status sat at intermediary or amber-level threat, but this could be upgraded quickly, resources permitting. Suzuki avoided incarceration on this prior occasion, having retained the best legal counsel. Privileges of money. Slippery character.

Jake drank water and contemplated a strategy. If Suzuki were local, in a reachable location, Jake suspected a high-level security detail. The Lape warehouse and office might be an easier mark to infiltrate initially. Once inside, he could make an accurate assessment of the risk involved.

A lot depended on his new contact, Riku. Suzuki could be the angle and person he sought. He read and switched browser tabs.

The search narrowed on Suzuki's career: well educated at a

private secondary school, then a prestigious Japanese university. Graduated with honors and headhunted by fortune five-hundred business leaders. In the early years, a stint in Dubai, followed by Arab Emirates as chief financial officer: interesting possible connection. Perhaps a sheik with big pockets and an unmissable opportunity. He filed names of the main owners in these businesses. Involvement across tech startups in Asia, Ge obtained investment from private sources which led to the birth of Lape.

One bad decision or trading partner? The legal battle had been the only blemish on an otherwise stellar career. Jake rubbed his neck, a cramp forming from his poor reading posture. He straightened his spine.

An address showed up for Suzuki in Tokyo. An upmarket apartment in a trendy high-rise. The desirable and expensive Shibuya in the west part of the city. A part-time pad. Stable of supercars, including a red Lamborghini garaged in the basement. Leisure activities included a gym membership, spin class, and VIP customer at upscale restaurants.

He dug further. Suzuki had an exclusive membership of an upscale escort club. Situated in Ginza, a trendy shopping district in the heart of Tokyo, 'Ginza Elite' catered for the richest of the rich. The highest quality of international escorts, according to their website. A sprawling, two-level club with a top-shelf bar and annual fee of five hundred thousand USD. Women circuited a dance floor with podiums, like a strip club format, and the client bought drinks to invite a conversation with the lady.

The more details Jake uncovered, the easier the target was to locate. Staking out the apartment to check movements and habits was a first port of call. He carried his empty glass to the sink. The terror link bugged him. He turned off the computer and prepared for bed, peering into the vanity mirror. His stubble had grown to a short beard in the past few days, a status he decided to leave. Pass off as a modern accessory in the corporate world.

A beep from his burner. He pressed in the code and read the text.

Meet Asakusa shrine tomorrow morning eight. Bring 70000 yen. Tanaka.

From the hotel safe, he removed seven ten-thousand yen bills and a few thousand singles more. He folded the seven and placed it in an inner pocket of his jacket.

Tired, he climbed into bed. As he pulled the duvet over his body, he tried to turn off the day's thoughts. Neon broke in wafer-thin cracks. He wondered how anyone slept normally in this city.

Mist churned thick in waves, warping his vision. Someone yelled his name. "Jake." He peered into the fog, tried to focus on the source. Nothing. Smoky but tasteless, and no smell.

A light shone, tunnel-like illusion. Maybe death coming to collect his soul.

"Jake. Jake." The voice changed. Man. No, female. He squinted, tried to make sense of it all. Could not rationalize.

He woke damp, the sweatshirt stuck to his chest. Nightmares returned. He shrugged off the soggy garment, took a warm shower.

At seven-thirty downstairs, the hotel breakfast had started, so he went in and grabbed three mandarins and an apple. On the walk to meet Tanaka, he peeled the mandarins and ate them one-by-one. At this hour, he beat the tourists who were still tucked in their beds or eating breakfast.

A parade of taverns came into view and he passed a 7-Eleven store. The temple grounds rose over the gate like a trip back in time. He veered for the north-east corner and arrived at seventy-fifty-five.

Tanaka held a light gym bag in his right hand. He appeared from a bunch of trees and strolled up alongside.

Jake handed over the cash roll.

"Thanks." Tanaka casually put the money in his pocket. "The money is a token amount for expenses. It is much more economical than owing me favor. You will know this if we work together in the future." A slight upturn in the corner of Tanaka's mouth formed. "Do not get caught with the weapon. Our gun laws are very strict. It will be difficult to get you off an offense."

"I'll take your word for it," Jake said. "Hope this will be a quick in and out."

"We can accommodate requests on intel. I may not be able to assist every time, but will do my best. A successful outcome from this assignment is beneficial for us too, for obvious reasons. We want to minimize collateral damage. Let's walk over there and sit." He chinned in the direction of a shaded seat opposite the gate.

Tanaka positioned the bag on the surface between them. Black-tailed gulls glided toward a feast of bread scraps littered on the uneven path.

"This has been a pleasant conversation. Let me know if you require anything else."

"Most certainly." Jake stared straight ahead at the deserted shrine, populated only by them and birds.

Tanaka rose from the seat and wandered slowly off, as if going fishing at a nearby river.

Jake took the eastern path out of the grounds. The exit had a black spot with surveillance cameras. Nearby he located a large public toilet with private areas. He pressed the button and went inside.

In the restroom, he unzipped the bag. A Nambu M60, nine-millimeter, swing-out cylinder for five rounds. Not his favorite, but common law enforcement issue in Japan. They were small, so easier to conceal. A bulletproof vest, three flash grenades, tactical binoculars, and night vision goggles he packed away. He shoved micro-transmitters and a small monitor into his pockets, pulled off his hoodie and strapped on the vest. It fitted snugly. He loaded the bullets into the cylinder and pushed the weapon into the small of his back. A box of spare rounds remained; he put them in another bag.

He wiped down Tanaka's bag with paper towels and fit it into the bathroom trash can. He gazed at the mirror and checked his appearance. Nothing out of place or conspicuous. The smallest thing could give you away: a gun handle protruding at the wrong angle or the top of the armor showing above your collar.

Armed and ready to go, he pressed the electronic button to open the door.

Chapter 26

THE LIGHT SHONE on Katerina's table. Her elbows balanced on the surface, head in palms trying to recollect. An LED went dark in the far corner of the office. She glanced at the clock. Six-twenty P.M. A hand touched her shoulder. Most employees of the Rotterdam Times head office had gone home.

"Come-on, let's get out of here."

Katerina pivoted. "Hey, yes, sounds like a plan. I lost myself there: did not realize it was after six."

Mia smiled and straightened. The cubicles were mainly deserted, a vacuum pushed by a cleaner the only sound echoing on the floor. She noticed three workers at their desks still.

"I'll turn off this machine." Katerina hit shut down and lifted her bag. Her head ached a little from the previous night. The extra glass or two of red wine had affected her sleep. Energy sapped from a day of staring at a monitor, or the accumulated stress of Syria and helping Jake find answers to Japan. She followed Mia into the kitchen and washed her last mug.

They walked to the elevator and rode to the ground floor. A guard waved and opened the sliders manually.

"Haff a goot evening," the tall man said in a Dutch accent.

"You too, Jan. See you tomorrow." Mia placed her cell phone in her bag. "I know a great bar only five minutes' walk from here." Mia put an arm over her shoulder. "Don't worry, we will find the answers you're searching for. We are two of the world's most persistent journalists."

"Thanks for your support, Mia. I really appreciate it."

"Think nothing of it. This is fun anyway." Mia pointed at the next traffic light. "Over the rise past the pizza shop."

A chic cocktail bar with open, bi-fold doors pointed at the canal.

Mia ordered two passionfruit killers and they chose stools. They placed the drinks on the bench and stared at the darkened city winking and flickering.

"Jake replied to my email. The lead on Suzuki is promising and he is excited to follow it up. He has made a new corporate contact." She paused and her brow furrowed. "I am not convinced about the terror angle yet, as I cannot see the motive. It's a real conundrum at this stage."

Mai sipped and watched a group of patrons enter the bar. "I agree. There are facts but we have no proof."

"A strike point event will put us in the right direction. Flush out the motives for this geography."

"Japan is an unlikely location to stage a potential disaster or bloodshed."

In the background, a waiter activated a gas heater stand. A gust carried off the inky-black canal, bringing a chill to the cozy bar. Clusters of drinkers filled the small tables as surround sound music played.

Katerina tightened her scarf. "Jake will find a way in; he's really good at that."

"Tomorrow we can dig deeper on Suzuki, connected events and pinpoint links."

"I still have some tricks up my sleeve," Katerina said defiantly.

Mia smiled. "I am sure you do." She finished her drink and pushed it aside. "Would you like another?"

"It's tempting, but I must decline. Last night I had a few glasses of red thinking about Jake. Woke up a bit shady this morning."

"Let's leave, shall we? Would you like to sleep at my apartment tonight?"

"Are you sure it's not an inconvenience?" Katerina said.

"Not at all. Love to have the company."

"It's settled then."

They stood on the sidewalk as drizzle began. The pizzeria wood-fired oven aroma wafted in the cold air.

"What about a pizza to cap off the evening?" Mia perused the shop window.

"Love that idea."

The pizza shop bustled with customers. Three small tables in the corner were full, orders flowing at the counter.

"What do you feel like?"

"I am partial to a marinara, as we're in a port city."

Mia laughed. "Yes, I like seafood too. Let's get the big size."

"Agreed. I'm famished. You bought the drinks, so I'll get this."

They waited in line and ordered.

Mia and Katerina sat side-by-side. The warmth of the oven and confined waiting area made them forget the cold outside.

Katerina collected the box and they walked to the basement parking lot under the publisher.

"That's me." Mia unlocked a red hatchback and climbed inside. Katerina joined her. Mia flicked the de-mist switch as they emerged from cover into traffic. The drizzle turned into a pour, wipers swiping on the fastest speed.

"Let's swing by the hotel and you can pack a change of clothes."

"I'll get my laptop too."

Mia waited on the curb as Katerina gathered her things. "Got everything you need?"

"Yes thanks."

Mia joined the lane and sat on a steady speed. The rain pattered the car, floating headlamps blurred yellow and white.

By the time they reached the apartment the drops were nearly hail. They parked underground and climbed the stairs into the lobby.

The food overpowered the elevator cabin.

"I am soaked." Inside, Mia took off her coat and hung it on a rack. "Should I open a red?" Mia winked, poised at the pantry.

"Just one for me." Katerina laughed. "You are a bad influence."

"I try." Mia held two plates and Katerina opened the box and separated a piece of pizza. She hovered over a plate, nibbling from the end.

Mia twisted the top off a wine bottle. "Cheers."

Glasses clinked. In the window, the black canal glistened and heaved, a snake in a vast swamp. Laughter came easy as they ate and talked.

"We demolished that pizza." Mia laughed and topped up her wine glass. Katerina declined a second and put both plates in the washer, the empty box in the bin.

"I better get a clean set of sheets."

"Let me help you."

Mia set up a bed in the spare room. "This is ready to go when you are tired."

They channel surfed and settled on a rom com.

Chapter 27

JAKE DESCENDED THE narrow staircase to the subway. He figured a train was a better way to travel Tokyo anonymously. Suzuki's apartment sat near Shibuya station, a modern and busy ward.

He bought an all-day pass and followed the flow of commuters. An overhead board displayed the line timetables. Steel-colored beams supported the ultra-modern platform. It curved and waved in an aesthetic sculpture. An art piece.

The rush of a bullet train braking to the station gave Jake a shiver in his spine, the gust stronger than the noise of the transport somehow. It didn't entirely make sense. Wonders of technology. He jostled with bodies as they squeezed into the cabin, a single organism slithering and sliding. Standing room only.

Tunnels and tiles flicked by in still motion, flashes of white. The train stopped and started, the flood of passengers in endless motion.

Shibuya station materialized and he exited into a larger cavern with an impossibly high ceiling. The elevator took him to the turnstile. He clicked through and out into a cluster of high-rises and blue steel.

He followed the Hachiko exit, massive screens and billboards dominating the sky. The intersection of Shibuya crossing reminded him of Times Square in New York. It had a marked crosswalk capped by an edge of four smaller crossings. Hundreds of people walked in all directions, covering the large area like an ant colony. He continued north and turned right into rows of more affluent residential towers.

Suzuki's building abutted a restaurant complex with more apartments. Neon signs covered the other side, a multi-colored wall he could stare at for only ten seconds. The reception maintained the standard security level, nothing overly sophisticated. He walked around the block to get a feel for the neighborhood.

A trendy bar filled with young corporates wrapped the east junction. It grew into a five-star glass-and-steel hotel, a phallic symbol of wealth. Tokyo town planners did not do things by halves.

Jake inched to the far corner, careful not to accidentally run into Suzuki. Further surveillance outside the perimeter would give better clarity on Suzuki's habits and routines.

From across the street, he took photos with his burner of the foyer and layout. He sat at a table in a small shop and ordered a small sushi and a bottle of water. Through the glass, he watched the residents coming and going. Most people didn't appear to know each other and the guard ignored them as they passed, the rent-a-cop disinterested in his duties.

Jake worked through initial strategies of getting into the rooms: worst case scenario if he could not gain access another way.

A young woman placed his meal on the table and he ate slowly, alternating his gaze from the cell phone to the high rise. The sky cleared, a strong reflection on the window blocking him from being noticed by passersby.

No sign of Suzuki. The demographic consisted mainly of corporates: equal mix of men and women, power suits in blues or grays. The waitress took away the empty plates. He asked for a pot of tea. It came straight away, piping hot. A little cup accompanied the steaming beverage. He poured and blew on it for a minute.

The burner vibrated.

"Hello."

"Hi, George, it's Riku. We met at the bar."

"Hi, Riku. How are things with you?"

"Good. I called people and we are in luck. An executive I met before wants to chat tonight. Cyber security is a hot issue right now with these guys."

"That's doable." Jake stayed cool and measured. "Where did you have in mind?"

"A late-night entertainment venue. Upscale host club in Ginza. You need a membership, so you would be my guest."

"Intriguing. I'm up for that."

"There will be other corporates, including a major one from Lape Industries. He loves this place in Ginza. Practically lives there when he is in town. It is not in the traditional red-light districts in Shinjuko. Classier. Women from all around the world, not just Japan." Riku cleared his throat. "They have a dress code. You need a collar and jacket. Is that cool?"

"Understood and no problem."

"This place is call Ginza Elite. Meet me there at nine-thirty P.M. Text when you're out the front."

"Sure will."

"Get ready for a big one. These guys like to party hard. Unless a woman really takes their fancy, they will go all night."

"I am looking forward to it, Riku. See you tonight."

"Hai."

The call cut out and he finished the tea.

He walked over the pedestrian crossing and into the corner mall. On ground level, he found two menswear places on opposite sides. The bigger one had a sale on jackets. He tried on a few until a salesman came over.

"Can I help you?"

"Do you have this jacket in a forty-two, western size?" He held a navy-blue, single-breasted brand.

"Let me check."

The sales attendant retreated into a door marked private. He returned with the correct jacket. "Here you go."

"Thanks." Jake chose a cream-colored shirt and entered the dressing room. The ensemble had a casual but formal edge. Enough room around the ribs and waist to carry, if necessary. Not black tie, but modern and chic.

A wall displayed formal shoes. He picked a gray pair in a modern take on a classic style and tested a pair with soft heels. A must in his line of work not to announce your presence with noisy shoes. The shop attendant folded them into a bag.

At midday, the subway congestion had not lessened at Shibuya station. He took the next Ginza line train. Six stops to Ginza station. Reconnaissance on the escort entertainment venue for tonight. A gun was not practical and they may conduct searches. The knife might be strapped to his lower leg. A stroke of luck if Suzuki happened to be one of the executives.

The train pulled up to the platform. The JR pass beeped and displayed the green light as he came out into the open air. A mix of stately buildings and older residential blocks blended with modern towers. More median strips with spaced trees.

A large black umbrella marked the entrance of Ginza Elite, the words in neon-white script. Subtle compared to many areas of Tokyo covered with signage. Two doormen who doubled as Yakuza bookended the entrance. Organized crime syndicates controlled all the entertainment venues of this nature in the city.

The venue opened one room at this time of day for high-ranking members and private parties. Women in cocktail dresses entered individually with the occasional heavyset man in a brand-name suit. He checked the alley to the rear; all keypads and secure, so he didn't venture down in case of surveillance cameras. Shopping precincts were packed into Ginza, glittering over the sidewalks. This was an out-of-place venue, hidden in a side street near the main station.

He returned to the subway and rode the train to the temple grounds. He wandered the outer streets near the hotel, paused at shop windows checking for reflections, doubling back to catch familiar faces or suspicious behavior. His counter-surveillance had been slack, so he increased the duration to forty minutes on this occasion. The density of pedestrians made this challenging at points.

A smattering of guests gathered in the hotel restaurant. He climbed the stairs to his room and activated the lights with the key card. He hoped the event tonight could potentially reveal high-ranking executives at Lape and get him close to the motives of these buyers.

On the burner, he wrote a text to McCallister:

Getting nearer. Unsure of strike point. Breakthrough tonight? Your man came through with gear. Update when know more. Sphinx.

Jake flipped open the laptop and loaded the main menu. The inbox had only a few emails, none from Katerina. He sent a quick one to her, telling her not to stress too much, that she'd already given him invaluable leads, he had progressed, and would send more tomorrow.

On the floor, he pressed sets of push-ups. He limbered up with light stretching, alternated with planking for his core. Sweat dripped down his brow as he pushed the repetitions to failure. Five sets of both exercises and he warmed down. He performed basic kata movements from his kickboxing form, then took a shower and cleaned up, shaving the stubble off to change his appearance again. Time read seven-thirty-two. The cream shirt had many creases. He erected the hotel-supplied ironing board and switched on the iron. He pressed the shirt smooth and placed it on a hanger.

He chose spaghetti Bolognese and an entrée of spring rolls. He wanted to get carbs for energy and to absorb the night's alcohol.

He ate the food quietly with devices turned off or in sleep mode. Stillness covered the room. Darkness fell and the city lit up with hundreds of brands blinking.

A meditation session would calm his mind after the physical exertion. He lowered to the floor and crossed his legs. His mind emptied as he focused within.

Chapter 28

EIGHT A.M. MACHINERY and industrial sounds permeated the apartment. Katerina roused and stared at the ceiling. A moment lapsed while she recognized Mia's spare room. Her friend's support had proved invaluable so far. Dawn light spanned the white duvet, making prison-bar shapes on the fabric cover. She moved positions to relieve tension in her lower back.

The mattress had been comfortable; she'd slept the whole night. A percolator sat on the stove, the surface still warm. She poured the contents into a cup and crossed her legs on the couch.

A click and the front door cracked open. Mia stepped inside and padded to the living room. She wore a sweatsuit and sneakers, hair covered with a cap: no makeup.

"Hi there."

"Hey. You're up early, Mia."

"I went for an early morning jog." She leaned against the wall. "Tiring, but feels great. Going to make fruit smoothies with other healthy stuff. You want some?"

"Thanks. Sure, why not?"

Mia went to work cutting up fruit on a kitchen board. She pulled a blender from an overhead cupboard and plugged it into the wall socket. A tub of yoghurt sat side-by-side with the fruit. Big spoons of the yoghurt went into the blender.

Dark clouds hovered low in the sky, the morning gray filtered in off the water, and the usual breeze. Katerina did laps around the furniture. She opened her laptop. Jake had sent a message. Not an update. She scanned the text. Her chest warmed despite the cold. This made being separated from him worth the effort.

"Here you go." Mia stood opposite with a tall glass in her hand.

"If this doesn't give you an energy boost, nothing will."

Katerina viewed the pinkish red concoction and swallowed. "This does taste fantastic."

"I aim to please." Mia moved around organizing the kitchen. "It's mostly fruit: berries, bananas, and low-fat yoghurt. Occasionally I add chia seeds or other natural ingredients."

"Interesting." She drank the liquid steadily until the glass was empty. Her stomach felt full and content. "I feel healthier already."

"You can stay here if you like: move out of the hotel." Mia rinsed the blender, placed the device in the dishwasher.

"That would be lovely. Are you sure I won't cramp your style?"

"Not at all. Besides, what style? I am just me."

"Ok. I'll go and pack and checkout now. See you in a bit."

"I'll be at the office. Here's the spare key and I'll tell reception you're staying. Make yourself at home or join me at work."

Katerina hugged Mia. "Thanks so much, Mia. Really appreciate your support."

"No problem, like I said."

Jake locked the hotel room and descended the stairs two at a time. The workout had invigorated his body, a spring ready to jump at a moments' notice, his mind rested and alert. Outside the temperature had cooled from the afternoon rays, but not to an unpleasant degree.

He descended the station elevator unarmed except for his hands. Groups chatted on the platform, Friday night revelry. A light wind preceded the train. He sat at the window, the next seat vacant. Scanning the passengers, he saw no one that set off his radar. He came prepared for a big drinking session. To keep his wits on his buying round, he would alternate with soft drink only in his glass.

Ginza came up; he disembarked. Gangs of late-night shoppers, bags hanging from both hands, boarded the carriage. He maneuvered in the gaps, aiming at the exits. At nine-twelve P.M. he performed a circuit. Counter-surveillance. The challenge of higher street traffic numbers was both an advantage and disadvantage. He could vanish in the crowd, if necessary, but a follower could do the same, or hang back and be covered by pedestrians.

Nine-twenty-five. At the front, he texted Riku:

Hi, Riku, waiting out front. Guests accompany members or I am on guest list? Cheers, George.

Heavy-set corporates in brand-name suits queued up to a rope. The doorman allowed a new group entry every five minutes.

Riku passed the opening and contemplated the people outside. Jake moved from the shadows. He signaled Riku, who nodded and spoke to the main security guy. Riku waved to him. He crossed the road and came to the rope.

"You're a guest of Riku. No trouble or fights and we will get along fine."

Jake agreed. The man undid the rope latch.

"Glad you came, Jake." Riku patted him on the back.

"Should be a good night. Thanks for inviting me."

They went into a reception area with a marble top and faux fireplace. A glamorous receptionist was stationed in a recessed booth.

"He's with me, Tanya," Riku said.

Tanya barely acknowledged him. He wondered if she blinked either.

"This way. Follow me." Riku lead him through an archway and into a huge space. The room enlarged to impossible size. On the thirty-feet high ceiling hung a massive chandelier. He swiveled to take in the establishment and decor. Circular balconies layered the three levels to the top. Gorgeous women roamed the floor with trays. Dressed in lingerie and heels, these females could strip you bare in an instant.

Riku stopped at the circular bar and ordered two shots of tequila. Upscale backsplash rose to meet glass supports. Single malt whiskies. Jake scanned the wall from left to right: Suntory Yamazaki, Glenfiddich, Midleton, Seppeltsfield, Macallan, Old Rip Van Winkle. The line extended too far to see remaining labels.

The second row were the vodkas: Belvedere, Chopin, Gray Goose, Royal Dragon tapered off like the whiskies. Most started at two-hundred-plus a glass.

"Big night, guys." The female bartender poured the drinks and gave them a smile. Riku produced rolled-up notes and pressed them into her hand. He included a generous tip.

They leaned with their backs against the bar. Jake played it cool. For fifteen minutes he nodded while Riku talked nonstop about the everyday job as a lackey to the big guns. Beautiful women paraded the main space, weaving between the booths and tables. Men leaned and gyrated, peacocks with words and wallets, vying to catch the ear or attention of a female.

"Let's go to the booth." Riku pointed. "That's my contact at Lape and an executive he's with; The big, sleazy suit who is a bit too hands on with the females. He'll get thrown out if he's not careful."

At the table edge, Riku nodded. "I'd like you to meet a friend. George Perry."

"Hi, George, my name is Haruto."

Jake shook hands with the Lape executive. "Haruto. Good to meet you."

"Likewise."

Followed by the big guy.

"This is Minato," Riku said.

"Hi." The men shared a handshake.

They sat in the booth with drinks in hand.

"The talent is fantastic tonight." Minato drained his glass.

"How's everything at Lape: keeping you busy?"

"Coming along, but we need specialists to take it to the next level. What are you in, George?"

"Consultant. Cyber Security."

"That's something we need to do better. Are you working on a project here in Tokyo?"

"Government contract. Can't discuss the finer detail, of course."

The music changed tempo to a faster, hard-energy genre. A woman curled her finger at Haruto. He reached out as she took his hand and pulled him to the bar.

Minato cheered and waved his hand. He waved for a refill and pointed at Riku and Jake.

A tall Japanese woman sauntered to the table.

"Single malt. Suntory three. Put it on my tab. Thanks."

She smiled and signalled to the bar.

"The firewalls and protocols must be tighter on the internal network. Our contracts are highly classified and cargo requires privacy. Too many breaches and attacks recently. One DDoS attack last month wiped us out for over three hours." Minato tapped sausage fingers on the table. "I can't have this type of risk in our business."

"I wouldn't accept that either."

"Is this something you would be open to discuss?"

Jake stared at his glass, contemplating the answer, dramatic pause to hide the eagerness within. He glanced at Riku and across at Minato. "I could perform an initial assessment to gauge the size and scope of the project."

"Good man." Minato chinned at the hostess strutting their way with a tray. "Here she comes. Drink up everybody."

She placed the glasses down with expert grace and ease. Minato stared at her statuesque figure, his gaze in absolute awe of her beauty.

"Why don't you come over and buy me a drink?" she said.

The big man rose. He bent over the table. "If I don't come back, I'll get your number from Riku tomorrow."

"Have a good night," Jake said.

"Use my tab on the table, Riku."

Minato went behind the flock of suits and stunning females. A strobe flickered colors over a train of glittering cocktail dresses. Jake had a challenging time to drag his head from the endless stream of beauty.

"Great first impression. You have a meeting that quick." Riku raised his drink. "*Kanpai*. Or cheers, as you say in America."

"*Kanpai*." Jake touched his glass.

Different women walked the floor as the night progressed. A central raised podium served to give a panoramic angle. At near midnight, a pair of Japanese men entered and did a circuit. Jake recognized Suzuki and waited to see Riku's reaction.

He leaned back in the leather seats. The pair came from behind. Riku tilted his head and became animated.

"That's Suzuki, a high corporate executive. He sits on more than one board, including Lape."

"Interesting." Jake sipped Suntory. The delicious burn trickled his throat.

"He wields great influence in corporate Tokyo. Stock exchange and politicians. If we get the chance, I'll introduce you." Riku tilted his glass to his lips. "This Suntory is amazing, isn't it?"

"One of the very best single malts. And aged to perfection."

"Do you indulge in this variety of female?"

"I have a partner currently, so no."

"Is she in Japan?"

"In Europe doing work. How about you?"

Riku laughed. "Many are out of my price range. Besides I have a girl that has been on and off for eighteen months. I come here to socialize and network with powerful people."

"This is the right venue for that. It must be hard sometimes to maintain perspective among all this glamor."

"True. Tempting on occasion. Speaking of powerful people." Riku gained his feet. "Wait here." He weaved into the bodies, aiming at the bar.

Under the lights, Jake saw him tap Suzuki on the back. The man turned and shook his hand. Riku chatted and bantered, playing the game.

Jake enjoyed the whisky, eased back in his chair. He saw Riku point at their booth. Suzuki and his associate crossed towards him, the party beelining the impromptu dance floor.

"Haruto Suzuki, this is George Perry."

"Good to meet you," Suzuki said in a deep voice. "What brings you to Tokyo?"

"An IT contract."

"That could be useful. Are you available in the short term?"

"I'm working on a contract but will be meeting with Minato in the coming days."

Suzuki pivoted to his associate. "I will attend this discussion. Arrange it with Minato."

The associate nodded and made a note.

"I look forward to it." Jake motioned to the booth. "Will you join us?"

"I would like to, but have a pressing engagement to attend at another location soon."

"Some other time."

"Goodbye for now." Suzuki gave a short bow to Jake and Riku, then turned to the crowd.

Riku slid in opposite Jake with two more whiskies. He passed one across the table.

"You are on a roll tonight."

"Suntory again?"

"It's the best."

"Cannot argue with that. I going to use the bathroom." Jake stood and headed to the corner.

Chapter 29

DRIZZLE TRICKLED DOWN the windows in long threads. Katerina clutched her purse. It took time to get used to living in the port city with the weather. Slick road reflections made it difficult to ascertain lines.

The hotel entrance was covered by a lone doorman. She paid and stepped out under the sheltered awning. Water gushed in the gutter channels. Umbrellas bobbed past her line of sight as she entered the lobby.

She boarded the elevator and pressed her floor number. Her mind ran over the databases left at her disposal. There had to be more data on Suzuki and Lape she could dig. Links to reveal the identity of the buyer. Or buyers.

In the room she gathered her belongings, shoving them into the luggage. Bangs and clangs echoed from the ports. Zipped the bag and did a circuit of the room. Travelling with two bags had advantages. A sweep of the bedroom and wardrobes proved nothing was left behind.

She wheeled the luggage to the elevator and presented herself to the service desk.

The cab's tires sliced the wet as the downpour continued relentlessly. A fog curled from the water, moving across the built-up city. She settled back in the seat. In the rearview, she noticed a blue SUV that had circled past the hotel earlier. The plates were too far away to read.

"Please detour down a street."

"There's one coming up."

"Perfect."

The driver put on the blinker and slowly took the curve. She watched the mirror. The blue SUV turned into the street. Her pulse quickened.

"I think someone is following me. Can you merge with the main road and see if we can lose them?"

"There's a route around the canal which has heavier traffic." The driver watched his GPS updates. "We can weave in and out and see if it works."

Low visibility helped her cause. The cab braked at an intersection and joined the flow on an amber signal. In their wake, the dark blue SUV caught the red light and braked. Bicycles surged across between. They changed lanes to create distance.

In the mirror, she saw the SUV nudge into the traffic, passing a red light. A horn beeped. Someone yelled an obscenity.

The cab driver slammed the accelerator and edged the next intersection. He angled over a gas station and exited the other side. A side alley ran between four-story structures, speed limit reduced for pedestrians. The cab slowed to twenty miles, no sign of the pursuer.

"We are five minutes away from your destination."

"You can drop me there." She pointed at a mall entrance. The complex ran west to the next block. She could dash through the center to Mia's apartment undetected. She checked the meter fare and had the cash and a tip ready.

"Here you go." The driver eased to the curb. She watched mirrors. No SUV in sight. "I'll keep driving west and come around from the south. Hopefully that will keep them guessing for a while."

"Thanks so much for your help." Katerina put the money in his hand and slid across the seat.

Wasting no time, she entered the sliding doors. Shoppers created cover but slowed her pace. A food court with stools and tables. People carried trays filled with meals. She powerwalked around obstacles but not too hurriedly. Her peripheral vision monitored the scene, and head checks at the elevators and doors behind her. No one suspicious.

She aimed at the sliding glass. This would take her to the opposite block from Mia's apartment. A family of five gathered on a seat, a girl of six dropping a bag of sweets. The youngster cried as

Katerina veered to avoid the spill.

No SUVs waited at the entrance. The rain had abated, sky remaining dark. A breeze brought back the chill. She scrambled over the pedestrian crossing and made it up to the corner. Mia's apartment foyer was empty bar an elderly woman peering into her mailbox. She pressed the lift button, heart rate elevated from the pursuit. The doors receded and she yanked her luggage into the cabin.

Numbers lit up until she found the right floor. She rushed to the threshold and pulled out the key. Her hand shook as she shoved it into the lock. The door swung in her wake. Cool air greeted her in the living space. Blood pounded between her ears from the near encounter. Luggage left at the foot of the island bench.

Katerina quickly regained her composure. Cars moved in lanes below. She retreated to the couch. A stalker had to be related to their research, or a separate matter with Mia. She yanked her cell from her pocket and stared at the device.

The cell phone rang and rang.

Finally, Mia answered. "Hey, how's it going? Got your stuff yet?"

"Hi, Mia. I am at your apartment." She paused to gather her thoughts. "Listen, I'm sure that a dark-color SUV tailed me on the return."

The sound of a sharp inhale. "Oh lord! Are you positive?"

"Yes. I saw a dark blue SUV earlier near the hotel. When I packed and hailed a cab, it was following us. The driver turned quickly, and it did too. We managed to lose them and I got out at the other side of the mall near your place."

"We need to be more careful. Please stay in the apartment and I will drop by later."

"OK, was thinking the same thing. Let's send update texts every one to two hours. Be on the alert for a dark blue SUV. Or any cars you see again."

"Bye." The line cut out.

Rain pattered the glass. Katerina checked the balcony door was locked. She paced the living room, possibilities running through her mind. The investigation she did for Jake in Japan did not reach this far. If it did, it must be a powerful network.

Who was the enemy? How did they find me?

She sat at the table and fired up her computer. The latest data results loaded in spreadsheets. Numbers and tables combined dates, events, and personnel. She analyzed the details, trying to uncover the possible link.

Suzuki's involvement in the matter had to be limited, hard evidence scarce. She broadened the search over two decades. Suzuki had run a now defunct company called Satcom. The co-founder named Kanji Sato had an interesting background in chemicals. She ran an advanced search on Sato. The information came up standard on the surface. An ivy-leaguer like Suzuki, Sato had a physics PHD from a prestigious university.

Glossy cover. What's underneath?

She ramped up the search tentacles in open and closed media sources. He'd avoided an environmental inquiry some ten years back. Unrelated. Benefactor in a few local causes. Chaired a chemical manufacturing board for three years.

An article surfaced from 2012.

Sato visited a man in prison named Shoko Asahara, a terrorist on death row. She scanned the story and her stomach lurched. Asahara had led a doomsday terror cult known as *Aum Shinrikyo*. The criminal had masterminded a sarin gas attack on the Tokyo subway.

Katerina placed her elbows on the table. She palmed her eyes and inhaled. This had to be the link they were searching for.

For the attack and other offences, Asahara was convicted and sentenced to death in 2004. The last appeal was rejected some years later. They arrested more members of the religious cult. In 2018, Asahara was executed by hanging.

A search on company titles associated with Sato showed a

registration that had used Lape warehouses in the last twelve months. Storage and shipping fees. Suzuki ran these invoices by a shelf company in his name.

She hacked the overall balance sheets. This took ten more minutes. Using password cracking software from a dark web forum, she located the reports in cloud storage. She scanned the spreadsheets for the date range and numbers.

Not accounted for in Lape industries' revenue. This relationship turned murkier by the minute: arms dealing with the oligarch, chemical manufacturing linked to terrorism, international crime syndicates and importation of contraband.

She wrote an email to Jake outlining Suzuki's offshore private link with Sato's company. Also the fact that Lape assets were being used to transport, manufacture and store. The email included the attached article. She wrote a brief summary and a bio of Asahara.

The email sent, she rose and stretched. A seagull glided to the balcony and gripped the rail. She watched and rubbed a cramp in her neck. The evidence pointed to a major terrorist attack in Tokyo. A sarin gas attack on the subway or something worse?

She shook her head, as if part of her was unwilling to face facts.

Where was the intended target? She picked up her water bottle and drank. Her phone beeped: a message from Mia.

Hey there, update to check you're ok?

Katerina typed a reply:

Thanks, Mia. I am good. Hope you are too.

The words echoed in her mind as she stared at the expected storm front. She saved the new discovery to show it to Mia.

Chapter 30

THE NIGHT AT Elites wore on into the early morning. Whisky and conversation flowed in equal measure, elevating the party atmosphere. Suits were fist pumping and gorgeous females strutted their stuff. The adrenaline and competitive energy ran thick in the atmosphere. Security materialized out of thin air if patrons became rowdy. Tabs and cash were pumped to maximum effect.

At one-twenty A.M. two women caught eye contact from the bar and approached.

"Here we go. Incoming at five o'clock. Two live ones and they are hot." Riku contemplated the dance floor.

The Asian one was first to their booth. Both women were international model standard on any catwalk.

"Hi I'm Sylvia," said the tall Japanese woman in a tight-hugging red dress. "This is Adriana."

Adriana had European features with long brown hair and blue eyes. She smiled demurely with her hand on her hip.

"Would you like to join us?" Riku gestured at the table.

"That would be lovely."

Sylvia sat next to Riku and Adriana slid in by Jake.

"I am Riku and this George."

They took turns shaking hands.

"What should I order for you ladies? We are having Suntory whisky and it is divine."

Adriana said, "I love Suntory. One for me, please."

"I'll have the Belvedere vodka, thanks," Sylvia said. "I don't mix this late."

Riku waved at a waitress who came over promptly. He confirmed the tab and their order.

The group chatted about corporate life in general and Japan's economy. A round of drinks came. Jake nodded when appropriate. He suppressed a yawn and declined a refill on the next order. The morning approached quickly and he wanted to get some rest. Riku paired off with Sylvia and they conducted their own conversation.

It seemed like foreplay for the rich, but he carried the interaction happily. Katerina entered his thoughts and he felt a touch guilty for sitting there with beautiful women. His intentions were honorable, but it still felt wrong. He'd explain everything in the next communication tomorrow.

Adriana angled to face Jake and fidgeted with her glass. Not wanting to be rude, he faced her, but left a gap in the seat. He smiled attentively and asked her about her background if, of course, it wasn't a personal question.

"Not at all. I'm from Prague and have travelled through Europe for the past five years." Adriana stirred her whisky with a straw. "I worked in clubs and pubs and even a stint as a DJ in a club in Spain."

"Spain must have been one massive party." Jake shifted his drink. "I'm in cyber security, so nothing as exciting as your life. Although I have travelled to some cities in Europe, but mainly for work."

"True, but the pace can be overwhelming. At twenty, with so much falling in your lap, it's hard to gain perspective. For a moment I think I lost mine to youthful folly."

"I see your point." Her attractiveness was undeniable. He reminded himself that his intention was purely to gain intel and nothing more.

"Your industry is a necessity to keep all our information safe. Back in Prague, I did the first year of a business degree. Have thought about returning at some later point. Finish the course and have a normal job during daylight hours." She smiled wistfully.

"A good option to fall back on when you are ready. The world of commerce is equally cutthroat and competitive." Jake waved his hand. "Take all the corporate suits here tonight. Powerful and dominant personalities. It is like a battlefield here and the richest person always wins. The boardrooms are the same."

"Tell me about it." She nodded attentively, eyeing the patrons. "We can't escape this way of life."

"What do you do outside of work?"

"I go to the gym: have to maintain fitness, especially for this job." She winked. "I can see you work out, George. Impressive for a corporate man."

"I try to fit it in when I can."

"It shows. Keep it up." She smiled again.

The conversation diverted and more than once, she smiled seductively. He sought a segue to leave before the evening escalated.

A waitress checked the table for a refill. Riku and Sylvia ordered one each. He looked at Adriana, who pouted her lips.

"One last drink."

The waitress retreated. The time showed two A.M.

"I think we have a lot in common, George. Fitness and corporate aspirations."

Jake nodded as the alcohol caught up in his system.

The round of fresh drinks arrived. Adriana lifted hers and they drank in unison. She snugged close to his body, the warmth going to his crotch as her hand squeezed his thigh gently. He caught her eye and knew he'd had one too many. She was gorgeous and his defenses were weak.

"Adriana, it has been a pleasure but..." His protest sounded lame.

"Let's go back to my place. Normally I don't suggest this so early, but I feel such an attraction to you." Her hand caressed his stomach. "Let's go." He hesitated, even in his alcohol-fueled state, wondering what her game was. He turned. "Thanks for a great evening, Riku."

"I'll give you a call, George. Thanks for coming tonight."

Jake grasped her hand and moved through the artificial brightness, bling, and adrenaline. She clung to him as they hunted for the door. The doormen had the same expressionless faces. One nodded but he could not be sure. Outside a breeze churned. The temperature had dropped further. He raised his collar around his neck, sought out a ride. Adriana wrapped her hands around her arms. He removed his jacket and put it over her scantily clad shoulders.

"Thanks."

"Cabs over there." She pointed forward.

They walked to the next bend. Thirty feet from the venue, a cab rank extended beyond the glow of streetlights. Music pumped from Elites in their wake. He got to the first cab and opened the door. She slid inside. The journey saw little traffic, neon colors in full force. He watched for shadows. There were none he spotted.

"It's down this road and left," she said in French.

The driver braked at the curb. A semi-modern apartment block. He paid for the cab and she led into the foyer. They crossed the tiled floor to the stairs. Ambient yellow lit up the corridor paintings. His head felt like cotton wool from the whisky. His fortitude with alcohol had diminished with age but he could still hold his own. The keycard passed over the reader twice before it bleeped green.

He straightened his posture in the living space, took a glass, and held it under the faucet. The water tumbled down his throat in gulps. Dehydration had set in fast. He swallowed two vitamin B12 tablets he'd brought in his pocket. Closing the blinds, she shut out the electronic billboards.

"My bedroom is there on the right and the bathroom that way." She shrugged off his jacket and hung it on a chair. "I'm going right to the bedroom."

Adriana unzipped her dress and let it fall to the floor. Her shapely hourglass curves were perfection. He pulled off his shoes and unbuttoned his shirt. His self-control was overpowered by lust. She embraced him and they fell to the bed.

They had heated sex for nearly an hour. The sheets damp with sweat, Adriana mounted him and thrust, groaning. Finally, they separated and lay, shoulders touching, on their backs.

"That was amazing." Adriana grinned. She traced a finger over his arm and noticed his outstretched leg. "Your shins have dents and lumps. That means hardcore Muay Thai training."

"I did martial arts years ago. Just a hobby."

"My ex was a professional kickboxer and his shins were similar to yours." She propped her head on her bent elbow. "Who are you, George Perry? IT consultants normally are not this fit and into advanced fighting skills."

"You are very knowledgeable for a woman who works in a cocktail dress at a bar. Do you know Suzuki?"

"I have seen your business partners at Elites many times."

My business partners? Jake started to think this could be more dangerous than a one-night fling. *Did Suzuki hire her to find out more about him?*

"We could do this for a few hours more." She rubbed her flat stomach.

"It's tempting, I must admit." His arousal was almost immediate. He had to be rational and control his urges.

Three-forty. He forced himself out of bed. "I have to leave."

"That's a shame. I'll order an Uber. You can put the destination in."

He put a hotel a block south of his. "It will be here in three minutes. I better wait outside."

She put on a dressing gown to let him out. "Here's my number. If you are around, give me a call."

Under the hallway lights, they kissed goodbye.

He walked to his hotel. In the bathroom, he freshened up. His face felt clean, but numb, eyes slightly red. Nothing that a bit of sleep would not fix.

An email login through encryption placed his inbox on the screen. His comprehensive security measures meant it bounced from different locations to mask his own. Katerina had sent an email marked important. He opened it and scanned the text. His pulse quickened. Suzuki was not only linked, but in business with a terrorist supporter.

The article she'd attached saved him time finding the history. He sucked in breath as he read, stopped a moment to calm. Sato sits on a board for chemical manufacturing. Suzuki and Sato are still major partners in a business, importing and exporting in suspicious channels. Connect the dots.

Jake leaned back in his chair, ran his fingers through his hair. He had to meet Suzuki and his team—and fast. He sent a brief email to Katerina.

Thanks so much. Next level intel. Timely. Take care. Ring soon.

Sleep first. He shut down the computer. The doorway silhouette shadowed the hall. He trundled over the carpet and entered the bedroom.

Colors broke from the blind gaps, casting long shards on the comforter. He shrugged off the jacket and pants and lay in bed. The night at Elites had been productive. An introduction which led to an invitation with the right executives.

He rolled onto his side. His cyber knowledge was sufficient to run a strategic presentation: enough to get him into the boardroom and into the contract. If he wanted that much. A glimpse into their IT infrastructure would prove how much compromise and culpability there had been. He was edging closer to the assignment objective. Motive.

The whisky acted as an anesthetic. His head floated in the clouds. An illusion, but a nice sensation. He pictured Adriana.

A deep breath, hold and exhale. He repeated the process and thought of Katerina.

Eyes heavy, he drifted off to a deep sleep.

Chapter 31

A NOTIFICATION BEEPED from the inbox. Nine-ten P.M. Katerina checked and read the reply from Jake. They were seven hours ahead. It must be around four A.M. in Tokyo. She picked up the cell and rang his number.

"Hi." Jake sounded groggy.

"Hey. Were you asleep? Your email just came so I thought you might be awake."

"Fell into bed now. It is good to hear your voice. A big night with the Japanese executives. Riku invited me to an exclusive bar. The guy I met at the bar opposite Lape's warehouse. Minato and Suzuki hang out there regularly drinking top-shelf whisky and vodka. All a big show of testosterone and competition." Jake stifled a yawn. Guilt gathered about his tryst with Adriana. He pushed it away.

"Ah, ok."

"Held back on drinking too much whisky. Took it slow. Suntory. Still knocked back plenty enough to feel the effects."

"Did it work being there? I am sure you charmed them all."

Jake laughed. "I was introduced to Minato and Suzuki. We are talking an IT contract on their cyber security."

"Wow. That is worth the effort."

"After staking out Suzuki's apartment yesterday afternoon, this is easier. I'll probably need your help though." He rubbed his eyes, relieved Katerina was in good spirits. "With the technical jargon and skill set. You're the real expert."

She chuckled. "Of course I will help. If you send across the details, I can put together a basic report that will easily pass their IT team. You can refine it or read over so you don't get caught out on questions."

"Thanks so much for that."

"No problem." She hesitated. "Try not to be alarmed, but I think I was followed this morning."

Jake inhaled sharply. "Where?"

"I checked out of the hotel today and moved my things to Mia's apartment." She gathered her thoughts. "A dark blue SUV tailed the cab. Tinted windows. I know I saw it earlier. Told the driver to hang a right into a lane and it followed. We lost it by weaving into different streets. Lucky the driver helped me."

"Happy you got away. These people could be lurking about. Please be safe and be on alert."

"Don't worry, I will." Her voice cracked slightly. She placed a hand over the microphone and swallowed her drink. "You sound tired. I'll let you go back to bed."

"Thanks for the understanding and support. Really appreciate it." Jake was hesitant to end the call. "Good to hear your voice."

"You too. Ciao."

Katerina placed the burner on the table. She stared out at the darkened shapes. They hung like apparitions in mist, glittering lights dimmed in the background. She battled a sudden sense of melancholy. The SUV chase reminded her of the seriousness of this task. These people could reach out anywhere with limitless resources.

The oligarch goes and others step up to replace him.

Her resolve firmed as she examined the data. A rumble came from her stomach. She hadn't eaten since lunch. Mia texted she had a late meeting about an article with the editor.

Katerina boiled some rice on the stove and opened a tin of curry-flavored tuna from the pantry. After the incident earlier, she didn't want to leave in the dark to look for food.

A basic meal but it would have to do. Under the circumstances she did not mind. She spooned the meal slowly, rolling over the possible events that could precipitate the arms deals. A large transaction of this size had to have a motive and end game.

The call came at nine A.M. sharp. One eye opened, Jake hovered over the nightstand and retrieved his burner. He pressed the answer button.

"Hello."

"Morning, George. Minato here. How did you pull up from our adventures in Ginza?"

"I got back around four A.M." He pulled up out of the sheets and rested his spine against the headboard.

"Well done. Can you be available this morning for a chat in our office?"

He cradled the cell on his shoulder and shrugged on a pair of jeans. "Sure, what about eleven A.M.?"

"That works for me. Suzuki wants to be there, so I'll put in his diary."

"It would have to be casual wear at this short notice. I am working remotely now from a hotel, so will come straight over when finished."

"No issue. It's your expertise that matters, not fashion sense. I'll text the address."

His burner beeped with the location of their head office.

The bathroom lights flickered. He undressed and opened the shower door. A warm flow massaged his face, trickling over his pores. His brain buzzed from the whisky. Dehydration had been partially avoided with the B12 supplement.

In the restaurant, A hot breakfast menu was being served. The waiter took his room number and said he could sit anywhere. The warmer had scrambled eggs. He half-filled his plate, added a piece of toast and mushrooms. He ate slowly, brushing up on his protocols and cyber security terminology. The hacking he'd undertaken on assignments, especially in recent years, gave him knowledge in the field.

Outside the air remained chilly as rays started to pierce through the landscape. He doubled back on a route to the Asakusa station subway to detect any watchers. A JR train pass cost the same fee and covered him all day. He descended the stairs with a flow of commuters. The peak hour bustle on the platform had not died yet.

He caught the orange Ginza line to Shibuya station. The corporate office sat in a cluster of high-rises a block from the subway exit. It had a fast-paced vibe, the neighborhood being a major business district in Tokyo. He walked outside to a major junction of five pedestrian crossings that connected the streets. It was the biggest of its kind in Japan. He did a circuit, checked reflections and faces.

Automatic glass sliders opened into an upscale reception. A marble wrap-around dominated the wall and a young woman with a headset smiled.

"Can I help you?"

"I have an appointment with Minato. It's George Perry."

She rang and spoke into her microphone.

"He will be with you soon."

"Thank you." Jake waited and scoped the security measures. Seemed to be minimal visual recording. No biometrics, just a fixed camera pointed near the sliding glass.

Minato entered the reception. "Welcome, George, good to see you again. Come with me."

A series of checkpoints required a security pass. Minato held his card to the reader and a corridor led to a conference room. He cracked the door and flipped the light switch.

"Make yourself comfortable."

Jake placed his bag on the table. A large flatscreen, wall-mounted, hung next to speakers. In the corner a small bar fridge purred. He pulled a chair out. On the table was a conferencing handset with a microphone and speakers. The room was otherwise minimalist.

Suzuki entered and outstretched his hand. "Good to see you

again, George."

"Likewise." He lowered into the swivel chair.

"Water?" Suzuki pondered the contents of the fridge.

"Yes, thanks."

Minato sat opposite Jake and Suzuki at the end.

"Tell us more about your consulting services." Suzuki eased back in the chair.

"I'll keep this light. First I conduct a Q and A format with the administrator to ascertain specific requirements: shortcomings and strengths, threats and vulnerabilities from their perspective. I can get a deeper insight of the business needs. Then I put it together and shape out how an audit framework will develop."

"Good." Suzuki nodded. "This is what Lape requires to move forward and tighten all layers of our online presence. What are your inferences so far?"

"The biggest threat these days is high-level coders that can data tunnel over channels without detection. Secure channels such as DNS and ICMP, for example. You are vulnerable without a solid, ongoing plan and protection that can evolve with your architecture. The maintenance is equally important to the fix."

"Keep talking."

"I can tighten your protocols and secure firewalls, but you need ongoing support at this level to maintain security." Jake addressed the room. "The only constraint is my time."

Suzuki chinned Minato, who nodded and said, "We are interested in progressing. What is the first step?"

"An infrastructure audit on your systems. I am on a contract, but I can fit this first stage project around it in the next few days. The invoice will be on an hourly rate initially until I see what is required."

"That is reasonable, and we can run some numbers through finance." Minato smiled. "What access will you need?"

"Administrator level to begin." Jake checked his calendar. "Can someone get me started today? I have three hours to spare now. It will help fast track the report for you."

"That's possible. I'll ring IT and tell them the situation. Minato will take you over." Suzuki waved his hand. "I am impressed with your willingness to start immediately."

"I will be in touch." Jake gained his feet.

Minato gestured and Jake followed him down the corridor. They got in the elevator and went to level four.

"Take this temporary pass. Normally they give you a security clearance at reception."

They walked into an open layout with rows of cubicles on either side. House plants sprung from pots. Standard prints of iconic scenes and decor dotted the outer ends. Minato stopped halfway at an opening. A diminutive Indian man with glasses peered at three monitors of streaming data.

"Gurash, meet George. Gurash is our system administrator and can answer all those IT queries you will have. I am a dummy in this area and won't be any help."

"Pleased to meet you, George."

"Likewise."

"Will you be in Tokyo long?"

"Probably short term. Two to three weeks."

"George is here to help with cyber security. Iron those bugs and stop attacks. I'll leave you guys to it. You have my number. Let me know if you need anything."

Gurash took Jake into the administration of their site and showed him the infrastructure. The system had high-level protection and an effective firewall. He could probably breach security with three days to spare and Katerina's help.

Jake wrote notes, took passwords in code. There were opportunities for data tunnels. He could use these to get in undetected and search personnel records and transactions. Gurash talked about the upgrades and changes they had implemented in the last twelve months. The conversation became monotonous, but he let the administrator talk to gain his trust.

The computer clock glowed one-fifteen P.M. Jake placed his pen aside and closed the book.

"That's enough to get started. Thanks, Gurash, for you time."

"Anytime, George. I might see you again if you come aboard."

"Is the kitchen over there?" Jake said.

"Yes, follow the aisle to the end." Gurash pointed at an archway.

He did a lap of the level to the staff kitchen. On the way, he checked surveillance. Two low-tech, fixed cameras at each end of the open plan layout. He walked out of range. A water cooler was positioned in the corner. He released a plastic cup and filled it. A cluster of workers chatted at the sink. One spotted him and nodded. He drained the contents and put the cup in the trash compartment. Gurash was talking into his headset, transfixed on one of the monitors. A relaxed atmosphere, no one working too hard.

On the ground floor, he handed back the visitor security pass. The sun had increased its stake on the day, but not by much. He did a reverse circuit of the block before heading to the subway.

Chapter 32

AT EIGHT-THIRTY P.M. Katerina sat on the sofa and eyed her laptop.

The lock clicked and Mia walked in. She released her carry bag onto the table.

"How are you?"

Katerina relaxed her posture. "I'm fine, thanks."

Mia held her hands and gave her a hug "Sorry I couldn't come earlier. The editor meeting dragged on, as they do."

"I'm fine, Mia. Really. You have been so supportive, letting me stay." She hesitated, gathering her emotions. "I could not ask for a better friend."

"So sweet. It's nothing really." Mia opened her bag and lifted out a carton. "I bought some takeaway rice."

"I had some already. Boiled on the stovetop and added a tin of tuna."

Mia laughed and took a bottle of white wine from the fridge. "Feel like a Sav Blanc?"

"I'll pass tonight, thanks. I exposed another lead for Jake. This corporation are connected to an executed terrorist."

"No way. Suzuki?"

"Yes. A business partner, who is a chemical manufacturer, did a prison visit to Shoko Asahara. This guy was the mastermind behind the sarin gas attack on the Tokyo subway. Injured five thousand people and killed twelve."

Mia transferred her takeout into a bowl, using a spoon to scrape the corners. "That is curious, isn't it?" She poured a glass of wine.

"Definitely way too convenient. Why would he risk such a visit to a terrorist about to be executed?" Katerina shook her head.

"Must have a really strong motive." Mia ate in silence for a minute as the words sat.

"Jake went to an upmarket bar last night where these Japanese businessmen all hang out."

"Sounds like he can hold his own."

"Yes."

"Hostess bar?"

"Didn't say. I trust him completely. He went home in the early hours after slugging top-shelf whisky."

"Those Japanese corporate types get up to all sorts, don't they? Even the married ones." Mia laughed.

"Especially the married ones." Katerina smiled.

"I think you're right."

Katerina moved to the couch and checked the TV menu. She surfed channels for a while, the latest information running through her mind. Reruns of American sitcoms were mostly playing: nothing of interest. She clicked the TV off and noticed a cramp in her left leg.

This terrorist link scared her. To think Jake could be near an attack. Wrong time, wrong place scenario. Accidentally present or not, to be killed like that would be awful.

"What's wrong?"

Katerina realized she'd been twisting a cushion tassel with her fingers. "Thinking about terrorists and Jake. We escaped from all this danger five months ago. It has all come back to haunt us, and with interest. First the oligarch resurfaces and Jake's roped back into service. Now we have terrorists importing chemicals and planning deadly mass attacks."

"That's why he has us super journalists. To help get to the bottom of all this. Think how much we've found so far. I realize the danger, but we are uncovering the truth slowly. Then Jake can do what he does to stop the bad guys." Hand on hip, she sipped from the wine glass. "This is a great drop."

"You are always so positive, Mia." Katerina smiled despite herself. "Jake is resourceful and connected with the right people. We are an effective team."

"See. You go, girl." Mia stared out at the blinking night-colors. "Are you sure you won't have some wine?"

"Thanks, but no. I need my head right for tomorrow to hit the research."

"I get it and understand completely." Mia packed the leftovers into the carton. She moved around the island bench, wine in hand, and claimed the armchair.

"You seem a little weary too," Katerina said.

"Big day with editorial deadlines on a few stories. One is an exclusive that we had to push out. Political scandal with the opposition leader."

"I guess I'll read about it in tomorrow's news."

"It's no big deal for us foreigners, but the locals will lap it up. Keeps the subscribers and audience interested. Shareholders too. Pays the bills."

"I know what that's like. You must jump on every exclusive you can." Katerina crossed her legs. "No matter how minor it might appear."

"Yeah. The assistant editor can be a stress case sometimes. Really highly strung. Everything must be perfect. As long as the spelling and grammar are correct, the rest is hype and creativity. We do not live in a perfect world."

"Parts of a small publishing house I do not miss."

"I won't rant anymore."

"Happy to chat about work." Katerina stood. "I am going to lie down. Ready to crash any minute. Had a shower just before you came home."

"Not far behind you. Sleep well and see you in the morning."

Shibuya station entrance lay around the corner. Jake had performed enough counter-surveillance to be reasonably satisfied he was not being tailed. He took the stairs and sought the turnstiles. Commuters shrugged by as he stepped on the platform.

The threat of an attack had been upgraded to red with Katerina's intel on the terror link with Suzuki's partner. Move fast and carefully to avoid suspicion. He would consult all contacts, including McCallister.

He boarded the carriage and sat alone in a section of four seats. The panels slid shut and the bullet train started. If the strike point event was uncovered, he'd reverse engineer the attackers and their associates. It was crucial to discover the location with enough time to prevent beforehand.

Tourists congregated in a large group at Asakusa station. The elevator put him on the ground floor. He strolled into the temple grounds. A circuit of the monuments relieved his sense of security. He doubled back the same path and exited the complex at the other side.

A pair of white-cheeked starlings swooped low near the shop window. Jake ducked and headed southeast back to his room. The clock read three-thirty. Cracked blinds warmed the couch fabric. Housekeeping had cleaned the room.

Loading the laptop, he performed scans and security checks first. Satisfied the system was secure he logged into email. He wrote a quick summary of Lape's architecture and some passwords. The information had been verified, he explained. He encrypted and sent the email to Katerina, requesting she tell him her opinion.

The burner lay on the table surface. Thoughts veered to McCallister. His trust in the man had not increased since starting the mission. It had to be done.

He picked up the device and analyzed the contents. Important call numbers had been memorized for security. No saved contacts. He pressed the buttons in the burner and thumbed send.

"Hello." McCallister sounded clear.

"Sphinx."

"How's it going?"

"Good. I'm entering a cyber security contract with the company in question."

"Great progress. Anything we can help with?"

"It is complex. Can you find any major events happening in Tokyo? Especially classified ones involving US diplomats and not announced to the public and established media. These guys are a chemical manufacturer who were in comms with a terrorist on death row a few years back. The terrorist was executed soon after for a sarin gas attack on the Tokyo subway. I am thinking political. Need to find out soon. Could be happening any day."

"Got it. Will get back ASAP."

Chapter 33

AT TWO HUNDRED pushups, Jake started on a set of hovers. Resting on his elbows, he held the position until the burn flooded his core. He did butterfly stretches, warmed down with other exercises. Sweat trickled to his eyebrows.

The orange disc sunk behind the cityscape as the evening darkened. He paced the room, body limber and more relaxed, joints tight and flexible. Laptop open, he flicked into the main menu. With the acquired information, he tested methods of using the passwords without detection. Any mistake would set off alarm bells but for the excuse, he was testing the system, considering stage one.

He ran diagnostics to the site and created a backdoor into the system. Trading information on spreadsheets sat in the drives. Lape had international cargo coming from major ports around the world. Shipments from Rotterdam were registered as from the same supplier on a monthly basis. He loaded the inventories and manifest. A list of chemical agents and byproducts surfaced. Some of these materials could be lethal and used for attacks. He copied the items, storing them on a document. A further search in databases would show if they were of concern.

The names behind the supply companies were his next target. He searched the files, but they listed only company numbers and names registered, keeping these details anonymous. Surprise, surprise.

His burner vibrated. Jake picked up the device. "Hello."

"I have the information you requested," McCallister said.

"Let's hear it."

"Took some digging and signoff. I am glad you asked. There is a major meeting occurring in Tokyo called The Quadrilateral Security Dialogue."

"What is that?"

"An alliance formed sixteen years ago between four countries—US, India, Japan, and Australia—to secure and protect the Indo-Pacific region, particularly the South China Sea. Shinzo Abe, the former Japanese prime minister, initiated the dialogue."

"The Japanese Prime Minister that was assassinated last year?"

"Correct. Extremism for sure."

The pulse in Jake's neck increased. "Go on."

"It disbanded for some years, but reformed in 2017, mainly due to increased foreign military presence in the region from certain Asian countries."

"I can read between lines. When is the dialogue scheduled and will all leaders be present?"

"It will meet in three days in Tokyo. The US President and Indian President, with Japanese and Australian Prime Ministers, will all be there."

"This is the strike point. What's the location?"

"Kasumigaseki Building. It has thirty-six floors above ground and three below. It's on level ten and the ministers will access from the basement in a private elevator."

"I haven't come across it."

"You won't unless you are seeking it. Intentionally under the radar. It is 800 meters to the Prime Minister's historical residence and in a discreet location to hold important conferences privately. Considered Tokyo's first modern skyscraper. The prime minister can come and go without being seen by the press or public. The challenge is that there are companies occupying many of the levels, such as Price Waterhouse Coopers. Staff and workers coming and going. That is the reason for the exclusive elevator and the basement access."

"Makes sense. When is the meeting held?"

"This Thursday at one P.M. I know you understand it is highly classified."

"This time allows 60 hours to prepare. Can you let their team know I will be around? Get the sign-off now with secret service in case they get the wrong idea. Give them my physicals, same as you gave those dead mercs you sent to find me."

"You won't let that rest, will you?"

"Not likely. I'll be in touch." Jake cut the line.

He typed up an email to Katerina about the Quadrilateral Security Dialogue meeting. The date left limited research time. He asked her to please investigate who might be connected via transactions, including Lape. The more information, the better.

An idea struck him and he called the number.

The cell rang three times.

"Tanaka."

"It's Perry. How are you?"

"I'm good. What I can do for you?"

"I've made contact with executives from a chemical importer that might be a threat to national security. Need a security pass for the Kasumigaseki Building."

Tanaka hesitated, as if to gather his thoughts. "Do you have hard evidence?"

"Not at this stage. It's a strong hunch based on circumstantial evidence and the suspect has past collaboration with known terrorists. We need to monitor the activity covertly."

"Are you aware of the political significance and purpose of the building?"

"Yes. That's why it's imperative I have this clearance. I would advise not elevating military presence or it will wave a red flag."

"We may not have a choice, given the calendar."

"It's up to you, but I think no more security level than is expected."

"You want it under the name of George Perry?"

"Correct."

"Understood. Leave it with me."

At ten-forty, Jake stripped and showered. In the mirror, he trimmed the stubble to a three-day growth. Lights off, he lay in bed and cleared his mind of the day's turmoil.

He quietly repeated the mantra, "I am energized and fully protected." The aches left his body as he imagined floating in water.

The phone alarm beeped from somewhere near her ear. Katerina scrambled to locate it. It had fallen off the nightstand and onto the floor. She squinted at the face: seven A.M. The mattress creaked in unison with her sigh. She tumbled out of the sheets and straightened the duvet.

The lounge lay in silence, first signs of dawn highlighting the furniture. She walked softly so as not to wake Mia. In the kitchen, she fetched a cereal breakfast.

Determined to find more answers, she switched on the laptop. The screen flashed as it loaded. She pressed on the fingerprint recognition button. A crane swung in the background, lifting a heavy load at the ports. She crunched on a spoonful of cereal.

The inbox had a new message from Jake. She eased forward on her elbows and scanned the contents. A ministerial meeting with the US President and three other country leaders in seventy-two hours. In Tokyo. The history of the Quadrilateral Dialogue fitted the terrorist scenario. She touched her hair. The dialogue founder, former prime minister of Japan, executed last year. Too coincidental to not be part of this conspiracy. She searched up profiles and background of the dialogues, acquainted herself with more detail about the current leaders.

She made a strong coffee in the kitchen. With the data Jake sent her, she hacked into Lape's system. The menus were easy to navigate, storage systems made sense.

Narrowing on transactions with foreign entities, she triangulated possible links to Kanji Sato through background checks, associates, and deals. The software searched out keywords and references. Sato had greased palms to gain favorable political outcomes. He had given references for controversial figures before and after his environmental enquiries.

A log of transcripts showed a recent export from Rotterdam, a route that followed the same path as the others, but detoured on the last leg of the journey. The original shipment had been dropped off in favor of a smaller dock and missed a major customs checkpoint.

She pulled up the import document and examined the time and date stamps. Shizuoka outer customs authority at Shimizu harbor approved the goods and duty payment. The goods were separated and taken by road transport north-east to Tokyo.

Why would this shipment unload at a different dock to all other containers? The closest one to Tokyo's main port.

On the map, she calculated the distance from Tokyo to Shimizu via road: 180 kilometers. Under three hours in normal traffic conditions.

At eight, Mia came in the doorway. "Hi. Early riser today. You were not kidding last night. Straight into it."

"Hi, Mia." She put her hand to her mouth and yawned. "I think this is something important."

"Nice one. Can't wait to hear." Mia had a sweatsuit on, and hair tied in a ponytail. "I'm going to the gym. Be back in forty minutes. Bye."

"See you soon."

The door clicked. Katerina rinsed her bowl. Seagulls squawked on the balcony, seeking early morning food scraps. She opened a new toothbrush in her vanity and brushed her teeth.

She returned and clicked from standby mode. Lape were deeply involved in this potential threat in Tokyo. She clicked the mouse and plunged into the internal records for any detail on the contents of the cargo. Every avenue led to nothing. Someone had omitted the electronic record of the manifest, if it had ever been there. She laced her fingers behind her head and flexed her lower back. The back stiffness required regular movement.

Spreadsheets she read contained basic details, but not enough to give her clarity. She combed the databases for loose and remote connections, just in case.

At 9:10, the door clicked. Mia clunked the keys on the countertop and vanished into the bathroom. The water in the shower gushed. She emerged from the bathroom in a navy power suit, skipped breakfast, and waved goodbye.

"I am off to the office."

"You go for it, Mia."

"Please keep in touch during the day. I will try to help you search this afternoon again from work, as my morning is back-to-back meetings. Sorry I can't do more today."

"Not a problem, Mia. Thanks again. You are a great help."

"Ciao."

Stiffness had crept into her legs. She did a circuit of the living area. Rain smattered the glass in heavy doses, wind gusts forcing the droplets sideways in long streamers. Her progress on the background was undeniable. Whether this shipment turned into the contraband they sought did not matter.

She continued around the space, sidestepped the island bench. The laps reinvigorated her body. Blood pumped into her leg muscles, numb like her backside, from excessive sitting. Sounds from outside reverberated in the windows. She glanced into the glass wall at the streetscape below.

It occurred to her that Jake needed the report. She used the same flaws in Lape's security to compile a summary of possible threats and vulnerabilities. A solid start to page one followed with positive statistics. The report grew as she included examples of how breaches could occur, leaving out specifics, with advanced coding skills and knowledge. A framework evolved on the opportunities to tighten the plugs and the contract hours required. The objective was to achieve a minimum threshold of sixty percent decrease in external attacks and virus risk. She concluded with an upgrade package and two options on the implementation process.

Satisfied with the document, she saved it to the drive and attached the report to an email. In the body, she included an explanation to Jake on the import shipment that stopped at Shimizu and was sent by truck to the Tokyo marina. She added the name of the Customs official who signed off, checked it over, and sent it to Jake.

Her burner beeped. Mia had sent a text.

Hey, friend, let me know how you are. Finished last meeting soon, then can help. Leftovers in ridge. Do not starve yourself.

Katerina replied:

Thanks heaps. I am fine. Done report for Lape. Jake had breakthrough on major event. Too much to type. Tell more later.

Chapter 34

THE MORNING LIGHT broke the blinds at 7:16. Jake trundled into the living room and read an email from Katerina. She'd created a professional and comprehensive report for Lape. He noticed her separate note with a name of a Customs official in Shimizu port. This guy had to be taking bribes. He thanked her and summarized the expected day's events. The laptop closed with a click and he packed it in a carry case.

The outside chill hit his cheeks. He shoved his hands in his pockets. Morning mist still swirled on the ground as he walked to the subway.

A bullet train arrives every seven minutes at Asakusa station. Doors open and commuters squeeze into the limited space. The train speeds by eleven stations, packed with mainly executive types in white-collar attire. No one was out of place or showing special interest in him.

He alighted at Toranomon station. Gingko trees shrouded the sidewalk edges, shaded by larger seventies-built office towers in browns and grays. He tracked a public walkway which spilled onto a plaza facing the Kasumigaseki Building.

A box of concrete, glass and steel loomed over the flat landscape. Jake studied it from the opposite side of the thoroughfare. A thick tree canopy hung above his head, lending his presence to the shadows. He circled the silver star sculpture resting grandly in the forecourt. Visitors posed for photos and congregated in groups, pointing at various structures.

The building had housed local and international brands for decades. He took photos with his burner, acting like a sightseer. A fountain with layers of flowers decorated the other side. The lack of direct street access might prove challenging for a terrorist attack. That would not stop these maniacs from trying. Plenty of ways to smuggle a smaller denotation or gas into the basement and bring it up to higher levels.

He noticed fixed-point cameras on the roof eves and walls. If they had biometric technology, such as facial or gait recognition, he would remain out of range. Secret service may not be sufficient to protect the US President, much less the other ministers. Once word got around about the prime ministers and presidents, or they were sighted, it may go public. All it takes to go viral is for a teenager to video record on their cell phone and post it on Facebook, YouTube or TikTok.

His burner rang.

"Tanaka here. I have the clearance."

"Great. Does it need a photo?"

"No. The card is issued with a name only." Tanaka cleared his throat, traffic noise in the background.

"I am right outside the building now."

"Meet you in the forecourt in fifteen minutes. Stay out on the perimeter as they are building up heightened security. No point getting clicked onto the system until we have it registered."

"Will do."

The line went dead. He walked to a public seat south of the front section. Among the pedestrians, he spotted four loners and people out of place. Those with too much purpose and interest in illogical aspects of the tower. Steady streams of couples and groups meandered in and out of the grounds.

If the security cameras were vulnerable, he'd scrutinize the recordings for identifiable suspects and make a list. Tanaka's answer might be a no on getting access, so he had to find another way. He repeated the trail around the end.

Tanaka appeared on the edge of the forecourt. He seemed invisible sometimes and allowed you to see him when it suited. An effective espionage practitioner. A flock of small birds squawked and squabbled over food scraps scattered on the pavers.

Jake turned back to see Tanaka make a beeline toward his

position. The crowd condensed with workers arriving. He kept his eyes peeled. Tanaka wore a wide-brimmed, recreational hat, a flannelette shirt and casual cargo pants.

"Hi there."

"Nice outfit. I nearly missed you."

"So it works really well." Tanaka strolled toward the sidewalk, hands in his pockets.

"It's a tourist spot here. More than I expected."

"Funny what people come to see in Tokyo sometimes."

They walked northwest through a paved section between structures. Gingko trees lined the embankments. Stone steps and landscaping led to a café-like building with an overhang.

"The Prime Minister's office." He pointed at a smaller, older brick house. "The original residence next door."

"They haven't used the residential part in over ten years," Jake noted, having seen the location yesterday. "The Kasumigaseki Building is almost an obvious choice for such functions, being so close to the minister's office. Is it safe?"

"It does present challenges. A drone landed on the helipad roof some eight years back. Contained radiation. No one was hurt."

"Interesting."

From the site, the pair traced south-east. The flank of the Kasumigaseki rose, nestled between two larger modern towers. They circled clockwise down an avenue and returned to the forecourt.

"Here is your card." Tanaka held the key pass. "The access level will allow you to come and go like a normal office worker. It has you registered as a government administration officer on level six."

"Do you have guys stationed here in the next thirty hours?"

"We are working that out now. Covert and formal."

"Access to the cameras would be advantageous. Can you get that for me?"

"That's higher than my paygrade. I'll apply pressure in certain places and see what happens. More proof would be beneficial, but it makes sense this building would be an ideal target."

"We need eyes on every single person as of yesterday. Facial recognition at a minimum. Best chance of catching members of this radical group."

"I agree. Unfortunately, a lot of bureaucracy in Japan holds us up. Remember I am a contractor."

"An effective one."

"Compliments will get you everywhere."

"Thanks for the key pass. I will go in now and try it."

"Bye." Tanaka broke away and walked toward the main road.

Jake pulled his cap straight and aimed for the sliding doors. The entrance opened to a mosaic-tiled floor. An information counter sat in marble on the left. Triangular-patterned lights shaped the modernized ceiling.

The black directory board gave him the company name and level. He scanned the lines to familiarize himself with the layout. Blank on level ten and no hire option either. Level six listed a local government office, as Tanaka had confirmed.

He sought the elevator bay and used the card to go to level eight. Two other people joined him in the cabin; one smiled and he returned the gesture. At eight, he got out in a corridor. A consulting firm had a sign on the south end. At the opposite end, an architect and engineer had a business.

In the corridor, he noticed a public toilet. He opened the door and found three basins under a long, continuous mirror. A urinal row formed a niche curve. The end wall formed the first of three cubicle stalls. Standard layout. He washed his hands and exited.

At the lounge, he sat in a bank of comfortable armchairs and couches. He waited to see the traffic flow that came to the foyer. Workers dressed in neat casual clothes up to power suits with button-down shirts.

He strolled outside. A food truck parked on a concrete apron faced the street. He bought a chicken and rice combination pack and ate the takeout on a seat. A plan formed in his mind to conduct surveillance on the building. Any irregularities would be identified and solved. He threw the carton in the trash and headed back to the Kasumigaseki forecourt.

Chapter 35

AT FOUR-THIRTY, Katerina contemplated getting a snack from the shopping strip outside the apartment block. Her cell phone beeped. She read the text. Mia had left work early and was in the foyer downstairs.

She tied her hair back, put on a jacket, grabbed her bag, and locked the entrance with the spare key. Mia waited in the reception area, a smile on her face.

"How are you feeling?"

"Fine, thanks. I got the report done for Jake today. Feeling relaxed after a long sleep last night."

"Nice. You feel like heading for a drink and an antipasto?"

"Why not?"

The rain had cleared but the roads were still slick. Mia hailed a cab and they ventured north to a cozier section of the city, further from the machinery and coastal breezes. Katerina watched for tails, but didn't recognize any.

They stopped outside an Italian restaurant.

A tall, young man showed them to a red-cushioned booth against the east wall. The exit faced opposite so they could keep an eye on customers.

The waiter placed two menus on the table. "I will come back in five minutes to take your order."

"I might start with a glass of this French shiraz. It is divine."

"Great choice. I will join you."

Mia signaled the waiter and ordered a bottle of the wine and a serve of bruschetta.

"Fantastic to leave early today after yesterday's twelve-hour marathon shift. I scrutinized the files for more on Suzuki and Sato, but nothing new has come up."

"You just keep going, Mia. Amazing fortitude." Katerina stared at her wine glass. "I cracked Lape's internal system with passwords and coding. There's a corrupt Customs official who let a shipment through in Shizuoka. It is 180 kilometers from Tokyo's main port. They transport by road to the dock. He's got to be on the take."

"That is big news." Mia lowered her voice and leaned over the table. "Lape are in deep with these terrorists."

"I sent Jake the Customs guy's details. He will investigate."

The waiter returned, placed the bruschetta on the table. "What would you like to order?"

Mia chose a chicken risotto and Katerina ordered spaghetti carbonara.

"This network is broad and international, considering the mounting evidence. The Russian oligarch traded with these people and led us to Paris first. Multiple shipments to Rotterdam, Japan, and other cities as well," Katerina said.

"The chemical manufacturing could be on a grand scale too. Targeting the US President along with three other top country ministers is the ultimate attack." Mia sipped her wine. "Lucky you're such a good hacker to find the corrupt custom transaction in time."

"I get the horrible feeling there's more at stake."

"How big can it get?" Mia shook her head. "These radical groups infiltrate every society and level destruction on innocent lives with no remorse. One of the reasons I stay in journalism: to expose killers and murderers with twisted morals."

"I agree, Mia."

A young woman brought their meals, topped up the wine and took the tray.

They ate in silence, enjoying the food and soaking up the atmosphere. Katerina let the background music and the tastes take over her senses. She would be back to digging up information on the internet soon enough.

Mia finished her glass and broke the silence. "That shiraz was delicious. I could go another, but must do a workout tomorrow morning."

"I couldn't drink anymore despite the fantastic taste. A cappuccino might go down well though." Katerina raised her hand and the waiter came over. "Can I please have a cappuccino?"

"Make that two."

The waiter collected their empty plates.

"A man approached me today with a potential scoop." Mia paused and her brow furrowed. "I asked him the subject. He told me it's regarding chemical imports to Japan."

"What? How did he know you were investigating?"

"Not sure. He walked up to me as I entered the building this morning. As if he knew not only my workplace, but was also tracking me."

"This organization is dangerous." Katerina rested her elbows on the table, head in her hands. "I should not have got you involved."

"Nonsense. I can take care of myself and knew this could be risky. My job is fraught with threats and danger." Mia leaned over and placed her hand on Katerina's shoulder. "I would do it all again."

The cappuccinos came. Mia broke open a sugar sachet and shook it into her cup, stirring the sweetener in with a spoon.

Katerina blew on the foamy top, but left it sugar free. "What do we do from here? I mean if I cannot convince you of the danger."

"You are stuck with me, girl. See the evidence this guy has. He's not asking for money yet, so he has an ulterior motive. If we watch our backs, we should be fine. I have a security guy who can watch over the meeting, and any other times for protection."

"I didn't think they could find us this far away. We need to keep our guard. He could be in league with this network. Anything else you noticed about this man?"

Mia nodded with a grimace. "When he left, he got into a dark blue SUV."

"We need to be careful around these people. I say we meet him, but with your security present. At least we now know who that was stalking me yesterday."

"Agreed."

Katerina finished her wine. "Do you feel like getting out of here?"

"Yeah, let's go."

Outside, a gust kicked up. Katerina pulled her jacket closer around her body. A cab came and they jumped inside.

Chapter 36

THE KASUMIGASEKI BUILDING had no suspicious visitors that Jake could ascertain in the hour since his lunch. An idea regarding the Customs official nagged him into action. She had sent his name and the office address. The rest he would put together himself. He checked Google maps for the nearest hire car rental and found one east of his location. On the main thoroughfare, he hailed a cab.

They sliced west across town and slowed into the verge of a car rental shop front. It took seven minutes: light traffic. He walked over the lot to the counter.

"I need a car for two days, please. Something with smoked windows. Medium size, room in the back. An SUV?"

"We can help you with that."

The sales attendant led him to the yard and showed him a Mazda CX5 in dark gray. "This has maximum tint. Turbo two-point-five liter. Extra power pickup in the larger engine."

Jake opened the rear door and the guy pointed inside.

"Plenty of storage space in the trunk, as you can see. It is classified as a station wagon. We have a special on these today, thirty percent off the daily rate. How many days do you think you need?"

He wanted to get on the road and the vehicle ticked all the boxes. The salesman wouldn't be quiet until he said yes.

"I'll take it for three days."

He filled out the touch screen contract and digital signatures under Perry and paid in cash.

The traffic thinned as he merged onto the expressway. Signs for the Shibuya AH1 fork guided him south-west. White-tipped mountains soared above, a constant fixture on the horizon. It led him to the E1

Tomei Expressway which snaked along the coast to Shimizu.

A recent photo of the official showed him to be mid-thirties. Yuto Endo. No glasses and five-ten tall. Unmarried and lived alone. He resided in an apartment in the center of the city. Moonlighting as a corrupt official meant he had to launder or hide his ill-gotten gains.

Jake slowed at a gas station and filled the tank. He bought supplies: food and water. A stakeout could be on the calendar for tonight. The GPS issued an update in a female voice; they were thirty minutes to their destination. Taking the slip road back to the expressway, he maintained a rhythm on the speed limit. The sun receded behind mottled clouds as he moved closer to the destination. In the distance the landscape undulated, wrapping a coastal town grown into a modern city.

Snow-capped Mt. Fuji loomed in the sky, an ancient Mona Lisa-like volcano that followed you everywhere. He slowed to the shoulder and checked the GPS. The road curved to the water. He blinkered left and saw the entrance to an open-air parking lot the workers used. A machine issued a ticket at the boom gate. The time read four forty-seven P.M. At five, Endo would finish his shift and most likely head home.

He drove around to see if he could find Endo's car, last year's black Toyota Century Crown SUV: only nine months old. Discreet laps without arousing suspicion. In an aisle near the south-east corner, he saw the gleaming car and plates. Slick. Business was booming for the humble Customs official. Reversing into position nearby, he faced the exit for marina employees.

The lot was deserted. Jake got out and pretended to check the rear tire. He crouched and lay on the ground, peering in each direction. No legs or shoes as far as he could see. He stayed low, crab-walked to the Century Toyota. In the wheel well, he attached a micro transmitter.

Doubling back, he returned to his car and shut the door. He took the tracker handset monitor from his bag and switched the power. The display flickered and found the grid map. The device worked and the icon was positioned accurately on the display.

A seven-foot hurricane-wire fence separated the harbor from the lot. Fixed cameras pointed from the eve above the building. None were in the lot. The path snaked from the building to a cutout swing door.

Staff began to emerge at four-forty. Males and females in casual to smart business attire. He checked everyone as they passed. At five-sixteen, a man fitting Endo's description opened the gate and tracked toward his position. Other workers were getting into vehicles. Jake fired the engine and the headlamps flicked on as per the auto setting.

The target got in and pulled out, driving slowly to the nearest exit. He did the same, careful not to rush or be eager. Jake raked the ticket over the reader and stuffed notes in the slot. The machine counted the cash and the boom gate rose. By the time he'd finished, Endo had taken a right. He accelerated to catch up, leaving one car between them. There was sufficient traffic to enable him to blend.

Daylight faded as Endo entered the main junction and passed around the S-Pulse Dream Plaza. A blue-and-white Ferris wheel rose from the base. Dark blue lapped the concrete retaining wall on the south verge of an entertainment precinct. They continued north and steered right toward a strip of restaurants. Endo parked outside a sushi takeout place and went inside.

Lights over the plaza lit up; an Eiffel Tower replica streamed yellow.

In ten minutes, Endo left with a paper bag. He reversed from the park and headed west. Jake followed carefully, a gap of two cars separating them. They weaved by traffic heading to the apartment tower. The last turn put Endo at the base of the building. He vanished into the basement parking lot.

Pedestrians came and went in a decent stream on the sidewalk. The theme park S-Pulse attracted customers from all over the city. Jake took a parking spot on a right-angle near to the basement exit. This avoided being obvious in case Endo became paranoid and checked his windows. The visual remained viable as he lowered the seat and settled in for a long wait.

By ten-twenty, there were still enough cars on the street so Jake's camouflaged with the rest. Endo had not left the building by car, and he hadn't seen him come through the lobby. The tracking console had the car icon stationary.

He eased back in the seat and waited.

Chapter 37

PAST MIDNIGHT JAKE woke with a jolt. Confronted with a darkened windshield, he quickly recalled the task. Watching Endo's apartment, he had catnapped; thankfully a light one without intense dreaming. The monitor light blinked. He pressed the button, bringing it to life. The blue icon had the car situated in the basement.

He cracked the door, an ache setting into his back. Outside the vehicle, he stretched his legs. Red brake lights blurred in shopfront reflections. He stayed out of sight in case Endo spotted the car out the window.

The sun would start to rise soon. Neck rotations helped the blood flow. He did another lap around the car and returned to the seat. The dash display had five-thirty-eight. Hopefully some movement from Endo in the next few hours would prove useful to his case.

He ate a sandwich he'd brought. Patience was paramount in staking a target. The traffic started to stir, trucks and larger vehicles moving toward destinations and deliveries. A grocery van blinkered and drove in between two towers.

Over his shoulder, a thin orange line broke over the city scape, piercing gaps in the skyrises. Glass windows brightened and blinked, as if sending morse code. The neon strobes of S-Pulse Dream Plaza and the wheel faded out. Mount Fuji hung over the city again.

He flipped the laptop open, logged into his secured platform and checked his inbox. No updates from Katerina since the last one. The specialized anti-virus software ran checks and cleans on his system. He engaged the highest possible security, but it didn't hurt to run a second one every so often.

The tracking handset chirped; Jake angled the display. Endo's car moved in the basement, aimed at the exit. He started the engine and pulled his cap on his head. The sectional door peeled, revealing the Toyota headlamps.

It had to be a personal rendezvous as it was too early for his shift to start. Endo blinkered to the left, opposite direction to his workplace. The lights were green for Endo and red for Jake. He waited and casually necked to the line. A Nexus pulled up beside him.

The lights went green, he turned right. Endo drove at the city limit, so he tailed from a safe distance. Shop fronts flickered, melting lights and signs. They bowed right into a smaller avenue in the northern section. Residential living spaces decreased in density and streets narrowed.

Endo roamed the block and parked on a smaller side street. He opened the door and walked out onto the sidewalk. On the next bend, he sat at an al fresco table at a café. A young waitress came and asked for his order.

Jake did a lap. A modern, gentrified area probably under the radar for criminal enterprise. He found a parking space opposite the mouth of the lane.

At the café, Endo sat waiting. A woman with a graying pony-tail approached from the south. She shook hands and sat down at the table with Endo: an older woman in her middle to late fifties. Dressed conservatively in brown trousers with a pastel cardigan. She could be an aunt or relative.

Endo fidgeted with a salt-shaker. He ordered a coffee and acted bored.

Jake avoided moving closer to the conversation in case he got made. The pair talked, and at one stage he saw her point her finger at his chest. He waited out the chat.

At seven-thirty, she rose. No peck on the cheek or even a hug: not friends or close.

Jake hurried to Endo's car. He found a concealed position two meters from the front fender. The rear of an apartment tower had an empty setback allowing cover. He strapped a COVID mask on his face, drew the pistol, and backed up against the brick.

Endo fobbed his car. Jake stepped from the recess with his gun aimed at hip level. The Customs officer startled and held up his hands.

"Get in the car, Endo. Quietly, with no fuss." Jake opened the passenger door and sat down.

The shock was evident on Endo's face. Weapon aimed across the console at the open door, Endo complied and sat behind the wheel.

"Shut the door and start the engine."

"What do you want?" Endo's confidence increased as he pressed the ignition button.

"All in good time. Let's drive first and chat." Jake knew that Endo would be too busy concentrating to launch an escape. The man was a bureaucrat; they usually did not have fertile imaginations.

Endo nodded numbly. He steered the vehicle into the single lane. They cruised just under the speed limit.

"I know you've been helping corrupt businesses get stock inspection free through the port here. This is a dangerous hobby, Endo, especially if you knew the people you were dealing with better."

Endo's mouth slackened. "You can't prove this."

"I have digital trails and other documents. That's how I located you to begin with." Jake watched Endo. "But in exchange for my silence, I am asking you for information."

"Which information?"

"Names of people who paid you to turn a blind eye to a particular shipment. Monthly from Rotterdam."

Endo straightened in the seat. He stared forward, struggling with the request. "I don't know enough about these people. Secured messages and just dead drops for my payment."

"If I don't get an answer, the price is your life."

The car wavered slightly as sweat trickled over Endo's brow. He swiped it with his palm.

"When we first started this transacting, a man and woman came to see me. At the start, they spent thousands on entertainment.

I got used to the lifestyle. It worked, of course. I overheard a few conversations. The woman's name was Vera James. From what I can gather, it's the same person running the show from the sidelines."

The lights changed. Endo drove the Toyota in silence as Jake digested the information.

"What did she look like?"

"Tall for a woman, at least 170 centimeters. Dark hair. I estimate in her late twenties or early thirties. I only meet them once face to face."

"That's all you have?"

"I swear it."

Heading south, Endo curved left and drove by the shopping precinct and into the slip road.

"Drop me off down here." Jake pointed at the road shoulder.

Endo braked and his face flushed with concern. "What should I do?"

"You can figure that out for yourself. No one twisted your arm to take these bribes, did they?" Jake slammed the door and watched Endo drive off. He returned to the car after doing a lap to shake any potential watchers. He deactivated the car alarm and watched the pedestrians walk by.

With a little over forty hours until the Quadrilateral Security Dialogue, he needed solid leads. The coastal trip may not be a waste of time if this information turned out to be solid.

He rang Tanaka's number.

"Tanaka."

"Hi, it's me."

A pause. "What's going on?"

"I need an ID please, fast, on this female. I had a chat with the Customs official. It may be crucial for uncovering the suspects in the Dialogue meeting in two days. Vera James is the name she's using. Five feet seven with dark hair."

"I am working it now ASAP."

"Nice, thanks."

The line went dead.

At nine-forty he bought a takeout coffee and sat at an outdoor bench. The rays were sparse as lunchtime caught up, a cool breeze shifting westerly off the shoreline. He put on the sunglasses and drank the caffeine. The woman's face from earlier flashed through his mind. She did not appear to be a terrorist, rather a government agent. Which country did her allegiance fall to?

He called Riku and it rang out to voicemail. A short message and a beep.

"Hi, Riku, it's George Perry. I hope you're well and recovered from the night at Elite. Thanks for inviting me. I had a great time. Give me a call when you can."

In the laptop, he located the Lape report Katerina had sent. He attached her findings along with an email note. In the address window, he included both Minato and Suzuki. The summary stated that should they engage his services for the second stage, he could not start work on this project for two weeks. This was due to prior commitments and a busy schedule. He did a final proofread of the document and pressed send.

On the monitor, Endo's car remained in the work parking lot. He refreshed the inbox. No reply from Tanaka.

The clouds parted to let a patch of warmth hit his shoulders. He debated whether to hang around for Endo to make another move, if he did at all, or return to Tokyo. With forty-eight hours till the minister's meeting, he risked valuable surveillance time.

He threw the coffee cup in the trash and got behind the wheel. The priority had to be the meeting in Tokyo. The expressway back to the capital lay two kilometers away and he headed straight for it.

Chapter 38

SLANTED RAIN PUMMELED the windshield, pushed by the wind drafts. Lights blurred and shimmered the city like a continuous storm in an aquarium seen through the glass.

"How do you stand the weather here?" Katerina stared out the window. "I think it's colder than Siberia."

"Being English, let's say I am accustomed to this climate." Mia laughed. "You do get used to it after a while."

They reached the tower and paid the cab driver. Mia walked by the mailboxes, Katerina followed. A lone guard behind a desk watched a sitcom with canned laughter. He tipped his head in greeting. The tiled floor was slick with wet shoeprints. She sidestepped the puddles.

An elderly woman shared the ride, Mia smiling as the elevator pinged at her level. Katerina and Mia stepped into an empty corridor, unlocked the door, and plunged into the living room.

"I am off for a shower unless you would like one first?" Mia placed her bag on the table.

"No, thanks. Go ahead."

Katerina took off her coat and hung it on the hallway rack. On a pantry shelf, she took a tin of chocolate powder, poured low-fat milk. The drink went in the microwave. She plonked down on the couch and closed her eyes. A vision of Jake passed through her mind and she fought to let it go. She tried to relax and shut the bad possibilities out. The drink was comforting.

Mia came out in pajamas, her brown hair slicked back. "That's much better."

"Now for my turn." Katerina showered and put on her thick, long-sleeved night clothes. In the kitchen she made another warm drink. They sat on the couch with the heater going. The patter of rain mixed with the blinking city lights.

"Do you want to meet this mystery guy tomorrow?" Mia said. "I could do with the moral support. It might also have something to do with our Japan case."

"Sure, I'll come along. Do you think we need some muscle this time?"

"His name is Walker. I'll arrange Richard, my protection contractor. He's reliable and skilled."

The mountains receded to the west, lying like miniature stones at the foot of Fuji. Jake sat on the speed limit, taking in the gradual slope. In his other peripheral, the Pacific Ocean glistened in the early afternoon glare. Tokyo was ninety minutes, the ministerial meeting in less than forty-eight hours.

He studied the horizon. An urgency churned in his stomach as he inhaled and held his breath.

The sign had the city of Atami next exit. He entered the ramp and followed it to a length of shoreline. Yachts lined the marina, separated by a man-made built-up area. Steps descended to a beach strip which meet the water. Families and beach-goers erected umbrellas and tents, making the most of the limited warmth.

He cut north west along the coast, Mount Fuji came and went with the undulations. The city neon welcomed him with hundreds of messages. On the drive he considered changing hotels.

The Imperial Hotel Tokyo was a seven-minute walk to the Kasumigaseki building. A relocation to this venue would be ideal to stakeout and monitor the area.

His hotel lobby had a scattering of people late afternoon. Being too early for dinner meant people were still sightseeing and doing outdoor activities. He took the stairs for exercise after driving for three hours. His limited possessions made packing up easy and quick. The gear from Tanaka he hid in the suitcase but shoved the weapon in the small of his back.

A quick checkout with all the usual pleasantries and they gave him a discount for the additional night as it was after checkout time. He got to the Imperial just before five-thirty. A valet parked the rental car in the hotel's secured lot. Greeted by an attractive young woman behind a desk, he checked into a level one room that faced west. The attendant took a bag filled with two pairs of jeans and three pairs of underwear and sweat shirts for clean and press.

In the bathroom he ran a shower in lieu of missing one yesterday and staying in the car. The soothing sensation convinced him to let it run until his skin went prune like. He dried, pulled on fresh underwear and a sweat shirt. A pair of jeans were folded in his bag which he balanced in each leg and pulled up. He added a loose jacket and zipped it up.

Outside the main avenue traffic thickened with the oncoming evening. He walked west to the forecourt of Kasumigaseki building. The total travel time read seven minutes at a reasonable walking rate. The tourists had mostly gone now with a colder wind and sun disappearing behind the mountains. Beyond the star monument he saw a man in a suit and straight posture near the main exit. Plain clothes agent. The man ran guard detail, pacing back and forth with purpose and a serious expression.

Good to see security but that won't be enough to stop our determined terrorists.

Jake lapped the perimeter as the sky darkened. He found no one else of interest.

Halfway over the foyer his burner beeped with a text message from Tanaka:

We need to chat: can you call me?

Wanting to talk in a private he climbed the stairs to his room. The key pass clicked, he placed the burner on the table, and sat at the table to make the call.

Chapter 39

BLACK CLOUDS HUNG low as the car pulled into a parking lot. The position was an hour inland and secluded. Katerina undid her seat belt, unsure of the isolation of their position. The driver, a protection specialist named Richard, stepped out of the vehicle, and began surveillance. Mia and Katerina crossed the gravel to the lawn embankment. A solitary figure sat at a timber outdoor setting covered by a shelter. Trees thickened around the west side sloping up a rise.

"Hello. Thanks for meeting me here." The man chinned at Richard who scoped the surroundings. "Under the circumstances I completely understand the need for protection. I can assure you I came alone."

"Good to meet you Mr. Walker. My name is Mia and this is my colleague Katerina. It is not only your people we are concerned about. How did you find us?"

Mia lowered into the seat facing Walker and Katerina straddled beside her.

"I went to a friend who has experience with media and told her my situation. She recommended I go to your publisher. Incidentally she met you on an assignment. You were very approachable."

"Thanks, just being myself. What is her name?"

"Jansen. The story was about an attack by hijackers on a boat."

After a minute of deliberation, she answered. "Yes, I recall that incident. What did you want to talk about today?"

"Relieve my conscious from this dilemma. I work for the Port of Rotterdam authority. Most of the time I process paperwork like a bureaucrat. While it's not uncommon to receive bribes we send them on to the relevant authorities if there is enough evidence or cause."

"Go on." Mia shifted her position.

"A man and woman approached me from a large manufacturer.

They ship within Europe and to parts of Asia. We have dealt with containers from the organization for years. However, this time they were representing foreign shareholders. They offered me a large sum to make this happen. Turn a blind eye with inspections and make sure no parties intervened. The process was to take forty-hours."

"Where were the goods imported from?"

"France but I don't think that was the original source. The contents remain unknown to many.

"You haven't identified the goods?" Katerina's eyes were opened wide.

"This is the strange part. I am not sure there is goods." He adjusted his glasses. "A new technology or contraband are my best guesses. The incoming documents have been altered by other authorities. But within the maritime industry as they are authentic. The containers were sitting there on a ship docked. They wanted them checked and stamped but not inspected by our authority."

Mia glanced at Katerina.

"Do you know the destination?" Katerina analyzed his body language.

"Asia. Japan, I suspect. My superior removed me from the case last week and it came from above her."

"Why did you bring this to the media? This puts your life at risk."

"I felt it was my duty to bring this to the attention of the public. The people need to know the truth. If there's a threat, I could not live myself if I knew I could have prevented it." Walker paused; his shoulders slumped with apparent exhaustion. "This is worth such a risk."

"Can you get access to the system anymore?" Katerina said. "If we can find out where it came from that would help immensely."

"They locked me out and cancelled my password." Walker swiveled his head left and right, a symptom of paranoia. "Please keep my identity anonymous."

"We will Mr. Walker rest assured. All sources remain confidential."

"She had long blond hair. A man joined her to negotiate the terms. Rather it turned out a dictation of terms. I suspect the man was a bodyguard as he did not say much."

"Any other details?"

Walker shoved his had in a pocket and pushed a folded paper over the tabletop. "This is a still image from one of the cameras; footage I managed to get from the hard drive."

Katerina opened it and they both studied it. A printout in grainy ink-jet.

"That's all I have. I must get going." Walker gained his feet, anxious to wrap up the conversation. "Please do not use my name."

"You have my word. Thanks for taking the time to speak to us. We will investigate further and again your name will be not be published."

Walker nodded and treaded on the loose stones to the lawn.

The women rounded the embankment, aiming at the car. Rain threatened overhead as Katerina tugged her coat zip up to her neck. They walked the slope to the edge.

Richard watched from the parking area. He had been doing laps, checking for signs of trouble. Mia rounded the embankment. A fob sounded as Walker unlocked a car on the east side.

A gun shot sounded, echoing through the clearing. Katerina ducked, watching over the lawn. Pink spray bloomed from Walker's chest. He keeled forward at his door, head butting the windshield.

"Get in the car." Richard said running with his weapon outstretched. He aimed at the woods for the sniper unseen for the canopies, gaze locked on Mia.

Katerina yanked the driver's door and dived inside. She pushed the start button, the key sat in the console. Straightened her posture, hands on the wheel. Mia fell into the rear. Sprinting at them, Richard fired into the woods, a guess at the position of the sniper. Three meters away he vaulted the gap and wrestled the handle with his free hand. He sat in the passenger seat and gripped the door closed.

She slammed into reverse and revved out of the spot. The car swung one-eighty, pointing at the exit. A round sparked on the gravel. First sign the sniper had them in their sights. Richard opened the window, shot a round at the trees. She hit the accelerator.

The car plunged forward to the slope. A stone retaining wall rose, hiding their descent. Katerina clutched the steering, teeth grit with concentration. Richard clicked the safety on his pistol. She navigated the curves, careful not to over adjust or speed. Gaps in the trees flashed as the car turned and shook. She maintained speed and breathed deep in-and-out. The road levelled out to farming paddocks, trees shrunk to pastures. They reached the bottom of the loose gravel road, a three-exit roundabout ahead.

Richard broke the silence. "Take the left at the fork. It will get us to the city quicker." He ducked at the rearview, scanning the exit for tails.

"Lucky, we had you here Richard." Mia said.

"I didn't do much yet." He put the gun back behind his jacket. "But I need to stick with you ladies until this is finished."

"We need to locate this contact." Katerina pulled into the shoulder. "You can take the wheel Richard. I want a break."

Chapter 40

TANAKA'S NUMBER RANG twice before he picked up.

"Hi Tanaka." Jake said.

"Hey. An update: I have been deep diving nonstop on that woman." Tanaka stopped as if pained to reveal the truth. "I cannot get a solid ID on her yet."

"This is concerning."

"With the name and basic physical, you gave we tried every facial recognition database in the country and international. She's a ghost."

"That's a red flag in itself. I might try my sources but it is a last resort." Jake paced the carpet, restless about the development.

"Another specialist I can try who has a broader network scope. Hope I can get ahold of him this late. It's our last chance."

"Thanks. Let me know."

The phone beeped and he placed in on the counter. He stood at the window pointing west at the darkness, the direction of the strike point. A tunnel of colors weaved into a sea of brake lights, contrasted by dark patches of greenery. This side of town had fewer neon signs.

Thirty-six hours until the dialogue meeting.

He loaded the laptop and backdoored the NSA databases. Using the woman's name and description, he put out queries and match technology. The system streamed the data but no hits over sixty-five percent. He walked the floor, musing over other avenues. She had to be someone trackable in the system.

The screen flickered an answer. He leaned over the chair. The latest searches were the same: not enough detail to get a higher score. How could she be this invisible. He typed up the results and sifted through for anomalies. This uncovered nothing new.

At the bar fridge he contemplated a vodka. He sifted the options and decided he would pass on a drink. A workout would be beneficial. He dropped to the floor and did one hundred push-ups. Last night sleeping in the car made him stiff. Warmups and slow breathing helped to diminish the symptoms and limber up. The chair provided a good position to do dips. He did hover exercises in between and finished off with a warm down.

He turned on the tap, filled a glass with water and moved back to the table. His inbox had no important messages. He sent one to Katerina describing his trip to Shimizu port to chase her lead on Endo's corrupt custom practices. At the end he mentioned the mystery woman Endo mentioned. She might be able to find something out in her channels. He leaned back in the chair, ran fingers in his hair. McCallister was a last resort option. Relying on the general was a habit he didn't want to fall into.

At least not on a regular basis.

The burner rang. He checked the number. Riku.

"Hello."

"George it's Riku. Got your message. It's been a busy day."

"I understand that. How did you pull up from Elites?"

"A bit seedy. I went past four A.M. We're going again this Friday night. You want to join?"

"Sounds tempting but neck deep in work. Thanks for the invite. I managed to get that report off today for Lape."

"No problem let me know if you want in."

"Cheers and thanks again for the introductions."

"Talk soon."

A mist lingered two feet above the ground as Rotterdam came into scope. Richard dropped them at the apartment and escorted Mia and Katerina upstairs to make sure they were not followed.

"I am going to perform surveillance in this block."

"Thanks Richard keep in touch please."

"Will do."

Mia closed the door and they sat in the living room.

"I think I am going to relax for a while before I jump back to work." Katerina sighed.

"Agreed. That chase finds me a little rattled. Maybe they were only after Walker. It still concerns me they might know who and where we are." Mia collapsed in the armchair. "And it is too early in the day for a drink."

Katerina surfed the TV channels and they watched some reruns of 'Friends.' The comedy helped them both to unwind.

At one P.M. Richard sent a text and confirmed the vicinity seemed to be clear. He'd wait outside in the car and watch the front for three hours and report back.

The third episode of the sitcom ended. Katerina got up and opened the lid to her computer.

"I'm going to do another search on this woman." She typed in her password and the main menu flashed. "Hope we can find something on her. I'll check the inbox too."

"Don't like sitting around at home but as Richard is securing the place I won't risk going to work. Who knows where the shooters are now." Mia squatted at her work bag and lifted her laptop. "See what I can dig up. No one likes to get shot at."

"There's an email from Jake. He staked out the Customs official named Endo I sent." Katerina scanned the message. "Endo gave him some information on a woman that could be involved."

Mia leaned over her shoulder and squinted at the computer. "Vera James. She's tall and about the right age."

Katerina flattened the printout Walker gave on the table. "She looks like a physical match and the hair could be a wig. They might be the same person. Disguises are probably part of the territory. If we can find this woman on a database and compare a photo."

"There would be no doubt. We have motive as well." Mia

placed her hands on her hips. "Who is Vera James? Everybody leaves a footprint somewhere. We only need to discover it."

"And how did she fit into this transaction?" Katerina held her cell phone over the printout and clicked. She emailed it to herself. "I will reply to Jake and send him this picture."

The message took Katerina thirty minutes to complete. Mia's cell phone rang and she transferred to the couch. She put Richard on loud speaker.

"Hi Richard I have you on loudspeaker."

"Sure. The landscape out here is safe. No suspects yet and pedestrian traffic is all smooth. You can usually spot oddities no matter how subtle. Hopefully we were too quick to escape although they could have got my plates on their scope. It is a company vehicle that traces back to a rotating fleet of fifty SUVs anyway so perfect dead end for them."

"Thank goodness we have you on the job."

"Happy to help you out Mia." Richard cleared his throat.

Silence ensued in the room.

"Anyway, I'll keep out here just an update."

"Thanks, from me too." Katerina said. "Really appreciate your efforts."

"No problem bye."

The call cut out.

Mia grimaced. "No drinks for me tonight. I need an alcohol-free day occasionally."

"You always know how to lighten the mood, Mia."

"Do my best." Mia shrugged. "What about we order a delivery of something as a late lunch?"

"Sounds good to me." Katerina smiled.

"Right, I know I put those menus in a kitchen drawer."

Chapter 41

A NOTIFICATION BEEP came from Jake's inbox. New mail. He moved from the window to the chair and examined the subject line. Katerina and Mia found a port authority informant named Walker. He met up at great risk to give them information.

His pulse slammed in his head as he read the rest of the message. The threat for Katerina and Mia had increased exponentially. He wanted them out of danger but diplomacy would be required to convince her. She sent a profile photo of James given by Walker.

He opened the attached printout. Inkjet made it a little pixelated. He put the image to basic biometric tests. Not exact science as he had only the one angle and partial front of her face. He would put this Tanaka for ID and facial recognition.

Jake picked up his burner and hit redial. It rang at the other end.

"Tanaka."

"Yes." Tanaka sounded alert despite the hour.

"Can you run a check on this photo see if it matches our name or description? Maybe an alias but might put us a step nearer to her location."

"Will do. Anything else?"

"No, I am at the Imperial hotel as of tonight. Want to be closer to the strike point. It all hinges on finding something fast or we are going to have a disaster on our hands."

"Good idea. Talk soon."

Jake typed the name into databases and searches but little came to light. He'd have to deep dive to have a chance of a hit. The platform flickered with results as he typed in matches. A prompt sorted the data, streaming in vertical columns. He rubbed his temples, elbows resting on the table surface. Fatigue overwhelmed his senses, his eyes blurred.

He let the program operate on auto, gained his feet, and worked his hamstrings. His muscles fired into action which masked his lethargy.

Tokyo twinkled in the window like a mound of dragon treasure. The thought of Katerina getting shot at frustrated and worried him. Being in Rotterdam had the illusion of a safe haven; far away from Tokyo but this group had an international reach. A whistle blower killed by a sniper who opened fire on Katerina, Mia and Richard. Impossible to protect her from here.

The laptop whirred in the background. If Japan brought in their counterterrorism unit to the Kasumigaseki Building all hell would erupt. All eyes in Tokyo focused on the security dialogue and the four country leaders. Communications and meeting ceased. The enemy would disperse and their opportunity dashed.

An alert beeped from the computer. He expected a donut from this latest search and leaned at the screen. A hit. The mouse cursor flickered over the prompt. He double-clicked. It loaded the data sequence. Nine days ago, a woman fitting ninety percent facial biometrics to his suspect arrived from a European city to Haneda Airport. Jake requested additional information from the system. A list popped onto the screen. He loaded the name on the travel document. Joanne Patterson. UK passport. In the picture she had brunette hair and Eurasian features. Travel reason: Business. Multiple identities. Training unknown. Alliances yet to be confirmed.

The grainy photo from Katerina depicted Johnson's facial profile. He held up the passport photo and compared the two. A very strong indication this could be the same person.

He straightened and exhaled. This female had connections and a network. Calling in McCallister pained him to no end. It always led to further obligations and sunk him in deeper. They were dealing with a serious covert operation. Terrorists or not, something was going down in Tokyo and soon.

Tanaka had to get her facial points up on the Tokyo security network for recognition. All parties would be informed if they were detected, including Jake. It was the only fail-safe way to find her location.

At ten-thirty-eight P.M. the burner rang.

Jake vetted the caller ID and picked up the call, "Hello."

"It's Tanaka. Still working on something solid."

"I noticed a military contractor out there yesterday. Is he one of yours?"

"He's agency but part of the wider local presence."

"The body language is obvious, I made him straight away."

"I am asking for more covert operators."

"Can we get her biometrics flagged on the Tokyo surveillance camera system? If this Vera James comes up, they send us an alert and location in real time. I need to know straight away no delays. Might be crucial in crashing the terrorist's plan."

"You are asking a big call. I can see the logic though."

"It's now or never. If we don't get on top of this, they are more likely to succeed."

"Agreed. Leave the bureaucrats to me. Meanwhile you keep using your regular methods until I get this stamped." Tanaka took a breath. "By regular I mean as responsibly as possible too."

"Always." Jake hung up and placed the burner on the counter.

He tapped the tracking pad and typed a new protocol on Joanne Patterson. The platform went to work on all open and closed sources. Checking all databases and corners of the globe. Even the dark web. If there was something else on her, they needed to know and fast.

The toilet flushed quietly. He freshened up in the bathroom and brushed his teeth. Tomorrow morning he'd stake out the neighborhood and perimeter of the forecourt. A check of the program to see if there were any more links to the new name. Nothing. He stared at the prompt. Enough data had come to light to progress forward.

He turned off the device and clicked the lid over the keyboard. The burner sat on the table. Since reading her message, he contemplated calling Katerina. He calculated the time at five P.M. in Rotterdam. She would be in a secured location and mentioned a protection specialist. He grasped his cell phone.

"Can I please order a large nasi goreng and a separate large chicken? Better add a beef dish for Richard. What do you recommend?" Mia nodded. "For delivery. You just opened the kitchen? Thirty minutes is no problem."

Katerina pressed the mute button for the TV and snuggled under a rug. Mia lifted the heating remote and beeped it into action.

"I put it on three quarter fan strength." Mia said.

"Nice. The forecast on the expected cold front is extra powerful today."

Warm air caressed Katerina's cheek, taking the chill out of the air. Her cell phone rang and she shifted from under the blanket.

"Hello."

"Hi it's me."

"Hi me lovely to hear from you. What time is it there?" Katerina adjusted her position.

"Eleven P.M. I saw your email earlier and I had to call."

"Don't stress too much. We escaped unharmed as they were after the whistle blower."

"That doesn't mean you are not in danger. I feel like it's my fault for involving you."

"I make my own decisions." She took a breath. "Mia's editor has Richard, their security personnel, watching her building. I am staying with Mia so we are both protected. Save that we will go straight to a hotel if there is any more attacks."

"This puts my mind at ease. Thanks for the leads."

"No problem."

"Vera James has another alias. Joanne Patterson. She entered

Tokyo using a travel document with this name."

"You found this out after I gave you the profile?"

"Yes, a few hours ago. Thanks to your photo. It helped us identify her. There's an important event here the day after tomorrow. If my hunch is correct, we can catch her and the group and stop whatever is being planned."

"Is that it though? Or there will be more assignment with that old commander of yours?"

"Hopefully not. I told my contact who dragged me into this it's the last time. I want out of this too. The money will set us up for a while."

Katerina sighed quietly. "I just hope we don't get killed in the meantime."

"We will back on the boat in no time. Please go to the yacht with Mia the next sign of trouble. It is in Manila, Singapore main dock ten. I will send you the code now. I have a patrol service setup and can notify them."

"Good idea. Miss you."

"Miss you too."

She pressed end.

Chapter 42

HIS PHONE ALARM buzzed, pulling Jake into consciousness. Dawn lines breached the blinds, stretching bars over the floor. He tumbled out of bed and stepped into the bathroom. A shower and fresh set of clothes put him on the path to the living room. The Kevlar vest went on under his sweat shirt. He checked the cylinder and slide of the Nambu M60, shoved it in his belt. Loose hoodie went on the top, good for concealing when carrying a weapon.

Outside the door, housekeeping had left the laundry. He placed the bag on the table. It contained his jeans, sweatshirts and underwear cleaned, pressed, and neatly folded. Downstairs had a small activity of transitional behavior. Two guests at the front desk, an older couple waiting in line and a family on the couches.

He drove the rental car out of the hotel lot and returned it to the hire venue. The traffic appeared mixed; too early for peak morning at six-thirty A.M. and already attracting large trucks and trade utility vehicles. He watched his mirrors every so often for shadows. Encountering a bottleneck near the rental place held him up ten minutes. He filled the tank at a gas station and pulled into the driveway of the shop.

A young woman sat behind the front counter. He placed the key fob down.

"How was the vehicle?" She clicked the mouse.

"Fine thanks. Enough room in the rear and comfortable for a coastal trip."

"I'll have a quick inspection then you can be on your way."

Jake lowered into a seat in the waiting room. She hurried off to the lot grasping a clip board in her left hand. He watched her circle the car squinting and ticking her sheet as she moved.

She returned to the waiting room.

"All good to go. Here is your copy for your records." She peeled off the duplicate. "Please leave us a rating online as feedback is always welcome and do come again."

"Thanks."

The nearest underground subway station was Sumiyoshi, a five-minute walk. He bustled into a pre-work stampede on the platform, managing to board the next train. Settling into a seat, he only had three stops to travel. The route followed the Hanzomon line where it intersected with the Ginza line. He alighted and caught the southbound train to Toranomon station. The elevators hummed as he rose to the ground floor and into the morning air.

A quick stroll west placed him at the forecourt. The strike point had fewer tourists at this early morning time. A guard in a navy suit patrolled the main entrance, a different guy from yesterday. Equally stiff in posture and with a serious gaze. He circuited the flank and checked the northwest wall. Another guy in a gray suit and short haircut monitored the personnel entrance. Even the shades were styled in military issue. These recruits must be clones as they dressed and acted the same.

His burner vibrated at eight-forty-three A.M. He pushed the pickup button and put it too his ear.

"Yeah."

"It's Tanaka. I have a green light on the facial recognition for our mystery woman. Her specs and particulars are on the system and I have a direct line to the operators."

"Great. Now all we need is an accurate hit. I am thinking the chances are good of spotting her."

"We have forty-thousand cameras in Tokyo. The tech and infrastructure have been upgraded recently so hopefully we will find her location in the next twenty-four hours."

"Amen." Jake said. "Do you have manpower at your disposal if I need backup?"

"We are flexible and ready to move out if necessary. Where are you now?"

"At the rear side of the building with your clone agent doing laps. Do they make these guys in a factory? Or is it a storm trooper Star Wars thing where the aliens can manipulate the DNA and clone?"

Tanaka chuckled and his voice lowered. "I have some more operatives coming in and they use more covert methods."

"That's what we need. I want to be challenged trying to spot them. Like you and your fishing hat. So that the enemy will have trouble spotting them too. Any delay is crucial on the battlefield and could lose the war. We need the upper hand as much as possible. How many secret service agents do you expect will be here?"

"A small team with the president and pairs covering interior and exterior."

"Easier to manage and a less visible footprint to the enemy. Wise move."

"Few people know about the helipad there so we are likely to keep it a secret. It does get checked regularly and they will up the frequency tomorrow."

"Safe with me don't worry. I'm staying here for two to three hours. Anything irregular, no matter the size and I will be waiting."

"Keep your phone on."

The call went to tone.

As the morning led into eleven A.M. nothing out of the ordinary occurred near the Kasumigaseki building. For a moment he began to doubt the mission imperative. Moreover, his tenuous situation. The weight of a major bust and arrest seemed problematic in Tokyo. If he were caught in a red alert scenario tomorrow, he wondered if he could trust the intelligence community to release him if it all went pear shaped. Does Tanaka have the power to get him out undetected?

A group of sightseers clustered in a huddle, taking happy

snaps, and smiling at the camera. The new guy might toss him to the lions to save his own skin. McCallister has no morals, as seen with the expendable hit men he sent to the yacht. He also was deemed expendable and whoever would be promoted to his job, on the event of his death, would inherit the burden. What did Plato say about only the dead will see the end of war? In this business, the cycle goes on and on.

He watched the main entrance, still unsettled by the shooting in Rotterdam. Katerina and Mia were lucky not to have gotten killed or injured. In Tokyo he was unable to help them and probably the cause of the incident in the first place. They were investigating the same shipments and company. He hoped they would sit tight and stay safe at the apartment with their security personnel.

The agency guy at the front dipped his chin down. Talking on a mike. Amateur hour for these guys. Jake swept the crowds in the forecourt. Nothing unusual or different.

His phone burner rang at eleven-forty A.M.

"Hi Tanaka."

"We have a hit on the woman."

Chapter 43

THE LIGHT TRUCK covered all the necessary requirements for the job. Vera assessed the cargo hold once more to be certain. A seven-ton capacity. Small enough not to bring too much attention on the road. She shut the doors and bolted the latches. The white body panels had no dents or scratches. She inspected the front. Straight and clean.

She zipped a backpack filled with spare clothes, makeup, and disguises. A Glock forty-three, the best small pistol for concealment. The barrel was threaded and less than eighty-seven millimeters in length. It took six nine-millimeter rounds in the magazine. She checked the magazine was full. In her pocket she put the gun and an Omega 9k suppressor.

Her burner vibrated against her leg. She held it up. "Yes."

"Are you good to speak?" A female voice said.

"Give me a minute." Vera threaded by a wall of shelves and into a private office suite. She closed the door and sat. "Go ahead."

"Are we on schedule for the next phase?" Laurent's thick French accent came over the microphone.

"All set to go."

"Good. How effective are the Japanese team there?"

"Average at best. They get in the way more than help." Vera contemplated the warehouse. "I will persevere."

"We need to keep them on side in the short term. Until this assignment is completed." Laurent gathered her words. "Our main customs man has talked to someone. He knows way too much about the operation."

"When?" Vera squared her shoulders.

"In the last twenty-four hours. We believe under duress. He sent a message through to the handler stating that he's done. The heat too high. He said to cool off all communication until further notice." She sighed. "I think he may sing. He's weak and will fold under pressure again. It leaves the syndicate vulnerable and exposed."

"I will take care of it."

"We won't allow any loose ends."

Vera clicked off and climbed behind the wheel of a Toyota. She steered south west, kept on the expressway. Frustration mounted as she mused over the extra fixing she had to do. A tight schedule stretched her limits. Mistakes are easier to make under stress. She gripped the steering wheel and maintained the speed limit. The traffic varied as she neared her destination. Dusk formed over the port city of Shimizu as lights twinkled. She cruised the shop fronts dwarfed by the row of high rises. A block away from the tower she parked the car. She fitted a blond wig and applied a prosthetic chin.

Strolling twice past the entrance gave Vera an indication of the basement activity. She stopped at the neighboring window to monitor. The garage door rose as a car emerged and turned left. She slipped under the gap as it lowered to the ground. Endo's spot sat against a cement pillar in the east quarter. She walked briskly with a confident and relaxed manner to avoid attracting attention. It was vacant and he hadn't got home from work yet.

She crouched on the cement against the wall. Fastening a pair of gloves on her hands, she checked the time. Six-twenty P.M. Fifteen minutes past with two arrivals and a departure. Endo's parking spot stayed vacant. The exit door whirred again. Lights shone into the basement. A car engine became louder. The fender and tires rolled into Endo's spot. He killed the engine and the door opened.

Rising upright she levelled opposite. He turned front on in surprise. Vera pointed the weapon and shot him in the chest. His eyes were glazed and lids open wide with shock. A suppressor masked some of the noise but the report echoed. He fell backward, blood spattered on the panel. Picking him by the shoulders she bundled him into the vehicle.

His body collapsed like a jelly fish on the seat. She rotated to the opposite door and pulled his collar from the other side. Endo was fading fast. She shot him again and folded his feet into the footwell. Rummaging in the glove compartment she found a terry cloth and wiped the blood spots off the panel. The basement gate remote lay in the console. She pressed open and replaced it. A silence fell on the basement as she gently closed the rear car door. The exit yawned revealing the lights and traffic noise. She touched the internal wall button to activate the door before slipping into the night. A cold breeze carried from the nearby water. Outside she shoved her hands in her pockets and returned to the Toyota.

Chapter 44

THE LOBBY INTERCOM chimed and Mia answered. "Yes."

"The Chinese food is here."

"Ok send them up."

Mia let Richard know in a text that food had arrived and to join them in the apartment.

"I am famished." Katerina folded the blanket she used on the couch.

"There's plenty of food and Richard is coming."

"Sounds good. He's a great help, isn't he?"

"Sure is."

The bell rang. Mia left the living room and padded down the corridor. She cracked the door and a young Caucasian man held white takeout bags.

"Your Chinese order."

"Thanks." Mia balanced the door with her shoulder and reached out.

"Mia watch out." A scream came from the right near the elevator bay.

She turned in surprise to see Richard bolting toward her. The delivery man released the takeout and fumbled behind his back.

"Shut the door now!" Richard yelled.

Mia retreated inside the apartment, the door slammed shut in her wake. She spun and sprinted at the living room. "He's armed."

"Get down in case he shoots the door." Katerina pulled her to the kitchen.

A gun shot ripped in the corridor, a thump as a body hit the carpet. The gun fire sounded like thunder. No suppressor. Footsteps and a crack sounded. Mia turned to Katerina.

A sharp knock. "You can open up." Richard said.

Katerina cracked the door and peered into the passageway. A man's body lay prone, a dark red circle expanding in his leg. Richard kneeled beside and held the shooter's wrist.

"Is he dead?"

"No. I aimed at his leg and hit him on the head with the gun handle." Richard dropped the arm and gathered his cell phone.

"Hello police there's been an attempted shooting. I have apprehended the perpetrator and he's out cold. The man entered an apartment under false pretenses and is armed."

"Yes, he's injured, I shot him in the leg." He hesitated. "My name is Richard Stringer. I am licensed to carry a weapon. I was providing protection for the intended target."

"Ok thanks." He terminated the call.

Richard said urgently. "Police are coming. This guy must have mugged the delivery person and posed as them."

"Which means they probably tapped the mobile reception."

"Ï will wait with the body until the police come. If he wakes, he will try to escape."

"Richard, I think we should not mention this morning's events to law enforcement."

"Yes, I agree. They will find Walker's body soon enough and we did not see the sniper. The car did not get hit and no witnesses at the scene."

"Good idea." Katerina looked at the body and the scattered delivery. "Let's go inside Mia."

"Another near miss. Two in one day." Mia sat upright in the couch and tucked her legs. "It's too close for comfort."

Sirens sounded as the police arrived. An ambulance brought a stretcher and carried the shooter away. Two police officers spoke

English with thick Dutch accents. They interviewed Mia and Katerina who kept their explanations brief. Mia clarified she was a journalist and it may have something to do with one of her current stories. The officers listened and wrote notes. Mia was vague on specific details regarding the imports and did not mention Rotterdam or any information from Walker.

The officers thanked them for their time and left. Katerina gathered the spilled food containers on the floor and placed them into the bag. She carried it into the kitchen and dumped in the trash.

"Mia I am going to our yacht. I'd like you to join me. At least for a few days until this trouble blows over. They know where you live as well. Who knows how far their network reaches."

"Sounds like a good plan."

"But please do not tell anyone where it is. If you take leave from work, they cannot know either. It's too risky." Katerina leaned over and held Mia's hands.

Mia nodded, her mind off in the distance. She had never seen her friend so shaken. Normally she was the extroverted one.

"Yeah sure. I won't tell them."

"Are you OK?"

Mia shook her head as if to dispel the mental haze that overtook her brain. She gained her feet and put her hands on her hips. "Takes more than this to get at me. Let me find my luggage and we can catch the next available flight."

"That's the Mia I know." Katerina opened her computer and loaded a browser. "I will check flights and we can get out of here."

"My credit card is in my purse on the counter." Mia shuffled her luggage into the bedroom.

"I will pay for you it's the least I can do."

"No please I would not dream of it. I need a break anyway. I haven't had a vacation for over two years. Since before COVID started."

"Do you want to fly business class?" Katerina glimpsed over

her laptop. "There's a discount sale running with one of the major airlines."

"After this stress we both deserve a bit of luxury."

A pair of sparrow birds nose-dived at a tree setback from the garden edge. Jake faced a group of holidaymakers, cell phone to his ear. "Where is the location of our target?"

"A shopping strip twenty minutes from the building."

"What was she doing?"

"Getting supplies from a home-improvement center."

"Did they get the registration of her car?"

"Out of range. But a score of ninety-two percent says it is her."

"At least she doesn't know how I am."

"I would not take anything for granted." Tanaka said.

He sat on a bench and crossed his legs. "Can we track her probable direction at this stage?"

"If we get another sighting quickly then we can project a travel path. Triangulate the signal."

"Let's work towards that."

Jake pocketed the burner. The sidewalk led past the sculptures and to the glass frontage. For the first time since getting the pass, he entered the sliding doors. Workers gathered in social groups to chat and go about their leisure time. He used the security pass on the reader and pushed the elevator button for level ten. The light flashed but it denied access to the floor. He pressed eleven and it accepted.

The doors retracted and he stepped onto level eleven. Staff were arranging furniture in the corridor. Signs were up for an industry conference planned for next week.

A security guy patrolled the corridor. Jake nodded and stepped back into the cabin and pressed the second highest floor. He climbed a small set of stairs to the rooftop. A door swung open to a modernized platform. The original edge frames were reinforced. He took in the raised steel skeleton that held a helipad. Mount Fuji blocked the horizon. If terrorists planned an attack, did they know about this landing option?

Winds roared around his ears. Jake shoved through the door and descended the steps. A guard came out of the elevator and strode at the direction of the rooftop stairs. He rode the cabin to the ground floor. A man and a woman in guard uniforms circulated the foyer from opposite ends. The lunch crowd started to thin. He did a quick round of the main sections, noted the staff and body language. Nothing out of place or noteworthy.

He exited and walked out to the forecourt. Chatter in foreign language carried in the wind. A sensation that someone watched his back travelled in his spine. The foliage shook from the garden section. As the sun dropped in the west, he noticed a glint in the trees. Jake's instincts kicked in. He jumped at a raised monument. A bullet ricocheted off the pavers. Meters aways a woman screamed. He crawled to the monument base and pushed against the brick. The rail above his head sparked with multiple rounds. A sniper hid in the trees somewhere near the glint.

People scattered from his vicinity, scared of becoming collateral damage. Chatter in Japanese diminished in volume. He waited for more activity. No movement. He rose and fired a round into the tree trucks, hoping to get a random hit. Or scare the person into fleeing. He dropped back to a crouching position.

The forecourt went quiet. One minute went by slowly.

He lifted his head over the top, searching the gaps. No glint. He circled the raised section. Hidden from view of the woods he snuck around the verge. The wall structure provided him with sufficient cover.

A tall security guard came out of the building. Jake indicated at the woods. The man nodded and cautiously approached the overhang. He followed from the other side, remaining low. No sounds came from the trees. The sniper fled.

In the park he found the guard bent at a bush. The man spoke in Japanese.

"Do you speak English?" Jake said.

"A little bit." The tall man held up a spent jacket. "The sniper shot from this position."

"He opened fire on the courtyard. I will call the authorities."

Jake rang Tanaka. The guard spoke Japanese into a radio.

"I just had a sniper shoot at me from the woods. Here now with a guard from the building."

"I'll be down straight away."

He hunted on the path and dirt around the shrubs. Two more jackets. Tanaka arrived in five minutes.

"Hey." Jake said.

"Hey. What do we have?"

"These spent jackets." Jake held them in his palm. "High powered rifle."

"Did you see him?"

"No by the time it was clear the shooter escaped."

Tanaka put the rounds in a clear bag. He looked around for more evidence but could not find anything.

"No more sighting of the woman. Like she disappeared of the face of the earth." Tanaka said.

"I was afraid that might happen." Jake paced the sidewalk taking in the fading warmth. "Chances are she's an expert in espionage. Easy to change appearance and disappear."

"We are on alert for her. As soon as we detect her, I'll let you know."

"Sure thing."

Jake dialed McCallister's number.

"It's Sphinx. As you know the security dialogue is tomorrow."

"What can I do to help?"

"Have you cleared me with the secret service team?"

"All good to go. I take it you don't require a formal introduction?"

"No, I will most probably be in the background. Depends on what goes down."

"Makes sense. Let me know if you need anything."

The dial tone sounded.

He walked the full circuit twice taking in the commuters and the scenery. On the west end walkway, a man and woman were loitering. He aimed the burner camera at himself, clicking a selfie. The tourist act gave him a good angle to get photos of the two without arousing suspicion. He walked a few meters to the right and did the same from the other side. Again, he captured the couple unaware. The pair eventually walked off hand in hand laughing to one another. Unlikely to be intelligence operatives but he had to make sure.

The cell phone rang.

"Hi."

"She just booked into the Imperial." Tanaka paused. "Your hotel."

Jake's stomach flipped. "Can you find out what number room she's in?"

"I'll try."

He stood on the sidewalk, a ringing in his ear from the last conversation. What was she playing at? He began to doubt she did not know his identity. Or she planned an attack on the Kasumigaseki Building and the Imperial happened to be the closest hotel. He started walking east toward the hotel, cap pulled lower.

His phone displayed five-fifteen P.M. If he returned to the hotel, he might run into her accidentally. That would have possible ramifications in the future. He had to be careful how he entered the building. Hopefully Tanaka got back to him quickly about her room number.

Chapter 45

THE EVENING DARKENED slowly, a thin orange line the only evidence left of the day. A wind swayed the tree leaves. Jake powered the long way on the path in Hibiya Park, on alert for followers. Elm trees threw elongated shadows on the forest floor. Street lights flickered. Nothing out of the ordinary or suspicious. He assessed the hotel entrance from the opposite side of the street. Guests filled from the lobby into the restaurant for the six o'clock menu. Enough people to camouflage but not too many to stop Jake from evaluating each person.

He gently shouldered by the bodies, nodding and mumbling apologies every so often. Vera James' face was not apparent in the vicinity. The people were like hungry zombies with blinkers wrapped around their heads.

An elderly couple brushed past and he waited for them. He pushed the stairwell door, and ascended cautiously. This way he had a head start if he saw James. The landing rail cold to touch. Level one corridor was empty. He walked to his room and swiped the reader.

Against the living room wall, he lowered to the bar fridge and shelved the food items. A modified strategy had to be formed. Intercepting her at the hotel gave advantages and disadvantages. He was not sure of her role in a potential attack tomorrow at the security dialogue. If he located her and tracked covertly, he might discover her intentions. This plan hinged on Tanaka finding her room number.

There were so many variables that he may have to wing it tomorrow if he did not learn new information about her.

He searched on the laptop for data on both names Patterson and James. Deep diving into various databases, he inputted wide ranges for any remote connections. The system gave no new data.

His burner rang with a familiar number.

"Hello."

"Hi. We have the room number: it's two hundred and fifteen. She's in under Joanne Patterson." Tanaka said.

"Thanks that will help. Do you think you could put a static watcher outside the Imperial entrance here? We need to know her whereabouts and I will have trouble getting to her room undetected by cameras."

"It should be doable considering the severity of the threat."

"Give them my cell number, I will leave it on all night. As soon as I get the message I will come down. They can follow from a safe distance. Any more hits on facial recognition?"

"None. Let you as soon as I know."

"Cheers."

He leaned back and ran a hand through his hair. Just above him on level two Vera James was planning and plotting a major terrorist attack. In the window neon flared in all colors like a distant galaxy.

A coffee table sat in front of the couch. He moved the table aside and crossed his legs in a meditative position.

Staring at the wall, he recited the mantra, "I am energized and fully protected." He repeated the mantra over and over until a calmness fell over his mind like a blanket. His extremities were weightless, almost as if he had left his body. Heart beat slowed. He stayed in this state repeating the mantra. Still conscious but completely relaxed. If an idea or image flickered, he extinguished it for blankness. His breathing was the only thing he could hear. He floated as if on a cloud.

Slowly he brought himself back to the room and the present. He sat up and extended his arms, as if waking from a deep but cleansing sleep. The furnishings materialized: table, chairs, TV and cabinet. He focused on his balance, feet finding a solid stance.

He waited a moment at the glass, reflecting on the darkness beyond his room. The weight of a major catastrophe sitting on his shoulders. He undressed in the bathroom and turned on the shower taps. The soap lathered all over his skin, the warm water trickled. Fog obscured the mirror, he swiped with a spare towel. He dried and dressed in fresh jeans, sweatshirt, and a hoodie to sleep. He would be prepared to leave straight away if she left the hotel.

In the living room he packed his equipment ready for tomorrow.

The cell phone beeped and he read the message:

A watcher will be there in ten minutes. Tanaka.

Jake replied:

If they spot the target call or text me straight away. My cell phone will be on. Perry.

On the couch he made himself comfortable. He plugged the burner into the charger and put it on the coffee table within reach. The weapon positioned beside the cell phone. A movie played on the screen at low volume. An action thriller starring Bruce Willis with Japanese sub titles.

He snoozed and woke to the twinkling Tokyo lights. The time read eleven-forty P.M. Been out for over one hour. The water bottle was half full and he swigged a mouthful. He texted Tanaka and asked for the watcher's cell phone number. Tanaka answered in five minutes. The watcher's name was Kaito.

Jake sent a text to the watcher. Outside had dropped to eight degrees Celsius. Kaito the watcher got back quickly confirmed no sightings of James yet. He would keep him updated on any developments as soon as they happen. The blanket had fallen on the floor and the heater still giving warmth to the room. He pulled up the cover and went back to a light sleep.

Chapter 46

RAIN BATTERED THE road as the uber pulled into the airport drop off zone. Katerina and Mia got out and paid the driver. They entered the international departure terminal and each found a ticket kiosk. After five minutes of options and pressing buttons a luggage tag printed and dropped in the dispenser.

"Rotterdam to Singapore transfer at Heathrow for four hour and half hours." Katerina stared up at the electronic board. "We are at counter eighteen."

Mia pointed to a roped barrier curving across the tiled floor. "Over here."

The queue lines for check-in were moving quickly. They wheeled their luggage behind the next person in line. An elderly couple spoke in Dutch. Three young backpackers gathered in a huddle talking to one and another, huge bags strapped over their shoulders.

"I am feeling better already and we have not left Rotterdam." Mia smiled gazing at the passengers in transit.

"Wait until we are in the air then the feeling will really kick in."

A blond female attendant waved and they presented at the counter. Katerina and Mia both handed over their passports and loaded the bags onto the belt. She processed their check-in luggage with a bright smile on her face. The x-ray machines were a quick affair.

Mia pointed to a corridor on the left. "Through here."

The lounges were a ten-minute walk by all the duty-free shops. Katerina sent a quick email to Jake while she still had internet. She avoided too much detail as they were on a public service.

Two hours went by quickly. They boarded the plane and settled in their business pods side-by-side.

A glass of wine for takeoff. The pilot's message was music to Katerina's ears. She had been daydreaming about the yacht and being with Jake for weeks. At least this was the first part of that fantasy. She fastened her seat belt.

The plane screeched of the tarmac and pointed straight up in the air. Mia snuggled into her pillow and held up her glass wine.

The beep chirped in the room. Jake picked up the burner in a semi-daze and read it under the glow of the muted TV. Kaito had reported that the target was on the move. Time display: four thirty-three A.M.

He scrambled off the couch, plunged the pistol into his belt and shut the door. A draft came from the wall vents. He jumped the steps three at a time. Emerging into the lobby he maintained a composed walk to the exit. He called Kaito as he casually exited the hotel.

"Hey. Where are you?"

"I am a block west chasing on foot." Kaito said in low volume. "Not sure if she's carrying: it is a possibility with loose clothing."

He quickened his pace, watching for other people out at this early time of morning. Not fast, to avoid attracting attention or make excessive noise. Clumps of flora overhanging the lawn strips. He pounded the sidewalk. Rounding a bend, a cluster of high rises loomed in the darkness. Only silver glinted on a few windows. The Kasumigaseki Building sat one kilometer northwest.

Under a streetlamp he squinted at the road. A truck had pulled into the shoulder, blinker flashing. Thirty meters behind a hand waved. A figure stepped out from the cover of a Gingko.

Must be Kaito. Jake indicated with his right palm and hugged the embankment. He kept from sight as he met the watcher in a paved area offset from the sidewalk.

"She is in the cabin talking to the driver." Kaito said.

"What is your take on this? Are they executing an attack here?"

Kaito shook his head. "I don't know, too early to call. Tanaka just brought me in on this." He hesitated as if weighing up what to reveal. "I've been investigating this company's operations for six months in Tokyo. Something is going down but I'm short on material evidence."

"I am with you on that. Hopefully we can get a bust on this before it goes live and you can take the credit here." Jake turned and watched the scene.

A second truck pulled up behind the first. Two men dropped out of the passenger side. The driver slid the rear latch bolt. A click sounded as they eased apart the doors. The liftgate buzzed slowly to the ground.

"She's definitely the leader of this crew." Jake said.

Vera James lowered out of the rear truck and rounded the flank of the vehicle. She paused at the front truck. A cranking sound emanated from the enclosure. She gestured to the man and said something inaudible. The pair disappeared in the cargo hold.

"What are these guys doing at this time of the morning so close to the location of the security meeting?" Kaito said. "The license plates are covered."

"This must be related. What's the enforcement protocol as far as you're concerned?"

"It's too hot. We must move on this." Kaito pulled out his pistol. "You carrying?"

"Sure am. What's my liability as a foreigner if I get caught by law enforcement who want to run it by the book?"

"This case is as serious as it gets. National security. Tanaka will have your back. Shoot to maim but kill if we have too."

"That's my kind of attitude. You mind if I tell you an approach plan?"

"Go for it."

"Each take a side then you do the arrest. I will cover you from the east to gauge their reaction. If it's a peaceful surrender, great. If they respond with aggression, I will start taking them out."

Kaito nodded. "Let's do this."

Jake snuck on the inside passenger side. A streetlight provided enough sight to get him past a bend. He canned the notion of holding back on the enemy. The visuals were limited. Muffled voices from the cabin. He could not risk getting closer without exposing his position. The second pair of men could be heavily armed; they are outnumbered and possibly outgunned. He chinned at Kaito and pointed to the ground.

A cluster of trees and embankment gave Kaito cover on the opposite sidewalk. The Japanese agent signaled Jake with his fingers: a three-two-one countdown. He walked out into the open, weapon pointed.

"Hold it there." Kaito raised his voice and repeated it in Japanese. The passenger of the front truck appeared from the shadows and held up his hands. A black beanie obscured his facial features and mask covered his mouth and cheeks. Vera remained out of visual.

"Stop walking." Kaito gripped the pistol with both hands, eyes trained on the beanie guy.

A second figure emerged from the driver side. Jake could see the profile but not their hands.

"Come on, come out." Jake said under his breath.

Dressed in dark clothes with a face mask the second man's elbow extended with a weapon. Jake pointed and shot. The man's shoulder sliced back, dropped to his right knee. His gun clattered on the concrete. The man rolled out of sight.

The sound of scuffling feet as a third smaller man entered the scene. A burst of rounds sparked the sidewalk. Semi-automatic. Kaito fired and retreated to cover. Jake stayed at the embankment. He ducked behind a retaining wall. The first man waited at the flank of the truck.

Another spray from the smaller guy spread over the road. Jake guessed he was stalling, holding them at bay. He fired at the third shooter to try and distract him.

The liftgate moved up and folded back in the truck. Gunfire

from the third shooter chipped the ground. The man aimed over the road firing a Kalashnikov. Rounds went wild as Jake returned fire. He held position with the Kalashnikov. From the rear the first man fired in Jake's direction.

Kaito emerged from the east and shot at the third guy. The shooter must need to reload a fresh magazine soon.

An engine fired into life, the scent of brake fluid and diesel followed. The front truck squealed into the lane almost fishtailing the back tires. Two hundred meters ahead of Jake's position he could not risk exposing himself. The first guy shot at Kaito from the rear truck. Jake fired at the man. He collapsed on the ground. He picked the man's weapon and cabled his hands together.

The automatic spray finally ceased as the third guy dumped his empty magazine. The front truck reached a distance of four-hundred meters. Kaito chased and shot at the driver side mirror. The bullet went wide. A bend in the road with thick trees deprived him of a second chance.

"Missed damn it!" Kaito eyes lost in the distance where the truck had been moments ago.

Footsteps pattered as the third shooter fled on foot. The man cut into the path, made a beeline up the steps. Jake aimed and hit the assailant in the back of the leg. The man stumbled and fell. He caught up to him.

"Thought you were going somewhere?" Jake said to his captive. "You can stay with us for a while." He hauled the man onto the sidewalk. They secured cuffs around the third fugitive's wrists, tied with a cable. The man lay face down on the sidewalk.

"We nearly got her." Kaito said over the prone body of the first man.

"Don't stress there will be another chance. Let's get these guys into questioning." Jake said and peered into the darkness.

"What about her and the other one?" Kaito gestured at the remaining truck.

"Good point. We will call it in to Tanaka and go from there."

Jake dialed a number on his cell. "Tanaka, it's Perry. James got away with an injured man. We have two accomplices here that have bullet wounds."

"Where are you?"

"Near the Imperial on the main street." Jake checked a street sign and gave him the location.

"See you soon."

Kaito unlocked the cargo hold on the abandoned truck. They yanked open the doors. Empty. The passenger cabin had nothing of note but they searched it anyway. Jake stood with the captured thugs.

"Do you think they were going to transfer weapons?"

"Who can say for sure." Jake shook his head.

"We nearly had her." Kaito said.

Jake spotted oncoming headlamps. "Here comes Tanaka."

Chapter 47

THE TRANSFER AT Heathrow went quickly. Katerina and Mia occupied the lounge until the announcement came over the speakers. They boarded the next flight and got comfortable in their seats. A meal was served soon after takeoff. They chatted for a few hours until falling asleep. An attendant gently woke them both with an hour until landing in Manila.

Katerina adjusted her seat and stowed away her bag. The flight attendants were tidying up and getting ready to descend. Her stomach lurched at the thought of leaving Rotterdam behind and returning to the yacht. The angst of nefarious people tailing her and the murder of the whistle blower Walker in broad daylight gave her flashbacks to Saint Petersburg. She hoped deeply that Jake's mission would be completed in one to two days so he could join them at the boat.

"Nearly there, I cannot wait to relax on your yacht." Mia said.

"You read my mind. It will be fun, especially with you there."

Mia reached out and touched Katerina's leg. She looked away and wondered if Mia had another motive for being so nice to her. The idea became silly the more she thought about it.

The wheels hit the tarmac with a series of screeches and the passengers disembarked in an orderly fashion. Katerina and Mia navigated the arrival section and came to the elevators. The belts brought their luggage and they passed into customs. Out in the fresh afternoon air, Manila sun warmed Katerina's shoulders.

"The weather has improved from the Netherlands."

"Definitely." Katerina guided them toward the cab rank. "A twenty-minute drive in this traffic to the docks."

"I am ready for a lot of rest and relaxation." Mia sighed reflecting at the horizon. "And some cocktails."

Manila had movement and rush everywhere. People flocked to

and from the high and medium rises. A high-density city. They got into a cab and directed the driver. Eateries, laundromats, and shop fronts flashed on either side. Residential towers dominated the skyline in every direction. Neon and LEDs pulsated constantly with brands and slogans.

A road sign with 'port' directed the traffic left. Blue patches of water shimmered every so often. Gulls flew overhead seeking the best places for scraps. The driver turned at an intersection and drove along the harbor edge with boats moored in rows.

"Just drop us here please." Katerina pointed at a ramp to the main pier.

The driver slowed to the end of the parking lot. Katerina paid him and stepped out into the ocean breeze. He lifted the luggage from the trunk and bid them farewell.

"The yacht is over on that row. Will alert security that we are here so they don't get the wrong idea."

"Right behind you girl." Mia gazed at the orange trail reflecting from the horizon onto the water.

Katerina spied at a kiosk on a concrete apron. She confirmed with security that it was her yacht and her and her friend would be staying. The attendant asked if they would like to continue the checkups and she said yes.

Fifty meters west they found the yacht and walked on board. The water gently lapped the hull. She led Mia downstairs to the main living room and flipped the light switch.

"It's magnificent Katerina. Thanks for inviting me." Mia circled the couches admiring the furnishings.

"Please make yourself at home." Katerina moved behind the island bench and placed a bottle opener on the counter. "We have champagne in the fridge. Would you like a glass?"

"Would I ever!"

"Coming right up."

A black tinted Toyota SUV pulled up curbside. Tanaka opened the passenger door and stepped onto the sidewalk. No hat this time. A plain blue sweatsuit with sneakers as if he had been working out at the gym. He surveyed the scene in thoughtful silence for a moment.

"So, these are our henchman."

"Japanese citizens I think." Kaito eyed the prone figures on the ground.

"I shot one in the leg. We wrapped a cloth around the wound. Another one got away injured with James: round in the shoulder."

"I'll call an ambulance."

The driver came out to join Tanaka.

"Hiro. Please put this guy in the back."

"Sure." The driver helped the first guy to stand and led him to the back of the SUV.

Tanaka rang an ambulance and gave the operator the address. He hung up and faced Jake. "You better get back to the hotel. This area will be swarming with cops and I don't want to have to explain your presence to the powers that be. I will try to keep it quiet."

"Sure, no problem." Jake chinned at Kaito. "Thanks for your help this morning."

"Likewise. Might see you again."

"I will be around the building in a few hours but I will keep a good distance. Vera James didn't see me properly."

He started off east to the hotel. The sky hung inky black with artificial city color dotted on the horizon. A call on whether she would show up today at the security meeting he could not make either way. Too many questions were left unanswered. Her involvement in an attack was imminent that much was guaranteed. Presence in the company of armed thugs so close to the strike point and time wasn't a coincidence. But she could not afford another slip up now and realized the law had caught up with her activities.

Shapes danced as he cut across to the Imperial. This time she escaped an arrest and with causalities in her crew that could talk under pressure. Her strategy and plans may have changed. They were dealing with vast resources and capabilities. To withdraw from the battle to win the war might be the smartest resolution for James. He did a circuit on the hotel block, watching for familiar faces. The streets were deserted so easy to monitor. No suspicious cars lurking for an ambush. In the lobby window he gauged if she had returned. All quiet.

The dimly lit lobby resonated with a calm vibe. A security person had their head in a book and kept on reading. He ascended the stairs. A sensor light flicked on as he reached level one. He bleeped the reader and sank down on the couch for a few more hours of sleep. The adrenaline subsided from the earlier action but his mind raced. Possibilities and outcomes regarding James flashed by. He pushed them away and tried to get a few hours rest.

Chapter 48

AT FOUR-FIFTY A.M. the truck eased to a halt at an intersection. Vera James had replaced the fake license plates at a dimly lit parking lot with no surveillance cameras. She cased the location earlier on the event of an emergency. That very need arose. The skyline flickered so much neon she swore she saw stars when she closed her eyes. Lack of sleep didn't help the situation.

Daiki sat slumped in the passenger seat, a miserable expression on his face. She tried to ignore him and drove south toward the water.

"My shoulder is bleeding out." The man grimaced as he stared out the windshield. "Those guys came out of nowhere. Bam, bam we were out for the count."

"It happens sometimes; you are a gunman comes with the job. I'll get the surgeon onto it as soon as we get to the warehouse. Keep the pressure on with your hand."

A series of smaller roads carried them into the industrial section of the port. She slowed at a boom gate and cracked the window. The card bleeped as it passed over the reader. They cut across the yard, staying in the single lane. In the east quadrant, she found the triple fronted gate. Headlamps illuminated the concrete, the roller door buzzed. She eased into the bay slowly, expecting a confrontation from the director. Stacks of steel shelves receded into the gloom. Brakes squeaked as they came to a stop. His shadow cast long over the dispatch area.

The roller door dropped in their wake. She removed her hands from the steering wheel.

Suzuki propped on the mezzanine ramp, backlit by LED lights, his face wore a grim expression. "What happened out there?"

Vera shut the door and peered up at him. The simmering anger inside her subsided as she gained perspective and put on one of her many personas. She mounted the steel steps to greet him at his level. He treated every woman like those whores he paid at that place in Ginza. Suzuki thought Elites was his little secret amongst the boys. She checked out everyone she worked with down to the last detail.

"We were ambushed at the exchange. The main one is Japanese but I am not sure. He fired straight away. We had it under control until a sniper shot from cover. I couldn't see their position until we fled. The tech is safe in the truck. Two men were captured and we escaped." She waved at the truck.

"This puts us back considerably. We have but one opportunity to make this work."

"I disagree. Plan B can still be executed. I will go and perform the actions alone."

"You've been seen by law enforcement. I hope the other two don't talk under pressure."

"I wore a face mask. If they know who I am it's because I was followed. That means they may already know my name here. The two gunmen know nothing, your local hired muscle. The police won't be able to get further information."

Daiko stumbled from the truck cabin, eyes pleading. "I need help."

"The surgeon is in the spare office." Suzuki stared down in partial disgust. "You better get him patched up."

"Come on then." She strode at a corridor entrance beyond the walls of product. A ledge ladled with store equipment ran two meters to the archway. He followed her clutching his shoulder.

The dispatch zone broke into a section of partitioned walls. Perspex windows revealed rooms with a desk and swivel chairs. Vera led the injured man deeper into the complex. She identified the back exit and opened a door. The scent of disinfectant and hospital grade cleaners wafted in the air. A good sign. She didn't want any further complications or bodies to dispose.

A short Japanese woman in a white gown bent over a trolley of surgical instruments. Vera motioned to Daiko who staggered past her.

The surgeon straightened. "Welcome." She gestured at a gurney in the center of the room. An IV drip bag balanced on a stand. She plucked on a pair of rubber gloves.

Daiko collapsed on the white sheets and closed his eyes. His face was pale and beads of sweat ran down the edge of his face. The woman cut open his shirt and told him to relax. A dark red stain surrounded his upper chest at the clavicle.

She armed a syringe and angled it at Daiko's wound. "A local anesthetic for the pain. I may have to dig deep to find this bullet."

"I will leave you to it." Vera closed the door and weaved toward the front. She followed the passage back to the main section. The last room had a locker which she fingered in a code. It clicked open. She removed a bag and placed it on the table. Contingency supplies. She unzipped it, lifted a change of clothes, and laid them on the table surface. A black dress and dark jacket to match.

She swiveled at an archway that led to a small bathroom. At the basin she washed her face and dried it with paper towel. A mirror sat above the facets. She applied basic makeup; eyeliner, lipstick, and a toner to dim her cheekbones. Her black hair slicked back in a ponytail. She took off the pants and slipped on the dress. A holster strapped on her shoulder, the jacket over the top. The weapon tucked neatly inside, hidden from view. She put sneakers on her feet and tied the laces. A wedge in one shoe would change her bearing in case they had her on gait recognition. For the office she had a pair of low pumps in the bag.

She added a pair of glasses for effect and examined herself in the reflection. Professional and attractive but not too beautiful she would stun every man. Too much attention was a negative. Part of a corporate team here to do business. She put the glasses in a case. Her black hair blended in with the Japanese population. A high-powered rifle, disassembled in parts, went in the carry bag beside the pumps and a box of rounds. She placed a small backpack inside, swung the bag over her shoulder and headed into the open dispatch area.

A Honda SUV was parked in the west corner. She ignored Suzuki's glare from the platform above as she powerwalked to the car. He had delusions of grandeur and knew very well she did not report to him. Soon his usefulness would expire. As far as she was concerned, he'd always been useless.

The key fob nestled in the tray between the seats. She dropped the pumps into the passenger footwell. Carry bag went into a secret compartment built in under the seat. In case she got stopped by law enforcement at least they would not find the rifle. She hit the roller button on the wall and sunk into the driver seat. A discreet vehicle, common on the streets of Tokyo. Clean registration. Last year's model.

The crisp morning revealed itself slowly as the door rose. She revved onto the crossover and drove north. Dawn started to break, a line of yellow pierced the eastern high rises. Her hand rummaged in the bag for her sunglasses. She sought the case and wrapped them around her ears. Neon faded in her periphery as the night dissipated to day.

Paradoxically, she found Tokyo both glamorous and tacky at once. The neon lights versus ancient temples. High rise upon office tower next to palaces and ancient monuments.

An office building near the bungled exchange was her destination. Soon she would complete unfinished business.

Chapter 49

TANAKA RANG AT eight-fifty A.M.

Jake had hustled into the bathroom already and taken a quick shower. He put on a different jacket and pair of slacks. A pair of sneakers that were effective for running long distances. In case he had to use stairwells or chase someone.

"Hi. How's it going?" Tanaka spoke softly like he had been up all morning processing paperwork and interrogating suspects.

"Not bad. Did we manage to get any confessions from our shooters?"

"Nothing. I don't think they know details. As we thought hired goons to do a job. Anyway we will keep them here and press charges to keep them off the streets for a few years."

"What's the flight plan for the Japanese prime minister today?"

"This is highly classified. Only three people know the agenda."

"I have a strong hunch so work with me." Jake paused. "I need to know his movements beforehand. Two to three hours prior."

"He's in a meeting with the U.S. President in an undisclosed location."

"Now we ambushed Vera and her crew she will execute an alternative attack. The strike point will change. We must assume they have extremely reliable and accurate intel. Otherwise, they are not a serious threat."

"Makes sense. You think it will happen beforehand?"

"Depends on the circumstances you are about to tell me. But yes, now this attack has rattled cages it must be. I would do that in her shoes. In fact, to get local help, which she assuredly has, probability is she will attack the US President and Japanese Prime Minister together. The Australian and Indian leaders are not as valuable to take down."

Jake said.

Tanaka remained silent but the cogs were turning.

Jake kept going. "The mode of transport to the prior engagement is helicopter? Tokyo has the most helipads of any city in the world."

"Correct."

"The venue is within half a mile from the Kasumigaseki Building?"

A long stretch of silence. "If I reveal the location and something happens…"

"Can you afford not too? You are protecting the Japanese Prime Minister and I'm protecting the US President. My credentials are proven beyond doubt." Jake said.

Tanaka cleared his throat. "The InterContinental ANA hotel on Akasaka. The US President will helicopter in at eleven A.M. and meet the Japanese Prime Minister in the private executive rooms."

"That's the new strike point. I will go straight there and do surveillance."

"Do you need backup?"

"I will go solo at this stage but please be on standby. Send the same small contingency of trusted soldiers and agents to the Kasumigaseki Building. Kaito is reliable and good enough to go there. He cannot come with me as he's been made."

"I agree and it has been arranged."

"If Vera James comes up on the cameras let me know."

"Will do."

The call went to dial tone.

Imperial lobby had the stragglers from the end of breakfast crowd. He made the shortcut among the pet owners in Hibiya Park out for their morning stroll. Kasumigaseki subway station contained remnants of the peak hour rush. He shouldered to the booth and bought a ticket. A two-stop ride to Toranomon Hills station where he alighted and faced east. The fresh morning breeze made him numb in spots, cold enough to take away any drowsiness. Halfway, over he located the Natural Lawson convenience store and bought two salad wraps, a bottle of water and a banana. He walked and ate, weary of his surroundings.

A street surrounding the strike point, he did a lap of the block, stopping at various points. One time he did a one-eighty turn and forged back the other way. Countersurveillance was crucial to perform. Positive outcome to avoid a preventable mistake. He had to be sure there were no followers he wasn't aware of before tracking a target.

The InterContinental ANA rose like a beacon from the cluster of smaller buildings. A revolving door served as the main access point to the lobby. He claimed an arm chair, not in the main queuing area, with a view of the entrance. The other side had a large open archway to a restaurant. Every man and woman that entered and approached the marble countertop he evaluated.

Several key factors broke the process to a more basic level. Inferences have a high probability of predicting an individual's core traits and choices including intelligence, health, interests, and social habits. A powerful but dangerous tool used by giant tech companies.

He utilized a similar and simplified process to spot followers and on this occasion to try and detect Vera James. Lifestyle and fashion magazines were stacked on a coffee table. He picked one up and flipped through the pages. This activity provided him adequate cover. Intermittently he vetted at the incoming guests. She would come in the main revolving door if his hunch was correct after already having scoped the perimeter.

An elderly couple booked into a suite at the counter. A string of American tourists talking loudly and pointing out the windows. He waited and watched the traffic. Turned a page in the periodical. An interview with a European celebrity chef he had never heard of before today. The guy made it big in Europe then America after growing up in a small remote town in Italy. Rags to riches. That story was almost a cliché these days.

The wall clock displayed ten past ten A.M. A pair of well-groomed men entered and sized up the facilities. Mid-thirties with lots of luggage. They moved slowly to reception taking in the décor. Could be a couple. A receptionist became free and the pair approached. She asked their names. The lead one spoke and Jake could make out the voice. Out-of-towners for sure.

The lobby cleared as the last guests checked out of their rooms. He read more of the articles. A flurry of Japanese families came in to book. Children running about playing and laughing. He glanced away, shifted positions in the seat.

More couples and people came to the counter. He ruled out all of them one-by-one for one reason or another. The edged closer and past ten-thirty.

In the window he noticed a woman powerwalking on the opposite sidewalk. She had sports footwear with corporate attire. A dress and a brand name jacket. Out for a dose of morning exercise on her break. Fit and tall for a female. She wore glasses. Her black hair tied back in a pony tail. He tilted his head away so as not to stare and draw attention.

The wall continued after the revolving door. He angled to spot her in the glass reflection. She waited at the pedestrian crossing and came over when the traffic subsided. Her attire was completely standard with executive Japan styles. The fact that she camouflaged so well in the urban environment made her stick out to him. He could not leave to chase her as she would make him quickly and he needed to stay in the hotel in case it was not the target.

She passed behind the restaurant. Jake raised the magazine, scanned the words. He trained back on the lobby, no one of interest. The restaurant floated between breakfast and lunch periods and had minimal customers and one staff member.

He switched to the door. The female power walker stepped on the revolving axis and onto the tiles. Without checking her surroundings, she marched up to the receptionist. Her shoes had changed to low heel pumps and a gym bag hung from her shoulder. His pulse quickened as he worked on his next move.

The time hit ten-forty. Jake replaced the periodical on the

stack and joined the line as she moved to the counter. The space between them was two meters. He strained to listen to the conversation.

In his mind, the chances of this being Vera James went up considerably.

Chapter 50

A MIDDLE-AGED man in an impeccable black suit served the woman he suspected to be Vera James. Jake heard her request a room on the thirty-fifth floor. He relaxed his posture and tipped his cap, decreasing his presence. Vera was intent on completing the booking due to the time factor, he guessed. She paid in cash, another a red flag, and nodded at the attendant. The man processed it and gave her the key. She did not turn back as she clipped away from the desk to the elevator bay.

"May I help you?" The man pivoted from his terminal and grinned with perfect white teeth.

Jake smiled in return as he approached. "Can I please book a room and check-in now?"

"Certainly. Do you have a preference on the floor?"

"What's the highest you have available. I like a long view."

"We have one on thirty-five. It's an executive suite. Forty-three thousand Yen or three hundred and twenty USD a night. Whichever currency you would prefer."

"I'll take it thanks and will pay in Yen. Cash. I am travelling light."

"Very well, I'll will book that and process the rest."

Jake rummaged in the carry bag and found his wallet. He removed the Yen notes and slid them across the counter.

The man typed up the details and produced an electronic card. "Here is your key pass. Room number eight hundred and twenty-two. You'll need it in the lift as well as the room. Let us know if you need anything and have a good stay. The elevator bay is over there."

"Thanks." He waited two minutes and pressed the up button on the wall. The elevator arrived at thirty-four and he disembarked. A stairwell started in the west corner which he took to thirty-five. It continued to the rooftop.

The corridor had lush carpet and classy landscape oil paintings hung between doors. He beeped the key pass and entered the room. A pleasant scent of sandalwood hung in the air. He sent a text to Tanaka requesting a watcher for outside the hotel's main entrance.

A large living room with a big screen TV greeted him. The bedroom was large with a queen size bed. This led to a high-end bathroom contained a chic floating basin, modern tapware, feature mosaic tiles and a frameless shower. Pity he would not be staying.

He placed his carry bag on the table surface. Everything he needed was on his person, the bag more for impressions that he owned something. He listened at the front door for sounds. Nothing.

Out in the hallway, he walked beyond the elevator bay to the other end. He figured another flight of stairs for the helipad. Instead, he discovered a private elevator for the rooftop. The time read ten-fifty-eight. The stairwell at the end was empty still. A small cupboard for the janitor sat opposite the stairwell entrance in a nook. He picked the lock and moved aside a broom and a bucket of cleaning products. The doors closed and darkness fell in the confined space.

The slapping and whirring came faintly in the dark. Up above. A helicopter. The thud as the feet pads touched the surface. Voices ushered and diminished. He opened the crack between the panels. A faint ding. They were in the rooftop elevator. The lack of security unusual under the circumstances.

A second ding as doors screeched. Four to five people cramming in the lift to go down. He saw a flash of gray hair. A burly giant blocked out visuals. The president. No sign of Vera James.

Doors slammed shut. The bay emptied. He leaned in silence, weighing up his next move. For ten minutes nothing happened on thirty-fifth floor in the corridor. He must be missing something. It had to be her booked into this hotel.

He opened the panel and clicked the pass to his room. Slumped against the door he lowered to the floor. So close yet so far.

The burner vibrated as he had it on silent since hiding in the janitor cupboard. Tanaka replied that he had someone, a female, watching the lobby on the bench outside. He texted Jake her cell number and a map indicated a large conference room on the thirtieth floor.

Her room overlooked the main road and a tranquil park. Vera James wished to avoid this scenario but no other option was available since her crew were ambuscaded earlier. Ambient light reflected off her tablet. The morning's event caught her unaware. Two men down and another injured. A major blow she had not expected, perhaps the biggest in her career to date. She never dwelled on failure and realized it was a necessary component that led to success. Her inbox beeped with an email notification. She read the message from Suzuki demanding success today in his usual acidic and unrelenting tone.

But she'd bounce back with renewed determination. The flights leaving Tokyo today were numerous. She always had an exit strategy, just in case. An alternate schedule should plans go awry. She scanned her top three destinations; Hong Kong, Beijing or Amsterdam.

The US President will rendezvous on the rooftop to join with the Japanese Prime Minister at eleven o'clock. He would descend to one of the conference rooms in this hotel. A chat before the dialogue scheduled for one P.M.

An attack as the president landed provided little odds for success. Escaping such an event would prove impossible with so little preparation. She still needed to find the Japanese Prime Minister to satisfy her Tokyo based partners and complete the assignment. The bonus was her freedom and enough of a payday to execute the next plan. She still had a few tools at her disposal. If she could pull it off with all parties none the wiser. That was the hard part.

She paced the carpet and worked the numbers. The floor that the president and prime minister were meeting here was believed to be thirty but unconfirmed yet. Suzuki's contact might come through with the location in time to act. If that happened, she stocked the right equipment to cause additional confusion and distraction.

Otherwise, let the president attend the conference room. The classified meeting put them in a predictable path. She unzipped the backpack and filled it with clothes, makeup kit and a wig. Bide her time until he returned to the rooftop for the flight to the security dialogue at one P.M.

Chapter 51

THE EXPLOSION SHOOK the floors, rocking the table. His chair jumped and fell, leg points smacked the flooring. Jake pushed into the corridor and bolted to the stairwell. Broken prints in frames scattered in his path. He regarded the elevator as unreliable at this stage. Bounding over the steps, hand sliding on the rail as he descended.

He made it five floors down and touched the handle for thirty. Smoke billowed from the door crack. He zipped up the hoodie over his face and pushed into the space. Two burly secret service guys pulled weapons, aiming into the mist. One coughed and spluttered as they squinted at the walls. A third formed a protective ring around the bay. Searching for an unseen enemy, stunned by the chaos.

Visual dimmed as he searched for assailants. Footfall somewhere close. He could not discern the source. A gray-haired, tall figure in a suit materialized. He wore a COVID face mask bookended by men in suits. The US President.

A lithe figure in black emerged from the shadow. The person wore a proper face mask. Vera James. She pointed at the huddle, like a gridiron scrum. A burly hand extended and stabbed the lift button frantically. Doors staggered apart. Air sucked into the cabin creating a void. Jake maintained sights on the figure in black.

Shot fired. One of the secret service guys crumpled to the floor. Ambient light glowed from the elevator. The group fell past the doors. Jake spotted the president standing in the corner. Vera James' arm outstretched taking a wide aim.

He catapulted in the air at her position. She startled, broke to run, shooting wide. The tackle failed as he hit the carpet empty handed. His shoulder lanced with fire. A clear view to the elevator. The president held his arm, crimson dribbled down his sleeve. She missed.

The clack of the stairwell door reverberated. He forced himself upright and ran at the exit. Smoke drifted in clumps, filled his nostrils as he raised a forearm to protect his mouth. In his wake the elevator finally staggered to the roof.

Ears still rang from the gunshots, the relief short lived. He shouldered the door with his good side and hit the landing banister. Footsteps echoed faintly. Gazed upward. Cannot see her. His head swam from the gas inhalation. Gripping the rail, he steadied his stance. Must be fleeing to ground floor and making an escape.

Jake spiraled the banister, heading in a downward trajectory. A discarded gas mask lay on the step. At floor twenty-five he plunged through the door and ran up to the elevator bay. The doors expanded and he hit the button. He bet on her escaping on foot through the lobby.

A crammed elevator opened to greet him. Nodding at the wide-eyed faces he snuggled in the corner. Petrified guests transfixed at the mirrored walls and talk non-stop about the disruption. No one knows the cause of the disturbance.

The doors clambered open. Passengers spill out of the cabin. He rounded the bay and stumbled past the reception. Panic enveloped the lobby. He shrugged into the crowd of bolting guests, running in all directions. Outside he checked either side of the hotel perimeter for Vera James. Nothing.

He returned to the front. A hole in the wall-to-ceiling glass showed the explosion site. Curls of smoke and a burnt smell in the air. The restaurant flank had a jagged fissure on the exterior brick. Daylight flooded the floor, strewn with rubble.

The stairwell entrance sat in the west near the restaurant. He walked through the open section and stopped at a window panel. An unobstructed view from outside would be ideal. The opening provided this and the crowds milled further to the front. Trees dotted a sidewalk grass strip. The tree trunk allowed him visual but hid him from sight. He hoped his elevator trip had beaten her if she planned to escape.

Stragglers poured intermittently onto the tiled flooring. He flicked back and forth to minimize getting made. She might have paused briefly to change or shed clothes. A string of middle-aged couples staggered into the lobby. He strained and waited. Clumps of fleeing guests pushed and shoved. His lungs and shoulder burned.

At the end of a cluster, a woman with black hair down in dark active wear linked with the flow of bodies. He barely saw her in the bustle. She wore the same spectacles and makeup. James.

He bolted to the front keeping ten meters from the wall to avoid detection. Flashes of her face and torso as he rounded the bend. The revolving door turned like a faulty merry-go-round, jolting with the strain of users. Glass doors were bottlenecked as guests stampeded the narrow openings. He peered at the masses to spot her. Black hair bobbed everywhere as much of the population were of Asian descent. He strained, dodged, and pushed toward the exits.

Sirens wailed in the distance both police and ambulance rushed to the scene. He had five minutes maximum before law enforcement arrived and started cordoning off the perimeter. Questions would be asked of an American with his features. He dipped up and down.

In a group of tall men, Vera broke free from a pack. Jake maneuvered around the outside, keeping an eye on her position. She jogged east, as if not fatigued from the stairs. Incredible fitness and endurance. He pounded the sidewalk tailing her from one hundred meters. If he got closer, she may see him. Too far and he would lose her in the Tokyo streets.

She crossed the road and must have spotted him in a reflection. Drawing a pistol, she turned and fired. Jake dove to the concrete, somersaulting to lessen the impact. Glass shattered behind him. He came to his feet. She kept running, gaining distance. Tires screeched and a horn blared. Traffic at a standstill. He meandered amid fenders, ignoring angry motorists. Drivers yelled in Japanese. Coming up to her last position, James had already sprinted to the intersection.

Commuters stared and pointed at him. He chased on trying to make ground. Lights went red and he missed the signal. In the distance he trained on her head. Jake meandered in and out of high rises and towers. Shadows covered the paths and buildings, silver glinted from the windows and glass. He maintained the pace but could not close the gap.

Cars lined the busy roads, sidewalks thick with pedestrians. He strained to keep her in visual. She veered north moving around people with apparent ease. A mass of heads snaked between businesses. She went right at a restaurant, beyond al fresco tables and a-frame signs. Patrons commented and pointed at her. A waiter tried to catch her but she slipped his position. The other side led to a courtyard and thoroughfare. A sushi and juice bar bookended a second strip. Jake swerved around an elderly couple, stumbled on a loose concrete paver. Up ahead a throng of sightseers converged on a waiting bus. He realized he could not discern her face.

He had lost her.

The next right turn led to a mini shopping mall. Vera James checked for her pursuer. Gone. She slowed to a walk and found a food court with a block of toilets. She preferred not to risk boxing herself in a potential trap but was sure she shook the mystery man. A row of four cubicles formed the back end. The door swung on the last one. She locked it, shrugged off her backpack and lowered it to the toilet seat.

Her kill shot on the president had been foiled by this persistent man. She caught a glimpse and was sure he was not Asian. Brown hair medium height and build. Who was this guy? He'd located her again in the lobby and chased her a fair distance.

She yanked off her black top and pulled on a blouse and a jacket over the top. Her makeup set combined with a facial prosthetic changed her appearance sufficiently. At the basin she used a wipe to clean her cheeks. A nose prosthetic that extended to her cheekbones fooled facial recognition technology. She suspected that in Japan, authorities employed this method to find her. The ends pressed to her skin, attached by an adhesive. A different foundation and eyeliner streamlined the edges and she pulled her hair back in a short ponytail. A blond wig hid all traces of her natural strands. Blue contact lens for her eyes completed the transformation.

The rifle bag was stashed in a gym locker. With the president requiring medical attention the security dialogue would be called off or postponed. The Japanese Prime Minister either left earlier or had not been present at the hotel. Her intel lacked accuracy and consequently she failed the contract.

A Japanese woman passed her as she left the toilet. Shoppers increased in numbers at the food court as of lunch hour. She purchased a bento box and a bottle of water and sat on a stool. Two teams were out for her; law enforcement and Suzuki's henchmen. She chewed on salmon and rice. This did not scare her; she had witnessed worse odds and lived to see another day. It did give rise for an alternate strategy and cause to rethink her position.

She scanned the crowd but kept her head down. Unfinished business irritated her more than anything. For her, Tokyo was cursed with setback after setback. The Japanese contacts were impossible to work with. A rigid men's club mentality and culture she reasoned were unwilling to embrace the twenty-first century. She sat for a minute to regain her composure.

The trash bins were situated against the wall on the edge of the dining room. She shoved the food cartons in the chute and turned toward the exit.

Chapter 52

TORANOMON HILLS STATION, the nearest subway station, was two stations east to his destination. Jake disembarked at Kasumigaseki and walked to the building.

He called Tanaka who picked up on the second ring.

"Hey."

"That got complex at the InterContinental. An explosion injuring twenty people. The president shot in the arm."

"Vera James pulled the trigger." Jake inhaled a deep breath. "Had I not tackled her he might be dead.

"She killed a secret service agent."

"That was her first shot. The president was next. Did anyone see me?"

"No reports so far. They are still cordoning off and trying to make sense of it all."

"She's good Tanaka. I mean skilled."

"I trust your assessment. Where are you now?"

"Kasumigaseki forecourt."

"Kaito and a specialist undercover team have the perimeter surrounded." He paused. "Do you think she will show?"

"Cannot say for sure. I have got in her way more than once today. She'll be rooting for me in the future." Jake stopped and sat on a bench. "The president won't be showing in person now, will he?"

"He's getting patched up in an unknown location. Might be prudent to conference this one in." Tanaka hesitated. "The Customs official was found in his car. Shot twice."

"I am only surprised at how quick they did it. Talk later." Jake hung up the call.

A large incoming chopper sounded, banking to the right. It hovered over the roof, feet settling. Twelve-fifty P.M. Tanaka confirmed that the Indian President and the Australian Prime Minister were attending despite the chaos at the hotel. Jake decided to sit in the background on this occasion. He rubbed his shoulder. A text alert chimed. He thumbed open the message.

Kaito. The message confirmed that he was on the west side.

Jake replied stating he'd join him soon.

He did a circuit from the east, gave the grounds a wide berth of thirty meters. Undercovers and covert operators were in good numbers. Some were in suits and others in casual attire. So as not to set off any alarms he located Kaito to declare himself present.

Rounding the parkland area, he saw Kaito flanked by two burly guys in suits. At least Kaito wore jeans and a sweater. It gave him a relaxed holidaymaker vibe. Must be taking lessons from Tanaka.

"How's things?" Kaito held out his hand and they shook. He waved at the two burly Japanese guys, "This is Jiro and Sora."

"Not bad all things considered." He nodded at the two guys in suits. "Good to meet you. Any sign of our attackers?"

"So far so good. Security is tight without being too obvious." Kaito gestured at a group of tourists. "We are blending in with the crowds to keep this under control and quiet."

"Nice one. You heard what happened at the InterContinental?" Jake walked with Kaito after he signaled the suits to do laps.

"Explosion and a shootout. The explosion could not be controlled from leaking to the media but the shots are for now."

"The president took a bullet in the arm. Lucky it wasn't the chest. I think he will be a no show here."

"Same people?" Kaito raised an eyebrow.

"The female we caught this morning. She's a really good shot. I chased her into the city but eventually lost her in the crowds. She took a shot at me in public." Jake said.

"Sounds like quite a unit. We need her on our side."

"Not sure who we are dealing with anymore. It's too organized for the usual terror groups and the skills set on some of these people is well above average. Even for mercenaries."

"Maybe the president can phone all his meetings in the future. Too hard keeping him and Tokyo safe."

They rounded the east bend of the building.

"It's one-thirty and no disturbances." Kaito said. "Hope we caught these guys."

A scream echoed from the other side of the perimeter. Jake straightened as Kaito touched his sidearm. A gun shot broke the background traffic noise.

"You spoke too soon." Jake broke to a run. Kaito followed as they barreled past the trees. A group of three men and a woman huddled over a man prone on the pavers.

Kaito reached a guy in a suit, one of the agents Jake saw earlier. He tapped him on the shoulder. "What happened?"

"He was caught with a gun approaching the entrance. Jiro spotted the offender first and tackled him to the ground. He tried to pull the concealed weapon but we had him secured by then." Sora spoke in English for Jake's benefit.

Kaito checked the attacker's clothes for personal items. No ID or cell phone.

Sora led the cuffed man away as onlookers stared and pointed. Jiro had a word to the small gathering in Japanese probably to assure them that the situation was under control.

"I will check the foyer if you want to join me?" Kaito said.

"Sure, let's do it."

The pair entered the sliding glass and slowly monitored the reception area. A small toilet block near the rear required electronic access.

"This is for staff only but worth a walk-in." Kaito unlocked it and they found the cubicles were empty and the urinal. The door locked automatically in their wake.

"Lobby is all clear." Jake said. He and Kaito exited the interior and scanned the forecourt.

At two-thirty a helicopter rose from the roof and glided away from the sun.

"The ministers have departed safely. No further incidents." Jake wondered which ones were present since the catastrophe at the hotel.

"I will round up the men and women here and report to base." Kaito held out his hand. "Thanks for your help today."

Jake took his hand firmly. "You're welcome. Appreciate the backup."

"I hope your president recovers fast."

"Cheers." Jake turned and headed for Shibuya Park.

As he reached the tree line his burner rang.

"Hi Tanaka"

"Hi. We interrogated the man who brought the gun to the building." Tanaka pulled in a breath.

"What did you find?"

"First hour or so, he would not say a thing. Name is Isamu. We left him alone and built up the pressure. Then we sprung some evidence and gave polite threats. He folded under the pressure. Says he is part of a cult. A new branch of Aum Shinrikyo. Their leader was a man named Asahara was executed back in two-thousand-and-eighteen."

"I heard about this guy. Gas attack on the subway nearly three decades ago."

"Correct. Our man Isamu has a long criminal record; been picked up before for weapon charges. Protesting violently. Association with other extremists."

"How did this guy know about a classified dialogue meeting?"

Jake stood under a tree canopy and lowered his voice.

"We have not confirmed this yet."

"I don't buy it."

"What are you thinking?"

"Too convenient. A brain washed cult devotee stumbles onto a building with a highly classified meeting. He's a patsy. Someone set it up and sent him in armed."

"Motive?" Tanaka said.

"To divert attention and place the blame on an obsolete doomsday cult or fringe extremism. Hiding the real motive."

"I see your theory. We will charge him with as much as possible."

"That keeps one more lunatic behind bars."

"What are your plans now?"

"I will wrap things up here and get your gear back to you later today. Do not want to hang around too long."

"Let me know when you're free."

Jake hung up and nodded to the person at reception. He pressed the elevator button and had the cabin to himself. Up in the room he turned the American news channel on. A story on the InterContinental ANA started again on loop. A TV remote sat on the armrest. He collapsed on the couch and increased the volume.

The media report on the English news station confirmed that the US President was shot at a hotel. A second man was killed and believed to be part of the president's security detail. Sources reported an explosion occurred at this location minutes before the attack. Law enforcement are continuing to investigate if the incidents are linked. The perpetrators are unknown and still at large. Witnesses are still to be interviewed and more information as it comes.

A sparrow fluttered its wings and lifted off the balcony. The door clicked behind him as he descended the stairs and came out onto the sidewalk. He arrived at the subway station and boarded a train bound for the InterContinental ANA. The bag of gear he had to retrieve and check out of the room. A chat with McCallister was required and soon, to clarify the assignment with other unanswered questions.

Chapter 53

FIREWORKS CRACKLED AS a kaleidoscope of red and blue shot into the skyline. Jake sat on the third-floor restaurant and watched the spectacular display in the glass. He worked on the vodka. Not a fancy expensive brand, but a good solid one nonetheless. He figured he earnt it after the last few days. Tanaka approached, placed a glass of bourbon on the surface and slid onto the seat opposite.

"Great view."

"It's a festival downtown near the temples."

"You put on quite the light show here in Tokyo." Jake nudged the bag under the table. "Here's the gear. Appreciate the lend."

Tanaka dropped it between his feet. "It's been interesting working with you Perry. You're very resourceful. We could do with more of you here in Tokyo."

"Likewise. I appreciate the honorable conduct and keeping your word. That's a rare trait in this industry." Jake smiled. "But let's not get teary eyed."

Tanaka chuckled. "The humor alone is priceless. In Japan everybody is serious about every topic. I won't ask where to next."

"That's probably best then I don't have to lie. Truth be told I don't know besides home for some rest and relaxation."

A crackle and bang and the room glowed in greens and reds. Jake relished his drink and the atmosphere.

"Sounds nice and well deserved. I need a holiday too after this debacle. One disaster after another."

"You will be fine Tanaka. And probably get bored without the excitement."

They fell silent, enjoyed the moment, a respite from the tumultuous chaos that had engulfed Tokyo.

"I cannot find anything on the female after that chase you had. A shopping mall was the last detection. No more facial recognition anywhere. As if she disappeared into thin air."

"She probably used a facial prosthetic after I lost her. Changed again and applied a different disguise. If it was me, I would have gone straight to the airport and flown out. Can you check cameras surrounding the last place I saw her? Should be around twelve-thirty P.M."

"Yes. What are you thinking?"

"They should pick up someone similar of her height and gait leaving. Check for places like a toilet block in a mall. That is where she would go for privacy to change her clothes."

"Will do."

"Update me on how it goes."

Placing the empty glass on the table Tanaka stood, "Let me know if you are in Tokyo again. Till next time."

Jake shook his hand warmly. Tanaka picked up the bag, turned and sauntered toward the exit in his usual casual style.

In the darkness colors pulsated, explosions of a good kind. He sipped the vodka slowly, thinking about returning to Katerina and the boat. The alcohol burn diminished the ache in his shoulder. Business nearly completed here in Tokyo and unarmed he felt vulnerable.

He thumbed the burner and placed it to his ear.

"Hello."

"It's Sphinx." Jake used his handle.

"Hey there. Congratulations I hear the job is done."

"In a manner of speaking. The president got hit in the arm. Lucky it wasn't the chest. I tackled the shooter which is the only reason he's alive."

"The president at the hotel was a decoy."

"Come again?" Jake's voice cracked on the last syllable.

"After you alerted me, I told my director in Washington of the threat. The Secretary of State and the Secretary of Defense decided to send a decoy. That way we protect the most important person in the free world and flush out the enemy too."

Jake remained silent and let McCallister run with it for a while. He was appalled by McCallister's non-disclosure again but relieved to hear about the president.

"You risked everything including lives and a terror attack?"

"I had to make a call. No two-way about it only shades of gray."

Jake shook his head. "Did the security dialogue happen today with all four leaders?"

"The US President phoned it in from an undisclosed location. If it makes you feel better, they only let me know twelve hours ago."

"It's a mess here in Tokyo. We have an extremist cult group getting the blame for random acts of violence and terror. Not to mention a hotel lobby explosion."

"It's not only the US President's life at stake. They tried to kill the Japanese Prime Minister as well." McCallister's voice faded. "Did you get a name on our terrorist?"

"Vera James. It might be an alias and I'll send you a picture with physical stats. We've made eye contact and I foiled her plans twice in one day."

"Sounds vaguely familiar. I will put this through the wash to see what comes up. She won't forget your face."

"And me hers. Let me know how you go."

"I am transferring the balance of the fee now. Should clear straight away. Thanks again, you've done well."

The airport was surprising light on commuters which highlighted the need for surveillance. Vera James eyed the departure board, checking the nearest flights. She dumped the rifle bag in a locker near Lape's warehouse on the way. A flight that suited her departed in two-and-half hours. She paid cash at the counter for business class and confirmed that she had only carry on.

A quick circuit of the pre-custom zone showed no followers she suspected. The toilets were a good place to corner or expose potential tails. She entered the female one and took note of nearby commuters. Her disguise held up to the harsh LED lights and not overdone. She applied a light pastel colored lipstick. The effect enhanced her olive skin, changed her appearance slightly again.

On exit she scanned her periphery. No repeated passengers or watchers from prior to her bathroom stop. She walked briskly to the custom gates. A line moved quickly to the belts. She took out her tablet and placed it in a tray. The backpack went separately. She took off her shoes and added to a tray. A clear plastic toiletry bag held the makeup, transparent for ease as it entered x-ray examination.

The metal detector did not chime as she walked under. At the other end she collected her belongings off the conveyor belt and returned them to the bag. The attendant waved the backscatter scanner over a man and missed her as she shuttled past.

Her burner rang. Suzuki. She answered. "Yes."

"What happened out there? This is unacceptable."

"An American threw my aim. A trained operative. He was prepared and not part of the secret service." She gathered her thoughts. "In any case, I do not report to you. They have exposed the plot and the players. Cabinet Intel are involved. If I was you, I would lie low for a long time as I am sure this mystery man knows who you are."

Suzuki responded with harsh words in Japanese.

Vera James lowered the burner and terminated the call. She dialed a number from memory and waited for it to pick up.

"Bonjour." Laurent said.

"It's set in place. The American stopped the hit but Suzuki and his cohorts have taken the blame. Wang will be exposed more than ever now the terrorist cloak is lifted." Vera James said. "No one knows about us."

"Invisibility is our biggest strength. Maintain it at all costs." Laurent hesitated. "Wang has the network to identify the American."

"I will keep that relationship alive. I'm disposing of this burner and will make contact again soon."

"Ciao."

She switched the phone off and detached the SIM card. An announcement for late passengers blared over the loudspeakers. People brushed past on either side rushing to their flights. She smashed the card under her shoe heel and threw it in a trash can. With her sleeve she wiped the phone of prints. Up ahead she disposed of the burner in a different spot.

A sign for the business lounges lit up on the wall. She read the list for her chosen carrier. In ninety minutes, her plane would takeoff, jetting her from the jurisdiction of Tokyo. To gain admission she showed her passport and ticket to the lounge staff.

Chapter 54

SUZUKI HAD TO stop himself from throwing his cell phone at the wall. That woman infuriated him from the start. She failed her mission and now he had investors breathing down his neck for results. He took a deep breath. From an overhead shelf he grasped a bottle of nihonshu. Sake. His favorite in times of stress. He poured two fingers high into a tumbler and drank it straight.

One lesson he learned from a mentor long ago. There's always a solution to every dilemma; usually the answer is a small point missed. He perused the glass pane onto the floor. Something about the brown-haired American she mentioned niggled in his mind. He inputted a number and put the phone to his ear.

"Hello." The receiver answered. "Just wait a minute please." Footfall in the background as he walked away to gain privacy.

"Shoot."

"Do you know about an American involved today with Tanaka? Brown hair average height and build. Dressed almost like a tourist."

Sora hesitated to answer. "Why do you ask?"

"Listen Sora I pay you a lot of money for information. Not questions. Do you want me to cut you off?"

"Sorry just asking. Yes, I met a guy today at the Kasumigaseki Building stakeout. He fits that description."

"Where is he staying and for how long?"

"I don't know. He helped with surveillance and got involved at the hotel with the explosion earlier. One of the good guys for sure."

"We need to chase him down immediately."

"Is there a bonus if I can find out?"

"You greedy..." Tanaka rested and inhaled. He said through

gritted teeth. "Yes, if you catch and eliminate him, it's twenty thousand USD on top of your generous retainer. I want results this time."

"He is meeting with Tanaka tonight at seven-thirty P.M. I overheard the conversation. Could be the last time. I will wait outside the venue."

"Good idea. Call me when the task is done."

The second vodka went down Jake's throat more smoothly than the first. He felt naked without a weapon. His burner lay on the table surface and he considered texting Katerina. She'd confirmed her return to the boat on email so he knew she got back safely. He wanted to surprise her though and was torn between the two options.

He swilled the drink and realized he had barley eaten all day. With Vera James at large and various unanswered questions about the attacks he sensed unfinished business. He wondered how much Vera knew about him if at all. Their eyes met as he tackled her to save the president. A waiter stopped by the table and indicated whether he would like another. He shook his head.

One final sip and he headed to the elevator. On ground floor Jake exited the building. Outside a breeze kicked, he shoved his hands in his pockets. He noticed a man's figure in a suit across the road. A man in a suit in Tokyo wasn't unusual but the mannerisms were noticeable. As if trying too hard to be occupied.

Walking in the opposite direction he used shop reflections as mirrors. The man followed at the same pace, pretending to stare ahead. Jake let him tail for the next block. He knew up ahead the next lights were a major crossroad.

The intersection spread fifty feet away, glowed under a mirage of neon. He maintained an even pace, as if to not realize the guy was shadowing. The pedestrian signal changed to a green light. He stalled for a moment and turned out of sight. His follower might panic and rush, alerting Jake and impossible to ignore.

He tracked the buildings under the street lights. Shooting a weapon in public with witnesses would not be wise. The alleys and lanes trailed off regularly. He waited for a narrow one with numerous obstacles and rubbish bins. Plenty of alcoves for concealment. The two-story building ended with a gap; an L-shaped right angle that tapered to the intersecting road. He trailed the space past a stack of discarded cardboard boxes. Footfall sounded behind as the man entered the lane.

Steam tailed into the air from a wall vent. He took a right and assessed the spot for ambush positions. A row of recessed doorways lay ahead, Jake slipped into the middle one. The rustle of the suit moving as he came on the same path. He heard the man breathing as he rushed past Jake's position.

Jake stepped out of the archway. Two feet separated the men.

"Hey looking for me?"

"What?" the man twisted and Jake saw Sora, Kaito's agent at the building. Sora clenched his fists, a pretense for attack.

In a flash Jake stepped forward within the man's personal space and elbowed Sora in the nose.

Sora cried out, touched his face. Neck cranked he stumbled but recovered quickly.

Jake moved from striking range. "So, you're dirty."

"I can explain." Sora held out his palms. The other hand clutched his temple. He staggered away to give himself thinking time. Jake moved in as he was unarmed and needed to stay within his guard. They were about the same height but Saro had more bulk.

"Why are you following me?"

"I had too." Sora's elbow moved as his right hand slipped to his jacket. A service revolver.

Jake angled into Sora and snapped a short kick. The right knee joint cracked with a sickening sound. The burly agent screamed and collapsed to the ground.

"I could have gone harder. Smashed your joint completely." He circled around Sora as he writhed in pain. "That really hurts."

He positioned behind the man and pulled Sora into a choke hold. "Tell me who ordered you to tail me. It wasn't Tanaka."

"I won't." Sora gasped for air. "I cannot. What they would do to me."

Jake's forearm squeezed the windpipe, head forced against his chest. "That's a shame. Pity to die over such a thing."

"You can't, I am an agent. You are a foreign visitor."

"I do not care about small semantics. Do you think that will stop me?"

Sora stayed silent as Jake continued to apply pressure.

"Please don't kill me." Sora's face turned crimson as he managed to rasp the words.

"If you help me, I am happy to leave you just unconscious."

"Yes. Yes." Sora tried to nod.

Relaxing the grip, Jake released his hold enough to let him gasp for air.

Sora held up an arm signaling to catch his breath. His chest expanded as he gained his bearings. He sat in a squat position inhaling and exhaling. Suddenly Sora sprung backwards, ramming the top of his head at Jake's chin. The move was bold and savage with a lot of weight and impetus.

Jake saw it coming, sidestepped and with the momentum swung Sora ninety degrees. He had Sora in the same perspective and standing above him.

"I did warn you. Now we do it the hard way."

He resumed the choke hold from a squat position for enhanced leverage. Using his right arm, Jake tightened the strangle so the carotids were pinched shut at the front by his forearm and his bicep at the back. Sora gasped and tried to poke Jake in the eyes but he was out of reach.

The struggle became weaker and less effective. Jake let him fall unconscious. He laid the body prone facing upward. Sora lay peacefully. He applied enough force so as not to do any brain damage.

A search of his jacket and Jake found two phones. Neither had passwords or lock combinations. The first one had contacts including Tanaka's number. He opened the second one. One number in the received and sent calls.

He pressed the call button and listened to the ring.

"Yes, what is it: did you get him?" Suzuki sounded breathless, panting into the microphone. Jake recognized the voice.

"Hi Suzuki how have you been? You sound preoccupied up there. Important trip? Your man Sora is a little tied up right now."

Silence on the line only fireworks crackled in the skies. He waited for the reply. Suzuki finally said, "What do you want?"

"The attack failed and you have a dirty agent try kill me. Not the best of days."

"I can get to you by someone more reliable. We know your face." Suzuki whispered harshly into the phone.

"Really? Two agents have attempted in past twenty-four hours alone and I am still here."

"We will see."

"This is stimulating and I'd love to chat more but I have a ride to catch."

Jake hung up. He used his burner and called Tanaka.

"Hey Perry, did not think you would be calling so soon."

"Neither did I. Listen I have your man Sora lying in an alley. He tailed me from the restaurant tonight. I confronted him and he tried pulling his weapon. Not sure if he was shadowing or planning to kill me."

"Did not see this coming. Sora had me fooled."

"I separated his weapon and he is unconscious with a wrecked knee. An ambulance for sure. You need to organize the scene and collect him as I am not hanging around."

"What else do you know?" Tanaka said.

"He's been on the Lape informant payroll and funneling information to Suzuki. Working a second burner phone. That must be how they knew dates, times, and venues for the dialogue meetings." Jake drew breath. "I called the most recent number in his burner and got Suzuki. We had a little chat which became tense. Send a team into Lape's warehouse as he might flee anytime."

"Thanks, your help has been invaluable."

"Goodluck. I feel a mountain of paperwork coming your way." Jake peered down the street from the mouth of the alley. Headlamps and brake lights formed a flickering two-way chain of yellow and red. "The traffic is increasing."

Tanaka laughed. "Yes, but there will be solid arrests and evidence which I like. I am in the car now."

"I am throwing this burner when I leave Tokyo. To popular for this city. Will let you know when I do it. You can contact me on the email I used in case of emergencies."

"Got it. Take care."

Jake texted the location of Sora. He waited another three minutes and started off toward his hotel.

Chapter 55

SUZUKI WAITED AS files transferred to a portable drive. His heart beat rose as he scanned the office for incriminating physical evidence. Maybe the American bluffed as payback for the attempted attack. He swallowed another finger of nihonshu. The taste was bitter and harsh, perhaps in reflection of his current dilemma. His temple hammered with a killer headache. They would not send regular police to arrest him.

"Are you up there?" Minato's voice carried to the room.

Suzuki rounded the desk and stumbled onto the landing. Minato's sleeves were rolled up and his tie missing; uncharacteristically disheveled.

"Where have you been? I left a message one hour ago."

"Been busy with a personal matter. What's the big rush?"

"Sora has been caught by his employers. His Commanding Officer at the agency knows everything." A bead of sweat ran down Suzuki's brow and he swiped it with a backhand.

"Damn. We need to clear out of here."

"What do you think I am doing?" Suzuki shoved the laptop in a bag. "I am heading to the private jet and flying tonight. The pilot is ready to go and waiting."

Minato powered up the stairs. He had a computer in the adjoining room to Suzuki. Thrusting the door open he pulled the device from the power socket and rammed it in a carry bag. He gripped a cardboard box and loaded loose files and paperwork. The drawers were mainly rubbish but he rifled in each one. Loose papers scattered on the flooring as he dug to the bottom.

"How did they put it together?"

"That American we brought to Elites Ginza. He's not an IT

consultant, rather working with intelligence and law enforcement. I don't know what skin he's got in this besides his president's security but he's connected."

"This is crazy." Minato strained with the weight of the items. "I am going to take these away and come back."

Suzuki nodded, too absorbed in the getaway cleanup to listen properly.

Minato balanced his box and carried it downstairs to his car trunk. He loaded the personal effects in and slammed the hatch. The start button fired up with his foot on the brake pedal. The window lowered as headlamps revealed the lane stripes. He drove slow at thirty through the service area.

The computer chimed. Suzuki shoved a file in the box. He yanked the power cord from the wall socket and packed it in as well. A simple accelerant to set fire to the place could solve his problems. The idea rattled in his mind gaining popularity with his increasingly irrational thoughts. A realization hit that it lacked all merit and sanity. He grabbed his stuff and raced to the stairs.

Traffic signals flashed as the driver blinkered to the right lane. Tanaka sat in the front passenger seat of the lead Toyota SUV. The car led a team of three vehicles, sluicing the evening traffic. Fireworks started to ramp more volume, the masses enroute in a different part of the city. He watched a crane soar above the sheds, lit up like a giant praying mantis, the shipping container load swung from its chain.

The car weaved to the shoulder and into Tokyo's main port entrance. At the booth Tanaka displayed his badge at the duty guard and the boom gate lifted. Rows of warehouses with roller doors flickered in the bobbing headlamps. The storage lots vanished into the shadows. Branded signs blinking in the dark. According to the GPS the location was a larger complex of office and warehousing in the rear section of the compound.

The team formed a single file, taking a right bend and continuing straight for two meters. A dead end loomed ahead, capped with a triple level warehouse. The roller door down but a side access ajar. One car parked out the front which Tanaka identified as the managing director of Lape.

Darkness moved to form a silhouette. Suzuki.

"That's it over there." Tanka pointed to their left. Light shone from an upstairs window.

The fleet braked and created a triangle with Tanaka at the point. A lone figure clutched an armful of boxes and belongings. He squinted at the surrounding beams aimed at his position.

"Haruto Suzuki?" It was more a statement than a question. He had the man's file and police record balanced on the dashboard.

The man's lips moved but no audible noise came forth. A slight nod. Tanaka interpreted that as a yes.

"Put down the items and place your hands out where we can see them."

Suzuki positioned his load on the ground and held his arms in the air.

A quiet train carriage with majority vacant seats carried Jake two stops to Kasumigaseki station. The crowds must be enjoying the festival fireworks from an elevated viewing position not stuck underground on public transport. At least he could confirm there were no tails currently. A pleasant and unusual relief. That might change at any moment.

He stepped onto the platform and walked up the stairwell. The air mixed with a faint tinge of gunpowder. Electricity danced in the air as excited couples and families walked past enjoying the evening's entertainment. The city never sleeps.

The concrete steps were heavy under his feet, or perhaps a weariness overcame him. He lay on the couch with the laptop balanced on his chest. Flights to Singapore went every twelve to fifteen hours. The next one was at eight-twenty A.M. tomorrow morning.

His burner vibrated in his pocket.

"Hello."

"McCallister here. How's it going?"

"Fine."

"I did a check on our female friend. Deeply classified; had to pull a favor or two to get this across the line. The CIA are a secretive bunch at the best of times. You'd think we were not on the same team."

"What did you uncover?"

"Vera James is a non-official cover operative for the CIA. Or was is more accurate. She went native two months ago after a stella career in the field. She brought down more arms dealers and terrorists than most of the men. They are still not sure what turned her rogue. So undercover they had to wait to confirm her status before doing a search. You sure can pick your enemies."

"Any other information that could give me clues?" Jake said.

"Half a department of pencil-pushing bureaucrats has been searching for this female's location. Disguises, makeup, different accents. Facial prosthetics to beat recognition and even changes her gait sometimes. She'd been making up her own assignments on occasion but brilliant and resourceful."

"Probably contracting to the highest bidder. A Japanese terrorist with a few hundred million up your sleeve. It gives a lot flexibility."

"That is my line of thought."

"What is her cultural background?"

"Not much in her file on that either. Her mother was American but we believe half Chinese. She separated from her biological father when she was two years old. We believe he was first generation American with European roots. The man that became her step father was an American citizen and enlisted. He had a lot of influence on her in the early years."

"She's left Tokyo. The gravy train here has run out. Secret service is about to arrest the key players."

"Thanks to you."

"Makes me think she's working for a bigger outfit. I don't think she answers to the Japanese. A partnership with a foreign source."

"So not just local. Makes sense. Hopefully she's off the grid for now. Licking her wounds and answering to the person who gave out the orders."

"I'm leaving Tokyo in the next twenty-four hours. I will toss this burner."

"How can I reach you?"

"No more contracts for now McCallister. Consider me retired."

"If it's an emergency, can I at least put it to you obligation free?"

Jake did not want contractors stalking his boat again and kill people in the line of his own security.

"That email I used to send you information. But do not send contractors if I don't answer McCallister or next time the price will be your life."

"Understood. Till next time."

Jake lay down the burner and considered ordering food on room service. He dialed the number and spoke to the kitchen. A special on salmon penne caused his stomach to grumble. The meal came with a side salad and he added a serve of bruschetta.

The ink black sky popped and crackled with fireworks still. He stood and admired the show from the balcony. For some reason he procrastinated about booking the flight. His assailant Vera James would have fled the city in the afternoon soon after he lost her.

His shoulder flared up again, aching in the middle. He rubbed it tenderly and rotated it to relieve the pain. The burner rang and he read the screen. Tanaka's number came up.

"Hello again."

"I have something you might want to know. After the aid you provided me in the last few days it's the least I can offer. Also, to continue the intel sharing process."

"Great thanks."

"Since the arrest an hour ago we hacked into Suzuki's hard drive. There is a lot of communication in emails to various parties. Our analysts are examining as we speak. One of which is to a Chinese MSS agent. Ministry of State Security. We have a profile on this agent and been gathering intel from various sources for over a year."

"Suzuki is in league with the Chinese rather than a terrorist?" Jake nearly dropped the burner.

"This is a very strong indictor. We are building a case for international espionage to add to Suzuki's other offences." Tanaka cleared his throat. "His radical agenda opposes the Japanese Prime Minister. We knew that already and this is hard evidence of colluding with foreign enemies and espionage."

"China is hindering the security dialogue. It seeks to usurp their power and growing dominance over the Pacific region. The US alliance with India, Australia, and Japan is one of China's biggest obstructions. They wanted us to think it was terrorists. Hence the connection to Suzuki."

"Correct. And why they have gone to so much trouble to engage in terror activities. There is more. In the drive we found emails to Vera James routed to Chinese government servers. Sensitive information about Tokyo ports and access. Inspections and names of custom officials. Copies of federal documents. Suzuki attempted to wipe data off his system recently."

"She's contracting to China or defected outright and they would pay a fortune for her skills and knowledge." Jake exhaled. "All this time we have been fighting China. They are hellbent on dominating the world. It connects the dots perfectly and now you have the proof."

"It is cause for concern when they can get prominent Japanese citizens such as Suzuki and infiltrate the country at this level. Given his history with the environment and radical views makes him a soft target." Tanaka sighed.

"The enemy of my enemy is my friend. They executed like terrorists and nearly got away with it. Very well planned and implemented."

"But they ultimately failed. This time. Our team worked the cameras in that mall as you asked and they discovered her movements. She did it in the toilet block like you suggested. Completely different and marched right out again. Beats facial recognition. A real chameleon. They picked up her trail outside. She hailed a cab straight from the street and took a roundabout route to check for shadows. We tracked her to the other airport and she travelled business class to Hong Kong under another passport. Smart to cut her loses and leave quickly. I am sure she will try using Chinese intel resources to ID you."

"For sure Tanaka. Part of the job description."

"Don't I know it."

"Thanks again for the intel update. This gives me a lot more to work with." Jake said.

"Least I can do considering your aid in this matter." Tanaka hesitated. "These arrests are from your tenacious work. Not to mention the explosion at the InterContinental. Potential to be much worse."

"We are an effective team Tanaka and I enjoyed working with you. Stay safe until next time."

"Never can tell."

Jake dropped the phone to his hip.

Chapter 56

THE FAMILIAR SMELL of Hong Kong hit Vera James. A blend of traffic fumes, fast food, and a dense population living in cramped conditions. She asked directions from a small elderly woman who threw up her hands. The tiny shops bunched tightly together continued to the corner. She ignored the noise and focused on the mailboxes. A grocer stepped in her path and offered fruit. She waved him away and forged toward her destination. Both parties agreed Hong Kong was considered neutral territory. Pedestrians rushed either direction of the sidewalk. Traffic lights flashed overhead, she paused at an intersection, read a sign mounted on a bent pole. The grime covered half of the letters.

On the green signal she crossed the road and veered right. Painted shop fronts advertised products and services. She sidled the street searching for the address numbers. Her GPS showed it right in front. The wall was busy with stickers and advertisements she could not spot the original tiles underneath. Between a greengrocer and a suit shop, she sought concrete steps that led upward. She stared up at an open window, drapes fluttered in the breeze.

A narrow corridor followed as she stepped to the landing. She disliked these slum locations but the Chinese secret service insisted on choosing them. They figured no one would think to find them there. With all the limited dense living space and noise, eavesdropping became impossible.

She found a grimy door at the end marked 'accountant.' The handle turned as she pushed into the room.

A small Chinese man with a comb over sat in an old swivel chair behind a desk. "Sit please." He gestured at the only seat. A worn leather cushion base with hard arm rests. The room was bare except for the occupied furniture. On the desk surface a small electric fan pushed air onto his face. She dropped neatly in the seat and faced the assistant director of Chinese intelligence. MSS. She knew him as Wang.

"We may no longer have plausible deniability on this incident. This was a major directive in the assignment." He clasped his hands flat to form a triangle on the desk and rested his chin. "We hoped for a better outcome although I understand the limitations of our partners."

"Suzuki got in my way more than once. The Japanese agency had help from an American. A bullet I fired was inches away from the president's heart. I hate missing. I really hate making excuses." She gained her composure. "I need a match on a guy with brown hair. Five-ten. Average features and build but distinctive dark blue eyes."

Wang stared in a dimension seen only by him. "I rang our data people. The team scoured every system and database worldwide and came up with a few viable matches. After scrutinizing them one has the highest probability. I agree with their opinion after viewing the top three as well."

"Which one?" She tried not to sound too eager. "Do you have a picture?"

The assistant director diverted his eyes to the display. He clicked the mouse and angled the screen one-eighty degrees to face her. "Taken five years ago but I am told he hasn't aged in any major way since. Is this the man you saw?"

She grasped the table edge to lean into the photo. The hair looked right and a mask obscured the mouth and lips. Eyes were dark blue like the ocean at dusk. "That's him."

Wang leaned back and clasped his hands behind his head. His robotic expression remained the same regardless of the emotion.

"We suspect this operator was in Russia six months ago. A major catastrophe unfolded from a political conspiracy. Our allies were severely affected; a major setback for the trade of certain resources and arms. Underworld figures were shot. A veteran colonel allegedly fired two missiles in a residential zone. The media had a field day. Naturally. This event led to an oligarch and colonel fleeing the country. The world was exposed, via this individual's work, to an international cartel trade of weapons and uranium."

"I heard a bit about this." She sat upright. "But nothing

296

conclusive."

"This agent you pinpointed is single-handedly responsible for that disaster. He thwarted our attempts to secure the witness."

She nodded.

"This man fought in Afghanistan. Highly decorated. Most is classified even at the highest level. Five years ago, entered DoD intelligence and became a ghost. Completely off the books. Some say NSA contractor and moved on but nothing confirmed. The rumors are unreliable and inconsistent. He was reported dead two years ago by allied intel. Went native again from the effects of trauma. Thought to be retried or an external contractor. Then he popped up in Saint Petersburg." The chair squeaked and he held his hands in the air, the first sign of emotion. "My president wants our office to find him. Cost and resources are no issue."

"What is the pay on it?"

"Negotiable. Now this has happened it will be big. Really big. They want him caught and captured or worst-case scenario killed. Taken out of action. Preferably the former so we can interrogate him. Half a million plus expenses would be sellable."

The assignment tempted her beyond belief. She could take revenge on the man that caused the biggest and only failure of her career. But he was skilled like no other she had ever seen. He tracked her when the Japanese secret service could not. China provided massive intel resources at her disposal. She was torn. Every assignment she accepted drew her further into their web. It was like being institutionalized. A dictatorship big brother control from which escape or exit became increasingly impossible. The China regime rattled her and she really wanted to cut all ties. It felt like dependency. Their government tried to make drug addicts of the world. The same control they exert over the Pacific and Taiwan. No wonder there was a growing fertility issue in China with the current generation. Young couples opting out of starting a family. Preferring to be DINKs; double income and no kids. Who would want to be raised in their society?

She vowed after her school days in a strict private school she would never be brain washed again.

Ever.

A free agent who chose her own assignments and beholden to no one.

Wang sat silently gazing at his terminal. Sounds from the hectic traffic below reached the room despite the closed door. The little fan buzzed, doing little to relieve the stuffiness. Normally he would not give her past this meeting to decide on the contract. She could use the indecision on the money as an excuse to stall. Think it over at least for a few hours.

Finally, she replied. "I need a number on the money before I can give you an answer."

"I can have it for you within two hours." He did not blink or turn his head.

"Fine I'll wait around below till you confirm." She felt the irresistible pull of a challenge. A worthy opponent entered her sphere for next level combat. Wavering between helping herself and hating China she sought excuses to avoid this contract. If the money came in low, she'd say no straight away. If they offered an irresistible bounty, she'd ask for a deposit of half up front.

Until it became so good, she accepted the terms. Setting herself up for a trap.

"I will text you." Wang's voice floated out the door.

She descended the stairs and evaluated the restaurant menu taped on the glass. The numerous patrons feasted on a yum cha dining experience. Trays moved between aisles, servers offered bamboo steamer baskets of dim sims and other culinary treats.

For Hong Kong the place was popular with locals. Always a good sign.

A waiter ushered her inside and she pointed at a small table by the window. Opposite the entrance to spot all new customers. The first round of cuisine came immediately, happy to have her consuming quickly. She chose a seafood prawn basket and a chicken dumpling. A woman poured green tea from a jug into her cup. The waitress picked the pencil and ticked the items on her bill and replaced the paper on the spread. A trio of staff gave numerous nods and smiles as the help reversed away from the table.

Vera chewed and watched the organized chaos. Trolleys swept from the kitchen onto the floor, narrowly missing one coming the other direction. A large round table with three generations had a raised wheel in the center. Ten dishes rotated as the youngest of the family crawled under the table giggling. People talked and ate and the volume in the place rose. She concentrated on the meal and her discussion with Wang.

The food provided sustenance as she didn't feel that hungry. She sipped the green tea and agonized over a decision should the payday be good. Chances were the offer superseded any she had going currently. She put the fork in her mouth. A waiter offered another dish but she refused. She did not want a full stomach to make this decision. A child from the nearby table crawled under her leg. The boy made faces at her from under the table cloth. A parent scurried to rescue him, apologizing as she tugged the boy's arm.

Her cell phone beeped. Wang. She opened the message.

Six-hundred thousand USD. Half up front. Resources from central command if required.

She finished her meal and drained the tea cup. At the counter she paid the bill. Staff nodded and smiled again. She preferred a meet over texting but did not feel like another face to face so soon. On the sidewalk she called his number.

"Wang here."

"What else do you have on him?"

"His handle was Sphinx when he worked for the NSA. I need an answer in five minutes. They might change their mind on the rate."

His pushy attitude frustrated her but it was a huge payday to retire her biggest competitor.

"I will be up in four minutes with an answer."

Chapter 57

THE BUSINESS LOUNGE had started to thin as Jake fell into an arm chair. His back and shoulder ached. He tossed the burner in a trash can outside, five minutes before he entered the Tokyo airport grounds. The SIM card had been taken out and the phone broken up under his foot. It always gave him both elation and isolation to again be without a cell phone. In the modern tech world cell phones were disposal but it still did not shake the emotion. Perhaps he wanted to be a normal average Joe for once and not have to plan and strategize every detail to the nth degree. Keep the same number for a year or two or ten so old friends could call. Instead, he always watched his back and was suspicious of motives. Surveillance upon countersurveillance.

He meditated on this as planes glided past the glass pane on his left. Easy to slip into his mantra seated in a comfortable position and alone with his thoughts. The pleasant wave in his system eradicated negative thought and stress. The few minutes spent here and there brought him balance and peace. An announcement jarred him back to the room but in a refreshed state.

A variety of food and drink was available and on display. He strolled to the cold section and picked a cold imported beer from the fridge. It soothed his throat as he examined the sterility of airports. One level up from hospital whitewashed walls, uniforms and all the linen covering the beds.

The scheduled flight arrived at five-thirty A.M. He texted Mia to let her know he was coming after getting her number from Katerina when this debacle started. From Changi airport to the docks, he estimated a thirty-minute ride. He had no checked-in luggage so straight to customs which may still take thirty minutes or longer depending on the queues. He wanted to give Katerina a surprise when he stepped onto the bay, their boat in his sights, water lapping on the hull.

His stomach gave him butterflies thinking about a reunion. He missed her but was plagued again by the risks and threats that came with his job. More specifically how they affect loved ones. Could she cope with his lifestyle? At any moment he could be attacked or shot and she in the firing line. Collateral damage.

An inflight movie played starring the Rock and another action star. His seat laid horizontal and he fell asleep. In the dream he saw Katerina on a distant beach, out of reach. A forest of thick trees populated a remote island. He called her name over and over. Waved frantically to get her attention. Her face was drawn, still beautiful but missing happiness. He knew something had happened. It was his fault she was alone.

Jake stirred under the blanket. The blue glow of the TV monitor made him squint. Lights were off in the cabin as the passengers rested. He trundled to the bathroom to freshen up. The dream concerned him as he buzzed his seat to an upright position. A flight attendant brought him scrambled eggs, mushrooms, and toast for breakfast. He chewed pensively lacking in sleep and a little dazed.

In autopilot he trailed the wave of people to the escalators. He bypassed the conveyor belts exited the sliding doors.

"Where too?" A cab driver asked in English.

"The docks, thanks."

He opened the door and slid in the back seat. A blue sky radiated ahead and the dawn sun pierced the skyline.

The cab sliced toward the city streets. They emerged over a rise to see the blue ocean ahead. The familiar sight of the Marina Bay Sands soared to the south. He pushed the bad dream on the plane aside, mulling on the positives. The assignment from McCallister had been completed. If more came up, he'd refuse point plank. His most important task was to relax and be with Katerina. Be in the moment, live in the present.

"What part of the dock do you want to go?" the driver angled his head.

Jake told him the bay number situated in the north end. The driver nodded and cruised at a low speed. Seagulls dipped and glided over the water, seeking food scraps and other discarded edible treats. A car followed leaving a gap of three meters.

"Slow down a bit I want to check this car behind."

"Sure. I think it's an elderly couple."

The car drove close almost touching fenders. Jake saw the tops of their heads. Both gray.

Jake watched in the mirror until the reflection came off their windshield. "You are right. Elderly couple."

Always on alert.

At the next right the car blinkered left.

"There's the entrance." The driver pointed at the landing gap.

"Thanks." He paid the man in cash and lifted his bag from the trunk.

The walkways were inundated with groups of people. A jogger sped past as Jake wheeled his bag onto the path. Water spread in a brilliant blue beyond the moored boats, ripples dappling into the horizon. Planks of timber alternated to concrete as he walked. He checked the sign. It pointed right to a section he remembered mooring it too when he came to shore. The surprised first interaction with McCallister twenty meters south.

He continued northwest anticipating seeing Katerina after so many weeks. She'd been in Syria for two weeks before the assassins intruded onto their boat. The sun warmed his back in his wake, reflecting off the silver boat parts. He took the sea air into his lungs like it was the first time. How he missed it if only for a short period of time.

In the distance he spotted the sail of their yacht. A slight tremor in his chest as he neared. What if she has doubts about their relationship and safety? He had not thought if she formed the same concerns as him. Afterall helping her in Saint Petersburg did not obligate her to stay with him forever. Especially now with Vera James out there somewhere wanting revenge.

On the bridge a blond figure straightened. He quickened his

pace, the wheels jumping on the rough path. Only one way to solve his doubts.

Four boats separated him from his home. She turned in his direction, an elbow bent at her forehead to shield the glare. He waved an arm and she observed him. The realization must have hit as she hopped on the spot. She scrambled for the stairs as he rounded the last section of jetty.

"Jake." She called from the hull.

"Katerina." He let go of the bag handle. Broke into a jog. All doubt about safety and fears evaporated. A weight lifted from his chest as the future became clearer.

Her feet bounced on the gang plank. She jumped off the end and landed onto the concrete. Backlit by the sun, her silhouette like a mirage. He squinted and rushed to meet her. Arms outstretched he embraced her, filled with optimism for the future.

Book Three in the
Ties That Bind Series

by
Fay Lamb

Write Integrity
Press

Hope

Write Integrity Press
Hope
© 2017 Fay Lamb

ISBN-13: 978-1-944120-32-0
ISBN-10: 1-944120-32-7
E-Book ISBN: 978-1-944120-35-1

 Published by Write Integrity Press
PO Box 702852
Dallas, TX 75370
Find out more about the author, Fay Lamb,
at her website, **www.FayLamb.com**
www.WriteIntegrity.com
Printed in the United States of America.

Dedication

This story is dedicated to those who have fought the battle against breast cancer. Treatment plans may differ, and each experience is diverse, but your bravery is absolute, for no matter how scary the journey you did not ask to walk, you marched forward into the uncertain, you planned for the future, and you became a beacon to others you have gone before. Whether you survived or lost the fight, you are and were heroes extraordinaire.

Hope

Acknowledgements

Tracy Ruckman and Marji Laine are owed the gratitude of so many. They took chances on several unknown authors, of which I am one, and they brought our stories to life.

Thank you, ladies, for your faith in those who needed a place for their voices.

I know that they give God the glory, but I am so glad that He used both of these women in the writing lives of so many.

Hope

1

Hope donned the hospital gown, attempting to follow the instructions given to her by the technician. What arm went where, and what wrapped around what?

By the time she figured it out and stowed her clothes in the locker-style cabinet, she was certain someone would be looking for her. She turned the key and pulled it from the lock, carrying it with her to the room where she'd been told to return. She hadn't needed to worry. The room was full of women waiting for their own mammograms.

Making sure she tucked the gown under her, she sat and looked at the other ladies awaiting their turn. Each had graying hair. Even the youngest was well past her last dye job.

Hope was too young for this. At twenty-eight, she shouldn't be worrying about breast cancer. She'd get this over with. She was silly to expect it to be anything but pain from exertion. The lumps …? Well, she didn't have a medical degree. Still, there had to be a good reason.

Fiddling with the key, she turned it over, avoiding eye contact with the women about to face the same ordeal. One by one, a technician called the others until Hope was left alone. Her hand holding the key trembled.

An elderly woman entered the room and walked toward her. "Hello, honey. How are you this morning?" She sat in the chair beside Hope.

"Nervous," Hope admitted. "I don't know anything about the procedure."

"Oh, darling, the first thing you should know is it isn't a procedure. It's a test. It can be a little uncomfortable, but all you need to do is remind yourself that it will all be over soon, and breathe—except when they tell you not to." A sweet smile graced the woman's face, and she gave the slightest wink.

"You've had a mammogram?" Hope looked beyond the silver wire-framed glasses that blended well with the woman's beautiful hair of the same color.

"Oh, a few times. Once a year whether I want to or not. My doctor's insistence most likely saved my life."

"Then you've had …" Her lips quivered. Thinking of the word frightened her. Saying it was unthinkable.

"Yes, I have." The woman placed her hand over Hope's, and the marked warmth caused Hope to shiver against the cold. "And look at me." The woman smiled. "I'm a survivor. There may be times when you think you're not going to make it through, but you will." She gave Hope's hand a squeeze. "But there are many reasons for a mammogram, and not all of them end with a diagnosis of cancer."

"I'm so scared. I—I've had this soreness …" Hope swallowed back the terror rising in her. "And I did a self-exam. Then the doctor …" She was blubbering, spilling her all-consuming fear upon a woman she'd never met. The key she clenched dug into her hand.

"If you weren't worried or afraid, would you be here today?" She released Hope's hand with a small pat, and Hope loosened her hold on the key.

She shook her head and lowered her gaze. Her reddish-blond hair fell over her eyes.

The woman pushed it back from her face. "The Lord, He gives us good sense, and when that fails us, He uses our emotions to get us to react."

"But I'm too young." Somehow, those words had become Hope's mantra for today.

"See there. Your brain is telling you one thing, and your fear—your emotion—has made you react regardless. You're here, and you're making sure. That's all. You take one day at a time. One small step. Don't look to the end. Look to the Lord. No one knows what's coming around the corner, but He does. Whatever the outcome, if you know Him, you'll be fine." She placed her hand against Hope's cheek. Then she stood. "I'll be praying for you, dear." She left the same way she'd entered.

The technician held open a door. "Hope Astor."

Hope stood and moved toward her but stopped. The lady said she'd pray for her, but she never asked Hope for her name. "There was an older woman here. She just left. She was so sweet. I don't think she was here for the proce—test."

The technician smiled. "Seems you've met our Ms. Anne. She only speaks with special people."

"She said she'd pray for me, but she didn't get my name."

The technician beckoned for Hope to follow her. "Believe me. If Ms. Anne talked to you, she's knocking at God's door for you right now."

Hope shivered, and this time the cold wasn't the cause. What had Ms. Anne seen that made her feel she needed to approach God on Hope's behalf?

She followed the technician into the small, stark room. A tall rectangular box with what looked like the top of a giant's wrench attached to it stood against one wall. Hope stared at two clamp-like shelves.

In the other corner was a room with a curved wall. A large, tinted Plexiglas window sat in the middle of the wall like a giant eye surveying the starkness outside.

"Hope, I'm Mandy. I'm sorry I didn't introduce myself before. It's been a busy morning."

"I understand."

"Can I get you to step to the mark on the floor and slip the right side of your gown off your shoulder?"

Hope hesitated.

Mandy put her hands on Hope's shoulders and guided her. "Just let it slip off this side." She busied herself moving the clamps.

As instructed, Hope pushed the gown off of her shoulder. She closed her eyes. Heat seared her cheeks. Funny, once upon a time, she hadn't been this bashful. How many men—?

No. She wasn't going there. God didn't want her dwelling on the sins of the past. Her friend, Libby, who waited in the lobby, would sure give Hope an earful if she knew Hope had slipped back into those thoughts. Libby was right. Hope needed to move forward.

Mandy touched Hope's covered shoulder, and Hope jumped.

"It's better if you relax. This is how it works. Your breast will be placed in between these two plates. I'll leave you and go into the room there. I'll ask you to be very still and to hold your breath. You'll hear some clicks as the mammogram is taken. We'll do several views of both breasts. When we're done, I'll have you wait while I make sure the views are readable. We may or may not have to do another take or two, but my record is pretty good as long as the patient listens and relaxes."

Hope took a deep breath and wiggled her shoulders. "I'll try."

Mandy guided her up against the machine and maneuvered Hope into position. The clamp closed down, and Hope winced. Her breasts had been tender for months. She'd also noticed a purplish tint to them. If the right side hurt, the left side was sure to make her scream. She should have realized long before now that the pain was caused by more than the exertion of painting the new church. That had occurred a month ago. After the church's celebration of their first Sunday in their new building, the energy seemed to drain from her little by little, and the pain never went away.

Though Hope prided herself for a high tolerance for discomfort, she bit her tongue to keep from crying out with each change in position. Mandy was careful, talking her through each stage and each crushing clamp, telling her when to breathe and when to hold her breath. Hope clung to Ms. Anne's words. The ordeal would be over soon.

Mandy declared they were done for the moment, and Hope slipped the gown onto her shoulders, hugging her arms against her body. While Mandy checked the views, Hope stared at the torture device.

"Okay, Hope. We're done." Mandy walked with her to the door. You can change. Leave your gown on the bench."

"Did you see anything?" Hope wrung her hands. "Anything I should be worried over?"

"The doctor will talk to you." Mandy held the door.

Hope crossed the room where Ms. Anne had offered her such sweet encouragement and into the dressing area. She changed quickly but sat for a few minutes on the bench. "Lord, thank You for Ms. Anne. I know you sent her to me. Please be with that dear woman, and I pray for the opportunity to tell her thank you."

Opening the door to the outside hall, Hope allowed the door to close and smiled at the biggest encourager in her life. "Libby, you could have waited in the main lobby. You didn't have to stand out here the whole time."

Libby Carter tilted her head and smiled. "I wanted to be close. I knew you were nervous."

"Well, a delightful elderly woman came into the waiting room when I was alone. She sat and talked to me, said she'd be praying for me. The technician said her name was Ms. Anne."

Down the corridor, a man dropped some papers. As they floated to the floor, Hope met his cobalt gaze. "Danny," she whispered. He was a physician, likely to be here this early doing his rounds. Still, she had hoped not to run into him today. Too much had come between them, and she didn't expect any kindness from Dr. Daniel Duvall.

Danny ran a hand through his black hair then bent to pick up what he'd dropped.

Mandy opened the door. "Hope, I've talked to the radiologist. We're going to have the films and the report sent to Dr. Ramesh this afternoon. If she doesn't call you, please make an appointment as soon as possible."

Hope looked first to Danny, who turned away from her. Then she looked to Libby. What would she do if the news wasn't good? She had very little money left. For weeks, she'd been too tired to run a brush stroke over canvas let alone prepare to paint. She couldn't even think of booking an art show or craft exhibit. Insurance was non-existent. If not for the generous spirit of her good friends, she'd be starving and homeless.

Her mother always said her love for art would bring her to this. Connie Astor's prophecy had come true.

"Libby," she whispered. "I'm frightened."

Daniel never tired of hearing of Ms. Anne's exploits. The way the hospital staff acted whenever she came around could make most anyone a believer, but hearing her name on Hope Astor's beautiful lips wasn't what he'd expected. According to hospital gossip, Ms. Anne apparently had a direct line to God, knowing who needed prayer and showing up right when they needed it.

He'd wanted to get away without being seen, but the file had slipped from his clumsy grasp. Hope had turned those soft blue eyes in his direction, and his name had escaped her lips. Even after all that had happened between them, his traitorous heart sided against him. If he'd allowed it to have its desire, he'd have run to her, taken her into his arms, and would have done his best to assure her that she'd be okay.

Instead, he stuffed the patient's file back together, tucked it to his side, and walked past the two women as he fought to keep his eyes from betraying him as well.

"I don't think the news will be as good as we prayed."

At the demur tone of Hope's voice, he lost the battle and cast a quick look in her direction.

"You're young and have a can-do attitude. Whatever the news, God will get you through it," Hope's companion said while offering Daniel a smile.

Funny, the pretty dark-haired lady didn't look like she would stand a chance in the face of Hope's daring sarcasm. The only one who could have ever matched Hope was Daniel's sister, Tiffany, and perhaps their friend, Delilah James. He'd give almost anything he owned to hear one of Hope or Tiffany's quick retorts meant only to send him into uncontrollable laughter. He hadn't felt much like laughing in a very long while.

At the end of the hall, Daniel stopped. Despite his mind's best effort, his heart won out. He turned back for one more glance.

Hope straightened, seeming to wait for him to speak. She stopped, and her friend halted beside her.

What did she want him to say? While he might long for the old days, ache to be a part of the life they once shared, he could never offer her absolution, not after what Hope took from him.

Darkness circled Hope's eyes. She wore a pallor several shades lighter than her usual tanned skin, and her shoulders slumped. Added to that, she seemed cloaked in weariness.

Daniel shook his head. It would be like Hope Astor to

party all night and show up at the hospital for some routine tests. By nightfall, she'd look gorgeous again. She'd probably go home—wherever that happened to be now—and crawl into bed.

He knew via his mother's vitriol that Hope was no longer welcome in her parents' home—not since Tiffany's death. Hope's unwise decision had torn two families completely apart. And she seemed to be continuing in the lifestyle that cost her—cost him—everything.

He blinked.

How long had they been standing here, facing each other, saying nothing? He darted out of sight and around the corner, his emotions finally coming back to his side of things.

He took a deep breath to stall his heart before it could cross enemy lines once again. Yeah, a radiologist sending a report and films to a referring physician so quickly was rare. Hope could be ill and not playing her usual role of party animal. If Hope was sick, she had a better chance of survival than she'd given Tiffany. Because of Hope Astor, he'd never again see his sister's beautiful face or hear her wonderful, life-filled laughter.

No. Hope Astor had no place in his stony heart. He wouldn't let it betray him again.

2

Hope only wanted to go home, but Libby knew her too well. And her friend would be right to assume that if they left the hospital, Hope would return to Delilah James' apartment and wouldn't eat. Instead, Hope found herself behind Libby as they made their way through the cafeteria to dine on hospital cuisine.

"We'll take this one day at a time," Libby chattered as they moved through the buffet line.

Hope spooned a smattering of scrambled eggs onto her plate. Libby stopped her with a touch of her hand and added an extra helping. By the end of the line, Hope gave up and simply turned her plate in Libby's direction, allowing Libby to fill it up. She'd never known there was this much breakfast food. Not being a morning person, she never bothered much with that meal.

"You'll call Dr. Ramesh tomorrow morning, and we'll

get in to see her as soon as we can," Libby continued the conversation all the way to the table.

"You don't have to go with me. You have a business to run."

"Evan insisted I hire someone to help. She's very reliable, and he promised to check in whenever I have to be away for a length of time."

Libby's husband would move heaven and earth to help anyone in need. He'd done it for her on more than one occasion. Jokingly, Evan had said he would always take care of her. Once upon a time, she had thought they would marry. Instead, Libby had won Evan's heart. Good thing, too. She could pretend otherwise, but Hope had never truly relinquished hers to Evan. Daniel Duvall had always had possession of it. He probably always would.

Hope shook off the melancholy and slipped into a booth. "I can't thank you both enough."

"Hush up." Libby swatted at her. "We're family."

Hope lowered her head. *God, thank You for the unique group of people who call me theirs.* She kept her head bowed as Libby reached for her hand.

"Dear Lord, thank You for Your abundance, Your meal that nourishes, and for Your light that guides us. Father, show us Your will and Your way. We pray for Your healing hand upon Hope and upon others facing the same trials. Be with our Hope and comfort her, Lord, even while she waits, and cause her to know just why You have placed this obstacle in her path. In Jesus' precious name we pray, amen."

"Amen." Hope picked up her fork and stared at the massive amount of food her friend had chosen for her. Because the cafeteria charged by the weight of the tray, Libby must have shelled out a pretty penny. "Libby, this is so much."

"Eat what you can. You took so little."

"Libby, look at your plate compared to mine. Do I look like a Sumo wrestler?"

"No. Actually, you're beginning to favor a scarecrow with the stuffing beat out of it." Libby wrinkled her nose.

Hope crinkled her nose in reply and stopped just short of sticking out her tongue. You never knew what would come out of that woman's mouth. The only constant in what she said was truth and love.

"If Delilah can't make you eat, I'll be over to cook for you every night. I'll enlist Charisse, too, and you know what that means."

"Gideon and Evan will come with you."

"So, if you want to see Gideon and Delilah square off every night, you continue to eat like a bird. If you don't gain a pound a week, I'll keep my promise."

Hope raised her hands in surrender. "A pound a week. I hear you." Although, Gideon and Delilah's antics were about the only thing that made Hope laugh these days.

She bit into a cinnamon bun, figuring the fattier the better to keep Charisse and Libby from adding daily family meals to their already overcrowded schedules. For once, food tasted good. Maybe the reason she had no taste for food was the fact that neither she nor Delilah had a knack for cooking. The kitchen was the least utilized room in the condo they shared. Hope was tempted to ask Libby to cook for them, but Libby had so much to do.

Libby chewed fast and swallowed. "That good-looking doctor couldn't keep his eyes off you."

"Don't go there," Hope warned.

"You haven't dated since I've known you."

Sweet, wonderful, naive Libby. Dating to her was one thing. To Hope, it had been a temptation that would definitely pull her back into sins she'd rather avoid.

"Dating someone who finds you attractive and respects—"

If God had another man for her, he would have to laugh and love, to surprise her with unexpected gifts—little things that made her heart sing. He'd have to deal with Hope's love for sarcasm and dish it back at her, and he would have to except that she'd lived a life that left her far from pure. He'd have to steal her heart away from the man whom she modeled her ideal suitor after, and Hope didn't think that possible.

Danny Duvall was the man for her, and she'd done something that would keep him from her forever.

"Danny is the last man on earth who'd want to go out with me." Hope wiped her napkin across her mouth and looked around the cafeteria.

Her heart skipped a beat, pounded once, and skipped

another before continuing to pump more blood than she needed into her brain. Danny stood in line with a pretty young nurse beside him. He'd always shown Hope the greatest of respect, and she'd been infuriated more times than not at his gentlemanly ways.

As if feeling her stare, he turned in her direction. If hatred were concrete, his steely blue eyes erected a sturdy roadblock.

"The way he looked at you, I'd say he wanted to ask you out on a date," Libby pressed.

Libby clearly missed the glare he leveled at Hope now.

Hope slumped forward, resting her head in her hands. "Please, Libby. Drop it."

Her friend leaned back. Her eyes, always so vivid with emotion, stared back at Hope now with an unspoken apology. She opened her mouth to speak.

Hope raised her hand and forced a smile. "I apologize. You don't know the history."

"Oh, he's a friend of yours." Libby brightened, and her voice carried across the cafeteria.

Danny's stare narrowed. Once upon a time, that scowl would have prompted her into a fit of laughter. He'd mastered that acrid look on Hope and Tiffany, never truly meaning it. Now, Hope was fully aware of the anger seething beneath Danny's cool exterior. She'd known him long enough to realize he was fighting to stay in line beside his pretty companion and not come over and tell her—for the first time—exactly what he thought of her.

Hope examined her plate of food. Libby's money would be wasted today. She picked up her fork with a trembling hand and tried to get the food from her plate to her mouth. "Libby, Danny Duvall hates me. He's Tiffany's brother. His family blames me for her death. Let's drop it."

Libby's eyes widened. "Tiffany?"

"I'm the reason Tiffany's dead, and Danny and his family wish it had been me. The Lord has placed it on my heart to face their vengeance, but I've been a coward."

Libby remained silent, fixing Hope with one of her well-what-are-you-waiting-for stares.

Did the woman even realize some people struggled with doing God's will? "I can't," Hope murmured. "I can't bear to hear the loathing in Danny's voice."

Libby's gaze lifted upward. She widened her eyes and gulped.

In Hope's peripheral vision, she spied the doctor's white coat. She bit her lip and looked up.

Danny towered over her. She should have known. If she wasn't willing to go to the mountain, God would bring the mountain to her—using Libby's innocent outburst to quake Hope's foundation. Time for her retribution had arrived.

Daniel stepped back to allow Hope room to stand. She braced herself and rose as if fighting against an unseen hand pressing down upon her. He stared at her plate, packed high with food. She'd definitely lost weight. Maybe she lived in a shelter, and the woman with her had volunteered to drive her to the appointment. Feeling sorry for Hope, she'd offered to feed her, and Hope had taken advantage of the situation.

No matter her circumstances, he would not allow them to dissolve his determination. Time had come to tell Hope what he thought of her.

"Danny, I'd like you to meet my friend, Libby Carter. I'm not sure if you've heard, but Libby is Evan's wife."

"Daniel," he corrected then turned to the other woman.

Mrs. Carter stood and held out her hand.

He shook it.

The last time he'd seen Evan Carter had been at Tiffany's funeral. The time before that he'd been at Orlando Regional Medical Center the night his sister died and Hope had lived. Though Libby was pretty enough, this woman didn't any more fit Evan's type than she did Hope's idea of a friend. At one time, he actually feared Evan would marry Hope and take away any chance Daniel had. Now, he was glad Evan's interference kept him from doing something so foolish.

"Libby, as I was saying, Daniel is Tiffany's brother."

How did Libby Carter know his sister? Still, that was beside the point. "No, Hope. I *was* her brother."

"Dr. Duvall, I'm so sorry for your loss." Mrs. Carter's sentiment rang real enough. "Tiffany was such a wonderful person. I only knew her for a short while, but she always had a smile. She had a bounce to her step and carried sunshine with her wherever she went."

Daniel cleared his throat, unable to speak. Such an accurate description of Tiffany—a remembrance of his only sibling through the eyes of someone he'd never met. He kept his chin from quivering through strength of will alone. "Thank you, Mrs. Carter." He gave her a terse nod.

"Will you excuse me?" Libby moved around them.

"Where are you going?" Hope reached for the other woman.

"I can see that you and Dr. Duvall need some time. I'll wait over here." Mrs. Carter picked up her plate. "Dr. Duvall, she needs to eat. Maybe your encouragement will work better than mine." She moved to a table across the room.

Daniel folded his arms over his chest and waited. He didn't have an ounce of encouragement for Hope Astor.

Hope reached for the top of the booth. When she stretched out her arm, a wince played across her features. She backed up and clutched the leather seat. "Danny, I never got the chance to say how sorry I am for what happened to Tiffany."

Daniel stared at her. What did she want from him?

"I'm sorry," she repeated.

He didn't expect to see them, but tears washed over her eyes and streamed down her face.

No mascara. Why that occurred to him, he didn't

know, except that once when she'd laughed so hard she cried, her runny mascara made her look like a raccoon.

He shook the memory away. When he chose to remember times with his sister, he'd learned to cut Hope completely out of the picture.

Hope sank into the padded seat of the booth, almost as if it cost her too much energy to stay on her feet. She reached for a napkin and used it to wipe the tears from her face.

He stared down at her, wanting more, wanting to see her pain, to hear it put into words—something to justify the jagged edge of bitterness he kept caged in his soul.

"All this food. Libby filled my plate, and I'll never be able to eat it all." She looked up at him. "I can't do this. Danny, if I could …"

He said nothing.

"I'm so sorry," she cried.

Curiosity drove him into the seat Libby vacated. "What makes you sorry, Hope? Is it because Tiff died and you lived? Are you sorry you took her out drinking and had her drop you off with Evan so she was driving alone when she crashed into the tree? Or are you simply sorry because it happened, and you've had to pay a little for the death you caused?"

She blinked, and more tears fell from her blue eyes. She leaned back against the booth. "I'm sorry for the decisions I made that night. They cost me a dear friend. If continuing to pay for my sins would bring Tiffany back,

I'd gladly accept the penalty for all eternity, but no matter how hard you or anyone else punishes me, it won't bring her back."

"So, we just accept her death, forgive you, and move on."

"Those three actions are up to you, Dr. Duvall."

"Have you?"

"Have I what?" She stared at him.

"Accepted her death, forgiven yourself, moved on?"

"Truthfully, no, and that's why I can't expect the same from you. We loved her, Danny. I lived across the street from you all my life. Tiffany was like my sister. You were—you were our hero."

He stood. Some hero he'd made. He'd laughed at his sister's antics, at the lifestyle she and Hope loved so much, thinking they were just enjoying life. Daniel should have stood in front of the fast-moving train wreck, held his hands out, cape flying in the wind, and stopped the pending disaster that had taken his sister from him.

Hope was the one to always land on her feet unscathed. Daniel cut his gaze to Libby Carter who was picking up her tray and heading their way, and none too happy about something—probably because he'd made Hope cry.

Libby must have unending compassion. Based on Hope's appearance, she'd obviously gone out the night before, and still the other woman had made sure Hope kept her appointment.

He just prayed that Libby caught on to Hope's

recklessness before she lost someone she loved.

Without a word, he walked away and then turned back toward her. "I retired my hero's cape the night I could do nothing to bring my sister back to me." He pointed a finger at her. "And I'll never forget that you're responsible for it."

Hope

3

Hope studied her hands as she sat on the examination table. Paper rustled on the other side of the door, and seconds later came a knock and turn of the knob. "Hope, I'm sorry I couldn't get you in yesterday when you called." Dr. Mara Ramesh looked over the file in her hand.

"The technician at the hospital told me the radiologist was sending over the report and the films."

Dr. Ramesh looked up. Her eyes, the color of rich coal, studied Hope. "Yes, I have the report."

"And?"

A nurse knocked and entered.

"Lie down for me," the doctor instructed.

Hope did as she said, turning her eyes toward the ceiling as the doctor slipped her hand under the paper cover the nurse had placed over Hope's breast. "Ow," she said as the doctor's slender fingers pressed hard against first the left and then the right breast. Without a word, Dr. Ramesh lifted Hope's arm and pressed into her armpits.

Finished with her examination, the doctor stood back. She nodded to her nurse, and the woman left. Then she turned her attention back to Hope. "I'm sending you to see an interventional radiologist for a core biopsy. I'll have it scheduled as soon as possible."

Hope sat up. "I don't understand. I thought a radiologist took X-rays, did mammograms, tests like that. What does this entail?"

"You have masses in both breasts." She leveled her stare at Hope. "And I don't think you're taking care of yourself." She looked away and thumbed through Hope's chart. "A core biopsy, or biopsies in your case, will be a little more invasive, but I think time is of the essence."

"I don't—"

"Bottom line, here, Hope," Dr. Ramesh set her chart down and turned, arms folded. "While a lump or lumps can always be benign, I want to make absolutely sure. With the amount of abnormal tissue here, we could waste time with a fine needle aspiration, but a core biopsy will provide us more accurate information in a shorter period of time."

"Dr. Ramesh, I'm not able to …"

Dr. Ramesh held up her hand. "There is a slight chance with a core biopsy of pneumothora—"

"Pneumo … what?" Hope didn't like the sound of that word. Her grandmother had died from pneumonia.

"Relax." The doctor placed a hand on Hope's shoulder. "The chance is slight. All that means is that on rare occasions—very rare occasions—the needle used passes through the chest wall. Do you understand so far?"

"I'm in trouble." Hope shrugged. She was up to her neck in a black swamp, and the alligators were closing in on her.

Dr. Ramesh studied Hope for so long that Hope lowered her gaze. "You could be in trouble. That's true or …"

Dr. Ramesh's pause made Hope look up. The woman wore a smile.

"Hope, you and that friend of yours sitting out in the lobby, talk about your God and how powerful He is. If you believe in Him that strongly, now would be a time to put your faith into action."

So, the good doctor had paid attention to Libby during Hope's first visit when her friend had shared her faith—something Hope wasn't prone to do.

"As I said, we aren't sure at this point. Things don't look promising, but we need to take this a step at a time and plan for the worst. That way, we'll be prepared for everything." Dr. Ramesh raised her dark brows, and even Hope found enough energy to smile.

"We'll set this up ASAP. Another wonderful advantage to a core biopsy is that the results are returned quickly. Between now and then, you go home and get some rest. And eat nutritiously. In other words, take better care of yourself."

Hope remained silent. The doctor had her pegged. She

hadn't slept. Food was a necessary evil. Delilah had turned on Hope, telling Libby that Hope had not eaten last night. Always true to her promises, Libby had contacted Charisse, and plans had been set in action. Her new family would meet for dinner daily at Delilah's apartment, and nightly meals would be cooked, leaving leftovers for lunch the next day. Hope suspected that more than physical health, they wanted to surround her with their support to prevent depression from settling in.

They were a little too late.

"Hope, the biopsy will tell us our next step. I suspect you'll have some decisions to make, an oncology team, especially a good oncology surgeon, type of surgery, course of treatment, but I'm not going to overwhelm you today more than I already have."

Hope bit her lower lip. Nothing she could discuss would matter. One needed money or insurance for treatment. Hope had nothing. And a core biopsy didn't sound cheap.

"You need to eat well."

Nothing Hope hadn't heard from *Dr. Libby*.

"And you need to sleep. Do you need something to help you?"

Hope shook her head. "I—I'm prone to abuse them. I'd rather not."

"Then you need to get out and walk in the early afternoon, even if it's a short walk. Settle down with a boring book at night. Don't work on a computer or watch television before you turn out the lights. Those over stimulate the brain. You want to calm yourself, maybe even practice some breathing techniques."

Hope nodded.

"Do you have any questions?" Dr. Ramesh asked.

She had a hundred, but they were all useless to her now. Why waste the doctor's time? She shook her head.

"Wait here. Darla will return with your paperwork. I'll include some brochures on vitamin rich foods you need. I also have a list of oncology practices. We're fortunate to have the best cancer group in the country, headed by a surgeon I recommend highly. His name is Dr. Daniel Duvall."

Hope closed her eyes and then looked down at her hands. "And the second best?" Not that it mattered.

"I'll give you the list, and you can make your decision." Dr. Ramesh touched Hope's shoulder. "I've hit you with some scary stuff, and you need to strap yourself in. The ride may feel a little like a roller coaster plummeting both your physical and emotional levels, but if you listen to your doctors, we'll get the old ride chinking up the track to dock at wellness as soon as possible." She skirted out the door, chart in hand.

Would Dr. Ramesh order the tests and plan for treatment if she knew Hope had no means to pay?

Hope slid from the table and dressed while she waited for the nurse to return with all the information. Fully clothed, she sat in a chair and leafed through a magazine probably left by a previous patient. Starlets with low-cut gowns and perfect figures stared back as she turned the pages. She had once dressed like that, leaving little to the imagination.

She'd gained a new wardrobe from Libby's nice hand-me-down piles and some clothes Charisse had purchased for her. Now, those once nice fitting clothes were too big.

Well, God had probably closed the door on the slinky clothing. If a miracle occurred and she could afford the medical treatments, if they took her breasts, a strapless top would be useless anyway.

She tossed the magazine aside. One day at a time. That's what Ms. Anne said. Her mind had her jumping to a double mastectomy she couldn't afford, and she hadn't even had the biopsy.

She covered her face with her hands. There would be no more tests. She was done.

The door opened, and the nurse walked in. "Here you go, Hope. We've made you an appointment for the biopsy. Call and confirm. Here's a list of foods that you should be eating and a list of oncology surgeons and practices in the area. Dr. Ramesh wanted me to advise you, this is just a list to ponder until we get the results back from the biopsy.

Hope stared at the sheet. Daniel's name and the name of his practice were the first listed. Her reluctant hero had actually become a superhero.

"When we get the biopsy results, we'll refer you to a doctor of your choice." The nurse held open the door. Hope followed her down the hallway and out into the lobby. Stopping at the front desk, she pulled her debit card from her purse and slid it across the counter. She held her breath while the receptionist ran it through, and she breathed a sigh of relief when the woman handed her a receipt.

"Have a great day," the sweet girl said.

"You, too." Hope pushed open the door.

"Hope?" Libby followed her out.

She blinked. "Libby, I'm sorry. I was a million miles away. I forgot you were waiting for me."

"It's okay." Libby slipped her arm through Hope's. "How about some lunch?"

Hope shook her head. "You need to get back to work, and you're planning to cook dinner tonight."

"We're cooking dinner," Libby corrected. "Charisse and I have decided this plan of ours is a good opportunity to teach you and Delilah some culinary skills."

Hope opened the passenger door to Libby's new SUV. Several days after Hope's parents sent someone to pick up the Beemer, Evan had declared that Libby needed a vehicle to transport her equipment to and from her nursery, Happily Ever After Gardens. He'd then promptly handed Hope the keys to Libby's newer-model compact car.

Libby didn't press for the doctor's report, and Hope was thankful. They drove into the heart of downtown Orlando to Delilah's condominium.

God had given her a circle of friends, more dependent upon each other than Hope had ever realized—and she was the neediest.

Libby pulled into the parking garage and turned off the engine. "So, please tell me what's next for us."

Hope's lips trembled. "It's not good, Libby. I'm at the end of the line. No insurance. No money. No treatment. Dr. Ramesh scheduled a biopsy, but I can't afford it." She swiped at the tears in her eyes. "Now, I guess I wait to die."

Daniel maneuvered past an elderly patient and his nurse to get to his office. Every extra minute he managed to get during the day afforded time for his dictation. He picked up the three files from his chair, where his nurse made it a practice to leave them, and fell into the soft leather.

He slipped on the reading glasses he kept on his desk, but before he could start the recorder, his office phone buzzed. He picked it up. "Yeah, Terri."

"You have an old friend here to see you. Do you have a minute, or would you like me to set up another time?"

"Who is it?"

"Evan Carter."

Daniel leaned back in his chair and rubbed tired eyes. He hadn't slept well since seeing Hope at the hospital. The angry words he'd spilled out, thinking they would quench his desire for revenge, only added to some other emotion he couldn't quite place. Hope's quiet acceptance of his parting shot sank to the pit of his stomach like an anchor tossed into a hurricane-riddled sea.

"Dr. Duvall?"

Daniel sighed. "Send him back." He hung up the phone and stood.

Seconds later, Libby Carter peered around the corner. Evan came behind her, linking his hand with hers and entering the room. "Thanks for seeing us, Daniel." Evan released his wife and held out his hand.

Daniel gave it a shake and offered the woman a nod. "Sit down, please." He waited, and when the couple seemed comfortable, he sat.

"Libby tells me she met you at the hospital with Hope," Evan said.

Daniel watched Libby for any clue of what her husband knew of their meeting. "Yes. I was surprised when Hope told me Libby was your wife. I hadn't heard about the wedding."

Evan placed his hand over Libby's and smiled at her. "We had a treacherous courtship and a whirlwind engagement."

Libby blushed. "Hope had a lot to do with that."

"Both the treacherous courtship and the whirlwind engagement." Evan laughed.

Daniel could only imagine the havoc Hope could have wreaked if Libby had endangered Hope's relationship with Evan. Yet, they were both here smiling about it.

"Hope is like a sister to us, Dr. Duvall." Libby scooted

forward in the seat.

Daniel held up his hand. "I don't mean to be rude, Libby, but I'm not discussing Hope Astor. I'm sure she told you about our conversation at the hospital."

Libby shook her head. "She didn't say anything, and I didn't ask. I do know my friend, though, and whatever you said to her is heavy on her heart."

"Evan, does your wife know what Hope did to my family?"

Evan brushed back a strand of Libby's hair. His tenderness toward his wife elicited a yearning in Daniel—one that hadn't swept over him in months. Work wasn't all there was to life. He needed a wife, a family. Children—they'd help his parents cope with Tiffany's death, offer healing.

"That courtship I mentioned—Libby and I were in the middle of it when Tiffany died. Hope is a changed woman."

Even Daniel had noted some change in her. Hope spoke with a softer tone. Her dress had been a modest one, and she didn't argue or excuse her actions.

"You're a doctor." Evan broke into Daniel's thoughts "More specifically, you're an oncology surgeon. Hope may need your help. She won't ask you, so as her family, we're here to beg you to treat her."

When he'd left his parents' home after dinner on Sunday, Hope's father had been standing in the driveway across the street, beyond his gate, staring up at the leaves on the hundred-year-old oaks. Hope was once Stephen Astor's life. Both Stephen and Daniel's father had doted too much on their girls. Now, Evan and Libby claimed to be her family, and Stephen and Connie Astor pretended their only daughter didn't exist.

"Daniel, Dr. Ramesh is sending her for a—what type of biopsy was it, honey?" Evan fumbled for the words.

"A core biopsy," Libby answered.

Daniel picked up his pen and laid it down. Mara Ramesh had to be certain that wasted time was an enemy for Hope. She wouldn't have sent an indigent patient for a more invasive treatment unless she needed the results quickly.

"We've gotten Hope to agree to allow us to pay for the biopsy. No pun intended, but she's a starving artist." Evan leaned forward. "She's suffered from exhaustion for a long while, and now she's too weak to paint. She lives with Delilah James."

Daniel placed the pen on the desk. Hope and Delilah. What a pair. Life was probably lively in that place—at least when Hope felt better. Still, they were requesting too much of him.

"Dr. Duvall, if Hope is ill, we'll pay for her treatment. She doesn't have insurance. She doesn't have the support of her parents." Libby obviously wasn't beyond begging for her friend.

Daniel couldn't succumb to the likable woman's pleas. "You're asking me to treat the woman responsible for my sister's death—not only treat her—"

"You don't understand," Evan cut Daniel off. "A lot of things have changed in our life. I told you the night Tiffany died, I'd been clean and sober for a while. By God's grace, I continue to stay clean."

Evan Carter's change in lifestyle had come too late for Tiffany. Daniel pressed his lips together to bite back any hateful words. It would be better to remain quiet rather than to offend two people who obviously sought him out because they thought he cared.

Libby reached out and placed her hand on his desk. "Tiffany trusted Christ, and she's in heaven."

Daniel looked from her to Evan. Neither seemed embarrassed by such an idiotic statement.

"You've seen Hope and me at our worst," Evan said. "We lived selfish lives, using alcohol and parties to deaden hurts and not face our problems. We lived for what we thought were good times, but those days are over. We've all accepted Christ—Delilah, Hope, me, and your sister. Tiffany has gone to a better life, and while the rest of us remain here, we're now living a life of purpose."

Again, Daniel remained silent. Who was he to wake them from their fantasy? God didn't exist. Heaven was a man-made dream world meant to keep people from fearing death. He'd seen too much suffering at death's hand to believe a lie that said another life awaited after this one— whether it was this mystical heaven or a burning hell. Besides, one honest look at Hope should convince them she wasn't living a life of purpose. She looked awful.

Evan leaned forward. "We're not asking you to treat Hope for free. We'll pay all the expenses. We don't want her to know we're paying you, though. I'm sure allowing Hope to believe you would offer her any kindness is the last thing you want to do, but it's the very thing she needs."

"You haven't thought this through, Evan." Daniel ran a hand through his hair. "The costs associated with cancer—you'll have bills from the hospital, labs, chemo, radiation, pharmacies, and what if she requires hormonal therapy? The medications alone will cost a good sum, not to mention other unforeseen expenses. You're a successful businessman, but I doubt you have enough money to cover Hope's medical needs without taking out a significant loan."

Libby covered her mouth. Her choked cry wrenched Daniel's soul.

Evan put his arm around her. "What is money if we lose Hope? There are five of us covering her costs. We're only asking you to honor your oath and do everything you can to save her life."

Daniel brought his hands together, elbows resting on the arm of the chair. Then he brought the tips of his fingers to the edge of his nose and stared at the corner of his office. He weighed the pros and cons, allowed his traitorous heart to render an opinion.

"Give us some cause for optimism, Daniel. That's all we're asking. At least tell us you'll think about it."

Daniel slipped his glasses from his face and tossed them on the desk. "Why me?"

"Two reasons." Libby bounced in her seat like a hopeful child. "I've done research, and I've found out you're the best, and like it or not, Dr. Duvall, she doesn't have to tell me. Hope trusts you."

Daniel stood—an invitation for his visitors to do the same. He shook Evan's hand and then Libby's. "I'll think about it. You'll be hearing from me. The least I'll do is find her a doctor I trust."

The tears in Libby's eyes tugged at Daniel.

"Surely, you understand how difficult treating her would be for me."

Libby shot him an angry glare. "And do you think it will be any easier for Hope to humble herself before you when she knows how much she hurt you?"

"Libby, baby, Daniel's a fair man." Evan slipped his arm around his wife's waist. "We look forward to hearing from you."

As Evan led Libby from the room, she leaned against her husband for support.

Daniel dropped into his chair and closed his eyes. At the soft knock, he opened them. Libby stood in the doorway.

"Yes?"

"I apologize for my outburst, Dr. Duvall. I didn't want to leave here with you believing I don't see your side of things. I've never experienced a sudden loss of anyone, much less someone I loved. My mother lingered in her illness, but I had her with me. I can't begin to understand how you feel. My anger was uncalled for, and I hope you'll forgive me."

Daniel stood and walked to the door. "Libby, Evan Carter is a lucky man. You tell him I said so, and there's nothing to forgive."

Hope

4

Hope's heels clicked against the marble tile as the maid led her into the spacious living room. "Mr. and Mrs. Duvall will be with you momentarily." The maid closed the double doors, leaving Hope alone in the all-too familiar area of the stately Winter Park home. Here in this room, she and Tiffany spent their childhood hours playing with dolls, coloring, and scheming. And here in this living room, Daniel would pretend to ignore their antics. The more he tried, the more they would aggravate him.

Sitting was too presumptuous, so she stood. Smoothing her skirt, she moved to look out the floor-to-ceiling windows that allowed in the warmth of the Florida sun. Across the palm-tree lined street, on the other side of the wrought-iron gate, her father got into his car. The gates opened, and he backed out of his driveway.

Six months—six long months since she'd run into him at an art exhibit, and the pain of abandonment still ached within her. So much needed said. Time was running out. She didn't need a biopsy to know life was seeping from her like water through a small crack in a vase. She might have only one chance left. But the first breach she needed to attempt to heal was the one with Tiffany's parents.

The door opened and closed before Hope turned. When she did, the husband and wife staring back at her were aged and worn—not the couple that used to laugh with her and their daughter on the Riviera or other vacation spots, even here in this living room or in their kitchen.

"I can't imagine why you've come." Elsa Duvall spoke first. She stood behind the winged-back leather chair.

Jacob Duvall placed a hand on his wife's shoulder, but Elsa shrugged from beneath it.

"Hope," Jacob began, "you can understand that seeing you here after what occurred, well, it's a little like pulling the scab off a deep wound."

At least Jacob's eyes hadn't lost their kindness though each of his words threw invisible punches at Hope's gut.

"I know I've caused you both so much pain. Tiffany wouldn't have been out that night if I'd only listened to her." She bit into her lower lip. If only her chin would stop quivering. She'd never get through this if she cried. Her plan wasn't to garner their sympathy. She didn't expect a pardon from them any more than she had from their son.

"Why don't you say what you've come to say?" Elsa slammed a closed fist against the chair's fabric, but she did not move from behind the barrier the furniture provided.

Hope couldn't decide if that blockade was from or for her. "I came to tell you I'm truly sorry for your loss. I've been a long time in making my apology. I offer you no excuses. I don't expect you to forgive me. If there was some way I could make up for Tiffany's death I'd do it, but nothing I have—nothing I could ever do or be—could equal the value of her life." She took a deep breath. "I spent a lot of time in this house. You were always kind to me. I am sorry I repaid your kindness with such evil."

Jacob nodded.

Elsa stared, eyes wide, her face reddening.

"That's all I really wanted to say. I promise I won't bother you again." Hope made her way to the arched entrance into the foyer, closer to the people who used to treat her like a second daughter. Once, they seemed so strong, so together. A perfect contradiction to her own parents' embattled marriage. Now, they appeared alone and vulnerable even within each other's company.

"Hope, there is something you can do to make this up to us," Elsa said.

Hope waited, her heart ready to grasp any lifeline Elsa could offer her.

"Elsa, honey, let it go," Jacob said under this breath.

"No, Jacob. I want to hear what it is I can do." Hope nodded to Elsa.

Elsa straightened. With her open hand, she struck hard against Hope's face. "You can die. You can leave your mother with a hole in her heart as big as the one in mine. Your mother can wish she had one more moment, one more little space of time to share with you. Your father can wonder why his baby girl had to die—why he won't be able to walk you down the aisle at your wedding, why he'll never bounce upon his knee a grandchild that is as beautiful as the young girl he raised."

Hope covered the sting on her face. She gave one last nod before leaving. The maid waited for her, the front door opened. Hope walked through it. The soft click of the door's closure did nothing to ease her pain—not that she thought it would.

The last time she'd left this house, she'd pulled a reluctant friend with her. Tiffany Duvall never returned here.

Hope walked down the brick-paved drive to her car. Standing by her door, she stared across the street at her childhood home. Tears welled in her eyes as the living room curtain opened. She caught a momentary glimpse of her mother's beautiful face before Mother tugged the curtain closed.

Hope leaned against the back of the elevator as it climbed to the seventh floor. When the door finally opened, she pushed off the wall and made her way down the corridor. Standing outside, her key ready, she listened to the muffled voices and laughter and allowed it to lighten her mood.

Inside Delilah's condo, the aroma of a home-cooked meal met her. Green beans. Her favorite.

She hung her purse on the hat stand by the door. "Hi." She entered the living room.

Gideon Tabor and Evan Carter were seated in Delilah's leather chairs while Delilah intently listened to little V.J., Gideon and Charisse's son, talk about a group of metal objects spread across Delilah's coffee table.

Gideon motioned her inside as if the condo he'd sold to Delilah still belonged to him. They all acted this way. Seldom did they knock before entering each other's homes. Each abode was a comfortable extension of the place where they lived.

Family.

The five adults and the little boy in this house were all she had. The man who'd driven out of his driveway and the woman who'd peeked out her curtain—they'd disowned her.

If there were tears in heaven, she was sure to cry over losing this new family.

"Hey." Gideon jumped to his feet and slipped an arm over her shoulder. "You okay?"

She started to nod but shook her head instead.

"Come here." He pulled her into a hug, and she cried against him.

"Look what you've gone and done, you big ape."

Delilah tugged her out of Gideon's hold. "You've made her cry."

"Yeah, and she got my shirt wet," Gideon played.

Hope laughed as she wiped her tears. "I'm sorry, Gid." She leaned against Delilah.

"I didn't even get time to change. They all converged on me in the condo lobby," Delilah whispered. "Libby is so worried about you I doubt she's getting any rest. And she and Charisse are insisting we learn to cook."

"Yeah, my wife's gone insane." Gideon snarled. "I wouldn't let you within twenty feet of a sharp utensil."

"Oh, how nice, Giddy. You care."

"Yeah, I'm worried for the safety of anyone in the vicinity of you and anything lethal."

Delilah helped Hope into the living room. "I'm going to insist you get a break from the lessons tonight." Delilah's eyes twinkled with mischief. What was she up to now? "Evan bought V.J. the most fabulous toy." Delilah turned, so only Hope could see her, and rolled her eyes. "He's been telling me all about it since we arrived." She forced Hope to sit down on the couch. "V.J., tell Aunt Hope what you told me about Uncle Evan's gift."

Hope sat on the edge of the couch and looked at what she now recognized as a costly erector set. "Whatcha got here, buddy?"

"Uncle Evan bought it for me. I can build things."

"Trying to turn my son into an engineer. He's going into law," Gideon grumbled at Evan. "When you and Libby have your own kid, you can let him build things."

"Dad, I can be an engineer and a lawyer," V.J. protested.

"There you go." Evan nodded, as if that settled the matter.

"Is that so?" Gideon stooped beside V.J. "So, I guess you're telling me Mom and I need to put double into the old college fund."

V.J. gave a big nod.

"Done." Gideon hugged V.J. to him and with the boy's ears covered, he looked back at Evan. "Thanks a lot. I did have dreams of an early retirement."

Hope leaned back and closed her eyes. The light banter of her friends comforted and relaxed her. Her heavy eyelids closed, and the voices drifted off into the distance.

"Hope, come on. We can make it. Run."

Hope looked around her. Who had called? Where was she?

A girl nearly swallowed in a passing crowd motioned her forward. "Come on."

Hope ran to catch up. Energy she'd lacked for months surged through her body. She reached the girl who'd summoned her.

"Danny's waiting."

"Tiffany?" Happiness surged through Hope.

"Yeah, silly. Who else? Danny said you wanted to ride the carousel."

Hope turned around and around, gazing at her new

surroundings. What was she doing in the middle of the Central Florida Fairgrounds?

When she stopped her spinning, her gaze fell upon Danny. He stood on the ornate carousel, one hand grasping a pole, the other held out toward her. "Let's ride this before we head home."

Hope turned to her friend. Tiffany grabbed Hope's hand and pulled her to the carousel, but when Hope grasped Danny's hand, Tiffany released her, waving and fading into the background.

Hope turned to look at Danny.

"I've got you." He gazed upon her with such devotion she could have melted into the blueness of his eyes. "I've got you," he repeated.

"But Tiffany?" She forced her stare away from him to scan the crowd. Everything was gone—only a bright light remained.

"Let her sleep." Delilah's voice broke through Hope's dream.

Hope fought against waking, wanting to find Tiffany and Danny once again.

"She needs to eat," Libby argued.

"But she needs her rest, too."

"The doctor gave her this diet. We're going to make sure she sticks to it."

Hope blinked awake.

Delilah and Libby were standing over her.

"Libby, she hasn't slept in days," Delilah said.

"I'm awake, girls. Stop fussing." Hope pushed herself up. "I can't believe I went to sleep like that."

"Gideon bored you into a coma, I'm sure." Delilah offered her a hand, and Hope stood.

"It smells good." She sniffed the air.

"Salmon and potato cakes with some nice green vegetable stuff." Delilah winked.

"Those would be beans," Charisse entered the dining room from the kitchen. "And a fruit salad."

"Hope, I told you we shouldn't have gotten that extra leaf for the table." Delilah nudged Gideon as she made sure Hope was settled.

Gideon grabbed Delilah's hand and kissed the back of it. "I know you care about me."

"Delilah, is it okay if Gideon asks the blessing?" Charisse asked.

Delilah hesitated a moment then laughed. The entire group watched in silence. She stopped and waved her hand. "Oh, I'm sorry. I was just thinking about what I learned in Bible study the other night. God doesn't hear prayers if we have iniquity in our hearts."

"He must never hear yours." Gideon and Delilah's chorus of the exact same punch line brought them all into fits of laughter.

When the mirth died down, Libby reached for her husband's hand, and around the table, the others did the same. "Hope, will you say the blessing?" she asked.

She'd never been asked before, but she bowed her

head. "Lord, I thank You for the company I keep. I thank You for this new life with these wonderfully odd people. Thank You for the bounty You've provided and for the loved ones who fixed it. I—I—" She stopped, emotion overwhelming her. She cleared her throat and quieted her quivering lips. "I thank You for Your love and for Your mercy. Please be with us, and Lord, I ask You to heal the hurt I've caused for Jacob and Elsa, and to Daniel, and for my own parents. In Jesus' name, amen."

She looked up. Five dear faces stared back at her.

"Quite a prayer," Delilah helped herself to the green vegetable stuff and passed the bowl to Libby beside her.

"I went to see Tiff's parents this afternoon."

Delilah held the plate of salmon in mid-air.

"Here, Hope." Evan passed the platter of potato cakes to her.

"They're hurting, Dee." Hope took Evan's burden. "I needed to tell them how sorry I am."

"And do you think anything you said to them could help to heal the hurt?" Delilah pressed. "Elsa's a bitter woman. I was there when she demanded you not attend Tiffany's funeral. Nothing I could say would change her mind."

"No, I don't believe I helped, at least that I could see, but I did what I felt God wanted of me."

Silence stretched for an uncomfortable moment before Delilah passed the plate of salmon to Gideon. "Then there you go. God knows how to heal people. Maybe in time your apology will be the key."

"I'm proud of you." Evan leaned close. "Now, please eat everything on your plate, or Libby won't stop worrying about you."

She nodded. Each of the faces, including the little blond-haired boy, appeared concerned for her welfare. She took a bite of the fish. "This is delicious."

"Thank you," Delilah said. "I think it's the finest meal I've ever made."

Laughter erupted.

Charisse held up her drink. "Don't let her fool you, Hope. Dee's contribution to tonight's meal was putting ice into the glass and pouring the tea."

Gideon picked up his glass and looked inside. "And that's why there's green vegetable stuff in the bottom of mine."

Hope

5

Hope signed in for the biopsy and sat between Libby and Charisse. She looked around the hospital's lobby. People milled about the main room; some sought the elevators, and others stopped in the lobby to chat. Occasionally, a woman's voice would sound through overhead speakers to page a doctor or a nurse. Hospital staff walked past in their scrubs, some with equipment, and others with paperwork. All this commotion at only seven in the morning.

"Is it cold in here?" Hope laid the pager in Charisse's lap and wrapped her arms around her body to keep herself warm.

"They've got it a little chilly." Libby stood. "I think I have a sweater in my SUV."

"No. I'll be fine." Hope stopped her.

Libby sat down without argument.

"How'd you sleep?" Charisse asked Hope.

"Better than usual. I think all the good food we've

been cooking is making me fat and lazy."

"I think the sleep comes from the productivity, but no cooking for you tonight. Delilah is tired of the company. She said she's treating you to dinner." Charisse laughed.

Hope leaned her head back. If the tiredness stayed at bay, she might take Delilah up on the offer, although Dee already did so much for her—they all did. She suspected Delilah's motives were a lot less selfish than Charisse claimed. Delilah wanted to give the married couples a night alone. How could Hope repay any of them for their time and generosity?

Hope tried to fight Libby and Evan on the biopsy. Evan begged her to go through with it, and when Libby joined in, crying because she didn't want to lose Hope, she'd relented.

Hope shivered and not from the chill of the hospital's air conditioning. Dr. Ramesh told her the procedure was more invasive. She'd looked it up on line. They could make as many as five small incisions and stick a hollow needle inside to extract the tissue.

No. She wouldn't think about it. "I could sure use Ms. Anne," Hope murmured. She closed her eyes and tried to forget about what was to come.

"'Tis so sweet to trust in Jesus, And to take Him at His word; Just to rest upon His promise, And to know, Thus saith the Lord.'" Libby sang in a hushed tone beside her.

"'Jesus, Jesus, how I trust Him! How I've proved Him o'er and oe'r! Jesus, Jesus, precious Jesus! O for grace to trust Him more!'" Charisse held to Hope's hand, and her slightly off-key voice rang through the lobby.

Hope looked up. Everyone sitting and standing nearby stared in their direction.

"'I'm so glad I learned to trust Thee,'" Libby sang louder and nudged Hope with her shoulder.

"'I'm so glad I learned to trust Thee,'" Hope joined in to sing the second verse. "'Precious Jesus, Saviour Friend; And I know that Thou art with me, Wilt be with me to the end.'"

"'Jesus, Jesus ...'" Others in the lobby began to join in. "'How I trust Him! How I've proved Him o'er and o'er! Jesus, Jesus, precious Jesus! O for grace to trust Him more!'"

Applause filled the air. Hope lowered her head. Peace. Complete and absolute serenity filled her. And more than that, Libby's simple desire to remind her that God was with her had obviously comforted an entire room of people.

Ms. Anne had entered the waiting room on the day of her test, and she'd said for Hope to take it one step at a time. Hope could do this. Trust God. Let Him have the control.

"Ladies."

"Dr. Duvall," Libby said.

Hope raised her eyes. "Danny." He towered above her, so tall and handsome. She stood and still had to gaze upward. "You've met Libby." She turned toward her other friend who rose to stand beside her. "This is Charisse

Tabor."

"Gideon Tabor's wife." Danny held out his hand, and Charisse shook it. "I met you at my sister's funeral." He turned icy blue eyes upon Hope. "Have them send the results to my office."

"What?" She shook her head. Had she heard him correctly?

"Mara—Dr. Ramesh will get a report, but have them send a copy directly to my office. That is, if you want my help."

"Danny, I—I don't have money or insurance."

He shared a look with Libby. "Let me worry about it." He walked off.

Hope sank deeper into her seat and wrapped her arms tighter around herself. "So cold."

"The air or Dr. Duvall?" Charisse asked.

Charisse had understood her meaning. Danny was offering to help, but there was no warmth in his gift. "What was that all about?" she said more to herself and then looked at Libby. "Or should I be asking you? Libby, what have you done? He hates me. He'd never agree to help."

Libby shrugged. "All the more reason for you to listen to him, huh? God's giving you a chance to speak into his life, and maybe the life of his family. He's exactly what the Lord has ordered. And besides, he didn't correct you this time when you didn't use his oh-so-proper name. I think Mr. Sophisticated Doctor is softening."

Hope shook her head. Libby was ever the optimist, and

most often, she had a point. "You think? He just offered to help me. God is so good."

"Yes." Charisse hugged her. "Yes, He is."

Daniel swam through the cool water of his pool. He'd pushed himself beyond his limits. Five more strokes. He could do it. Just keep going. Four. Three. Two. One. He stretched to feel the decorative tile. Holding to the side, he plunged beneath the waters, coming up and shaking the water from his hair.

Forty-five laps. His limbs ached. His lungs strained. He floated on his back, moving his arms and legs for a cool down.

He stared up at the late afternoon clouds. He'd thought the exertion would release this restlessness within him. Wrong. His mind wouldn't settle.

Whom could he call—maybe have dinner, a movie? There was a pretty nurse at the hospital. She'd given him her number a few weeks back.

He allowed himself to slip beneath the water. Then he surfaced and made his way slowly back to the edge of the pool.

He'd seen professionals at the hospital end up in some pretty sticky situations when things went sour. Why start anything that might end in disaster? He couldn't think of a single friend who wasn't involved in a relationship. Most of his colleagues were married. They'd found their perfect someone while in school.

Not Daniel. He had an image of perfection in mind. The laugh pushed from him. As imperfect as she had turned out to be, Hope was the one he thought he'd marry.

His phone on the patio table rang, and he lifted himself out of the pool with wobbly arms and legs. He'd have to set forty-six as his goal. He couldn't let the waters best him. He grabbed his towel and his phone at the same time. "This is Dr. Duvall." He ran the towel over his head.

"Daniel, Mara Ramesh."

Daniel let the towel drop to the chair, and he sat hard in it. "Yes, Mara. What can I do for you?"

"I'm referring a patient to your group. She's signed the HIPAA and notified me today that you indicated you'd see her, authorized me to contact you. Hope Astor said she was once a friend of yours, and she wants you and I to work with both your oncologist and your radiologist. I plan to have the results of her core biopsy to your office tomorrow. I'm hoping you will confirm with the oncologist."

"And you wouldn't be calling me if there wasn't a good reason."

"I'm going to send the films from her mammogram and my applicable records." Silence stretched. Daniel stared at the water in his pool, fear gripping him. Hating Hope and living without her—two different ends of the spectrum.

"Daniel, this woman is a vulnerable mess right now."

Mara broke into his developing nightmare. "From her conversation with me today, I understand that your acceptance of her case is important to her, but she also confided in me that you are no longer friends."

Daniel closed his eyes and leaned forward. "I'm glad she understands that."

"I have to look out for the best interest of my patient, and while I know the answer, I have to ask you. Is your past relationship with Ms. Astor going to be a problem for you?"

He'd chastise her for his lack of faith in him, but he would have asked her the same question if he'd been in Mara's shoes. "Hope Astor is a patient of Duvall Cancer Group. Not only I, but Dr. Bambridge and Dr. Sullivan, will treat her as we do every patient in our care—with their total wellness as our goal. May I ask your diagnosis?"

"Inflammatory breast cancer. Stage II. No metastasis that I can see. Rapid growth, I suspect, since her symptoms only presented a month prior."

Daniel closed his eyes and breathed a sigh of relief. His traitorous heart again. "Prognosis seems good, then, I suspect."

"As good as it ever is. I'll leave that assessment to one of your brilliant oncologists, but I'd like to be kept apprised."

"Do I detect a fondness for Hope, Dr. Ramesh?"

"As I said, she's vulnerable. Those are the ones who need more than medical care, you know. She has a good support system in her friends, but she refuses to talk about family."

Daniel could tell Mara about Stephen and Connie Astor, but that would betray a confidence of a patient. "I'll take care of her, Mara, and we'll get her through this. Failure isn't an option. I cut the word out of my dictionary, and I suggest you do the same."

"Okay, Dr. Duvall. Not an option. Let's pool our resources, and let's see this patient through."

"I'll call you tomorrow after I receive the reports. I'll get her in to see David Bambridge as soon as I can. I'm sure he'll confirm your diagnosis. We'll consult with Dr. Sullivan for her radiologic care, and we'll set out a course of treatment for Hope. I'll keep you advised of all developments." Doctor mode: that was the safest place for him to be when talking about Hope.

"Sounds good, Daniel. Have a nice evening."

Daniel hung up the phone and leaned back against the chair. He stared up at the clouds for a long moment. One of the white puffs had formed into the perfect shape of a carousel horse.

If he believed in God, he might believe the coincidental formation a sign. He closed his eyes, and a single tear slid down the side of his face.

He'd allow his heart to grieve—but only for a moment.

6

The Citrus Restaurant was nearly empty. Daniel had hoped to run into a friend or two. Instead, he sat alone, staring out at the nightlife going on around him. The cars on the nearby overpass raced by. Just like his life. He'd taken his father's advice, waited to establish his career before giving in to the urge to pursue Hope, settle down, and marry.

And he would have pursued her with all he had. He'd have snatched her from Evan Carter, shown her how much he cared.

If only Hope hadn't caused his sister's death.

"Your meal will be out soon, sir." His waitress stopped by his table.

He nodded. He hadn't been here that long, and what did he have to do otherwise? She refilled his water glass. No ring on her finger.

She walked away, and Daniel's gaze followed. He

shook off the thought.

Again, he stared out at the downtown skyline. Two women walked by, and he held his breath, both hoping and dreading the fact that their destination was probably The Citrus.

Delilah held open the door for Hope, and they walked inside. Daniel pulled his glasses from his shirt pocket and put them on. Hope leaned against the wall. Her coloring was better. He'd noticed that this morning while he watched the three ladies sing that church song.

They'd created a mini-flash mob. He'd heard hospital staff still talking about it when he'd done his afternoon rounds.

Delilah said something to Hope, eliciting a weary smile in response.

The hostess gathered up two menus and led the women in his direction.

Hope flinched when her gaze collided with his. "Danny?"

Delilah followed the waitress, but Hope stopped beside his table, motioning for Delilah to give her a moment.

He stared at her. Then remembering his manners, he stood and indicated with the wave of his hand that she should feel free to sit.

She stared at the chair as if he'd placed a cobra on it.

"Have a seat, Hope." He heard himself say the words but couldn't believe it. He cleared his throat. "You're looking better today."

Her lips turned upward into a sad little curve. She sat, and he did the same.

Hope's wan smile faded. "They—all of them—my friends—they insist on having dinner every night. If not for them ..." She looked beyond him, and he turned.

Delilah was taking a seat at a table nearby.

"Dee wanted to go out tonight."

"Maybe you shouldn't be partying so much," he offered and took a drink of water.

Hope's face blanked like a blackboard being erased, almost as if she couldn't follow what he was saying. "Oh no, Danny. Nothing like that. Dinner. Dee and I both hate cooking. She says that she couldn't bear to have our friends in her condo one more night, but I think she knows as well as I do, that they needed a break from us—some time alone." She placed her hands on the table, one covering the other. "We're going straight home. I'm a little wiped out, and Libby worries enough as it is. They're really taking good care of me."

"Well, whatever they're doing, it's working."

"Besides, they made the maximum number of incisions. Even if I still lived the party life, I wouldn't feel like it, especially tonight." Pink graced her cheeks.

Daniel stared out at the dark sky again, watching life pass him by. Five incisions were the maximum, and most patients didn't require that many.

"Danny, I won't keep you, but thank you for agreeing

to look at my results and having your practice accept the referral. I don't know how you knew, but I believe Libby when she says you're exactly what the Lord ordered."

Did she actually believe God had moved him to a kindness he'd rather not have known he needed to bestow? He leaned forward. "God had nothing to do with this, Hope. Evan and his wife asked me to look after your care. I agreed. My partners and I will take excellent care of you."

As if he'd smacked her, Hope slammed back against her seat. Color drained from her face.

Daniel slipped off his glasses and dropped them into his pocket. Why did he have to go and open his mouth? She simply wanted to say thank you, and knowing her, the words must have been hard to get out. She was always so fiercely strong and independent—at least when she had her dad's money behind her.

"Well," she straightened, "whatever the reason, I do appreciate your generosity."

She wasn't wearing makeup, and her dress was modest, below her knee, no cleavage showing. And he found the look mesmerizing despite the fact Hope had seen better days. He shook the thought from his head. Hope would see better days. He'd make sure of it. "I made the commitment, Hope. I'll do whatever it takes."

Hope reached across the table and placed her hand over his. "Careful, Danny, you need to tuck in your hero's cape." As the waitress returned with his dinner, Hope left him alone, heading in the opposite direction of the table where Delilah sat. As she neared the restroom, she picked up her pace. He stared where the warmth of her hand had been.

"Daniel Duvall."

Daniel winced and looked up to maybe the only force more formidable than himself. "Delilah James, to what do I owe this pleasure?"

Without being asked, Delilah sat across from him. "Whatever you just said to Hope isn't helping her, but I think you know that."

He stared at her, unable to find an excuse.

"When your mother demanded Hope not attend Tiffany's funeral, that was a hard blow for her. I've never seen her so broken—not until she came home last night after her apologies to Jacob and Elsa. She won't tell me what they said, but I can see the pain it caused her."

Hope had apologized to his parents? Mother hadn't called him to rail about such audacity. "I can't make apologizes for my parents. They have every right to their anger."

"You can keep telling yourself that, or you can get over it." Delilah stood and leaned over him. "She was bowled over by your offer to treat her if it comes to that. She slept long and hard this afternoon. The first time in ages."

Behind Delilah, Hope walked from the restroom. She stopped and looked in their direction.

"Hope's coming back," he offered, grateful for the

reprieve.

"If you fail her, you'll never forgive yourself. Wouldn't you rather be the one carrying the grudge and not the one carrying the guilt? Think about it." Delilah straightened, meeting Hope at their table. "It's okay, Hope. I was telling him thank you." Delilah looked at him as she spoke. "He knows how much this means to us."

7

Daniel closed his office door and moved around the desk. He lifted the large envelope with Hope Astor's name written upon it and let it drop.

His glasses sat on his desk, and he put them on before picking up the files on his chair. His last patient of the morning was checking out, and as usual, he'd spend a few minutes on dictation before grabbing something to eat.

He opened the first file.

His gaze flitted to the envelope. He'd promised Mara he'd review it and get back to her, but the packet was his personal Pandora's Box.

With a deep breath, he reached for it, holding it up before letting it slip through his fingers, the edge smacking the desk once … twice … a third time.

A soft knock sounded at his door, and his nurse opened it. "Would you like me to bring you back something to eat?" Her brown eyes flitted to the envelope. Her features softened. She had always been perceptive, and Daniel was certain that though she'd never said anything, she remembered Hope and Tiffany's constant visits to steal him away for lunch in the early days of his practice.

"Thanks, Becky." He let Hope's info fall to the desk and dug into his back pocket for his wallet and then handed her a twenty. "Anything from wherever you go. You know what I like."

She nodded.

"I'm buying yours, too."

The worry he'd seen on her face vanished with her smile. "Well, it is your turn." Her teasing laughter stopped with the closing of the door.

He laid his wallet on the desk and picked up the package. With a deep breath, he unwound the string tying the flap. He turned his chair to use the window as a back light and studied the films for a moment. Then he reached inside the envelope and pulled out the radiologist report, finding nothing he couldn't guess from the mammogram.

He took a deep breath and pulled out the results of the core biopsy, reading them twice before he stood and moved to the window.

He didn't have a spectacular view—a vacant lot between medical plazas. The grass was withered and brown from the lack of rain and the hot Florida days. His heart was just as parched.

He leaned his head against the wall and continued to stare outside, heaving in harsh breaths. Why couldn't he hate her and act on that hatred? Why did she evoke an even stronger emotion in him—something he couldn't give a name, something foreign taking root inside of him—a mixture of grief and love—that he didn't want to feel.

Tiffany had danced through his dreams the night before, teasing him about Hope, laughing at his shyness, whispering the games of childhood, "Daniel and Hope sitting in a big, fat coconut tree …"

Something tickled his cheek. He swiped at it and looked at the moisture on his hand. Tears. For whom? Tiffany? Hope? Himself?

He pushed away from the window and picked up his wallet. The well-worn edge of a picture caught his eye, and he slipped it out—his sister and Hope posing in one of the mall photo booths. He'd been away at college, and they were still in high school. Tiffany had mailed it to him in a card. Before Tiffany's death, he'd kept it in his wallet because he loved to see the mischief in Hope's beautiful blue eyes. Now, he couldn't part with it because of the impish smile on his sister's lips—as if she knew a secret she would never divulge. He turned the picture over. "I've got you." He'd never learned what Tiffany meant. The three words were his—ones he'd always tell the girls if they needed his help or he needed to cover for some of their hi-jinxes.

Again, he wiped the moisture from his face. He never cried. "For you, Tiff. I'll get her through this for you."

Delilah had accused him of bearing a grudge. The

perceptive judge was right.

His sister had never harbored ill against anyone. She'd be in his face about his anger toward Hope, but therein lay his problem. The one who could help him forgive had been killed by the actions of the one to whom he could not offer forgiveness.

He'd talk to Mara later—after David Bambridge, the group's oncologist, examined Hope and they'd conferred with Scooter Sullivan, the group's radiologist. He let the picture fall, picked up the office phone, and talked to the receptionist in charge of Dr. Bambridge's appointments. Thankfully, Hope could be fit in today. Satisfied with the appointment time, he picked up his mobile phone. Scrolling through it, he finally found Hope's name and punched it for the call. He received a disconnect announcement. He set the phone down. Mara's office would have her number, but most doctors' offices closed for a few hours around lunchtime to allow their staff to clear the patients and take a much-needed break. He could call her answering service, but Mara wouldn't have the info with her.

Delilah.

He scrolled through his contacts and hit call when he found her name. Hopefully, she wasn't in court.

"This is Judge James."

"Delilah, Daniel Duvall. I'm trying to reach Hope."

"Hey, Danny, hold on."

A muffled conversation took place on the other end of

the line along with some static. "Hello?" Hope said.

"Hope, I'd like you in my office this afternoon." He picked up the report.

"Sure." Her voice came out in a soft whisper. "When?"

"Four. While I've scheduled the appointment for you, there might be a wait."

"That's okay."

"Hope." He laid down the report and picked up the photo, staring at his sister's face.

"Yes?"

"Have one of your friends bring you, okay?"

Except for her quivering breath, silence filled the line.

"I'll see you this afternoon," he said.

"Thank you, Danny."

Daniel clicked off the call. "You know, kiddo," he spoke to his sister's picture. "As most everything you and Hope convinced me to do, this is going to push Mom over the edge."

And why, when he preferred to be called Daniel, did the sound of his childhood nickname suddenly sound so sweet upon Hope's lips again? Given the battle ahead, he reasoned, he would let her wreak havoc with the traitor beating within him. Once he got her through the ordeal, he would put Hope Astor behind him and move on with his life.

Hope sat on the examination table while Libby took a seat in the extra chair in the room. Libby craned her neck to study the painting of the courtyard of an Italian villa.

"You know, he told me, don't you?" Hope asked her friend.

"Huh?" Libby stood and studied the painting.

"He said you and Evan talked to him about my condition."

Libby didn't bat an eye. Instead, she moved closer to the picture. "You painted this."

"Yes, it's on the Riviera. I went with the Duvalls in high school. I gave it to Danny for his birthday two years ago, but you're avoiding the conversation."

Libby drew near. "You were close, weren't you?"

Hope nodded. "Very. Tiffany and I often joined each other on family trips."

"Was Daniel with you when you visited there?"

"Yes. Better times for sure." Hope stared at her hands, not wanting to look at her painting or remember the whispered conversations of a couple on the cusp of adulthood, sharing their dreams of the future. She was thankful she'd not included the dark-haired man and the reddish-blonde haired woman-child she'd first wanted to place in the portrait.

"You know, Libby, I don't think I can do this." She slid from the table.

They'd been waiting for nearly two hours, not that she minded, but she could use it as an excuse. "I'm very tired.

I need to think this out. Danny shouldn't have to deal with me." She reached for her clothing. "I have to get out of here."

Libby stepped in front of her. "Sit down on that table, or I'll pick you up and put you there myself. What does it matter that Evan and I asked the man to do this? He had the option to say no. He even suggested finding you another doctor. Instead, Hope, he came to you. That's integrity. He may not want to do it, but he made up his mind to do the right thing."

"I hate that he sees I've come to this."

"Come to what?" Libby placed her hands on her hips. "To a place where God has you depending upon Him? That's not a bad place to be, you know."

"But I'm not depending on God. I have you, and Evan, Delilah, and those two lovable goofs, Charisse and Gideon."

"All put in your life at this time for such a purpose." Libby's green-eyed gaze bore into Hope as she pointed to the examination table. "My husband has brothers spread everywhere. He's tried to bring them back together, but he can't. So, he's adopted you as his sister. Delilah—she's always cared about you, even when she didn't realize she cared for anyone."

Hope half-laughed and half-cried. Brash Delilah, for some reason, always seemed to gravitate toward Hope's friendship.

"And Daniel—don't you even begin to think it was a

coincidence he was outside that room the day of your mammogram. God is in the details, and if you keep fighting against Him, you'll only be making it harder for yourself and easier for Daniel to avoid a God I'm sure he doesn't believe exists."

Hope stood her ground. She wanted her clothes. She needed to leave.

"Get on that table, Hope."

A light knock sounded on the door.

Libby narrowed her eyes at her as a balding man who wore a white coat, and sported a nice smile entered with a nurse. He held a file in his hand. "Are you going somewhere?" He looked from her to Libby.

"I—I'm here to see Dr. Duvall."

The man looked at his file. "I'm Dr. Bambridge, the oncologist for the Duvall Cancer Group. Dr. Duvall has asked that I take over for Dr. Ramesh."

Hope let her shoulders fall. "So, I do have cancer."

"Why don't you sit down and let the doctor tell you the results of your test?" Libby urged.

What could she do? She'd just let him tell her how bad it was, and then she'd begin to make arrangements for her funeral.

The doctor motioned. "Ms. Astor, please take a seat on the examination table."

Danny had tossed her problems to another physician in his practice. That truth hurt her.

Dr. Bambridge looked at his watch. "You're my last

patient, and I have rounds at the hospital. What's it going to be?"

"Please." Libby tugged at the sleeve of Hope's examination gown. "Please, Hope. Let him treat you."

Hope climbed back onto the examination table, and the nurse helped her to recline.

Libby dropped into her seat with a sigh.

Hope turned her face to the wall. She was ashamed that his hands had to touch her—that anyone had to see her like this. She should be thankful it wasn't Danny.

Dr. Bambridge moved aside the coverlet and began the examination. As with every examination she'd undergone lately, the poking and prodding made her cry out.

"Tender?" he asked.

She nodded.

"Oh, come on. Daniel told me you were tough. You can give me a better comeback. Give it another shot."

She turned to look at him.

The doctor's dark brown eyes gleamed with playful mischief.

"You think?" She smirked.

"I expect better from now on. There's no sarcasm you can throw at any of the doctors in this practice that we can't handle. We work with Daniel, remember?"

Her eyes filled with tears, and she looked away. "I remember." Her words came out in a whisper.

He completed the breast exam. "Come on. Sit up for me, crybaby."

She couldn't help the sob-filled laugh that escaped as the nurse helped her up.

His cold stethoscope touched the bare skin of her back. "Deep breath."

She obeyed.

He moved the stethoscope several times, asking her to take the same deep breath. Then he moved to the front. "Breathe normal for me."

Could he feel the pounding of her heart? Did he realize this was the last place she wanted to be, that she never thought she'd be in this position?

He lifted her arms and explored under her armpits. "Painful?" he asked.

"I feel it in the breasts because they're so tight but not there."

"Good." Stepping back, he studied her. "Hope, how much alcohol do you consume?"

She blinked at the suddenness of his question. "I haven't had a drink since ..." She faltered. She wasn't sure if the doctor knew Daniel had a sister who died. Still, she hadn't had a drink since that night. The last drink she'd had cost her too much.

The doctor studied her. "Drug use?"

"None since last year."

"You need to be straight with me," he pressed.

Danny must have told this man all her deep, dark secrets. "I promise."

"She's telling you the truth." Libby came to her aid.

Hope fought the smile. Libby was a fierce protector. "It's okay, Lib. Danny knew the old me too well. He probably told Dr. Bambridge to ask me. I'm a very capable liar, but this time, Dr. Bambridge, it's the truth."

He opened her chart and looked down at it. "Okay, why don't you get dressed? Then you ladies will wait for me in my office." He closed the file and walked out. His nurse followed.

"He's an infuriating man," Libby said.

"Dr. Bambridge? How so?" Hope began to dress.

"Not him. The other one who set you up for that interrogation. Dr. Danny is even pushing *my* buttons today."

Hope laughed. "And he'll tell you he doesn't know where Tiffany and I got our snarky attitudes. He's a good teacher, don't you think? Dr. Bambridge has learned his lesson well."

Daniel leaned on the wall by the window of Bambridge's office. As much as Daniel wanted to take control, this portion of Hope's treatment only brought him and Dr. Sullivan in to concur on the scope of treatment.

Sullivan stood against Bambridge's door, probably ready to head out for the evening but pausing a moment at Daniel's request.

Bambridge opened the file on his desk and clasped his

hands in front of him. He followed Hope's gaze out his office window and, meeting Daniel's gaze, offered a smile.

Hope didn't appear to notice his attention was on her—or she was embarrassed. Either way, the lift in her chin spoke volumes. Hope still held to her pride.

Funny, he'd always liked that in her, but this woman before him, she was softer, more demure, and he liked that part of her personality even better. He only wished she'd show him some of the audaciousness that attracted him to her. She would need it in this fight of her life.

What he hated seeing in her was the vulnerability that Mara had also recognized. Did it come from leaning upon the others who appeared to be pushing her through life? Their actions were generally a good thing, but if they prevented Hope from fighting her own battles, it could be a stumbling block to her treatment.

"Hope." He gained her attention. "I'm not going to lie to you. I believe Dr. Ramesh told you there's more than one mass. The core biopsy shows the tumors are malignant. The good news is that the sentinel node biopsy indicates the cancer has not spread into your lymph nodes."

Hope looked down at her hands, and Libby started to speak.

Daniel shook his head and nodded at Hope.

Libby sat back.

Daniel nodded to his partner.

"Hope, I need you to look at me," Bambridge said. "We have to communicate as a team. We need to have blood work done, some other testing prior to chemo."

She turned her blue eyes to Daniel, and for a moment he saw the little frightened girl he'd helped out of a tree when she'd climbed too high. *I've got you.* The words ran through his mind. Only then had she released her hold on the branch, and at nine years old, he'd become her hero. She'd told him so that day as he set her on the ground.

"So, I need chemo?" she asked.

"I recommend it, yes." Sullivan said, still leaning against the door. "After the chemo, Dr. Duvall will access the amount of surgery, if any, you need, and we'll discuss radiation at that point as well."

"You have a decision," Daniel gained her attention. "Depending upon the effectiveness of chemo, we can take out any remaining tumors or we can remove both breasts."

She swallowed hard and looked down at her shirt, pulling at it. "What do you recommend?"

He wished he could spare her, but he was never one to mince words with any patient. He wouldn't start with her. "A double mastectomy reduces the chance of reoccurrence. You need to be thinking of reconstruction. We can do it at the time of the mastectomy or any time after."

"My recommendation is that you wait until we see you through the treatments because radiation can do a number on implants, should you choose to go that way," Sullivan added.

"After surgery, we'll be able to examine the cells to determine if you need hormonal therapy," Bambridge said.

"What does that mean, hormonal therapy?"

"We determine if the cells are estrogen receptor positive. If they are, medications can help reduce estrogen levels. Something else to think about would be the temporary shutdown of your ovaries or even their removal."

Hope blanched white "You're saying I might never have children."

Daniel fought the urge to comfort her. If things had gone as he had planned, she might be his wife. They may have had a little one. Now, with so much between them, he wouldn't be the father of her children, but he'd never want her to feel the pain of childlessness. "Hope, many women with inflammatory breast cancer go on to have children."

"That's not something to worry about right now." Bambridge offered a caring smile. "Let's talk about chemo and radiation, Dr. Sullivan. When do you think Hope should begin?"

"Chemo? As soon as possible. If you'll order the blood tests, I'll get her scheduled."

"How long does that take?" Hope asked.

"Four to six months. We'll monitor you carefully. If we see the cancer disappear, one or two more cycles will get it done. If I see reduction, we'll go until it disappears, or I feel you can't tolerate the treatments."

"What happens if chemo doesn't work?" Libby wrung her hands.

"If it doesn't work, the tumors will grow. I'd have to

stop the treatment, and Dr. Bambridge would then look into other treatments to make Hope comfortable."

Daniel heaved a sigh. "We fully expect the chemo to do the job, the surgery to take out any potential future threats, and for radiation to do the rest."

"And radiation is how long?" Hope asked.

"I generally have the patient in therapy each weekday for five to eight weeks," Sullivan advised.

Hope pursed her lips together and stared between Libby and Daniel.

"Something wrong." Daniel lifted a brow.

Hope stayed silent for a long moment, but Daniel didn't miss the trembling of her hands.

"You've been wonderful to me, Danny. This offer to see me—when I first arrived, I thought you'd passed me on to Dr. Bambridge, but I see the extent of care you've offered. It's more than I ever hoped for, but the truth is, what you've just said—the surgery and all the other care—it's beyond the realm of my finances." She stood. "So, I won't be wasting your time."

"Your medical costs are covered." The words fell out of his mouth, and Libby held an arrow-tipped glance in his direction that would have killed him if she let it fly.

Hope headed for the door, the scared little girl needing someone to help her find her way yet too prideful to admit it.

Sullivan moved to allow Hope to leave.

"Hope, I've got you." The words flowed from deep

inside Daniel. Tiffany's words on the back of the photo. His words when he'd helped her out of so many scrapes and long ago predicaments.

She spun toward him. "What?"

"I've got you."

She stared at him for a long moment. "I can't—I can't take this charity. I've lost everything—but I won't lose my pride."

Libby pinned Hope with the same look she'd just given to him. "Your pride is a sin, and in this case a deadly one. And we're not offering you charity."

"How can I repay you?" Hope slumped. "I can't. I have no way of doing so."

"You can repay us by choosing to live," Daniel said, and his two partners nodded in agreement.

"And I have a few ideas. When it's time, I'll share them with you, but you have to listen to your doctors." Libby turned in her seat to face Hope, and after a long moment, Hope nodded.

Libby offered her a smile. "The treatment ahead is going to be rough for you, physically and psychologically, but I know you're a fighter. We can get you through this." She reached out and as Hope sat, she took Hope's hand in hers.

Daniel stared at Libby's hand clasped in Hope's tight grasp. Religious nut or not, this woman Evan Carter married was a pure gem.

"Here, Hope." Bambridge retrieved a Kleenex from

his credenza behind him and held it out to her.

She reached for it and sat back. "Thank you all so much."

"We can get you through this," Libby repeated. "And God is with us whatever the outcome."

Before this was all over, Daniel imagined his tongue would be bitten in half.

Hope looked at him, and he saw a gleam of mischief under the tears. "Danny doesn't believe in God, Libby."

Daniel pushed from the wall, choosing to ignore her. "As Dr. Sullivan said, you need to get the blood work done. The sooner you start chemo the better. You need to weigh the options of reconstruction, when, if, and how."

Once again, Hope pressed to her feet. She held out her hand. "Libby is right, Danny. I trust God. He used Evan and Libby to pull this together. You're telling me I have a greater chance of survival if I follow the entire course— chemo, double mastectomy, radiation, all of it. I'll accept the charity of others, and I'll believe God will allow me to repay it someday."

Daniel shook her hand. Why did he feel the sudden urge to pull her against him, to tangle his hands in the softness of her hair and whisper promises to do everything in his power to give her a chance of survival? Instead, he stood stock-still, unable to trust his emotions to keep his doctor-patient relationship as it should be.

Hope also shook hands with Bambridge and Sullivan. "Thank you. I'll be your best patient. I'll do everything you tell me to do."

"Mara—Dr. Ramesh—has asked to remain a part of our team. Dr. Bambridge, Dr. Sullivan, and I will treat her like a member of this group."

"If you'll wait in the lobby, I'll have my staff set up the therapy, allowing enough time for you to get the blood work complete." Sullivan held open the door for Hope.

Hope turned to Daniel. "I didn't need to hear Dr. Ramesh tell me you're the best. I know how hard you studied, how seriously you take medicine. I'm grateful you didn't let Tiffany and me pull you away from it too much." She turned and stopped at the door. "But I'm also grateful for the times you did, and I'm grateful to you both, Dr. Sullivan. Dr. Bambridge."

Hope moved around the corner, but Libby stayed.

"What is it, Libby?" Daniel ran his hand through his hair.

"Evan and I never asked you to take on the financial costs. After my initial wrong judgment of you—and I'm sorry for that—I figured out that must be what you meant. I'm right, aren't I?"

"Yes." He rubbed his eyes, hoping Evan's wife would think him only tired. He cleared his voice. "I've got her."

"We're all in this together, Dr. Duvall. We said we'd help with the costs. You're not alone anymore."

He jerked his gaze upward. How had this woman realized the all-consuming loneliness he'd felt lately?

"The sooner you understand that you can't hate her,

the sooner that pain inside you will go away."

Daniel looked away, unable to bear her scrutiny. When he looked back, Libby was gone, and his partners stared at him, mouths open.

"What?" he asked.

Bambridge snickered as he got to his feet. "Love her much, Daniel?"

Hope

8

The building still smelled of fresh wood and paint even though the church had been there for over seven months.

The design was nothing fancy, but it met their needs. The congregation had worked hard. Hope had even pulled her load. That's why she'd thought the pain she felt was muscle related, and she'd waited to seek a doctor, which she'd done six months ago.

Though still tired, the side effects of the chemo were behind her now. Dr. Sullivan had indicated he thought the tumors gone or at least shrunken to a size where Daniel could get everything during the mastectomy. Sullivan had stopped her treatments a month early. Even her hair had started to sprout. She no longer had to wait out the intense headaches and joint pain or deal with the mouth sores that made life miserable.

She should have felt she had a new lease on life, but she didn't.

Yes, Dr. Sullivan had indicated that he thought she'd done well with the chemotherapy, but she still had the surgery, and that scared her worse than anything.

Her thoughts had ping-ponged back and forth between taking a chance and having Danny perform only a lumpectomy—against his recommendation—but he'd looked her in the eye and indicated that he truly believed a double mastectomy would reduce the chance of reoccurrence.

Now, she simply needed to trust God to get her through the terrifying ordeal.

The Sunday evening sermon had ended, but the congregation remained in their seats. Gideon stood and moved to the platform as the pastor stepped down. "Thank you for staying," Gideon said. "James 5:16 tells us, 'Confess your faults one to another, and pray for one another, that ye may be healed. The effectual fervent prayer of a righteous man availeth much.' Tonight, we have a dear sister in Christ who is in need of healing. I'd like us to pause for a moment of silence to bring any lingering matters that might inhibit our prayers before the Lord. If you'll pray silently, I'll interrupt in a moment. If anyone else would like to pray for Hope as she prepares for surgery and for treatment for her cancer, please do so. We'll pause a few seconds before each prayer to give anyone who wishes to pray an opportunity. Once everyone who wishes to pray aloud has done so, Evan, would you close in a final prayer?"

Evan nodded, and heads bowed. The church was silent.

Hope stared around her. She slid off of her seat and onto her knees, clasping her hands on top of the chair and laying her head upon them.

Dear God, search my heart and show me any iniquity that I may not see. Help me to go forth in prayer with a right heart and a right mind, asking only for healing, Lord, because I have more to do to serve You. If, by my death, I serve You more, Lord, I will gladly leave this earthly realm to be with You, but don't make it that easy on me, Father. If I'm to die so that Danny and his family can live, let me be that conduit. If in order to seek Your favor, my parents need to lose their daughter the way Elsa and Jacob lost Tiffany—at my hands—I will gladly give my life, but Lord, I'm going to seek to live until You take my last breath from me. I will live from this day forward without complaint and in Your strength so long as You'll have me be a witness here on this earth.

Around her, Hope heard the words spoken on her behalf, some mumbled, but all comforting, even as she continued to pray.

Father, I have always loved Danny Duvall, but I have not always treasured him. Since my diagnosis, since he agreed to help me, I have thought of nothing else but his selflessness and my selfishness. He once told me he felt so alone even in the company of his own family. Dear God, I ask You today to fill that void. You are what he needs. And,

Hope

God, I'm going to presume so much in asking You to help me to be the one You use to show him Your love and Your tender care over him. Make me always mindful of the cost of my selfishness throughout the remainder of my treatment.

"Dear Father, please be with Hope." Evan's words cut into Hope's silent petition if only because they rang with such emotion.

Hope looked up. She'd been so deep in prayer she'd paid little attention to the petitions that were said on her behalf.

Libby had her arm around her husband holding him as he tried to find the words to speak. "She is knit to my heart like a sister to a brother. Dear God, guide the hands of her doctor and the nurses tomorrow. Be with Hope along each step of the way, and help us, her friends ..." Evan stopped to take a heavy breath. "... her family, to be towers of strength as she moves forward in Your will for her. Help us to be strong in whatever Your will, and help us to reach out to those who will be touched by You during this time. In Jesus' precious name we pray. Amen."

Delilah helped Hope to sit in the chair. Hope reached across both Delilah and Libby to hold Evan's hand. His eyes were moist, and she'd never loved him more than she did at this minute.

"You okay?" he asked her.

"I love you." She pushed past the other two women to sit beside Evan. She hugged him. "Evan, I know you've doubted your kindnesses at times, but you are the gentlest, sweetest man I've ever known." She kissed his cheek and reached for Libby's hand. "Thank you both for loving me so much and allowing the Lord to use you to move Mount Daniel and to garner his assistance." Hope stood. "Thank you, everyone." She told her church family even as her little eclectic family encircled her.

The pastor and his wife hugged Hope. Others in the congregation also told her they'd be praying for her and offered her words of encouragement.

"We'll be sure to pray for you right at six thirty tomorrow morning, covering you with prayer as you go into surgery." An elderly couple held her in an embrace.

"Thank you."

Delilah stretched. "Well, six thirty comes awfully early for a girl like me. I think I'll get Hope home. She needs her rest."

Hope stepped behind Delilah, following her outside. Libby slipped her hand in hers and Hope turned. "She's frightened for you," Libby whispered. "Be sure to pray with her before you go to sleep."

Hope smiled. If she didn't know better, she might think Delilah was more worried than she was.

"Dee," Gideon called. "Anything on your calendar I can sub for you in the morning."

Delilah shook her head. "I cleared my calendar, Gid. Thank you, though."

The lack of a parting shot by either one of them spoke

volumes. They were both burdened. At their cars, she gave them each a hug. They would meet her at the hospital in the morning, but she wasn't sure how quick the pre-op admittance would be. When she hugged Evan, she kissed his cheek. "'Night. I'll need you and Libby to hold my hand in the morning."

Evan gave her a simple nod and ducked into his car.

"He loves you, Hope," Libby said. "So, with God's help we're going to get you all better."

Hope sat in Delilah's car. "Don't take what she says lightly," Dee smiled. "I don't believe Libby Carter has ever had anything keeping her separated from God. If she's praying, all we have to do is add our words and sit back and watch." She started her car and stared out the window.

Hope didn't question her.

When her friend slammed her hand down on the steering wheel, Hope jumped.

"Hope, don't you die on me. Do you hear me? You don't dare die on me. I need you."

Hope smiled. "Now, why would a sophisticated, well-educated, legal mind need a sappy, little, sarcastic artist who never did anything with her life? Delilah, if God takes me away through any of this, you'll be fine."

"No." Delilah shook her head. "No, I won't be."

"Danny said he doesn't foresee any complications. Besides, you have Gideon and Charisse and Evan and Libby."

Tears streamed down Delilah's face as she looked at

Hope. "But you—you get me."

"Oh, honey, Gideon gets you, too."

Delilah gave a half-chuckle. "But you and I've been through so much." Delilah straightened and backed out of the church parking lot. "And I'm hoping one day you'll teach me the mannerisms I need to find a man."

Hope laughed. "Delilah, I already know the perfect man for you. And you won't need to change a thing."

Her friend gave her a brief look. "You're lying. You want to take my mind off my worries."

"Nope. I know exactly who he is, but here's the deal: once I'm on my feet after all of this, I'll tell you his name, and once I give you that information, I'll need to spend a couple of months convincing you I'm right. Then we can start convincing him I'm not crazy."

Delilah remained silent for a long moment then burst out laughing. "So long as it isn't Danny Duvall."

Not a chance. Though Danny and Delilah … No, not while God gave her breath. Besides, the guy Hope had in mind for Delilah was perfect—Dee just didn't realize it yet. She spent too much time antagonizing him in and out of court.

"Did you try your parents again?" Delilah broke into her thoughts.

Hope nodded. As the scenery passed, Hope's heart grew heavy. "Delilah, before we go home, can we make a brief stop?"

"Sure. Where?"

"I want to try one more time."

"Hope, they aren't answering your calls. They didn't even respond to your message about the cancer. Do you think they're going to let you in their house?"

"Just one more try?"

Delilah nodded. "Of course."

The Sunday meal was delicious as usual, but over time, Daniel's desire to be with his parents waned as they continued to seek solace only in grief and memories. At least his father had a thriving practice, and it kept him busy, but the house had become a prison for them. He wondered how much his mother actually went out these days.

Daniel had long gotten used to being the forgotten child—at least in his mother's eyes. Mom loved Tiffany. He'd been four when his sister had been born. He didn't remember her doting on him as much as she did his sister, but he didn't hold a grudge. Instead, he loved the quirky kid Tiffany had become.

Dad spent time with him. He'd coached Little League and Pop Warner football. His father helped him build a fort and even helped him fix up his first car, and the cardiologist had been proud of Daniel when he graduated from med school and took his internship in a local hospital.

Both his father and his mother had so many desires for their children. Daniel was sure he had not disappointed, and Tiffany had been coming around. That's why they took her loss so hard.

Mom's attention seemed to stay riveted on the empty chair. "Our baby would have been twenty-nine today."

Daniel winced. He hadn't remembered, and he had always remembered Tiffany's birthday. For twenty-seven years, he'd delighted her with unusual gifts or a great time somewhere. He'd never let her down.

Somehow, forgetting her special day only the second year after they'd lost her made him feel like a heel. He'd been so preoccupied with work—and with Hope's well-being—that Tiffany hadn't even come to mind lately.

This first mention of Tiffany coming so far into the meal was also a surprise. Mom must have wanted him to take note and to say something.

He'd failed her in that regard.

Mom lifted her gaze and put it on him. "Hope Astor," she spat. "If she ever dares come near me again, I swear, I'll kill her."

"Elsa," Dad placed a warning in his voice. "You know you wouldn't."

"Where did she ever get the idea that words were enough to garner forgiveness?" Mom looked to the ceiling, fighting emotion.

Daniel cast a look at his father. Had Hope tried to apologize to his parents again? He didn't think so. If not, his mother was pulling out bitterness for something that occurred months before. "When did you see Hope?" he asked.

"I don't know. She came by here some time back. She apologized." Mom slapped her napkin onto the table. "As if words could make up for what she did."

"Words are all she has, Mom." The words slipped out of Daniel's mouth before he could stop them. From where had they come? He wasn't exactly forgiving of Hope. Or was he?

He'd seen her a couple of times when she'd been in the office for her appointments with Scooter Sullivan, but he'd only recently had her in for her pre-surgery consult.

Surprisingly, he couldn't remember even thinking of Tiffany during Hope's visit. He'd been professional, but he'd loosened up with her. His back hadn't straightened with accusation. She'd been a patient and he her doctor.

Though, she hadn't left his mind much after she'd walked out of his office.

"Daniel!" Mom's raised tone pulled him from the thoughts he had of Hope even now.

"I'm sorry," he said. "What did you say?"

"I wanted to know why you'd take up for her like that."

"I don't know, Mom. Maybe because the anger you've held so long isn't good for you."

Dad remained quiet, but his face, set like granite, said more than words. The mighty Jacob Duvall was afraid to counter his wife, worried she'd start another session of crying.

The maid entered to clear away the dishes. Daniel

smiled at her as he always did. She left and returned with the final course.

Daniel stared at the cup of custard—Tiffany's favorite dessert. He swallowed hard. Tonight, of all nights, what was his mother thinking? Was she even trying to move on? After her last words, he didn't think her ready for this.

Each of them stared at the yellow dessert in the white bowls.

Having enough of the silence, Daniel picked up his spoon and dipped it into the dessert. "In honor of Tiffany." He raised his spoon and took a bite.

His mother's sad smile broke Daniel's heart. She picked up her spoon and brought a bite to her mouth. Then she dropped the spoon, allowing it to fall and splatter the custard over the white tablecloth before she rushed out of the dining room.

Daniel started to follow her.

"Daniel." His father's commanding voice stopped him. "Let her go."

"She's hurting …"

"Yes, she is, and she's destroying our family. If we keep comforting her, she's going to keep seeking it out. I'll go to her in a while."

Daniel sat down.

"Finish your dessert," his dad said. "Tiffany wouldn't want any of this wasted."

Daniel nodded in agreement and took another bite. "Do you mind if I ask you something?"

"Have I ever minded?"

"When Hope came here to apologize, what did you think?"

Dad stared at him for a long moment. "I think it took a lot of guts, and her showing up in person spoke louder to me than anything she could say. She could have sent a flower arrangement or mailed a card, but she faced us. That's something her parents have never done, and they only live across the street. I miss my friendship with Stephen."

"Bet you don't miss Connie much." Daniel offered a smirk.

"No, not so much. Stephen has always let Connie have way too much control. Sometimes I think I'd like to reach out to him, but …" he shook his head "… I guess the truth is, I'm a little henpecked as well. The wrath of Elsa Duvall at such treachery would end what's left of our failing marriage."

Ouch. Daniel had known things were stressed, but he had always thought his loving parents would find a way back to each other. Now, Daniel had to add to his father's burden. "Dad, Hope's a patient. Breast cancer. Both breasts. Somewhat aggressive, but no metastasis. I couldn't turn her away."

Color drained from his father's face. He closed his eyes and shook his head. "Then I know her apology was sincere. The words your mother chose for her couldn't have been easy to take, and Hope didn't retaliate in any way. She simply nodded and walked out. That couldn't have been easy for her at all."

Daniel put his spoon down. "What did Mom say to her?"

His father shook his head. "Son, you don't want to know the depths of your mother's bitterness. I never thought I could see a heart so hardened—especially my Elsa's heart."

Hope looked back at Delilah who sat in the car. She pushed the button on the intercom affixed to her parents' gate. She'd tried the code, but it had been changed, no doubt to keep her out.

"Yes."

"Mary, this is Hope," she announced to her parents' live-in maid. "Are Mother and Daddy in?"

"Let me check, Ms. Hope," the maid said in a near sigh.

In the glow of Delilah's headlights, Hope looked at her watch. Nine o'clock. Mother always hated phone calls or visitors after that hour.

"Ms. Hope," Mary said, "they aren't up to receiving visitors tonight. May I give them a message?"

Hope leaned against the gate. She'd allowed herself to dream, and the letdown took the energy from her.

"Hope." Delilah ran from her car. "Are you okay?"

Hope pushed herself upright.

"Ms. Hope, are you there?" Mary asked.

Delilah pushed Hope's hand away from the buzzer. "Yes, she is, and you tell her parents, if they don't open this gate …"

"I'm sorry, who are you?" Mary asked.

"Delilah, don't, please," Hope begged.

"You tell Connie and Stephen I want this gate opened now. Their daughter wants a few minutes of their precious time, and they'll give it to her, or they can call the cops. The headlines will be brilliant, and I'll tell them what a self-righteous coward Connie Astor has become."

"Dee …" Hope pulled on her friend. "This isn't the way to do this."

The buzzer sounded, and the gate opened. Hope widened her eyes. "I'll be back in just a min—"

"Not a chance." Dee took her by the arm. "I'll do my best not to say a word, but I'm not leaving you alone."

Mary opened the door.

Hope swiped her feet on the front mat and stepped inside.

"Oh, my." Mary's hand went to her face. "Are you okay?"

"Probably nothing that a little hangover cure won't resolve." Mother stepped into the foyer, a drink in her hand. She seemed to startle a moment.

Hope put her hands to her short, spiky hair. She'd stopped worrying about what people saw, but her mother's reaction brought on the self-consciousness. "Hope, you're looking absolutely awful. Couldn't you find a wig?"

Hope wanted to hug her mother, but Connie Astor didn't take public displays of affection very well at all. "Mother, is Daddy home?"

Mother turned without a word, and Hope followed her into the living room. Delilah dogged Hope's heels.

Hope's father stood when they entered the room. He seemed weary, his gaze darting between Hope and her mother. Once again, Hope feared she'd placed Daddy in the middle.

Mother made her way to the cold, dark fireplace that had been Hope's favorite spot on Christmas morning as a child. Back then Mother and Daddy had spoiled her with toys and clothes. Hope stared into the cavernous hole there now. Daddy had heaped the toys and the art supplies upon her, and Mother gifted her with essential items: books, the latest fashions, everything a young, practical woman would want.

But Hope had never been practical. She hadn't known it back then, but God had instilled in her a love for art.

Here in the midst of her family home, where she'd been barred from entrance for so long, Hope realized that truth. Any talent she had came from God, and she had yet to use it for Him.

"So, Hope. Have you come to your senses? Are you ready to come home, go to school, get a job in the practical world, stop following your father's fanciful fantasy that an artist can survive?"

"Mommy ..." The endearment fell from Hope's lips.

Her mother frowned. "Mother, Hope. Show respect."

Her father had yet to speak. Nothing new. Her mother ruled this home. Daddy's slumped shoulders and woe-filled eyes said it all.

"I—I came to tell you something."

"Well, get on with it. I'm sure that Judge James can testify that ex-parte hearings are only held early in the morning. I must be at the top of my game. Time is wasting. I have a file to review."

Delilah cleared her throat. Hope stared down at Dee's clenched fists. "Counselor, my office should have called. I canceled tomorrow morning's ex-parte hearings. They were rescheduled for next week. Something much more important has come up."

Hope allowed a brief smile. Delilah was no wilting flower. In ways very different from Libby Carter, she got her point across.

"So, I would appreciate it if you would spare your daughter the five minutes that your canceled hearing has provided. She has something on her mind."

"Please sit down," Daddy finally offered.

"No, Daddy, that's okay. I—we can't stay long. I just came to tell you that I love you. I won't keep you."

"That's it? Judge James, I should call the police."

Delilah narrowed her eyes. "You go right ahead, Mrs. Astor." She turned to Hope. "Tell them, or I'll do it."

"Tell us what?" Daddy stepped closer to her but stopped at a hateful glance from Mother.

"Daddy … Mother, I'm happy to announce that I've made it through chemo." She ran her hand over the bristle on top of her head. "But I'm having surgery tomorrow. I— I just wanted you to know in case … Well, the honest truth is, I'm a little afraid."

Silence reigned for a moment. "Hope, you always were so dramatic." Her mother waved her hand with the glass. The brown liquid sloshed to the tawny carpet. "Breast cancer isn't a death sentence. It's a wakeup call for you."

"You're. Not. Listening." Delilah ground out the words. "For once, hear what your daughter has to say, Connie." Dee stepped toward Hope's father. "This is serious."

"She's young. She'll overcome." Connie again waved the glass. "And if you think for one minute that we'll give you money for your medical treatment, you're mistaken."

Delilah gasped.

Hope braced herself for an onslaught of ugly words from her friend.

Delilah remained silent.

"Mother, I didn't come here to ask you for anything."

"I've always said that if you wanted to get this artistic foolishness out of your senses, realize that you control your destiny …" Mother cast a glare in Hope's father's direction. "Realize that a degree in business, in law, anything but the arts, will secure your foundation, then I'm right there. I'll help you pay your tuition."

"Connie, did you hear our daughter. She's having surgery."

"Well, I'd think this will be an incentive. She'll get herself beyond this medical problem, start school, and get a regular job to pay off her bills. Then and only then will she be welcome to move home."

"Mother," Hope whispered. "I love you." She moved to her father and wrapped her arms around him. "I love you, too, Daddy. I just wanted to have a chance to say so in case … in … case …"

"In case she dies!" Delilah's scream was like a woman gone mad. "Yes, she could. Things go wrong in surgery all the time. She's putting on a show of bravery, but she has to be scared to death. She should be able to seek comfort from her parents. We're praying for God's healing, but there's a chance that in all of this, God will choose to take her."

"God!" Mother cackled. "Better place your faith in a good surgeon … God doesn't exist, girls. He's a figment of weak minds."

Daddy held to Hope, and she relished being his little girl for one more moment. She backed away, planting a smile on her face. "Well, that God you say doesn't exist, He put me into the hands of the best surgeon in this area."

"And who might that be," Mother challenged.

"Danny Duvall, Mother. He's performing a full mastectomy tomorrow morning. I have a little ways to go, but with his help and the help of the physicians in his office and Dr. Mara Ramesh, I know that God has me in good hands." Hope backed away, pulling Delilah with her. "And Mommy, I'm aware that what you want for me stems from your love for me. You think you've carried the load because you believe Daddy's interior designs don't bring in the money to pay for this lavish house and the lifestyle you want for all of us, but for me, what Daddy did was much more important."

Her father straightened, his eyes wide.

"And what do you assume your father has done?" Connie brushed her hair back from her forehead, her body stiffening in what Hope's father once told her was the pole of pride that ran down her mother's back when she was being challenged.

"Daddy provided the love and warmth in this house. He provided color and creativity. He loves you despite your condescending and controlling nature, and he has always loved and supported me in whatever I choose to do. Right or wrong, that is more valuable than the money you bring in. His love was warm. Your money was cold, and while I used the creativity I inherited from Daddy to make beautiful paintings, I used your money to grow even colder. Still, I love you both." She spun toward the foyer. Only at the door did she realize that Delilah was not with her.

"You're both pieces of work," Delilah said. "I'd call you to let you know how the surgery goes, but I'd be wasting my breath."

"Dee, please," Hope begged.

Delilah was by her side in a moment.

"They may need you someday," Hope whispered as Mary opened the door. "Let's not go there now. Good-bye, Mary."

Hope walked into the muggy evening and down the driveway where Delilah's car remained on the other side of the gate. She wouldn't return to this house again any more than she'd enter Jacob and Elsa Duvall's manse. Why hurt her dad? He'd had a lifetime of misery, and the cost of his faithfulness to her mother had never been clearer to Hope in her life.

Hope made it to her car door but stopped.

Across the street, in his parents' driveway, Danny leaned against the trunk of his car, his legs crossed, his eyes taking in the action.

Hope lifted her hand, bowed her head, and ducked inside the car. Delilah took a minute to join her, and Hope spent the time praying her friend would not make any more of a scene.

When Delilah sat inside, she hitched her thumb toward Hope's window. The knock there startled Hope. "Danny," she breathed his name before rolling down the glass.

"You need to be home resting." Danny leaned down, his arms folded on the opening. He peered through the car and toward his parents' home.

"Danny, I know I've said it already, but I'm so sorry for all of this. Your kindness toward me is costing you. I know that, but I appreciate it."

His warm touch on her shoulder surprised her. "If you appreciate it so much, then I want you home and in bed. The next few months are going to drain you. I want you strong before radiation starts. The chances of infection increase."

Hope placed her hand over his. "I love you, Danny."

He yanked his touch from her. "Good night."

Hope rolled up the window. "Get me home, Delilah, before I die of embarrassment right here, and if you tell me 'I told you so ...'"

Delilah pulled away from the curb. "You won't hear it from me. Besides Libby Carter, you are the bravest woman I have ever known." She reached across, and her warm hand rested against Hope's face. "Not too long ago, I would have said you two were the weak ones, and I was the most courageous. Right now, I'm feeling a little like the scarecrow, the tin man, and the cowardly lion all rolled into one being."

"Oh, Dee, don't you know?"

"What?"

"All three of us: Libby, Charisse and me, we want to be just like you."

Delilah laughed. "You forget. I terrorized Charisse. I'm blessed she's my friend."

"We're all blessed."

Delilah took her hand away. "And we by you, my friend. And we by you."

Hope

9

Daniel couldn't believe it. They were all here with her. He pushed a smile into place. "Good morning." He snatched up the file lying at Hope's feet and read it carefully. Then he checked her IV. He ran his hand teasingly over Hope's spiky hair. She was beautiful with or without hair. Her blue eyes were the focal point, and everything else was just window dressing. "You doing okay?"

She nodded. "Is it time?"

"Not unless you want to do this without anesthesia." He winked at her.

"Do we have time to pray?" Evan Carter asked. "Danny, will you join us?"

Daniel nodded. He'd been through this ritual many times. Hope's friends held hands, and he nearly jerked from Delilah's touch. He managed to grip her hand, but his gaze met with Hope's.

"Dear Lord, we pray protection for Hope today," Evan

began. "We leave her in Your hands, and we pray that You guide Danny's hands. Father, may you help Danny to see the cancer and to rid Hope's body of this disease that she may live to serve you."

Hope closed her eyes. "Be with Danny, Lord. Be with Danny," she mouthed.

Daniel closed his eyes.

"Give Hope peace," Evan continued, "and Father as we wait to hear how she's doing, we pray You'll give us calmness of spirit, and in whatever comes, we give You the glory. In Jesus' name, amen." Evan patted Hope's shoulder. "We'll be here when you come out of surgery."

"And I'll be praying all morning," Gideon Tabor bent down and kissed her cheek. "I'll see you this evening."

"I can't wait." Hope smiled.

Gideon held out his hand. "Take good care of her."

Daniel shook his hand and gave him a nod.

A nurse entered. "Dr. Angelo will be here in just a moment. Ms. Astor, I'm going to slip a slight sedative into your IV."

"Dee?" Hope seemed anxious until Dee drew close. Hope reached for her friend's hands. "If anything happens, please tell my parents I'm sorry. Tell them I love them. I— I understand why they did what they did. Kiss my father for me. Tell him …" Tears welled in Hope's eyes.

Delilah gave Daniel a worried look.

Daniel nodded.

"I'll tell him anything you want," Dee said.

"Tell him all I ever wanted to do was make him proud of me, and I'm—I'm so sorry I didn't do that." She began to cry.

"I'm going to ask everyone to leave now." Daniel took control. "When the surgery is done and Hope is moved to recovery, someone will let you know."

They filed out, and Hope continued to cry. Daniel bent down. "Hope, I want you to listen to me."

Tears spilled from her eyes and onto the pillow.

"Look at me." He reached for her hand.

She stared first at his hand. Then her blue eyes turned to him. "Remember the day you got stuck up in the tree?"

She nodded, biting into her lower lip.

"You were scared then, too, weren't you?"

She nodded again.

"I had you then. I've got you now."

Her ragged breaths slowed. "Don't let me go. Please don't let me go."

Dr. Angelo entered the room, his heavyset lumbering a distraction for Daniel, a chance to gather his emotions.

"Ms. Astor." Angelo checked Hope's arm bracelet. "Good to meet you. Let me explain how this is going to work."

Hope's eyes were already becoming heavy from the sedative, but she focused on the anesthesiologist.

"We're going to wheel you into the operating room so that Dr. Duvall can do what he does best, but before that, I'm going to ask you to count down from a hundred. Don't worry about it. You won't make it all the way to one." Angelo winked. "You won't be aware of this, but I'll be placing a mask over your face and watching the nitrous oxide while it does its work to keep you asleep and pain free."

Hope cast a worried glance to Daniel.

"I've got you," he repeated.

Angelo gave Daniel a curious look but gained Hope's attention. "Are you ready?"

"Yes," Hope said.

They began to wheel her into the operating room. "Danny?"

"Uh-huh," he said.

"I love you."

"You only say that when you want something from me," he teased. "I wondered all night what that could be. You and Tiff always hounded me for something. 'We love you, Danny. Will you drive us to the mall? We love you, Danny. Will you cover for us so we can go to the movies?' What is it you want this time?"

Hope's eyes closed, and she fought against it.

"Okay, Hope," Angelo said. "Let's start counting down. One hundred, ninety-nine ..."

"I want you to have faith." Hope squeezed his hand. "Ninety-eight, ninety-seven, ninety-six ... ninety five ... ninety four ... ninety ... ninety three ..." And she was gone.

Daniel and Angelo went to scrub. At the sink, he

scoured his hands and arms, allowing a sudden wave of peace to wash over him. . . .*and we pray that You guide Danny's hands. Father, may you help Danny to see the cancer and to rid Hope's body of this disease that she may live to serve you.* He looked at his hands. Could it be that there was a God, and could that God help him get Hope through this? "If You're there, I would appreciate the help," he murmured.

"Didn't take you for a praying man," Angelo finished his scrubbing.

Daniel's face warmed. "I guess we can use all the help we can get."

Hands dried, the men made their way back into the OR.

"You okay, Daniel?" Angelo asked.

I want you to have faith. Hope's plea rang through his heart.

Daniel nodded. Never had he felt such peace, as if he were no longer alone. "I'm fine. Let's get started."

Daniel had changed back into his suit and headed out the door.

"Dr. Duvall." The OR nurse's shoes, free of their covering, squeaked as she made her way toward him. "I know you need to get back to your office, but Hope Astor's friends are waiting to talk to you."

"Didn't you let them know she's out of surgery?" he asked.

"Yeah, but the one woman, she's adamant that you speak with them."

Daniel gave a heavy sigh. Delilah would be adamant, but at least he had an excuse. "Tell them I'm only allowed to discuss the patient status with those listed on her HIPAA form."

The nurse handed him the form.

He read the list of names. All of them. A smile tugged at him, and he shook his head. "All right." He changed course, walking through the double doors and toward the waiting room. "Has she come out of anesthesia?" he asked the nurse who walked by his side.

"Not yet."

That worried him, but he pushed the thought away for the moment as he entered the waiting room.

Libby saw him first, and she touched her husband's arm. Evan had been dozing. He awoke and placed a tender hand against her face.

What was it about the way he looked at and touched his wife that caused so much melancholy for Daniel? Would this desire to have someone of his own to share the intimacies of life ever be fulfilled?

Delilah jumped to her feet before Evan rose. "How is she?" she demanded.

"She's in recovery. Two of you can go back when the nurse tells you."

Delilah placed her hands on her hips and tapped the toe of her stilettos against the waxed floor. "You know that's not all we want to know. What about the cancer? Were you able to get all of it?"

Daniel had a deep desire to pet Delilah's head like he would a small, worried child. He'd never seen her so shaken, had never known her to care for anyone—at least not much. Still, he'd keep his hand down. He'd like to keep it.

"What did you find during surgery?" she demanded.

"Exactly what we thought we'd find. The chemo had taken away most of the tumors. My trained eyes tell me we were able to get all of the cancer. She'll be taken to a room. I'm admitting her for a couple of days to get her body functioning and to make sure she's able to get up and move around."

"What else can we expect?" Evan made it to his feet.

"She'll be able to begin her radiation treatment soon. What I may not have gotten should be targeted and eliminated. In some ways, radiation can be more of a threat to her than chemo or even surgery. She'll need to get plenty of rest. Give her something to do to occupy her time between now and then because when the radiation starts, I'll be pulling the plug on a lot of her activities to keep her as germ-free as possible."

Delilah nodded and wiped her eyes with the back of her hand. Charisse slipped her arm around Dee, and Evan reached for his wife.

Daniel looked to each of them. "Your job is to keep her well-nourished and healthy and to keep her spirits up."

Libby nodded with a finality that Daniel suspected meant business. "She's prone to depression lately, but I have just the idea to make her feel productive."

"Thank you, Dr. Duvall," Charisse said.

"Everyone else calls me Daniel, don't be shy." Daniel turned to leave.

"Snarky," Libby Carter said loudly enough to gain his attention.

Daniel turned. "What?"

"That's what Hope called your attitude." Libby glared at him. "Snarky. I think it fits. Funny and rude at the same time—kind of the way Hope used to act." Libby walked up to him. She placed a warm hand on his arm and kissed his cheek. "She likes you that way, Daniel. Thank you for all you've done."

Daniel nodded and turned to go, allowing a smile to play on his lips.

"Daniel." Delilah came from behind him and pulled him to the side.

"What is it, Dee?"

"You want to keep her from going into a funk?"

"That's what I said now, isn't it?" He narrowed his eyes, forgetting he was dealing with someone who would never be intimidated by him.

"Well, you're as important to that plan as any of us. Gideon and I can only do so much to keep a smile on her face. That comes natural to us. We're always sparring. We like it because we like each other. You, however, are going to have to do something that isn't natural for you any longer."

"And what is that?"

"Care."

"And what makes you think I don't care about my patient?" he challenged.

"Care for her as the friend she used to be to you. Set aside your pettiness and get over her mistake that cost Tiffany her life. Evan and I have. Don't cling to your bitterness the way your mother and father have—the way Stephen and Connie do. The most important person in this world to her right now is you."

"Point taken."

"No." Delilah gripped his arm. "No, you haven't gotten the point. She told you she loves you, and you pulled away from her. Do you know how much that hurt? Let it go. Realize that Tiffany died, and there's nothing that any of us can do to bring her back. Look at the beautiful woman Hope has become. I'm not saying marry her. I'm saying love her like we do."

Daniel peered back toward the waiting room. No one was watching. He cleared his throat and leaned closer to Dee. "I. Have. Never. Stopped. Loving. Her." He stared at a spot over her head and then back to her. "And that's my biggest problem."

"Depends upon how you look at it." Delilah stood,

hands on her hips.

"What do you mean?"

"I would think that a man who is loved by the woman Hope has become is a blessed man. Are you sure you're not holding on to your mother's emotions? If you are, how are they working out for her? I saw her downtown a couple of weeks ago. She's aged. Anger and bitterness can do that to you. I don't want that for her or for Jacob. I certainly don't want it for you."

Daniel nodded and turned away.

"I know God's in control, Danny, but you do your best not to let Hope die," she called after him.

The chill ran through Hope. Her world was spinning. Colorful lights twirled around her, and she fought a bout of nausea. As if awakening from some distant place, she looked around her.

"I don't know what it is about the carousel, but we always loved them the best, didn't we?"

Hope blinked and looked to her right. Tiffany was on a carousel horse. The pink mane clashed against Tiffany's brown shirt and her auburn hair. "Tiff?"

"He loves you, you know." Tiffany leaned back, holding to the pole and letting the wind catch her auburn locks.

Hope shivered from the cool breeze. "Who?"

Tiffany sat up straight, her gaze on someone ahead on the ride.

Hope looked. For a moment, she didn't see anyone, but then Danny came into view, walking toward her, holding to each pole as he made his way along the moving carousel.

He drew nearer to her, and the intensity in his blue eyes flamed a smoldering ember inside of her.

"Love him, Hope. He needs you."

Hope fought to tear her eyes from Danny. Tiffany was gone.

"Hope?" Danny whispered to her. "Hope, you need to wake up."

Wake up? This couldn't be a dream. Tiffany? She was with her. She wanted to stay and wait for her friend to return. Besides, this feeling of drifting through air, the desire in Danny's eyes, she needed for all of it to be real.

"Hope."

She searched the carousel. Danny was gone, too. The ride slowed.

"Hope, I need you to wake up."

The ride stopped.

"Come on. I know you can hear me."

Hope blinked against the lights and then turned her head. "There you are," she whispered. "I thought I lost you."

Danny smiled down at her. "There she is, nurse. She'll be fine." He placed a warm hand over her cold one.

Hope shivered.

"Nurse, Ms. Astor needs another blanket." He turned to leave.

"Danny?" she called to him.

Danny stopped, but he didn't turn.

"Do you remember the carousel ride?"

Danny nodded, still not facing her.

"I've never forgotten it. When I'm better, we'll have to find one and ride it together." Her eyes drifted shut, and she drank in the darkness.

10

Hope bit her lip to quell the pain. She'd been waiting for it to lessen, fighting against calling for the nurse. The last thing she needed was to start on pain medication. She'd crave the effect.

She tried to focus on the arrangements of flowers sent by her friends at different times during the day. A pain shot through her. "Oh," she let the small cry escape between her lips. "Go away." She puffed breaths to lessen the hurt.

The round clock with the bold black letters showed only a minute had passed since she last looked. It seemed as if an hour had gone by. She fingered the call button, the desire to give in growing stronger by each tick of the second hand.

She turned as a young girl entered with a tray.

"Ms. Astor?" the girl asked.

Hope nodded.

The girl sat the tray in front of her and left.

Now how in the world was she supposed to sit up and eat?

She scooted upward in the bed and reached out to punch the up button. She let out a cry as the pain burned across the surgical area.

"Hope?" Danny came into the room. He dropped a clipboard on the foot of her bed. "Easy." He propped a pillow behind her, and with careful hands, he helped her to sit up. Then he removed the lid from the tray to reveal a very bland diet. "Yum," he teased.

"I'll share." She winced as another pain took the wind from her.

Danny picked up her chart and read through it. He stopped his reading and looked at her. "It says you refused pain meds. They'll help you rest."

"You and I know how easy it is for me to take them. I'm afraid."

Again, he sat the clipboard down. He pressed the call button and told the nurse to provide pain medication for Hope immediately. Within moments, the nurse slipped in and pushed the needle into Hope's IV. "Every four hours tonight no matter what my patient says. I'll re-evaluate in the morning."

The nurse nodded and walked out.

"Now, I want you to eat before the meds take you off to dreamland. If you hold this down, I'll have them put something more palatable on your plate for the next meal." He picked up her chart and read through. "Other than being a little stubborn on the pain meds, you seem to be doing well." He lowered the bar on the side of her bed and sat beside her. "I've got to say I'm impressed."

Hope opened the cellophane packing on her utensils. "Why, Danny, I thought nothing impressed you." She batted her eyes at him.

"With all the drinking and drugs you used to take, it must have been hard to shrug them off, and I see the desire in you to stay clean."

"Don't be impressed by me." She dipped her spoon into the cherry Jell-O. "I found it pretty easy. I leaned upon Christ, and I had motivation."

His eyes darkened at the name of her Savior. "What was the motivation?"

"I never want to hurt anyone the way I hurt Tiffany and you and your family and my family."

Danny stood so abruptly the clipboard clattered on the ground.

Hope reached for his hand.

Danny stared down at her touch. Then he gave her a slight squeeze. His thumb brushed across the top of her hand.

The familiar reaction to his touch returned. The heat of attraction rose in her face. She trembled, and she remembered a kiss from a long time ago.

But a searing pain stopped all thought. She tightened her hold on his hand. What would an attractive man do with a woman like her?

The days of dreaming of Danny as her hero, as the perfect man to make all her dreams come true, were over.

"Hope?"

"Sorry," she whispered. "Just a bit of pain."

"I'm sorry, too." He tucked her hand next to her body. "Please eat and try to rest, and no arguments with the nurses over pain medication. Tomorrow, I expect you out of the bed and sitting up, maybe even a lap down the corridor." He gathered his clipboard and walked out of the room.

"Yeah, right," she breathed. "You try walking with missing body parts, and I might make an effort."

He leaned back in, a smile deepening the laugh lines around his gorgeous blue eyes. "That's the attitude I want to hear."

She picked up her spoon and tossed it in his direction, and his laughter filled the hall outside her room. "Meds are working or else you'd have hit me." His laughter floated down the hallway.

Daniel stepped into the house when the maid answered the door. She led him into the Astors' living room. "Mr. Astor will be with you in a moment."

Daniel looked around the room and stepped to the wall to enjoy the paintings hanging there. Hope's work. She had such an eye for detail.

She'd given him a painting for his birthday. A rendering of the balcony of his family's Riviera hotel suite where they'd stayed the summer before he began med school. After Tiffany's death, he took it from his home and placed it in an examination room at the office—Dr. Bambridge's office—so he wouldn't have to see it. His first inclination had been to trash it, but he couldn't make himself completely let go. The painting was precious to him not for what she'd painted in the picture, but for what she'd left out. They'd shared a tender moment there, looking out over the Riviera.

Hope had only been eighteen that summer, and she'd seemed shy around him for some reason. Her demure behavior attracted him like the thought of mischief to an imp. When she looked up at him, her blue eyes showing such adoration, he could no longer resist the temptation that he'd fought since she and Tiffany turned sixteen. He'd kissed her with all the intensity of a man, and she'd returned to him the affections of a woman.

And that had frightened him.

"Daniel Duvall, to what do I owe the pleasure?" Stephen Astor strode into the room.

"I was hoping to meet with you and your wife." Daniel shook the man's hand.

Stephen cleared his throat. "Connie's not feeling well this evening. May I get you a drink? Bourbon, whiskey, scotch?"

Daniel shook his head. He hadn't had a drop of liquor

since Tiffany's death. "Nothing. How's business?"

"Doing well. I have some interior design work for a few homes in Islesworth. I've been asked to do some designs for models in a new exclusive neighborhood being built in Celebration. I can't complain. How's your practice?" Stephen motioned for Daniel to sit and took a seat on the floral sofa.

"Fine." Daniel took a chair and stared up at the portrait above the Astors' fireplace—Hope in the gown she'd worn as prom queen her senior year.

"Daniel, I'm assuming you're not visiting because you're in the neighborhood. I know your weekly dinner with your folks is on Sunday."

Daniel tore his gaze from the picture. "She's turned into a beautiful woman, Mr. Astor."

Stephen nodded and swallowed hard.

"She was here last night. She was very upset when she left. Is there a reason?"

"None that concerns you." Stephen wiped a piece of lint from his pants.

Had it been as easy for the man to brush his only daughter out of his life? "Well, sir, as her doctor it does concern me. I'm sure she told you she had major surgery this morning?"

Stephen nodded. "She told us."

Daniel couldn't help himself. He moved forward. "Excuse me. Your daughter—your only daughter—came to tell you that she was having a total mastectomy, and you not only let her walk out of this house, but you didn't think she might need to see you before the surgery?"

"How is she?" Stephen looked up, his gaze intent on Daniel.

Daniel shook it off. "I have to go."

"Daniel, did she make it through. Will she be okay?" Stephen stood and grabbed for Daniel's arm.

Daniel shook off the hold. He recalled the names listed on Hope's HIPAA form. She had not included her parents. "I guess I never realized what Hope lost when Tiffany died: a family—my family—that at one time did care deeply for her. I do realize she must have lost you and Connie long before that. I don't know why the two of you refused to see to your daughter's needs, but I'll give you a little relief from your anguish. She's better off without you, whether or not she survives whatever's ahead of her."

Daniel made his way to the door. "I never took you for a coward, Stephen. I know Connie runs this house. She always has, but I can't respect a man who would allow his daughter to go through what she did without her parents by her side. My dad, he's a little like you, but I know nothing could have kept him from Tiffany's side the night she died."

The maid rushed to the door and held it open for him. He walked out into the fading light of the day and to his car in the Astors' driveway. He pulled out and sped out of the plush Winter Park neighborhood. Life on these streets suddenly resembled a house of cards. When everything went well, the walls held strong, but let something interfere with the lives within these homes, and the walls tumbled down. Two houses of cards had fallen on the same date last year, and the people within the homes still tried to show the world everything was perfectly normal when nothing could be further from the truth.

Nothing was normal, and Daniel sensed his life would never be the same.

Daniel stepped out of the elevator usually taken by visitors and moved to the nurses' station. He stopped and punched in Hope's name on the computer, reading her vitals and the nurses' comments before moving down the hallway.

The room was semi-dark and quiet when he walked in. Five faces stared up at him. Libby Carter put her finger to her lips. Daniel peered around the curtain and smiled. Hope was asleep.

Evan nodded in his direction and then toward the door. Daniel followed him into the hall. "Thank you, Daniel."

Daniel slipped his hands into this pants pocket.

"I know this has been a struggle for you, but I'm not surprised you'd do this for her. You always admired Hope."

Admired her? He'd loved her. And Evan had taken her. "Why'd you leave her behind?"

Evan flinched. "Our previous relationship isn't something either of us are proud of. I can't offer an excuse, but one thing I know we both agree upon is that God had a greater purpose for both of us."

"Is it guilt?" Daniel asked.

Evan stepped back as if Daniel had fisted him in the stomach. "Excuse me?"

"Is it guilt that has you doing all this for her?" Daniel pleaded for an answer.

"No, Danny, it's love. My wife and I love Hope. All of us do. It's hard to explain how God can bring such a group of misfits together and allow us to call each other family, but He did, and we do." Evan leaned against the wall and stared at Daniel. "You still love her." He smiled.

"You can wipe that smarm off your face. I'm her doctor. I give my patients the best care possible, and I don't date them—ethics and all."

And the smile vanished. "What are you saying?"

"She has a little ways to go, and the last part of the journey is sometimes the most perilous."

"But you got all the cancer. Tell me you got all the cancer, and, if not, the radiation will eradicate any you may have missed." Evan gripped Daniel's shirt.

Maybe Evan still loved Hope.

"Evan?" Libby stepped out into the hallway. "Is everything okay?"

Evan reached for Libby and pulled her to him. "Everything's okay." Evan rested his chin on his wife's head and closed his eyes. "Why don't you tell the others we should leave? We'll get something to eat on the way home, and you can come back tomorrow morning."

Libby reached and squeezed Daniel's arm. "You really are her hero, you know." She left them.

"My wife loves that woman. And Dee—if anything happens to Hope—it will devastate them. Tell me what we can expect?"

"Her system has been and will be compromised by the treatments. The possibility of her getting pneumonitis is always there. Let's give her three weeks of freedom from the drudge of cancer before the radiation starts, knowing I've done my best and looking forward to the day when we can declare her cancer-free. Don't dwell on what could happen. Keep her busy. Give her purpose, something she can look forward to after radiation. Patients who have long-range goals or plans are often the ones who breeze through the treatments. Let's work for that end."

Evan nodded his understanding. "Libby has come up with a plan, and she'll contact you. I ask that you do your best to hide any remaining animosity. Hope may act tough, but she's fragile."

"You think I don't know that." Daniel folded his arms over his chest. "I didn't love her and leave her. If she'd have waited on me, I would have given her everything." Daniel coughed back the emotion.

Evan slapped a hand on his shoulder. "And if you'd have given her everything, Hope wouldn't be where she is today. She'd still be sick, but she wouldn't have Christ to lean upon."

Daniel bit his tongue. If Hope needed a God to prop her up, he'd let her believe one existed. Still, since the uttered prayers lifted over Hope, he'd felt a sense of peace he couldn't explain.

The others filed out of the room. Gideon shook his hand and each of the women gave him a hug.

Evan lingered behind. "You know, if you gave her everything now, she'd appreciate it a lot more than she would have before." He walked away. "Would you like to join us for dinner? Gid and I are always outvoted on the restaurant choice. Tonight, we might be able to finagle somewhere we like."

"I bet the big guy's favorite restaurant is Chuck E. Cheese." Daniel pushed a smile into place.

At the end of the hall, Gideon Tabor turned around. "Chuck E. Cheese!" He raised a thumb in the air.

"No!" the girls chorused.

Evan laughed. "Sure you won't join in the fun?"

Daniel was tempted, but he shook his head. "Have a good time. Buy some tokens. Play some skee-ball."

Hope

//

Today, both Hope's flesh and her spirit were weak. She had no desire to get out of the hospital bed.

"Hope." The beaked-nosed nurse peered down at her. "The more we get you up and around, the better you'll be."

She wanted to die, but she refrained from saying so.

"Take your time. Bring your legs around."

Hope slid one leg and then the other off of the side of the bed. Her gown was hiked up over her behind, but Hope didn't care.

The nurse helped her to sit up. "Next you'll scoot to where your feet can touch the floor."

Who'd have thought something as normal as getting out of bed would cause so much pain? "Easy for you to say," Hope said and then bit her lip.

Just because you feel it, that doesn't mean you need to say it. Libby's admonition ran through her memory. As if Libby never said outlandish things—the truth, but nonetheless outlandish.

Hope scooted as instructed. Her feet grazed the floor, and she pushed down with one hand for leverage. She shut her eyes and cried out.

"Use your lower body, not your arms, genius."

She opened her eyes. "Ha, ha." She stared at Danny who stood with his arms crossed over his chest. Now, the fact that her gown wasn't in place bothered her. "Would you turn around for just a sec?" she asked.

He did as she requested. "Modesty becomes you, Hope Astor."

"Oh, shut up." She bit her lip again as she tried to yank down the gown. The nurse brought her arm around her and helped Hope to her feet. "Thank you," she mumbled as the nurse straightened her gown and slipped Hope's robe over her shoulders.

"Decent now?" Danny asked.

"I think so."

"You have a visitor. I found him downstairs in the lobby. I think he's been there for a while. Let me tell him you're ready for a visit." He started for the door, and she followed him with her eyes.

Danny returned, her father beside him. "Daddy," she whispered. Her body trembled and she held out her hand. "Oh, Daddy."

Her father stood beside Danny, not moving forward, not taking her hand. "Hope, I'm glad you're okay."

Okay? Did he really think she was okay, as if she'd

only had her tonsils removed?

She stumbled backward at the weight of his refusal to give her what she so desperately wanted. Her daddy—he'd always been everything to her. Now, he seemed pitifully small.

"Mr. Astor, Hope needs to take a lap around the corridor. Why don't you go with her?"

Daddy jerked his head upward as if Danny had thrown an uppercut. "No. No. I just came by to let her know her mother and I are aware of the situation."

"Situation?" Hope straightened, though the pain seared through her.

Just because you feel it, that doesn't mean you need to say it.

Hope allowed her anger to seep away. "It's okay, Daddy. Thank you for coming."

"Well, take care."

"Tell Mother I miss her, will you?"

Daddy nodded and left them without another word.

"Come on." Danny came beside her.

Hope scuffed her feet along the carpet. "Where are we going?"

"We're going to take that lap around the floor."

"You don't have to. I suspect you want to get away from me as much as my father did."

"Yeah, yeah. I hear you. A ploy. I'll walk out the door, and you'll walk right back to that bed."

"Go," she urged. "I'll make the lap. I promise."

Danny stopped and a mischievous smile tipped his lips. "Let's make this fun."

Nothing could make this painful journey fun for her, but she waited.

"You make one lap around this floor, and I'll bring you a nice little surprise when I make my rounds this evening."

Oh, she'd always loved his little challenges and surprises. "Can I lean on you?" she asked.

He held out his arm. "I can't think of a wager we ever placed where I didn't give you the advantage."

Danny walked beside Hope, patiently waiting for her to take each step, and when she tired, he said nothing. He stood with his hand under her arm until she said she could go forward.

The silence between them wasn't awkward. Hope thought it companionable. Danny had a lot of practice staying quiet, listening to Hope and Tiffany ramble on. At times, the three of them would sit on the sandy beach and study the horizon for long stretches of time without a word passing between them.

As they reached the corner heading back to her room, Hope smiled. "Almost there."

"Yes, we are."

"Dr. Duvall." A pretty brunette nurse hurried down the hall, a file in hand.

"Excuse me." Danny made sure Hope was steady on her feet before turning to face the opposite direction. The conversation was muffled as Hope took tentative steps toward her room. When she looked up, the nurse tore her gaze away from her and back to Danny. Hope knew adoration when she saw it, and that nurse definitely adored the wonderful Dr. Duvall. She also knew jealousy, and she saw it in the penetrating glare as well.

"Thank you." Danny left the nurse and returned to her side. "What'd you take? About five steps, Speedy Gonzales?" he teased, holding out his arm once again.

"Forget it." She blew air between her lips and waved him off. "I'm going to do this last part without your help."

He laughed as they finally made it inside her room once again. "Okay, you win. I'll have to find a surprise for you."

Hope reached for his hand.

He pulled back as if she'd burned him with her touch.

She dropped her gaze to the floor. She had to remember all that they had between them—the least of it two missing breasts. "I don't need anything from you. Walking with me was the biggest surprise of all."

"Hope, I—"

She shook her head. "No, don't say anything. I know this was nothing more than a doctor wanting to encourage a patient, especially after Daddy ..."

Danny laced his fingers through hers. "It was a friend wanting to see another friend do well in her treatment, and I'm sorry about your dad."

Hope wiped the tears from her eyes before they could fall. "Let's not talk any more about it, and no surprise.

Okay? I'm fine."

"Why don't you sit up in the chair for a few minutes? I'm sure housekeeping will be in to change the bed."

Hope nodded. "Sure."

"Good morning." Libby breezed into the room with Charisse on her heels.

Danny dropped his hold on Hope's hand and placed space between them. "Good morning, ladies. I'm proud to announce that Hope walked the entire fourth floor this morning." He turned to look at Hope. "I'll see you during my evening rounds. Maybe another walk?"

Hope smiled. "Thank you."

Danny walked out the door.

Libby touched Hope's hair then dug in her over-large bag. She pulled out a catalog for art supplies. "Here's a wish list for you. Mark the things you'll need to start painting again. Don't worry about the money."

Hope scuffled over to the chair and lowered herself down. She flipped through the magazine. Everything she'd ever wanted had always come with the asking. A catalog meant a shopping spree at her father's expense. The thought saddened her, but she'd never let Libby know that.

She laid it aside. Today, she didn't care if she'd ever get a chance to paint again.

Daniel finished the last of his dictation and laid the file

on the corner of his desk. He peered out the window at the vacant lot next door.

Stephen Astor. The man hadn't been too far from Daniel's thoughts. He'd like to shake Hope's father. One only had to look into Hope's eyes to see she adored the man. And his actions had taken the wind from Hope.

That's why he'd stayed with her. He wanted to keep her mind off Stephan's shallowness.

At least that's what he told himself.

Truth was, he hadn't wanted to leave her. Maybe it had been her vulnerability. But he suspected something much more.

He leaned his head back and closed tired eyes.

The soft knock made him look up. "Yes," he called.

Becky slipped inside. "We're leaving. Do you need anything?"

Daniel stood. "No, I have rounds, and then I'm going home."

A mischievous smile lit Becky's face. "Tell me, Dr. Duvall, how should I answer my friends?"

Daniel shook his head. "About?"

"Well, there's word going around that the formidable stonewall that is Dr. Daniel Duvall is beginning to crumble. Everyone is asking if it's true."

"Is that how people see me … formidable?"

"Unapproachable."

"Snarky?" He narrowed his eyes.

Becky laughed. "I'm not really sure what snarky looks

like, but the word fits."

"And what do they surmise is the reason for the change in me?"

"We're not sure."

He laughed. "Becky, I'm sure glad I haven't run you off with my formidable, stonewall of a snarky attitude."

"No, Daniel. Not a chance. I've seen you through a lot. The loss of love. The death of a sister. Trying to hold your parents together. And now, trying to play savior to the woman whose love you lost. And just so you're aware. I've told everyone they must have seen another Dr. Duvall. As far as I'm concerned, you haven't changed, and they need to stop their gossip."

So, without ever mentioning a word to this woman, she knew all his secrets—and she'd protected him. "I appreciate all you've done." He reached for his jacket hanging on the back of the door.

"You do know you can't be her savior, don't you?" Becky waited, hands on hips. "Only God can save her, and from the incredible testimony I heard from her and her friend, He's already done that. The most you can do is allow God to work through you to give her healing, if He so desires."

He wouldn't argue with his fiercest protector.

"Daniel?" Becky stopped him as he started out the door.

"Yeah?" He turned back.

"Let God lead you." Becky reached for the bag in the

chair. "And don't forget this."

He took the brightly colored gift bag with pictures of floating balloons from her. The bright blue tissue paper hid the box inside the bag. "Thanks for everything." He walked out.

The drive to the hospital was a short one for him. He parked in the physician's parking lot and made his way inside.

He kept the gift bag with him as he did his rounds. The questions asked by patients and nurses alike brought several different teasing replies from him and garnered him several looks of surprise from nurses and aids attending the patients.

When he walked out of the room next to Hope's, booming laughter met him.

"You should have seen the look on the waitress's face when I approached her about it," Gideon expounded. "All those years of eating with Dee at The Citrus and having her complain about the steak being overdone. It took some convincing to get the waitress to go along. I mean Delilah used to treat them so badly I bet they suffer from post-traumatic stress disorder. They still flinch when she comes in. Have you noticed?"

"Gideon, what did you have the waitress do?" Hope's lighthearted question floated to Daniel.

"I had her serve Delilah a raw steak." Gideon again roared with laughter. "And you should have seen her face. She'd start to speak, and I'd shush her. She'd try to talk again, and I reminded her about her witness."

"Stop." Hope sounded out of breath. "I can't laugh like that. It hurts."

"On the contrary." Daniel entered. "Laughter is better than a pill for relieving pain."

Gideon stood. The big man was all alone and entertaining Hope.

"Well, I better get going. I need to meet Charisse and V.J. for the science fair exhibit. Evan and Libby are coming up as soon as they get cleaned up, and Delilah should be on her way."

"Kiss V.J. for me, and tell him Aunt Hope is proud of him." Hope hitched a thumb in Gideon's direction. "Gideon's son took first place at the science air."

Daniel smiled. "Congratulations."

"Don't congratulate me. His Uncle Evan helped him. Science wasn't my subject. He'd have grown a sweet potato if it'd been my call. Good night." Gideon placed a kiss on Hope's forehead. "'Night, Daniel." Hope's friend looked at the package in Daniel's hand and raised a brow.

Daniel shook Gideon's hand. "Good night, Gideon."

Hope sat up in bed, a half-eaten tray of food in front of her.

"What's wrong? You don't like the cuisine? And that's a step up from yesterday's meal."

Hope pushed the tray away. "I'm not very hungry."

"Uh-uh." He situated the tray in front of her. "Eat."

She picked up her fork and took a few bites before

setting it down. "I really don't feel like it."

Daniel held up the gift bag his nurse had chosen when she insisted the item had to be hidden to truly be a surprise. "Eat all of your mush, and you can have this."

Hope stared at the white puff of food on her plate and up to the package. "I told you I didn't expect you to do that."

"And you're telling me that Hope Astor, a present in sight, doesn't want to open it."

She smiled. "Oh, I want to open it. I just don't want to eat another bite."

He put the package on the chair and left to retrieve her chart. Looking it over, he discovered her vitals had been strong, but her temperature had varied a bit during the day. Her pain medication was due in less than an hour.

He pushed the tray out of his way. "Sit up for me just a bit. Can you?"

She did with effort. He asked her to breathe in and out as he pressed his stethoscope against her back and her chest. Then he helped her to sit back.

"I'm just tired, Danny. If I could just get the tiredness to go away, I might feel like I could live."

He picked up the bag and sat beside her on the bed. "Some of that is your body working overtime to protect you. The other is probably the medication."

She nodded her understanding.

"Eating is a big part of your getting your energy to return."

"I know." Her lips trembled. "I just don't feel like I can right now."

He offered her a smile. "Here you go."

"That's not like you, giving in like this. I must be dying."

"Hope!" The sharpness of his tone surprised him.

She looked up, eyes wide.

"You aren't dying." He lowered his voice. "And I never want to hear you say that. Our goal is life, a long and happy life for you."

She lowered her gaze.

He stood. "And I didn't give in. You met my requirements by making it around the hall today. Most of my patients need a wheelchair before they get halfway around."

She peered up at him. "You ... you ... stinker!" She tore into the gift bag and laughed aloud as she held up the paint by number set. "Oh, Danny, it's perfect." She covered her face and began to cry. "So wonderfully perfect."

"If you finish it, I'd like to frame it for a wall in my office."

She nodded without looking up to him.

"Hope, you won't believe what that jerk Gideon did to me." Delilah bounded into the room but stopped. She looked from the crying woman in the bed and back to him. She pushed past Daniel, and he slipped out of the room. "What is it?" Delilah asked.

"It's a carousel." Hope cried. "I need to live so that I

Fay Lamb

can paint Danny a carousel."

Hope

12

Daniel pulled into his parents' driveway, finished getting an update on one of his patients, and clicked off the handsfree-link. When had he taken a day off, and when had he enjoyed a weekend without an emergency?

He climbed from his car, readying for the usual Sunday night drama that had become his life since Tiffany's death. He closed his door and looked across the street.

Stephen Astor stood in his driveway. He held up his hand and walked toward the closed iron gate. "Do you have a minute, Daniel?" He pushed a button, and the same gate that had been closed to Stephen's daughter opened for Daniel.

"How are you?" Daniel asked.

"Connie—she wanted me to ask about Hope."

"Mr. Astor, I breached confidentiality when I came to you about Hope's surgery. Maybe you should call your daughter. She's staying with Delilah James, but I think you know that."

The man released a heavy sigh. "She's home then."

"No. I just told you she's at Delilah James. I think Hope would still consider this her home."

"I know you don't understand our position—"

Daniel raised his hand to stop the man. "I understand it's all about your position. What you don't understand is that your refusal to comfort and care for your daughter devalues your position in my eyes."

"Connie just doesn't want her to end up dependent on an artist income. She sees me as a failure."

Stephen Astor was anything but a failure. His interior designs had all the local celebrities, and the otherwise wealthy, clamoring for appointments. "Hard to believe." Daniel smirked. "Lawyers earn money, but interior designers demand their own price."

"But she made the man, Daniel. Without Connie, I'd be an artist on the street."

Daniel shook his head. "Don't you believe it. And don't let Connie try to control Hope's life the way she does you."

Stephen's face took on a hard glint.

Daniel straightened, challenging Stephen to say he was wrong in his assessment. "I think your wife has a lot of self-made pride, and it's hurting you, and it's hurting Hope, but don't you worry. Hope's a fighter. I expect her to handle radiation well. Barring any unforeseen complications, her friends will get her back on her feet in no time."

"How about you, Danny Boy? I know for a fact that you broke off communication with Hope after your sister ran herself into a tree. What made you decide to help her?"

Daniel took a deep breath. "Is your sarcasm because of Hope or because you know that your indulgence allowed her to live the life she lived? For the record, I do believe that Hope shouldn't have asked my sister to drive her to Evan Carter's house that night, but Tiffany had a choice in the matter. She shouldn't have been drinking and then gotten behind the wheel of that car."

Not before this very minute had he placed the blame on his sister—not aloud. "But the truth is, you aren't the only ones who indulged their child. Those girls were raised to be the life of the party, to be the popular girls in school, and popular girls didn't stay home on weekends and study. You and Connie and my parents were perfectly happy not knowing what those girls were getting into."

"That's not true." Stephen's face reddened.

"Don't tell me. I'm the one they ran to every time that wanted to skirt by you on something. The sad truth is, I knew that all of you would turn your eyes and look the other way. I thought it was a game the girls played, but I'm beginning to wonder if they weren't seeking direction from me. And I failed to provide it."

"This is about the death of your sister. How can we ever—?"

"Is it really about my sister's death with you? I mean you and Connie treated Tiff and me like your own." The same way his parents used to treat Hope. The way he had treated her—like his own, but not a sister—as if she belonged to him. Did she mean so little to him?

Daniel cleared his throat. "Stephen, have you ever thought that it's what you gave to Hope, what my parents gave to Tiffany, that put them in that car that night?"

Stephen blinked. "Are you saying you've forgiven her?"

"This isn't about me." Daniel rubbed his thumb over the palm of his left hand, not wanting to look into the man's face. "Hope is your daughter. She came to me seeking my help as a surgeon. I gave in to her despite my feelings for her. Can't you put your feelings aside and be the father she wants, encourage your wife to be the mother Hope needs?"

"And what about you?"

Daniel lifted his gaze. "I told you. I've done what I set out to do. I saw her through the surgery. I'll follow her through until my associate says she can be released back into the care of her treating physician."

Stephen shook his head. "You've loved Hope forever. Nothing's changed. Despite the fact that she's destroyed your family, you still care a little for her."

Daniel turned away from him. "No, you've got that wrong." He walked away.

At his parents' front door, he stopped and closed his eyes. Did she really mean so little to him? He rested his hand on the doorknob.

She meant everything to him. The truth hit him like a gale storm.

The door opened, and Daniel was surprised to see his mother and not their maid. "Daniel." She pressed her lips into a thin line.

"Mom." He kissed her cheek. "I'm honored by the fact you greeted me at the door." That would shut down any lecture he would receive about crossing enemy lines.

Hope put the finishing touches on the paint-by-number carousel picture. With careful hands, she held it up for Delilah's perusal. "What do you think?"

Dee looked up from the Sunday paper. A smile tipped the corner of her lips. "Only Hope Astor could put such flair to a child's paint-by-number kit. I suppose you're taking that to your follow-up appointment tomorrow."

"If I had the money to piece together a frame, I'd do it, but this is all he gets. We'll see if he lives up to his promise and puts it his office."

Dee laid the paper down and swung her legs over the back of the chair. She let her long dark hair hang over the arm of the oversize floral then lifted it in a ponytail only to let it fall down again.

A twinge of envy hit Hope. She couldn't wait for her hair to grow back. Would it still be as full? One woman in

Danny's office had said that when her hair grew in, the texture and fullness was greater than before. Another said that she had trouble adapting to the thinner, coarser growth. Though she'd made her mind up to be grateful for whatever God gave to her, Hope couldn't help but long for the time when she could surprise people with a gorgeous hairdo.

"I never got out of you just why that silly little gift means so much to you." Delilah broke into Hope's thoughts.

Hope leaned back, the energy she'd felt earlier while painting, spent. "Danny, Tiffany, and I used to enjoy the carousel at the Orange County Fair. I've been dreaming about it lately."

"And that little gift tells you Danny's been thinking about it, too." Delilah pinched her lips together as if fighting against saying something.

"What is it?" Hope pressed.

"Danny's a dedicated physician. I just don't want you to read too much into his actions. If I've seen anything in him lately it's that he knows how to motivate his patients to wellness."

Hope peered out the window of the high-rise condo. Time to change the subject. "How was church? I miss it so much."

Delilah laughed. "You've only skipped a week."

"But two services, three if you count tonight's."

Delilah stood. "Well, I suppose I should start something in the kitchen so Charisse and Libby don't feel that we're completely helpless. What would you suggest I do before they get here?"

"Put the ice in the glasses." Hope giggled. "That will impress them beyond words.

"Ha, ha." Delilah swatted at her with the newspaper. "I'll put up with your sassy attitude until you're better, but beyond that—forget it."

Hope again stared out the window. Tears spilled down her cheeks.

"What is it?" Delilah moved toward her. "Are you in pain?"

Hope turned to her and held out her hand. "I love you, Dee. That's all."

"Well, I don't get those words every day, so I'll treasure them."

"You deserve them. You're honest to a fault, and in my book, that translates into the deepest kind of love—for all of us. We're so lucky to have you, even if you can't cook."

Delilah dropped her hand and waved her off. "Being a lying deceiver wasn't too much fun. I thought I'd try the honest, direct route. I like it much better."

"You know, I couldn't stand to see you with him while I'm alive, but if something happens to me, you and Danny would be perfect for each other."

Delilah spun toward her. "Nothing's going to happen to you. You may not get your wishes where that—what does Libby call him?"

"Snarky." Hope laughed.

"Snarky idiot—that's more like it. You might not get to marry him, but you are going to be sitting on the beach with me in our old age, sagging bodies, turning all the old men's heads."

Hope laughed so hard she had to hold her chest. Finally, able to speak, she wiped the joyful tears. "It's a date, Dee."

Daniel waited for the maid to serve the soup. The woman's hand shook as she poured the broth from the ladle. Her eyes connected with his for the briefest of seconds, and Daniel saw the weariness in the lines of her face. "Are you doing well?" he asked.

The woman glanced quickly at his mother and nodded. "Very well, Dr. Duvall. Thank you." She backed away and left them.

His mother didn't seem to notice the exchange. "Daniel, why were you talking to Stephen Astor?"

"Why, Elsa, I didn't know it was a crime for our son to speak with the neighbors." His dad's face remained stoic while he ate his soup.

"You know what I mean. He motioned you over. I saw it. What did he want?"

Daniel didn't speak for a moment. He wiped the linen napkin across his mouth and returned it to the table. "It's not like you to play the part of the nosy neighbor."

"Was it about that worthless daughter of his? As if you could tell him anything."

"Elsa, that's enough. Daniel doesn't have to share your personal opinion about the Astors."

"My opinion? What about you? Their daughter killed ours."

Daniel stood abruptly. "Hope wasn't in the car with Tiffany, Mother."

"But she'd taken Hope to that dreadful boy's house."

Daniel closed his eyes and counted silently to ten. His mother's bitterness was driving her over the edge. "I haven't been in this house for dinner since Tiffany died where we didn't come around to this. Tiffany's gone, but I'm here, and I'm trying, but if you continue to bring her ghost into this room, I'm afraid I won't be much longer."

"She's all I had." Elsa burst into tears. "All I ever had."

Daniel exchanged a look with his father and moved toward the door. "I have somewhere I'd rather be."

"Daniel …" His mother reached for him.

"It's okay. I've understood how much you loved Tiffany for years. I just never heard you put it into words."

"You had your father; I had Tiffany."

"Yeah, I've always had Dad, and Tiffany had both of you." He stood in the doorway. "I loved her, you know. Loved being the big brother and covering for her and for Hope when they wanted to get into mischief. Why don't you just add me to the list of people who took Tiffany away from you, but while you're adding, take a good look at yourselves. You indulged her, too, just as much as the Astors indulged Hope."

"Don't you dare!" His mother stood, her eyes taking on the look of a wildcat. "Don't you dare tell me I had anything to do with Tiffany's death! Hope Astor—that's where the fault belongs."

"If you're going to blame Hope, Mother, you're going to have to let go of the halo you envision over Tiff's head."

"You don't talk ill of your sister. She's not here to defend herself."

"But Hope was, wasn't she!" Daniel stepped back into the room. "She stood in your living room and she asked for your forgiveness, not expecting it, and you threw your ugly words in her face." He stopped short of grasping his mother, shaking her to make her see her self-destructiveness. He raised his hands. "I'm done. Live with your bitterness and your memories. When you want to live life again, when you want to remember you have a son, and he loves you, I'll be around."

"Daniel ..." His father stood. "Son, please."

Daniel blinked back his emotions. "It's okay, Dad. I just need some time. Do me a favor and walk across the street and talk to Stephen Astor. He could probably use an old friend."

Hope closed her eyes and leaned back in the chair listening to the laughter and discussions around her. "Aunt Hope, are you okay?" V.J. tugged on her arm.

Hope opened one eye and put her finger to her lips. "Shh, if they know I'm awake, they'll make me work in the kitchen."

V.J. bounced beside her on the couch.

Hope winced but smiled. She ruffled his hair. "I heard that while I was in the hospital you won the science fair."

"Yeah. Uncle Evan and I did an experiment with yeast." He giggled.

"What's so funny?" She'd closed her eyes but opened them again.

"Yeast smells."

"And ...?"

"Evan and V.J. put the mess in my car after the science fair." Charisse came around the corner. "When V.J. says yeast smells, let me tell you, three-day old, bloated yeast, really smells."

"Oh, no." Hope sat up. "I hope you made Evan and V.J. clean it up."

"No, she didn't." Gideon stepped out of the kitchen with a carrot in his hand, probably unable to resist the chance to tease. "I lost three pounds to prove it. I think if you gave me the option of smelling a decaying body or that yeast, I'd opt for the body."

Behind Gideon, Evan laughed. "It would be impossible even for you, Hope, to create the shade of green of his face, and I saw him a couple hours after he finished cleaning it."

The doorbell rang, and they each looked to one another. Gideon moved to answer it.

"You or Dee expecting anyone?" Charisse asked.

Hope shook her head.

Charisse pushed Hope's hair from her face. "You look tired."

"I am tired, but I'm enjoying the—" She blinked as the tall, dark-haired doctor entered the room.

Danny raised a tentative hand to her.

"Another plate for dinner," Gideon called into the kitchen.

Libby peered around the corner. "Dr. Duvall, we're so glad to have you."

"I don't want to intrude. I just wanted to check on my patient."

"That lazy good for nothing. She doesn't need your attention," Delilah's voice boomed from the kitchen.

Danny ignored her. He walked toward Hope.

"What would you like to drink?" Charisse asked him and moved away.

"Are you sure?"

"We have plenty."

"If you have it, tea would be great."

"Hi." Beside her the little boy held out his hand toward Danny. "I'm V.J."

Danny looked surprised for a moment. Then he smiled

and shook the boy's hand. "Hi, I'm Daniel. Glad to meet you V.J."

"Veej, Mom says you have to set the table." Gideon motioned for him.

"No, she didn't," Delilah called. "She told your dad to do it."

"I'll help you, Dad." V.J. ran off.

Danny smiled down at Hope with a quick wink.

Hope patted the seat beside her as the room cleared. She imagined them huddled in the kitchen whispering about the good doctor's visit and what it meant. "Thanks for checking up on me."

Danny sat. "Are they always like this?" He looked over his shoulder.

She closed her eyes and nodded. "Pretty much, but I suspect they're working overtime to make me smile. The insanity is meant to prevent me from going mad with fear."

"I've got you, Hope." His soft touch on her hand surprised her, and she jerked from it. When his warmth left her she rued the action.

She'd clung to those very words throughout her hospital stay. Now, he'd given her another security blanket. "I'll hold you to it, Dr. Duvall." She put her hand over his now and squeezed. A tear slithered out from under her eyelashes. "I'm frightened, Danny."

"I'm going to do all I can to get you through this."

"I believe that, but it's what lays beyond the treatment that scares me. I've had illness as an excuse to sponge off of everyone. What will I do when I have to get out and earn a living?"

"You'll do whatever it takes. That's the least of my concerns about you."

Hope bit her lip. Once upon a time, she'd had drugs and alcohol to take away the fear she had of living life. Her father might have made it as an artist, but he'd had her mother's support.

Since the day in the hospital when Libby had insisted she mark the things she'd needed to resume her art career, a dread unlike any other had seeped into Hope's soul. She was uncertain of her talent and afraid that she'd never make it as an artist.

"I'm more afraid of living than I am of dying," she whispered.

13

Outside the examination room door, Daniel reviewed Hope's chart. Her post surgery blood work showed some iron and B12 deficiency, which he would remedy with iron and vitamin supplements. That surely attributed to her tiredness, but what about this lingering depression?

He started to knock but turned away.

"Something wrong?" Becky came behind him.

"Just need a minute." He closed his door without looking back. Moving to the window he stared out at the vacant lot.

Hope needed something to live for or she would dry up and blow away like the dead grass beyond his window. He had to think of something to give her purpose.

She'd surprised him with her words, spoken so low that only he could hear her, and when they'd called them to the table, she didn't act at all like a person contemplating death over life. Instead, she laughed and carried on with the rest of them.

For them.

He closed his eyes and shook his head. She'd done it because they were trying so hard.

For her.

She'd momentarily let her guard down with him, telling him the truth.

And why not? He knew her better than any of them— even Evan Carter, who'd walked outside with him, worried about Hope's lethargy. And all Daniel could give him was that before it was all over, Hope would hardly be able to go at times.

A knock sounded and the door opened. "Doctor?" Becky asked. "You have patients lining up to see you and staff that would like a lunch. What say you to that?"

He turned and pasted on a smile then followed her across the hallway. With a soft knock, he entered.

The first item he saw was the paint-by-number carousel in Hope's grasp. She held it out to him.

He took it from her and studied it. "I don't recall that this horse's mane was supposed to be pink or that horse was blue in the picture."

Hope beamed. "The carousel on the picture wasn't our carousel. Remember? Tiffany always liked the one with the pink mane. I liked the blue one." She leaned forward and pointed. "And there's the old white stallion you always gravitated toward."

She'd painted a perfect memory, and the gift made him

smile.

"Where's Ms. Libby this morning?"

"Libby is never far from me. She had a call and stepped out. We've been waiting for you long enough."

Becky gave a short snort and turned away.

"What? Do you think you're my only patient?" He turned away from her and offered Becky a wink. "Will you put this on my desk?" He handed his nurse the painting. "I need to get it framed."

Becky left him momentarily, and he turned to Hope. "Thank you. That means a lot to me." He cleared his throat. "Pleasant memories of good times with my sister."

He read her chart again, waiting for Becky to return. When his nurse opened the door, Libby was behind her.

"Hope, what's wrong?" Libby ran to Hope's side.

Daniel spun around and met Libby's glare.

Hope wiped her eyes, and Becky handed her a tissue.

What had he done or said that would create such a reaction in her?

Through her tears, Hope smiled up at him. "You're really going to frame it." She turned to Libby. "I'm fine. Really. Danny just made me happy."

The way she looked down at the soggy tissue, pulling it and wadding it up again told Daniel otherwise. She might like the fact he planned to frame the picture, but something else made her cry.

"You're just tired," Libby comforted. "That's why you're so emotional. Right, Dr. Duvall?"

"That's Snarky Dr. Duvall to you, Mrs. Carter." Daniel winked.

Hope rewarded him with a mini-snort laugh that used to send him into fits of laughter when they were younger, but the greatest gift was to see the pink rise on Libby Carter's face.

"I guess I deserve that." Libby peered up at him.

Daniel tilted his head toward Hope who continued to look down at the tissue, and Libby nodded her understanding.

"Let's take a look at my artistry." Daniel gained Hope's attention. "When is your next appointment with Dr. Sullivan?"

"Two and a half weeks from today. I think that's when the radiation starts."

Daniel waited for Hope to lie down. When she did, she turned her head toward Libby. Hope's friend grasped her hand, and when he pulled away the paper over her chest, Hope tensed. "Relax," he said as he examined the sutures. "Nothing I haven't seen before."

When he finished his examination, he covered her. His gaze settled on the ladies' clasped hands, Hope's trembling in Libby's grasp. "Cold?" he asked. "Libby can put your shirt around you if you'd like."

She shook her head. "I'm fine. Thanks."

"We're okay, Becky. I have Nursemaid Carter in here with me." He pulled his stethoscope from his pocket. "Sit up for me. Let's see if my trusty torture device can do its job. I get complaints all the time from patients that it's too cold."

"I don't need your stethoscope. I'm already tortured enough," she whispered.

Daniel shared another look with Libby. The woman's green eyes were not only beautiful but expressive. God help Evan Carter if he ever hurt his wife. He'd never be able to live with himself.

Now, those green eyes registered concern and sympathy. No wonder Hope tried so hard to keep them all from finding out the truth. She was in a dark place, and it was growing darker by the minute.

But she had been smiling when he entered—when she held his painting in her hands.

Daniel moved back to his chart, made a couple of notations, and turned back to the two women. "Hope, why don't you get dressed and meet me in my office?"

"I'll help you." Libby fussed beside her.

"Libby, I can do it," Hope snapped at her friend.

"Oh, okay. I'll wait for you out in the waiting room."

"No. I'm sorry." Hope shook her head as if she could change her mood. "But I'll be out in a minute."

Libby brushed a soft hand over Hope's straight reddish locks.

Daniel's gaze flickered to the painting he'd sneaked back onto his examination wall. On the Riviera, he'd touched Hope with that same tenderness ... only he had different thoughts in his head. Libby wanted to comfort

Hope. Daniel just wanted her.

She'd once wanted him as well.

So much passion in a woman barely of age.

"Dr. Duvall?" Libby cut into his thoughts. "Are you okay?"

He shook his head. "Sorry. Hope, I'll see you in a minute. Libby, I'd like to talk to her alone."

Libby nodded. "Like I said, I'll wait for you."

Daniel held the door open, and they walked out together. Libby started past him, but Daniel put a hand on her shoulder. "You're taking good care of her. All of you. Keep it up."

Libby dug in her purse and slipped out her own tissue. "She's so sad."

Daniel nodded. "But we're going to make her happy."

The woman smiled. "I've been working on a surprise for her, and I hope that you'll be a part of it when the time comes. A few things have to arrive, and then we'll be ready."

"Count me in," he promised. "I better get to another patient before the staff shoots me."

"I've watched them when you're not looking. They adore you, Dr. Duvall, snark and all."

Hope stared at the ragged piece of tissue in her hand and waited in Danny's office for him to finish with another patient. His muffled voice sounded through the wall of the examination room next door. She closed her eyes, taking in the sound, remembering how Danny had held her that night on the Riviera. With her ear pressed against his chest, his voice sounded as it did now.

"I love you, Hope," he'd said.

And she'd looked up in to his sincere blue eyes, fighting against the trembling. "I—I love you, too, Danny." She had to make him believe she was more experienced than she was. What would he think if he'd known she'd never kissed a boy? Up until that time, she'd saved her kisses for him.

His lips had met hers, and she'd wrapped her arms around his neck, clinging to him, giving into the overwhelming passion.

Then he'd pulled away from her, seeming to search her eyes for an answer to a question he never asked. He'd backed away from her. "I'm sorry, Hope. Maybe this isn't the best idea."

And with that, he had gone. The rest of their stay, he'd distanced himself from her, and when they'd returned home, she tried to pretend everything was as it had been before, but Danny had left her broken.

"Hope." Danny sat in his chair. She hadn't heard him come in. "You're a thousand miles away."

She forced a smile. "Yes, I was. Sorry."

"Basking in the sun somewhere, I bet."

"No," the whispered word left her with force. "Not

now."

"Well, yeah, because I'd be a little upset. But there won't be anything to stop you once we beat this thing, providing you use enough SPF." He turned his pencil and let it slip through his fingers to bring the lead to the desk. Then he turned it over, doing the same with the eraser.

"Don't, Danny."

He stopped his movement. "Don't what?"

"Placate me. Try to make me do something I don't feel like doing. I can't take that from you."

He leaned forward. "What do you want me to tell you—to go ahead and seep into despair? Not going to happen."

"And what has changed?" She shook her head. "If only God had allowed me to die instead of Tiffany. I know you miss her." His unguarded words before her examination told her so. His good memories of their time on the Rivera were about Tiffany. He'd excluded her from them so that he could hold Tiffany's memory near.

And his silence now confirmed it.

He stood and came around the desk.

Hope couldn't face him.

He whistled, gaining her attention. "You think if you'd died that night and if Tiffany had lived, I'd miss you any less than I do Tiff?"

She bounded to her feet and cried out from the pain.

Danny caught her arm, but he did not tug. His hold was enough to tell her she needed to face him, to listen to what he had to say, whether she liked it or not.

His blue eyes softened as he seemed to seek something deep within her. "I would have missed you more than you'll ever know."

"We've been here before." She tried to pull from his grasp.

"Yes, we have."

"Don't do this to me!" She stomped her foot and winced. "The first time left me completely undone."

Danny started to open his mouth but then shut it. Silence stretched between them for an uncomfortable moment before he stepped away from her. "Then I'm sorry, but I'm not going to accept the fact that you'd rather leave me here in grief than to fight your fears and live."

She lifted her chin. "What's left of me? You know me better than anyone." She moved to the door.

"Hope!" He reached the door before she could open it, placing his hand against it and leaning, so she couldn't get away.

"Let me go, please."

"I messed up. I got scared. Get through this for me. Make it out alive with my help, with the help of your other physicians, and those five goofs you call friends, and give me another try. I won't disappoint you."

She covered her mouth with her hand. "But don't you see. I'll disappoint you."

"I'll take what you have and cherish it, but I'm not going to give an inch. If you'll have me, it'll cost you."

She hiccupped a half-laugh. "Oh, yeah."

"You have to give up this insane idea that living is scarier than dying. You have to choose life—to choose me—and to fight for us both."

She reached for him.

He backed away waving his arms. "Nope. You said it. I don't give in easily." He leaned toward her, a smile on his face. "Besides, if I kissed my patient, I could lose my license. And guess what, I'm not releasing you from my care until I'm sure we're on the other side of this thing."

Hope smiled as Libby drove through downtown Orlando. She leaned back and closed her eyes. Danny loved her. He knew where she had been in life, what she had done … Hope looked down at the flatness beneath her shirt … all she had lost … and he still loved her.

"Care to tell me what the snarky doctor did or said that has you smiling for the first time without aid from Delilah or Gid's antics?"

"He said …" Hope folded her hands and pressed them under her chin, almost afraid to speak the words aloud. "That he loves me."

Libby nearly crossed the center line in the road as she turned to look at Hope. The smile Hope expected didn't appear.

"What's wrong?"

"Nothing at all. I'm shocked."

"You don't think that he said it just so I'd be encouraged?"

"I don't think him capable of that type of deception. If he said he loved you, it came from within that sarcastic heart of his, and it was sincere." Libby turned the SUV into the parking lot of the upscale restaurant, 310 Lakeside.

She and Tiffany used to spring by the place at least once a week. They'd known Hope's mother ate lunch here most days, and while Hope's relationship with Mother had always been strained, the woman would never fail to pick up their lunch tab. She couldn't have Tiffany thinking her less than a mother to Hope as Elsa was to both girls.

Boy, Hope had been a piece of work back then. She shook the thoughts away. "Why are we here?"

"Well, I just thought about it when you told me about Daniel."

Hope narrowed her eyes. A Libby-Lesson was about to commence. She'd never thought to name those times when Libby took her aside and spoke truth into her life, but that was a good title for what Libby poured into her. "Okay."

Libby wouldn't say anything until she was ready. Hope got out of the car and followed her friend into the restaurant. At eleven thirty, they'd arrived ahead of a usually full lunch crowd.

While they awaited a hostess, Libby's gaze lingered on the bench where Hope had met her for the second time in what seemed a lifetime ago. Hope swallowed hard. After the way Hope had treated her, she would have expected Libby to bring her here to get vengeance. But that was before. She'd learned that revenge was not in Libby's repertoire.

"Do you remember that evening when we ran into you and Tiffany here?"

Trepidation filled Hope. She did not want to go there. "I'd forgotten until we walked in just now."

"Why do you look so worried, silly? That was a good day."

Hope almost laughed, but Libby's scowl meant serious business.

A hostess asked them how many, and Hope almost let loose a "How many do you see?" Instead, she bit her lip. Maybe she did need a Libby-Lesson.

Libby motioned to the two of them, and the hostess led them to a table.

Soon a glass of water and a seafood salad sat in front of each of them. Libby held out her hand, and Hope closed her eyes. "Thank You, Father, for this food, and thank You for Daniel. We love him, too. May He come to love You as much as we do."

And in her prayer, Libby's lesson began. Hope kept her head bent forward. *Father, Daniel says he can't date me until my treatment is concluded—if I survive. I ask You only that He know You because I lived.* She lifted her gaze. "I understand your concern."

Libby smiled now. "Then I'm very happy for you, and we'll trust that God will hear our prayers, and we'll wait for Him to answer."

"You're amazing, Mrs. Carter."

Libby took a bite of salad and chewed before putting down her fork. "I don't think so. What's amazing is how much you've grown. You must have imagined that I was remembering that evening when we met because of what happened at that time."

"Well, that's all that I remember. I was very ugly to you, and I thought myself so smart when Evan got tongue-tied. Libby, I tormented you."

Libby laughed aloud. "Only because I allowed you to do it. I had a choice in how to respond. Instead, I had a singular focus."

"Evan?"

Libby took a deep breath and released it in a longing sigh. "I loved him. That night was the first time that a man had ever paid any attention to me, and the one giving me his time was the man I'd longed for, prayed for. Then this loud mouth redhead and her sweet bouncy friend jerked me back into what I thought was my reality."

Hope ate her salad, silently waiting for Libby to go on. When her friend remained silent, Hope leaned back in her chair and wiped her napkin across her mouth. "What did you think was your reality?"

"Loneliness. Not worthy of love. Rejected. Ugly. Stupid for thinking that Evan Carter could ever think of me, especially when I saw the competition."

Hope reached across the table. "I'm sorry for my hand in that."

"Don't be. Everything that you did and everything that happened only proved to me that Evan's love is unconditional and as deep and abiding as mine is for him. If God hadn't allowed you to torture us, I would have never gotten over the wounds of my childhood to realize the truth."

Hope waited again as Libby stared out the restaurant window, seemingly lost in her thoughts.

"Do you mind telling me what happened to make you feel that way?" Hope asked.

"Short and simple: my dad walked out on my mom and me on my fifth birthday. He pointed out that I was the reason. Little girls don't get over that kind of rejection very easily."

Hope's father's rejection stung, but Hope understood that he was caught in the middle. She respected her father. Her mother, though, had done nothing but drag Hope's dreams down in the same way that she'd killed Daddy's spark of genius. But in all the tug-o-war with her parents, Hope never lacked self-worth. In fact, her self-worth had once been highly inflated. Now, she was the daughter of the King and tried to remain humble about it. "I don't have to ask if you've forgiven your father, but may I ask how you did?"

"I still have trouble with it. Charisse and I talk about it

from time to time because we both suffered the same way. We remind each other to turn our anger and bitterness over to the Lord and to continue to forgive even though our fathers have never asked for that forgiveness."

"My dad, he's a good man. He loves me. I know he does. He's afraid of losing Mother."

Libby pushed her empty plate away and motioned for Hope to finish hers. "What was life like for you? I only had my mom. A good part of my life she was sick, but she loved me. I can't remember having two parents in the home."

"One word: miserable."

"Why so?"

"Mom is domineering, spiteful. She married an artist. She must have loved Daddy at some time, but it took her building her business to help him start his. I think she resents him for it. I don't think he can see through all her chatter to understand that he's as successful, if not more so, than Mother has ever been. Then I come along, and I'm just like the man she has apparently grown to hate. You want to know why I was so good at torturing you? I tortured my mother all my life by siding with Daddy, preferring his dreams for me over hers. Elsa Duvall was my encourager, not Connie Astor."

Libby again remained silent. She bowed her head as if in prayer, and Hope didn't dare interrupt. When her friend looked up, she reached across the table and held Hope's hands. "You need to forgive your mother and find a way to honor her."

"Libby, she's never been here for me."

Libby pursed her lips then shook her head. "She's been here, Hope. Just not in the way that you would have liked for her to be."

"I had," Hope lowered her voice, "chemotherapy, both of my breasts removed, and I'm facing radiation. She's not here. Did Dee tell you I went to see her and Daddy the night before surgery? They both knew. Daddy came to the hospital, but I really suspect Daniel had a hand in that."

"Dee didn't tell me you'd done that."

"Well, now you know. My mother is not here for me. She never has been."

"Careful," Libby countered. "All that torture you put me through, why'd you do it?"

"Jealousy." The word fell out of Hope's mouth without thought. "Anyone would be a fool not to have known Evan was in love with you, even that night when we all ran into each other here."

"Well, we've just established that I'm a fool." Libby narrowed her eyes but lost her fight to keep the giggle inside. She sobered. "Maybe a daughter who doesn't realize that her mother has lost her first love to her and then has lost her daughter to that first love would be foolish and believe her daughter and her husband didn't really love her."

"A mother who doesn't understand that her daughter isn't in competition for her husband's love is a sick woman."

"And a daughter who constantly pushes her mother away and honors only her father might not see what's deep inside her mother's heart."

"Connie Astor's heart is dark and evil, Libby. Let's leave it at that."

Libby laughed.

Hope slapped her hand on the table, making the fork on her plate clank against the dish. "Your Libby-Lessons have just crossed a line. Don't laugh at me."

"I wasn't laughing at you," Libby shot back. "I was laughing at the fact that the night when Gideon and Charisse drove me home from here, I thought the same thing about your heart."

Hope gasped.

"I can't tell you what you should do about the situation. I do believe you need to start with forgiveness, and you need to pray and ask God to heal this breach in your relationship with your mom … and your dad."

But they forsook me. The words stopped at the tip of Hope's tongue. What they had done didn't matter. What she would do did. How could she think that God wanted her to make amends with the Duvalls and not do the same with her family?

"Miss," a familiar voice called from a table across the room.

A waitress hurried past, and Hope turned. Her mother held up a plate, pointed at something, and waved her hand as if dismissing the poor woman who'd dared to serve the wrong dish.

Her mother's gaze met with Hope's. Mother seemed to startle, but she turned back to the computer on the table beside her.

Hope wasn't surprised to see her, but she did lift a silent prayer to God, daring to ask Him not to push so hard. Then, she lifted another prayer, asking Him for His forgiveness and asking Him to smooth the way for her. "Excuse me." Hope pushed back her chair and walked to her mother's table. "Mother, it's good to see you."

"I see you're out and about." Mother looked beyond Hope to where Libby sat.

"I'd like to introduce you to my friend, Libby. She's married to Evan Carter."

"That successful architect you ran after when Daniel dropped you? I don't care to meet his wife. If you'll excuse me, I have a hearing in an hour."

Hope nodded and turned away, her heart crushed. She'd gotten almost back to Libby before returning. She pulled out the chair across from her mom.

Several minutes passed before the woman looked to her, her arched eyebrows raised, a look that had always intimidated Hope.

"It has recently come to my attention that I have never sat across from you and told you exactly what I think of you."

Her mother lifted her hand from the computer and leaned forward, well-manicured hands clasped in front of her on the table. "Well, why don't you get it off your chest so I can get back to my work."

Hope stood, pushed in her chair, and leaned down to kiss her mother's cheek. "I admire you for your tenacity and your passion for the law. I remember the night you came home after a trial where you won that lawsuit against that company—the one where the little girl had died because the driver of their truck had fallen asleep at the wheel. You'd managed to prove that the company purposely left their drivers on the road for long periods of time and pressed them for quick deliveries. You cried that night. Daddy hugged you, and I remember at first thinking you were being typically happy about winning a lawsuit. Then you said something I'll never forget."

Mother didn't move, but her mouth opened just a bit.

"You said, 'All I could see was us without Hope, and I wouldn't give up for those parents.'" Hope swiped at her own tears. "Mother, I love you that much, too. I'm sorry if I ever made you think that Daddy was more important to me than you. He never has been. I just gave up trying to please you. Pleasing him was so easy because he and I are so much alike, but you need to understand … Daddy and me … you are the one that we most longed to please, and we never could, but we know everything you did for both of us showed your love, and I'm so very sorry I haven't told you that until this moment."

Her mother turned back to her computer.

Hope stood there for a moment, hoping the silence

would be broken by the woman she wished would hold her and tell her she loved her, too. When the action or the words didn't come, Hope walked away.

"Hope?"

Hope turned back.

"You're okay?"

Hope wiped her hands down her tear-ridden face. "I'll do fine, Mother."

"I know you will. You always have." Mother nodded. "But you really should wear a wig or a scarf at least. That look is not becoming on you."

Hope put her hands to her head. How was it that her mother could make her a self-conscious wreck in less than five minutes? She turned on legs made of Jell-O. She had to get out of the restaurant before she broke down.

In Hope's absence, Libby had obviously paid for their meal and left a generous tip on the table. She grasped Hope's arm and led her outside.

Libby started the car and turned on the air conditioning, but she didn't pull away. "You honored your mother in a very lovely way. I know she must have disappointed you, but you did what was right."

"How can I honor her when the life I live is not what she wants for me?"

"Honor doesn't always mean to obey. If your parents don't know the Lord or they haven't bothered to pray about your path in life, their ideas for you may be contrary to His. You honor them in the way you just did. You gave her a very lovely and personal gift, and I saw it touch her."

Hope peered out the window. She had nothing to say.

"Are you sure your mother didn't give Delilah up for adoption?" Libby asked.

Hope sat in silence. Libby's joke trickled into her thought process slowly. When she replayed the punch line, Hope burst into laughter. She swatted at Libby and cried out for her efforts. "You can be so bad."

They sat together laughing. When the fit of humor passed, Libby pulled out of the parking lot. Hope stared out her car window. "Danny and I have more than one obstacle when it comes to a relationship." Hope's sad reflection peered back at her through the closed car window. "I can't ask him to dishonor his mother and father by choosing me. I caused Jacob and Elsa a lot of pain, and I can never make it right for them. Elsa's hatred of me is so entrenched, and I don't blame her."

"Hope!" Libby bellowed.

Hope jumped and faced her friend.

"Pray. Nothing is too impossible for God: your life, your parents, the Duvalls' pain, your relationship with Daniel. God can do anything He wishes with them, but everything that happens is in God's hands and He means it for good."

Hope nodded. "He can move mountains." That wasn't the first time that the truth occurred to Hope. She just needed a reminder from time to time. After all, Mother had asked about her welfare.

Hope

Hope would rest in that, and she'd pray for more miracles to come. God had placed obstacles in her way, but she had to believe that He would help her to make her way over, above, and around them unless He had a good reason otherwise.

14

"Delilah?" Tiredness wore Hope down as she lagged behind her friend. "Where are we going? Why'd we have to leave so quick? Where're the others?" She stopped in the middle of the church parking lot and planted her hands on her hips. "And why are we not going to our car?"

The wind whipped, and Hope grabbed on to the scarf she had tied around her sprouting hair.

Delilah did a turn, acting more like a teenager than a circuit court judge. "It's a surprise."

A surprise? For her? At Libby's nursery garden located on the property next to the church? Hope picked up her pace, although with zapped energy levels, the light breeze remaining after the gust slowed her down. Hope halted at the gate. "Delilah, everyone has done so much for me. I can't ask for anything else from you."

"Oh, this is a surprise you'll have to earn."

That tweaked her interest. How long had it been since

she'd been able to contribute to anything? She was flat busted. She'd truly be a starving artist without the help of her friends.

No, that wasn't right. She'd be a dead artist.

"Come on." Delilah waved her into the gate.

Hope caught up with her friend and waited for her to open the door to the small building Libby used to showcase her floral arrangements and other items of interior design. The place looked like a small cottage on the outside and in. Stepping inside, Hope gazed over the homey fireplace mantel and up at a painting she'd sold to Evan for Libby when the couple was dating. She stopped and stared up at the portrait of a very young Hope and her grandmother. To think, she'd almost caused Evan to lose the woman he loved by withholding the treasure after Evan's purchase. A "definitely-not-for-sale" metal plate shined in the glow of the recessed lighting. Libby was probably the only one who would treasure that painting more than Hope.

And Libby had loved Hope even while she was wreaking havoc in their lives.

Delilah held out her hand.

Hope drew near to her friend. "Now what have they done?" she whispered.

Delilah remained silent, walking toward the back of the cottage and around the corner to the elegant solarium that took up the entire side of the building.

Hope stepped inside the room, which was filled with Hope's long-stored paintings either on the walls opposite the solarium glass or in easels, expertly placed. One easel held a beautiful sign. *Galleria of Hope*. Definitely some of Evan's gorgeous woodwork.

She covered her mouth with her hand.

"Surprise!" Her friends cheered from behind her.

Hope stepped forward as the others gathered inside. She walked the length of the room and back again, taking in, with new light, the pictures she'd painted some time ago.

"You like?" Evan asked her.

She turned toward him, throwing her arms around him. He embraced her. "Libby's idea," he whispered against her ear. "And Daniel approved."

Hope leaned from his embrace and searched the faces in the room. No Daniel.

Libby touched her arm. "I get an offer for the painting of you and your grandmother almost daily, and I got to thinking that you needed a gallery and a studio. Before you begin radiation, you can stay back here and work and greet your public and sell your paintings. While you're going through the radiation, your work will be here doing its job for you. Then when you're on your feet again, you have your own shop. We'll make sure you're incorporated. Until then, I'll keep the sales under the nursery and make sure I give you the money."

Hope grasped Libby's hand. "Taking out your cut for the rent, right?"

Libby pursed her lips and said nothing.

Hope

Hope hugged her as tightly as she'd held to Evan and cried against Libby's shoulder. She shouldn't have asked. Libby and Evan would never take a penny from her. She'd have to repay them in other ways, starting with showing a little more enthusiasm than she truly had the energy to give. She clasped her hands together and smiled. "You've always been too good to me."

"Nonsense." Libby pulled her away. "Nothing's too good for our Hope."

The door to the cottage opened and slammed shut. Someone ran toward the room. "Am I ...?" Danny stopped. "I am late." His shoulders sagged.

Hope moved to him, hands on her hips. "Daniel Duvall?"

He looked toward her friends.

"Don't you dare look at them. I want an answer. You knew about this and didn't tell me?" She spun in time to see Gideon nodding to Danny, giving him a hint of the answer he should provide. He stopped abruptly and shrugged.

"If you like Libby's idea, yeah. If you don't, it was Gideon's."

Hope laughed. "Oh, Danny, it's a wonderful idea." She stood on tiptoes and reached up with lips puckered to kiss his cheek.

He stepped back, hands up. "Uh-uh." Surprise and then a lazy smile crossed his face. "You're still under my care."

Hope stepped back, and her spirits fell. She forced herself not to look away from him, not to show any of them the truth. "Well, thank you just the same." She touched the scarf on her head and placed her hands to her chest—where nothing remained.

She'd nearly forgotten that Danny's love came with conditions that he'd imposed to give her incentive. And Danny still doubted the existence of God, and his mother wished Hope's existence would soon end.

"Hey," he reached down and took her hand in his, "I'm not giving in to you. There's too much at stake."

Hope stepped away from the group of friends, and he followed her into the corner. "There's something I should have told you. I have some conditions, too. I mean, if you really do love me, and you aren't just saying so to give me a reason to live so you can drop me when we're in the clear."

Danny looked back toward their friends and back to her. "What about me ever told you that I'd do something so low? Love has always been something profound for me. Outside of my family, you're the only other—"

Hope placed her hand to his face to stop his rambling. "I just wanted to get your attention, because what I have to say to you is very important."

He nodded. "I'm listening."

She caressed the face he would not let her kiss. "If getting cancer brought you back to me, I'd gladly do it all over again. But I'm worried about your parents and their feelings about me. We can't start a relationship without their approval."

"That's beyond our control, Hope. I'm sure Dad would come around, but Mom—that's not going to happen."

"Then you're not going to like what else I have to say. If cancer brought you to a relationship with God, I'd die happily because I know I'd see you again someday. I don't have that hope now because you claim God doesn't exist. I used to believe the same thing. But He does. I love you, but I can't commit to you until you commit to God."

He pressed his lips together tightly, his attention on the friends whose cheerful hum of voices sounded around them. "Okay."

"Okay?" She shook her head and had to straighten her scarf. "What does that mean?"

"I'll work on Mom and Dad, and I'll let God prove himself to me."

"That's so disrespectful of Him. Don't act like that."

"You mean He's so big, yet He can't live up to a challenge?"

"Don't …" she begged.

"Hope, if your God will prove to me that He exists, I'll follow Him anywhere with or without you."

The longing in his blue eyes spoke of some deep pain she hadn't noticed until this moment. Danny had become a part of her clique of friends, but he always seemed on the fringe. His clandestine plans for her made with Libby were beyond anything she believed he would do. She ached for him because, truth be told, she'd caused that emptiness in him when she'd allowed Tiffany to drive drunk, to hit the tree, and to die—alone as well.

She placed her hand against his shirt. His heart beat against her skin. "I have a challenge for you."

"Oh, yeah. Like the God-one wasn't enough."

She studied his features until the small lines at the corners of his eyes deepened with his smile.

"Try me," he said.

"Don't always look for God to show Himself only in the ways you believe He will."

"Don't you think that's part of the proof?"

Hope shook her head. "No. God will surpass your wildest dreams. He'll always do what's best for you, even if that means losing me."

"Not an option." He pressed his lips together and folded his arms over his chest.

"You are not God. You don't get to say. So, will you promise me?"

Danny reached out for her but stopped. "Yes."

The one word set her spirit soaring. *God, please forgive his brazenness and show him You love him. He needs You so much more than he needs me.*

Daniel studied Hope as she sat on the chaise lounge with the sunshine filtering through the glass. She closed her eyes and lifted her face to the sun. Her skin was paper thin and pasty, blue veins showing through. The scarf she used to hide her short hair matched perfectly with the outfit which hung on her like clothes on a scarecrow.

She was so fragile.

But yet resilient.

She leaned back against the white wicker. Weariness oozed from her.

She'd caught him off guard. Almost gotten the kiss, but he had plans. But, man, he could taste her lips, feel them brush against him. He was almost glad for the conditions she had imposed. They kept him from giving in. Even this God-thing she insisted upon. If it gave her hope to think he might one day believe, he'd let her believe.

He sat beside her on the lounge, listening to the other five in the small kitchen. "Do they do anything but eat?" He smiled.

Her lips turned upward but fell just as easily.

"Tired?" He took her hand in his.

"Today's been a good day. The service was refreshing. I hope you'll come with us one day soon."

"Hope, I—Yeah. I guess I should." He'd go, if only to give her some encouragement.

She turned a steady gaze upon him. "You think you're in control of what happens to me, don't you?"

He shook his head. "More so, I think than you are."

"Whether I live or die isn't up to me or to you. God knows my days. I might be tired, and I might think that it would be easier to die, but God has my days numbered. He could take me tomorrow, or he could grant me seventy more years to live."

Daniel swallowed hard. "I've never known you to give up so easily—on anything."

Yet he had. When he'd left her after their first and last intimate kiss, she'd never asked him why.

"Don't worry about me, Dr. Duvall. I'm getting better every day. You just work on Jacob and Elsa, and I'll keep petitioning God to show you Who He is."

Daniel tugged the scarf down over her face.

She pushed it back and rewarded him with a huge smile.

Gideon Tabor's loud laugh nearly shook the building followed by Evan's shout of "Jerk!"

Daniel laughed. "You know, you're very lucky to have them."

"Lonely much?" She tilted her precious face and peered through narrowed eyes.

He cleared his throat of the emotions welling inside. "How'd you guess?"

"You don't need to be. Not anymore. Not unless you want to be. They expect you to be here, just like we expect each other to be around. We're a quirky bunch, but we are family, and we've all come to think of you that way as well."

Warmth spread through him like a soothing balm. He hadn't known the depth of the drought of friendship he'd felt. "I appreciate that."

"Then do me a favor."

"What's that?"

"Let me stay here and rest in this wonderful little area that Libby designed for me, basking in this filtered sun, while you go and hang out with them for a bit. Tell them I'm just a little tired."

He stood. "Hope, are you okay?"

"I just want you to get to know them better, and I am a little tired. The sun will do me good, won't it, vitamin D and all?"

"You have been reading those pamphlets I gave you." He stared at her for a long moment. Then he bent down and ran his finger over her hand. "Rest. I'll go play."

She lifted a weary smile and closed her eyes, and worry stirred within him.

15

Hope hadn't felt much like getting out the last week, but she managed to make it to *Happily Ever After Gardens* and *Galleria of Hope* every morning. Libby had picked her up at Delilah's, and Dee had stopped by at lunch, bringing take-out for all three—four on Wednesday when Charisse had been able to join them. Delilah would then drive her home where Hope slept the afternoon away.

She'd sold two paintings since Monday, and making money had felt good. Still, Delilah wouldn't hear of her paying rent. Instead, she insisted Hope put it into savings so that when she felt better and could get on her feet, she'd have a nest egg. "Don't think of moving out, though. I never knew it would be so fun to have a roommate," she'd declared.

Saturday morning found her at the galleria. Business for the nursery and the décor shop had been brisk, and tiredness tugged at her like a child's insistent pull on a mother's shirt. Libby insisted she sit back in her corner where she could almost hide away from everyone but the most astute visitor to the gallery.

Hope stood back and eyed her latest painting, a gift for Evan and Libby. She smiled. The images of her friends were taking shape on the canvas. A whimsical scene. A favorite memory, she was sure, for all of them: the day Evan had proposed to Libby in front of all their friends.

Hope looked to the large roman numeral clock on the wall and saw that it was approaching noon. She'd worked her morning away.

"I'm sure Hope won't mind, sir," Libby's cheerful voice rang out.

Hope straightened her scarf and sat up straighter, not realizing until that moment, that her shoulders had slumped forward. Before this was all done, she'd have horrible posture, something her grandmother would have frowned upon.

"Hope," Libby rounded the corner, "this gentleman is looking for you."

Hope looked up. Her breath caught.

Her father walked into the gallery, his attention drawn to the paintings filling the room.

"Daddy? Is everything okay?"

"Sure," Daddy said without turning to her.

Hope tore a frantic gaze to Libby who stood, eyes wide. "I didn't know," she mouthed.

Hope waited to gain her father's attention.

He turned toward her and came to an abrupt stop. "Hope …" he whispered her name. "You don't look well." He stepped forward.

She held her trembling hand up, willing him to halt. She didn't want or need her father's pity. "I'm okay, Daddy."

"Are you sure?"

"She's doing well, sir. Hope's a warrior."

Daddy turned to Libby and back to Hope.

"This is my friend, Libby Carter. She married Evan. You remember him."

Daddy nodded and held out his hand. "Nice to meet you, Mrs. Carter."

"Libby's fine." Her friend beamed. "Mr. Astor, it is so nice to meet you. Hope's told me so much about you and Mrs. Astor."

"Oh, we're not all that bad," Daddy said. His chuckle had an edge to it.

Libby smiled. "She adores you. Well, I better see to my customers."

Daddy's gaze followed Libby around the corner. Then he gave his attention back to Hope. "You always were so talented." He waved his hand around. "I don't know what to say."

"You don't have to say anything. You taught me well."

"Your mother saw the advertisement in the paper. She said she ran into you in a restaurant or something."

"How is Mother?" Hope pulled out the stool she used

when painting and sat upon it. The tiredness continued to claw at her.

"Your mother is … well … she's your mom. You know how that is." He studied his hands. "Hope, I didn't want you to hear it from someone else, but your mother and I are getting a divorce."

Hope had spent her childhood wondering why her parents ever stayed together. The news of their estrangement was not a shock to her.

"Are you having a grand opening, anything, to celebrate?" Daddy moved on as if he'd not dropped a bombshell on her. He picked up a painting and held it at arms' length then placed it back on the easel and turned to look at the framed works on her wall. Evan, being Evan, had worked hard at surprising her with handmade frames, which were themselves works of art, and he'd promised that until she got her strength back, he'd frame any piece she wanted.

Her father didn't seem to notice she hadn't answered. He lifted a painting from the wall—her most expensive— the historic Thursby home at Blue Springs Park in Orange City, Florida. Daddy had taken her there early on in her training, and she'd learned how relaxing a day in the fresh air, paints by her side, canvas in front of her, could be. He started forward with it. "I want this one."

Hope waved him away. "You don't have to do that."

"No, I don't, and I wouldn't," he put the painting on the floor and propped it against his side, "but it has a special meaning for me." He opened his wallet and pulled out his credit card.

"Daddy, I can't charge you. If the painting means that much, I'll give it to you."

He shook his head and the card in his hand. "So, you didn't say. Are you having a grand opening?"

"No, not until I get through radiation and decide on reconstruction surgery, and since I'm not incorporated yet, Libby's ringing up all sales."

Her father paled. "So much." He held the bridge of his nose with his thumb and forefinger. "You've had to go through so much alone. Hope, I'm sorry, baby."

"You're here now." She threw her arms around him. "And I'm so very happy to see you."

He dug in his pocket and pulled out his ever-present handkerchief, wiping it over his face. "Daniel told me, and I just didn't get it." He touched her hair with a trembling hand. "You're so much stronger than I am, kiddo. I think your mother admires you, too, because you're a lot tougher than she is."

"Let's not over-exaggerate." Hope smiled. "I'll be happy if she would just give me a hug. It's been so long." The yearning sprang up from a well deep inside Hope. "Just one more hug."

"You're not hoping for much, are you?" Daddy teased.

"I'm not hoping at all. I'm praying," Hope told him.

Three women stepped into the gallery, and Daddy seemed to waken from a dream state. He cleared his throat, tucked his handkerchief back in place, and picked up the painting. "I'll pay Libby, and I'll stop by again. I promise."

Hope nodded. "I'd enjoy that. Where are you staying?"

"I'm renting a condo downtown. This will look great on my living room wall." He hugged her.

Hope went to the window and waited for him to walk outside. She watched him place the painting in his car. As if feeling her stare, he waved before getting inside and driving away.

She moved back to the stool and sat down, her body slumping forward. She'd just made a good week's pay in one sale. She should be exuberant.

Instead, she only wished that Dee would arrive and take her home.

Sunday dinners were getting harder and harder for Daniel to endure, and this one was no exception. He'd meant it when he'd walked out before. He didn't plan to come back, but Hope had asked him to win his mother over for them.

Mom's eyes were red. Her non-existent smile had become the norm these days. His father sat across from Daniel, his gaze settling somewhere on the dining room wall.

Before too long, Daniel expected them to announce

their estrangement. He wouldn't be surprised. Maybe it would be best for his mother to move away. Perhaps if his father could take her somewhere that Tiffany's ghost didn't linger, it would be better for all of them. Maybe Mom could find her way back from the land of grief.

The clank of his mother's fork against the fine china brought Daniel from his musing. "Did you know that Hope has her own gallery now? She's flaunting it in the paper. An advertisement. How could she?"

Daniel picked up his napkin from his lap and placed it on the table. "How could she do what? Go on living?"

His mother stared at him for a long moment. "What about Tiffany's dreams? Where would she be today? She could have done anything, and she would have been successful."

Dad continued to stare at the wall.

"But she's not here. She died," Daniel said. "Tiffany died. Not you. Not Hope. Not me. Do you even realize what your failure to deal with her death is causing you to lose?"

Mother gasped. "Haven't I lost enough?"

"Yes, you have, but there's so much left for you to enjoy. Your anger is choking the life out of you, and it isn't being too kind to Dad either."

His mother pushed away from the table but didn't stand. "You don't talk to me like that."

"Well, Dad isn't doing it. Someone needs to tell you. Let me ask you this: are you really still mourning Tiffany or does your miserableness give you a bit of comfort?"

"Jacob, do you hear how our son is talking to me?" His mother placed her hand to her chest.

"Yes, I do. Why don't you listen to him? He's asking you all the questions I want answers to, and here's another one: what good has your vitriol toward the Astors done for you?"

"I can't believe you think I should—do you think I should forgive them, go on with life without my daughter, forget her?"

"That's just it." Daniel sighed. "You seem to equate forgiveness with going on without Tiffany. That's not true. You can forgive Hope for any wrong you think she's done, and you can gain a second daughter."

His mother gasped again. "You expect me to …" She shook her head. "No."

"Let's put this into perspective." Daniel leaned on his elbows. "Hope grew up in this house. She loved you and Dad like surrogate parents. You never hesitated to take her on grand getaways with us—the Riviera, Alaska, the Canary Islands, Africa. She was always beside Tiffany, and you doted on her as much as you doted on me and Tiff. Didn't you notice that the Astors were too busy fighting their war with each other? Connie didn't bake cookies with the girls. She didn't take them to dance class or to cheerleading practice. She didn't haul them to concerts. We did all that. Us. Hope's family away from family."

"I don't see what that has to do with anything."

Daniel held up his hand to stop his mother from taking

over the conversation. "Tiffany died on that road, and I happen to know that a very big piece of Hope died that day as well. You didn't allow her to attend the funeral and to grieve over Tiffany. I'm not really sure she has yet to mourn her. Saying a proper good-bye would have gone a long way in helping her to move on."

His mother cried into her hands.

"Forgive her. Reach out to Hope, and tell her you're sorry."

"For what?" She shot a teary, steel-laced glare at him.

"You said some horrible words to her. I don't know exactly what, but I know they hurt her."

"How could you …?" His mother's eyes widened. "You've talked to her."

"Yes, I have."

Her face reddened. She slapped her hand onto the tablecloth and stood, leaning over like a dragon awakening and coming out of its cave. "Oh, why doesn't she just die? I told her that would make me happy." She banged her hand on the table. Her curls fell from their carefully coiffed confines and tumbled down.

Daniel and his father both stood.

"Elsa, that's enough," Dad said.

"She hasn't died because I wouldn't let her die. I plan on getting her through a serious bout with cancer, and I intend on marrying her."

His mother lifted her face so fast Daniel almost imagined his words as an upper cut.

"I don't understand her, but she wants your blessings. Even after she came to you and you treated her with so much hatred, she still wants to please you as much as she and Tiffany ever wanted to."

His mother sank back to her chair while Daniel and his father remained standing. "She was sick that day? She knew?"

"Yes, Mother. She knew."

Mother pushed to her feet more slowly this time. Without looking at Dad or Daniel, she exited the room. Her sobs trailed after her up the stairs.

Daniel sat and his father did the same.

"Is she going to make it?" Dad asked.

"Hope?"

Dad nodded.

"She's in radiation now. Her immune system is weakened. I had to compromise her physical health for her emotional health. The gallery was the idea of some of our friends. They opened it in a part of one of their businesses. Hope spent some time there rather than home alone between the surgery and the treatments."

"Tough call, I know." His dad ran a hand through his hair. "Prognosis."

Daniel started to tell his father the same half-truth he used on Hope's eclectic little family but decided against it. "Really? A lot of that depends on Hope not giving up hope."

His father's gaze locked with Daniel's. "You were

serious? You're going to marry that girl?"

"If she survives, yes."

Dad leaned forward and stretched out his hand. "Well, just see that she does."

Daniel grasped his father's hand and shook it hard. "Yes, sir."

Hope

16

As if chemo hadn't been bad enough with the fatigue and nausea combatting her stamina, radiation threatened to undo her.

Hope stood up from her seat in front of the porcelain throne and leaned against the bathroom counter, thankful her retching hadn't awoken Delilah. These days the judge seemed to have one ear listening for Hope's every move.

She ran water in the sink and grabbed a hand towel from the bar. She let the water flow over the cloth and then pressed it to her face, holding back the cough threatening to erupt.

The cool rag felt good against her skin. She stayed there for several minutes, attempting to summon the energy to walk down the hall and to her bedroom.

She used the wall for support and turned with her shoulder against the door as she arrived at her room.

Delilah sat on Hope's bed. Her friend stood and pulled

the covers back. "Do you need crackers, maybe some fizzy stuff to settle your stomach?"

Hope shook her head and climbed under the sheets and downy bed cover.

"You've been a trooper." Delilah sat on the bed beside her.

"Oh, I don't know about that." Hope laid back, thankful for the cool pillow beneath her. "I might not bore you with the details, and I don't want your pity ..." She waved her hands down her front and over her scraggy hair. "I'm swollen everywhere but my chest. My hair might be growing back, but it looks horrible. My eyes look like I've been battling with a heavyweight. Basically, I could have a role on one of those zombie shows and never need an ounce of makeup."

Delilah brought her legs up on the bed and sat cross-legged. Her gaze bored into Hope. "Do you still think your value comes from what the guys see in you?"

Hope hadn't thought of it that way, but Delilah was right. "It's a hard habit to break. Once upon a time, Danny used to look at me in this special way. Now when I see that look, I wonder if he isn't hiding his pity." She plucked her shirt out and peered downward at the place where she used to have breasts. "There's nothing about me to admire, and if Dr. Bambridge had recommended I have my ovaries and fallopian tubes removed, I'd have nothing to offer at all."

Delilah rocked back and forth for a moment. Then she leaned forward and cupped Hope's chin in her thumb and forefinger. "I don't ever want you to say that again. Could be God doesn't want either of us to marry, but if he does, the man, whether it's Daniel or not, won't understand what hit him when God places you on his heart"

Hope laughed at the thought, and Delilah released her, smiling again. "Feel like watching some television with me?"

"Right now, all I want to do is to sleep."

"Then don't worry about it."

"I feel awful about leaving my work at the nursery and making Libby take care of any sales. Are you sure it's not too much for her?"

"Libby had it all planned for you, and that's the beauty of your work being showcased at *Happily Ever After*. Libby's the only one who promotes your talent better than you."

"Ain't that the truth?" Hope ran her hand along the empty space beside her. "Delilah, do you believe God takes away those things we put pride in or used for bad?"

Delilah stopped at the door for a second. She drummed her fingers on the wall. The judge used to spout off whatever she thought, but lately, she'd been choosing her words very carefully. "You think He took your breasts?" she asked.

Hope nodded. Tears loosed from her eyes, and she used the palm of her hand to swipe them away.

Delilah stepped back toward her. "I think you got cancer. I think you and your doctors made the decision, and

I think God is walking you through the valley. Why He has you down so low, that's for God to answer. Besides," she winked, "there wasn't much to be proud of."

Hope laughed. "Is that so, Delilah James? What man on this earth would put up with your brash ways?"

Delilah stopped in the door. "According to what you told me before the surgery, there's at least one that you can think of. Care to enlighten?"

Hope shook her head. "I'll take that secret with me to the grave."

Delilah paled. She started to speak but closed her mouth. Shaking her head, she stomped out of the room.

Hope pushed back the covers. Another wave of nausea hit her. Instead of turning left toward Delilah's room, she beelined it to the right and to the bathroom, where if she didn't know better, she'd have claimed to have heaved out all of her insides.

Daniel slowed his pace for the last mile of his run. Lake Eola was a serene park in the heart of Orlando. The fountain in the middle of the lake pushed water toward the sky. Too early for the tourists to paddle out in the lake's famous swan boats. They sat inoperable near the shore in front of the Relax Bar and Grill.

Daniel jogged past. He'd spent a lot of time with Tiffany and Hope at the restaurants around the lake and at the lake itself. Perhaps a nice walk later would do Hope good, get her out a little. He'd keep her away from the crowds. Delilah had called, worried about the nausea and the lack of vitality in Hope. He'd assured her that it would pass once the treatments were ended.

Hope was taking the radiation better than most. His biggest concern was the compromise of her immune system. He'd been relieved to learn that Hope had taken his prescription for isolation seriously, staying home rather than going in to her gallery.

Footsteps thudded behind him.

Daniel moved to the side as a man ran past him, his leashed dog running out ahead of him. "Whoa, Cletus!" Gideon Tabor tugged on the red strap and came to a stop.

The dog sat obediently beside him.

Gideon stared down at it. "He's never obeyed like that before."

"Must be my commanding personality." Daniel held out his hand. "How are you?"

Gideon shook it. "Doing good. We missed you the last couple of days. Been busy?"

Daniel nodded. "I've been keeping in touch with Dee. She's a good nursemaid. Who would have thought?"

Gideon laughed. "She's worrying herself sick over Hope, same as Libby and Charisse."

Daniel concurred with Gideon's assessment. "Perhaps we should be more concerned with Dee and less concerned with Hope."

Gideon grounded his foot against the asphalt sidewalk. "She'll just knock any of that away. Making people think she's stronger than she is, that's Dee's way. So far, it's helped Hope. The two depend upon each other very much."

Daniel stared out over the blue waters of the lake. "Why don't I show up with some take-out for Hope tonight? The rest of you clear out. Take Delilah somewhere fun. Let her de-stress for a couple of hours."

"Sounds like a plan," Gideon agreed. "Look. It's simple to say a thank you. I know we've done it plenty of times, but those two words aren't enough to tell you how much we appreciate what you've done for Hope. After losing your sister, I can't imagine it's easy for you."

"Getting easier every day." Daniel patted the friendly dog's head.

"I didn't know your sister," Gideon says, "but the one thing I know is Hope loved her. She's sorry for what happened. That night plagues her. She knows God has forgiven her and Tiffany's in Heaven, but she lives daily with the pain she's bestowed on you and upon your parents and her own parents. Nothing we do encourages her."

Daniel remained silent.

"Tell me you're not harboring anger and love at the same time."

Daniel ran a hand through his hair. "Honestly, no. I think we've gotten past that. My parents—my mother especially—will probably never get over Tiff's passing. Hope is concerned about that. I'll need to talk her out of seeking approval, especially if that search is going to lead to my mother's complete undoing."

"What man can't do God has already done," Gideon said. "Perhaps God just wants you to bring it to Him so He can show you His awesomeness."

"I don't even know what that means."

Gideon laughed. "Church-speak for God is bigger than your problems. You can't change your mother, but God can. I don't think you've met Him yet. Why don't you join us for church on Sunday? Hope will love it."

"This Sunday, I'm on call. Maybe next."

Gideon slapped him on the back. "I'm looking forward to it." He looked at his watch. "We're both going to be late for work if we don't get a move on." He started off, but the dog stayed put. The taut leash acted as a spring, drawing Gideon backward. Daniel stopped his fall, leaned down and patted the dog once again, and laughed. "Good boy."

Hope

#

Hope sat next to Daniel on the couch. She hadn't been very hungry, but under Danny's careful watch, she'd eaten as much of the lobster and shrimp sauce that she could, delighted he'd remembered her favorite Chinese take-out.

Leaning back, she tilted her head and stared at the ceiling.

"Tired?" he asked.

Her gaze remained fixed on the white above her. "Yeah, I am."

"Your strength will return. Your body's been bombarded with chemicals and scalpels and radiation. It's working hard to get rid of all that stuff. You've been smart to stay home."

"The thought of walking from the condo to the garage and once there from the car to the gallery is too much for me."

Danny grasped her hand and ran his thumb over her

skin. She closed her eyes, enjoying the moment.

He released his hold, and the sound of papers crinkling gained her attention. "Danny, I …"

"I've got it. Let me throw this away. Have you decided what you want to watch?"

"I really don't want to watch anything on television. People living their lives … a little depressing for me."

Danny left her for a few moments and returned, a bottled water in hand. He twisted the top and gave it to her. "You need to stay hydrated, especially since you've lost fluids with the vomiting."

She took the bottle and drank it slowly. "How are your parents?" She placed the lid back on.

"Some good news of sorts." He winked. "Dad's coming around."

"And Elsa?"

He tilted his head, remaining silent for a bit. "Yeah. No. She continues to be lost in her own pity party."

"Don't be so judgmental. You haven't lost a child."

"I lost a sister, and in some ways, I think I've lost my mother as well. She was always partial to Tiff. Never bothered me before, but now, she doesn't try to hide her favoritism."

"You're jealous of Tiff?" She looked back at the ceiling.

Daniel scooted beside her. He laid back and lifted his gaze to where hers was fixed. "No. You know I could never be envious of her. She was a light in my life—like you are."

Hope snuggled close to him, slipping her arm through his and laying her head on his shoulder. In the past, she'd be on one side, and Tiffany would be on the other. They'd talk until the wee hours of the morning. "I miss her, you know."

"I know."

"She's come to me in my dreams a lot lately."

He turned to look at her. "Really. What mischief is she up to?"

"Trying to put us back together again."

He chuckled. "Same old Tiff." He moved a bit. Digging into his pocket, he pulled out his wallet, tugged a picture out of it, and handed it to her.

Hope laughed but then grew solemn. She turned the photo over and ran her fingers over the words Tiffany had written there. "I've got you," she whispered.

Silence fell between them. Hope pushed back tear after tear until she could no longer hold back the stream she'd dammed. "I've got you," she said with trembling lips.

"What is it?" He sat up and pulled her into an embrace.

"I keep telling myself that God knows what's best for us. Tiffany's death hadn't surprised Him. He knew what would come of her future. But I can't get over the fact that God let me live. I should have been the one to die. I talked her into going out with me. She didn't want to. When I fell and hit my head in that bar, I didn't think about Tiff at all. I only wanted to destroy Evan's love for Libby."

She stopped before her words could become a wail of

regret.

"Hope, she wouldn't want any of us to dwell on this. She certainly would have chastised your parents and mine for the way they're acting."

Despite the sadness, Hope giggled through her tears. "She was never one to fear my mom, that's for sure. Mom respected her because of it."

"Tiffany wouldn't blame you. The girl had no guile."

"I had enough for the both of us."

"That's true," he teased. "So, don't go there. Tiffany's forgiven you. I've forgiven you for a lapse in judgment. I've come to realize that my sister wasn't a tag-along. She went with you for a reason. She made the decision to drive drunk, and I don't put the blame on you."

Hope sat up and grasped Danny's arm. "You should put the blame on me. I asked her to drive me to Evan's house. I didn't keep control of my faculties. I was so drunk that night that I almost died because of my stupidity. I fell and hit my head before she drove me to Evan. If he hadn't been home, I'm sure he'd have found me dead on his doorstep when he returned. If Tiffany agreed to drive me anywhere, she was probably afraid. She had to have known I was hurt …" Hope wrung her hands. "Or did she not know? She didn't help me to Evan's door, or he would have stopped her. Still, she was doing me a favor, being my friend, and living out the 'I got you' in our lives." Hope choked back tears. "I didn't have her, not that night. I let her go."

Danny's warmth left Hope's side as he stood. He paced a few feet then returned.

"How could you love me?" Hope stared up at him, wanting the answer. "Are you being pushed to it by some need to get me through this?"

Danny crossed his arms. His blue eyes blazed with an intensity she had never seen in him. "You'll never know the truth of why I love you unless you decide to accept it for what it is. This fear you have of living is keeping you from doing so. I won't let it."

"You don't get to let anything happen, Danny. God does."

"And you think He wants you feeling sorry for yourself?"

"It's probably better than anything I deserve from Him."

Danny started to speak but sighed deeply inside. "Then I don't want anything from Him. I gotta go."

"I—Danny—"

"I gotta go." He stormed out the door.

Hope lifted her tired body out of the seat and moved to the door. She placed her hands against the wooden surface. She'd hurt him. Worst of all, she'd given him the impression that God sought vengeance upon her. She'd known it as soon as the words fell from her lips, but she couldn't stop them.

Was she trying to push the man away?

If so, she couldn't have done a better job of it.

She turned her back to the door and slid down it, weeping.

Daniel wandered in and out of his patients' rooms. If he went home, he'd never sleep. Hope was giving up, and he didn't like it. He'd been about to tell her what he thought of her God, but he couldn't.

But how could he let her continue to believe that some deity wanted to pull the plug on her life. In fact, he no longer held her accountable for his sister's death. He'd forgiven her.

Why couldn't she forgive herself?"

He stopped at the nurses' station where the pretty nurse who'd given him her number sat plunking away on the keyboard. She looked up, and the smile she gave him was warm. "Incident report," she murmured.

"Nothing too serious, I hope."

"Could have been worse." She gave him her full attention. "How are you tonight, Dr. Duvall?"

"Doing okay." He patted the counter twice. "I guess that does it for me. No more patients to look in on."

"We're always happy to see you."

"Likewise." He started off. His phone rang.

The caller ID announced someone other than Hope, and he sighed. She was a different woman now. She wouldn't pester him the way she had in her youth. He both liked that and despised it at the same time. However, the caller on the other end of the line wasn't someone he wanted to tangle with now. Delilah James had probably written his obituary and wanted to read it to him. After all, she probably planned on killing him.

He declined the call, tucked the phone in his pocket, and stepped into the staff elevator. In his car, he cranked up the air conditioning and turned up the music.

His car's blue tooth cancelled the music as a call came in. He looked at the caller ID on his dash. Great. Another person he didn't want to speak with. They were lining up tonight to make him miserable.

He pushed the button on his steering wheel. "Daniel Duvall."

"Hello," his mother's voice rang out. "Daniel, are you there?"

"I'm right here, Mother. What do you need?"

"I'd like to ask you to come over on Saturday morning bright and early. I have something I need for you to do."

"What's that?"

"You'll see when you get here."

"What I'm hearing is you won't tell me because if I knew I wouldn't come."

Her laughter, a rarity these days, tingled like fine crystal. "You've got that right."

"You've got me wondering now." He turned his blinker to maneuver off the main road and into his neighborhood.

"I bet I do. And so as not to inconvenience you, let's also have dinner here on Saturday and not Sunday."

"All right." He made the twists and turns along the neighborhood roads until he turned into his driveway, clicking his garage door opener and pulling inside. "And, Mother?"

"Yes?"

"It's good to hear you laugh."

"Did I?" she asked.

"Yes, you did."

"I'll try to do it more, Danny. Good night, son."

"'Night, Mom." He pushed in the button. The familiar *do-doot* told him that the call had disconnected. The chime on his phone as he walked into the house announced a text message. He tossed his keys on the kitchen counter and dug out his phone.

He leaned against the counter and smiled at the two-word apology from Hope and responded, YEAH, YEAH. I'LL RESERVE MY ACCEPTANCE FOR WHEN YOU'RE FEELING BETTER AND NOT FEELING SO SORRY FOR YOURSELF. I'M ANGRY WITH YOU. LOVE, DANIEL.

On Saturday, Daniel knocked and entered his parents' home.

The maid met him in the foyer and waved toward the stairs. "Hello, Dr. Duvall. Your mother's already started.

She asked that you join her in Miss Duvall's room."

Daniel halted on the bottom stairs and pointed. "How is she?" he whispered.

"She's in good spirits. Your father is with her." The maid smiled.

Daniel hurried up the stairs and went to the north wing of the huge home. Following the sound of opening and closing doors, he made his way toward Tiffany's room.

Outside of the door, he stopped and took a deep breath. He hadn't been in there since her death. Truth be told, he'd avoided coming upstairs. Sniffles tore him from his fear.

"Elsa, you okay, hon?" Dad asked.

Another sniffle was the only answer.

Daniel took a deep breath and stepped inside. The room presented him with a tightrope of emotions. One wrong word could send his family tumbling over the falls of remorse. He said nothing.

His mother looked up from her seat on the edge of Tiffany's bed. She catapulted toward him, wrapping him in a tight embrace. "I'm so sorry for what I've put you through."

"I understand." He hugged her. "We all grieve differently. I shouldn't have said anything."

"I had to set a date to do this, or it wouldn't get done. I need to let her go."

"Not completely." Daniel cleared his throat and fought the searing emotion branding his heart. "I couldn't even do that, but Tiff would never want you hiding away from the world and shutting out the people who love you."

His mother nodded and pulled away. "All the same, your father and I would appreciate your help."

Daniel touched his mother's face. She looked years younger than she had a week earlier. "I'm so sorry you had to go through all this. I miss her, too."

His father hadn't looked up from the drawer he sorted. His shoulders shook as if trying to bear a great weight. "She was an angel." The whispered words held more emotion than the loudest wail. "My angel."

Daniel clamped his father's shoulder. "She adored you, Dad."

"Both of you, from the moment you were born, held my heart. The only one I could love more was your mother."

Daniel embraced him. His mother's arms held him, and as a family they grieved together—something they had not done until now.

When their sorrow no longer had control over their emotions, they each stayed silent and went to work. Daniel chose his sister's mirror. Tiff had tucked pictures into the frame. He reached for one.

The Central Florida Fair Midway cast an aura of lights around them as they stood in front of the beautiful carousel of inanimate horses painted in brilliant colors. Daniel had his arms around both his girls.

He swiped at the pesky tears that wouldn't completely dry up before flowing again. Now that he'd begun to grieve, he wondered if he'd ever stop.

Hope's blue eyes shone with mischief. Above his head were the obligatory finger ears. Tiffany was oblivious to any of Hope's antics and stood beside him, a glow on her sweet-seventeen face.

His mother came beside him and lifted the picture carefully with her hands. Her fingers shook as she stared. "She's beautiful and bright. Strong but yet so needy." She tucked the photo back into his hand.

"You raised her right," Daniel agreed.

"Yes, I did. Tiffany, too." She winked. "Now, let's get to work. We're having your favorite meal tonight. I've already had mine."

"Oh, yeah. What did you have?"

She winked. "Crow, my boy. Crow."

His father's laugh probably startled the neighborhood, and Daniel joined in.

Hope

18

Her radiation treatments finally nearing their end, Hope suspected she should be overjoyed if not anxious to find out if they'd managed to eradicate her foe—this cancer that left her so undone. But she didn't feel much like eating … or sitting … or talking. Still, she pushed a smile into place for her friends gathered around the table. Libby and Charisse, no longer satisfied that they'd saved enough leftovers for Delilah and Hope to eat on their own, were back every night now.

Delilah had said she wasn't the instigator of their return, but Delilah's splotchy face gave her away. She cried—a lot. Hope could almost assume that Delilah thought she was closer to dying than Hope.

"Where's Danny Boy tonight?" Gideon asked.

Hope shrugged.

"He's at the hospital. One of his patients is touch and go," Delilah announced.

Gideon nodded. "I asked him to church a while back, but he hasn't made it yet."

"He honestly said he would come?" Libby asked.

"Yeah. I haven't reminded him of the promise. Something tells me his lack of follow-through is weighing heavy on him. He's kind of hiding from us."

He'd never told Hope of his plans. Perhaps he meant to surprise her.

He might not have been around them a lot, but he called and came by the condo on a regular basis, usually when she was home alone. His visits and hearing his voice were all Hope had to look forward to these days. He never spoke of their disagreement, but Daniel had maintained a distance from her—still caring but a little over-professional. In Hope's opinion, anyway.

She'd stopped getting excited over a good day every now and then. The next days were always harder on her because she'd gotten herself psyched for better times. With the radiation almost over, Hope doubted she'd ever feel like a human again. Tiredness weighed her down, and she did her best to protect Delilah's fraying nerves from the cough that would try to wrack her body. The last couple of days, that exercise alone took a lot from Hope's stamina.

"Hope?" Libby's worried voice broken into Hope's lethargy. "Do you want to lie down?"

Hope shook her head and peeked at Delilah who sat, lips pressed tightly together, her right hand gripping her fork. Hope shook her head and took a bite of the salmon cakes she'd come to love. "Charisse, you need to open up a restaurant," she managed.

"Thank you. That'd be a losing proposition, though, don't you think? Gideon would eat away my profits."

Gideon laughed. "All the better to keep your fine cuisine in our kitchen and at our table or one of the family's tables." He motioned to those around him. "Right, Veej?"

Beside her, V.J. nodded and continued to chow down.

Hope brushed her hand over his almost too-long bangs.

V.J. offered her a smile, but even the kid's eyes held worry.

"I'm okay, Veej. Honest." The lie rolled out of her too easily, worrying her. Where was her faith these days? She'd clung to it to help her make good decisions, like persevering when hopelessness churned deep inside. In prayer, she reasoned that God drew close when she petitioned Him on behalf of others. Pleas on her own behalf seemed as hollow as a chocolate Easter bunny.

V.J.'s warm hand settled over hers on the table. She almost drew back but kept it there a moment before placing hers on top of his and giving him a pat of encouragement.

Tomorrow's radiation would be the last. She was on a high wire without a net beneath her. Either she was cancer free or—

She didn't want to think about it.

Or the fact that she might not ever be able to have children and that she still had to go through reconstruction surgery since Dr. Sullivan and Danny had suggested she wait until after the radiation. Funny. She'd never given children much thought until holding her own flesh and blood might be out of the question.

A cough threatened to erupt. Hope pushed away from the table. "Excuse me," she said as she scurried down the hall.

Inside the bathroom, she ran the water in the sink, covered her mouth with her hands, and tried to keep the sounds of her cough to a minimum. She sank to the toilet's seat and waited for the problem to pass. Then she stood and took a good look at herself in the mirror.

What she saw staring back frightened her. Her skin hung off of her. Her eyes sported dark circles, and her pallor was a little left of dead. She closed her eyes and leaned against the counter. "Lord, help me," she whispered. Give me something to cling to, something to cause me to fight."

The doorbell rang, and Hope listened.

"Danny Boy," Gideon said, "Come in. We've saved some food for you."

Daniel's murmured voice brought Hope from the bathroom. She stopped at the end of the hall.

A chair rasped against the carpet as Daniel apparently sat.

Hope leaned her head against the wall and smiled. If she didn't know better, God was about to give her that reason she needed to trudge forward. Daniel Duvall wasn't usually so pliable. In the past, he'd have offered a good excuse to avoid eating with them. But he had to sense it, too. He was a part of this little strange family of misfit professionals, of which she was the most unsuited for the group. Unless she could call her art a profession.

And she could.

Libby had made that dream happen, and she needed to stay alive to repay the love and kindness they'd given to her.

"About church," Daniel said, "I think I'm free Sunday morning. May I join you?"

Hope stepped out of her hiding place, a genuine smile on her face. Sunday would be her return to church, even if she had to wear a mask. She'd missed services. "That's a great idea. You know where to find us. Ten o'clock sharp." She wouldn't tell him that was Sunday school. He could find out once he arrived. She took her seat between the little boy and the handsome man she loved and silently thanked God for His fast reply.

Hope

19

Daniel straightened his tie and tugged at his suit. He hadn't been in a church in years. He had no idea how to behave. This certainly wasn't his element.

Yet something about his mother's change of heart and Hope's completion of radiation made him believe that God might be responsible. Everyone had been praying for Hope's health and for their parents. Hope said she'd pounded at God's door, asking him for a change of heart in both their parents.

At least his parents seemed to be coming around.

And entertaining the thought of a loving, caring deity who answered purposeful requests—as Hope had described Him the night before—was a way of staying in Hope's good graces.

He pulled open the wooden door of the building and entered a foyer buzzing with people and with coffee and donuts.

"Hi, Dr. Duvall," V.J. Tabor held out his hand. "I'm the greeter for our Sunday school class today, but since I know you, I can show you to the class where my dad teaches."

"Class. Isn't there church?"

"Yes, in an hour."

Ten o'clock. Right. Hope had corralled him to arrive early, and what could he do but go with the little boy. "I'd appreciate you showing me the way."

V.J. beamed as he led the way. The place was beautiful with three lights hanging down on straight poles in the middle rows of each of the three sections. Chairs, and not the obligatory pews, formed the rows. The stage at the front of the sanctuary housed a pulpit and a choir loft with three long rows of chairs. To the left of the stage was what he could only describe as an orchestra section. But the guitars, violins, horns, and small percussion instruments told him the music could be a little lively—maybe they called themselves an ensemble. A set of drums behind Plexi-glass confirmed that he'd probably hear some upbeat worship music before he left today.

"This way." V.J. opened the door and led him down a long hall. A couple of turns later, and the boy ushered him into a classroom.

The murmur of voices stopped, and Gideon looked up from something he studied. "Daniel. Come in. Good job, V.J." He ruffled his son's hair. "Better get out there. You might miss a new classmate."

V.J. ran off without a word.

Gideon motioned for Daniel to pick a seat.

Daniel choose a chair in the back.

"Good to see you this morning. Hope should be here any minute."

A bell rang outside in the hallway, and a couple of minutes later, the room filled. Charisse hurried in last. Gideon pointed to Daniel, and she made her way to sit on one side of him, leaving a chair open, he supposed, for Hope.

Gideon introduced Daniel to the class, and he was welcomed with enthusiasm. Charisse then took down prayer requests from the class. Daniel shrugged when Charisse glanced at him. Hope was on the forefront of everyone's mind, and since she hadn't appeared with the bell, Daniel couldn't shake her from his thoughts.

He'd set his phone on vibrate, and she hadn't called him.

Gideon's gaze traveled with Daniel's more than once during the hour-long study in which Gideon confirmed Hope's declaration that they needed to seek his parents' approval. A woman in the front row had asked if honoring and obeying were the same principle. With ease, Gideon had explained that while honoring meant to never bring down shame upon a parent, that sometimes—especially when parents didn't know the Lord—obeying them would run contrary to God's will in an adult child's life. The Holy Spirit, he said, would help you to discern. However, as a child, under a parents' authority, that disobeying a parent would most often not honor them.

Food for thought, but more on his mind was the absence of Hope, and Delilah, from the room.

After class, Daniel hung around, hoping to follow Charisse and Gideon into the auditorium. He'd checked his phone again. No message.

"Dee would let us know if something was wrong. Maybe she's just tired or had a restless night," Charisse offered.

"Wouldn't Dee let you know?" Daniel grasped for a sensible reason Hope would not show up to church. Since he'd known her, she'd only missed church when necessary.

They entered the sanctuary, and Libby and Evan hurried forward to greet him. "We're so glad to see you." Evan held out his hand.

Daniel shook it and then allowed Libby to wrap him in a hug. "We substituted for the teens' class today," she advised. "If you want to have your faith renewed, you should try it. Those kids are hungry for God's Word."

Evan chuckled. "And Libby was hungry for them to grasp the teaching. They asked good questions that make me hopeful they'll go home with a renewed respect for Mom and Dad."

So, each class must have been taught from the same scripture. Daniel would admit, he'd enjoyed Gideon's knack for teaching. If not for Hope's absence, he would have delved deeper into what he'd learned.

"We can sit here." Libby pointed. "Join us. We have enough room." She counted the chairs. "Just right."

Daniel motioned for Libby and Evan to take a seat first. Then he did the same to Charisse and Gideon, who sat side-by-side, leaving two seats open, apparently for Delilah and Hope. Daniel sat on the edge of the row, something he often did when given the choice. He never knew when he'd be called to the hospital by one of his patients.

He lifted an uneasy smile down the row of friends. A melancholy stirred within him. Evan and Gideon had peace in their marriages. They took for granted what Daniel longed to have.

Lord, if I could sit in this pew every Sunday—every time Hope wanted to be here—I'd be content. Just let her get beyond this cancer.

The service progressed from some nice worship music into a sermon and then to a closing prayer and announcements. Daniel couldn't tell what the preacher said. His entire mind had been focused on the reason why Hope wouldn't come to church, especially when she knew he planned to attend.

Charisse jumped, catching Daniel's attention. She dug into her purse and pulled out her vibrating phone. She shot Daniel a look and showed him the message.

On the podium, the preacher said, "Amen."

Before anyone could get into the aisle, and not waiting for the others to follow, Daniel bolted to his car.

Hope needed him.

Daniel's world sat on the edge of a precipice, and he wasn't in charge of pulling it back. David Bambridge had that duty. All Daniel could do was sit idly by while all his hopes and dreams of so many years threatened to topple into a deep cavern.

He wiped his hands over his face to still the emotion. He needed to talk to Bambridge as a colleague and not as someone who stood to lose the only women who'd ever come close to stealing his heart.

Who was he kidding? Hope had stolen his desires for any other away from him. All he could see, even when he was angry with her, was his love for her.

He tried to speak but couldn't.

Bambridge motioned him away from the ICU nurses' station. "We've sedated her. She's on oxygen, and she needs to rest."

"Prognosis?" Daniel managed to get the word out between trembling lips.

"Failure is not an option." The good doctor offered him a wan smile. "Isn't that our new motto? At least Mara Ramesh thinks it is."

Daniel nodded. "Did you talk to Hope?"

An emotion that Daniel had never seen before played on his associate's face. "She's worried about you. Said she was afraid you'd blame God or me or even yourself."

Hope had pegged him. He'd blame all three if she died.

"She doesn't want you to do that, Daniel. She wants you to be there for her family—whether she lives or dies."

"Family?"

Bambridge leaned forward and looked through the small pane in the ICU door leading to the waiting room. "That family."

Daniel closed his eyes and took a deep breath. "Mind if I see her?"

Bambridge patted his back. "Tell her whatever she needs to hear. I believe that her well-being is dependent upon her mental health. I talked to her friend, Delilah, and she says that she's been up and down lately. Have you noticed anything?"

Yes, he had, and he'd added to that burden by walking out on her and keeping her at a distance. "I have. Delilah's description is adequate. I chalked it up to fatigue, but it probably went deeper than that."

"Let me deal with her medical. You deal with her emotions; give her a desire to live, Dr. Duvall."

Daniel made his way to the third cubicle room in front of the nursing station.

He stepped inside and drew the curtain. Stopping at the foot of the bed, he took a deep breath. No matter how he felt—this seeming depth of loss—he had to put a smile into his voice. He touched Hope's foot, which was covered by a hospital blanket, then forced himself to look in the face of grave illness.

He would blame the hospital lighting on her deepened pallor if only to give himself a little comfort.

Her hand was cold to his touch. He held it between his, trying to infuse his warmth into hers. She took long, slow breaths as if it cost her great effort. He checked the IV dripping into her veins for antibiotics and was satisfied that Hope remained in good hands with his partner.

Still, would the antibiotics be enough; would he ever see those blue eyes of hers again?

"Hey, Sleepyhead. I went to church this morning, and you're here lounging. I guess I'll have to make plans to go again with you. I didn't get much from the service because I was worried about why you and Dee didn't show. Oh, and thanks for tricking me into showing up an hour before the actual service. I guess you knew I'd enjoy Gideon's class. He's a great teacher, by the way."

Daniel cleared his throat of the growing emotions. He literally held her life in his hands, and there was nothing he could do to save her. He'd done his part. He'd gotten her through the surgery. He'd also stayed by her side through chemo and radiation.

Her hair was growing back, and she looked like a lovely little pixie, ready to play the role of Peter Pan. Emotions wanting to burst forward but held back burned his throat. "Hope," he bent close to her ear, "Don't go to Neverland. I need you here." His prayer uttered during church, which seemed a little like casting stones into a pond to see if they'd float, now gripped him. "I prayed," he said.

"I asked God to be allowed to sit beside you in church anytime you wanted to go."

He started to tell her that was his challenge to God, but he stopped. She'd made it clear that his challenges rattled her.

"You don't want to leave now, do you? Mom's coming around. You'll see. Eventually, she'll be championing us to get married. I'd like that. Wouldn't you? Me and you together. I think it's always supposed to have been that way. No. I don't think it. I know that's the way it's supposed to be. Don't check out on me, baby, when we're so close."

Through his meandering words, Hope's labored breath continued with the rise and fall of her chest.

"Oh, dear God, don't take her away from me. Let her live. Please, let her live." He cried out. "Hope, you have to live."

Daniel was a grown man. So why was he standing at his parents' door at 2:00 AM waiting for them to let him inside. The light had come on in his parents' room, and he didn't knock again.

"Who is it?" his father asked.

"It's me, Dad."

The door opened, and his father peered outside. "Daniel, is something wrong?"

Daniel's lips trembled, and he couldn't speak. He gave a curt nod.

Dad pulled the door open and ushered him inside.

Daniel followed him into the living room. He sat hard on the couch and stared ahead. Why had he come here? Hope had been here once, and she'd been horribly treated.

"Is it Hope?" His mother entered, her robe billowing after her. "Daniel?"

"I could lose her." Daniel peered up at her expecting to see a smirk.

His father sat in the chair opposite him.

His mother pushed in beside him, making him move over. She wrapped her arm around his shoulder. "I'm sorry, Daniel."

The sincerity in her voice was his undoing. He sobbed into his hands.

"Is there anything I can do?" Dad asked.

His father was a cardiologist—the best in the state, perhaps the U.S. and maybe even the world. He was the reason Daniel strived to be the best. A patient's survival was the only notch in their belts that mattered to either of them. Hope didn't need a cardiologist.

And Daniel couldn't help her either.

She was in the hands of Bambridge, and he was sure that the man had run out of miracles. Hope's condition had worsened.

And what had he done. He'd fled. She could die without him by her side.

"I need to go." He bounded up.

"No, sir." His mother grasped his arm. "You're not driving in this state. You're going up to take a power nap. You need to rest."

Daniel's heart went cold. He yanked from her hold. "This is what you wanted, isn't it?"

"Daniel, I—"

"She might die. Isn't that what you told her she could do to repay you for Tiffany's death?"

Mother blanched and shrunk away from him.

"Daniel!" A warning edge fell into his father's voice. Jacob Duvall seldom used it, but when he had, his kids—even his wife—had paid attention.

Daniel jerked his gaze to his dad.

"You're hurting, son. I'm going to let that slide, but when people are hurting they don't always say what they mean."

"Did you mean it, Mom?" He ran his hands through his hair.

"I did," she whispered the words.

"Do you know how much they must have hurt her, and she never said a thing to you. Never mentioned it to me."

His mother nodded. A tear fell down her cheek. She worried her hands, covering one with the other and switching.

She looked worn and defeated like she had the night in the ER when they'd come out to tell them that Tiffany had died.

Daniel placed his hands on top of hers and gave a slight squeeze. "The truth is, without a doubt I know that Hope has forgiven you. When I told her I loved her, she told me that we had to have the blessing of you and Dad before we moved forward. Hope didn't cause Tiffany's death. Let's stop casting blame on her and Tiffany. For whatever reason, God took her from us."

"Daniel …" his father sighed. "You can't believe in that fantasy."

Daniel looked down at the plush beige carpet. "I'm open to the possibility," he admitted. "I've set out a challenge for Him, and I hope that He will meet it. Admitting the possibility of God is a step of faith for me."

His mother brushed his face with the back of her fingers. "Keep the faith, Danny, and I will do my best to push my anger with Hope aside."

"Give her a chance. If you do, you'll see how easy it is to love her. She's changed. She has a strength that despite her present condition, oozes from her."

"And if she dies," his father said. "Will you still believe there is a God?"

Daniel took a deep, quivering breath. "Hope asked me to. I'll try my best if only to grant her final wish." Daniel patted his mother's hand and stood. "I'm better now, and I need to go home, shower, and change my clothes so that I can be productive."

He moved to the door, opened it, and stopped. "I love you both. I never want to hurt you or dishonor you. I crave your blessing. If Hope makes it out of this, I plan to ask her to be my wife. She's stubborn, and she won't accept my proposal if it means that I go against your wishes."

"You're a grown man, Daniel." Dad grasped the door, holding it in place. "You can do what you like."

Daniel shook his head. "No. Hope's right. If we start marriage out with a strain between you and me, that's just one of the things that can pull us apart. Like I said, she's changed. She's become a wise woman. The reckless teenager in her has been replaced with a thoughtful, caring woman."

His mother came to stand beside his father.

"You know," Daniel said, "she reminds me a lot of the person who raised her." He kissed his mother's cheek. "That's you." He ducked out the door and hurried to his car, halting outside to peer at the home across the street.

Stephen and Connie Astor's house lay dark except for the lights at the entrance and the orange glow on their porch. He'd seen the way they treated their daughter. Did Hope want their blessing, too? She'd told him that Stephen had moved out.

He stared up at the heavens. "Lord, can you pull this family together for us? Remove all obstacles to our happiness?" He opened the door. "And that's a request and not a challenge."

Hope

20

Rather than taking the staff elevator, as he'd done when he escaped to his parents' home, Daniel walked into the ICU waiting room with no doubt that some or all of their friends would be there, wanting answers from him—answers he hadn't wanted to face earlier that morning.

Delilah rushed toward him. "How is she? They won't let us in."

"They will, two at a time, during visitation minutes every hour. Hope needs to rest. She's receiving oxygen and being kept under sedation to allow for proper oxygen saturation. When you're allowed back, keep the conversation to a minimum, yes and no questions for head movements and don't let her talk."

"What's the prognosis?" she demanded.

He thought about lying to her, but Delilah had been Hope's champion. She didn't deserve to be misled. "Pray, Dee. Get the rest of the family together and pray."

Delilah stepped back, her mouth parted. She gave a curt nod and turned on her heels, grabbing her purse and pulling out her phone. "I'll be in the chapel, and I'll have them join me. If you'd like, please meet us there."

Daniel nodded before he opened the ICU entrance.

Mara Ramesh stood at the nurses' station inputting information. She looked up as Daniel neared. Her gaze was one of sympathy.

"Bambridge called you? How is she?" he asked.

"He did. Seems we're in a critical period. I'm afraid the odds aren't in our favor."

Daniel fell against the counter. His world tilted, but he managed to hold on. "Organ failure?"

"Not that dire yet. But I don't see any improvement. Her lungs are congested."

"No change at all?"

The doctor shook her head. "She's held steady since her last round of medication, but she's weakened by the radiation."

Daniel grasped Mara's arm, squeezing in his encouragement. "Failure is not an option, Mara."

Mara closed her eyes and took a deep breath. "We're not saviors, Daniel. That, I believe, belongs to a higher power. We're not even physical engineers. I may not worship this God that Hope declares, but I do have faith that we are not in control. Whatever happens to Hope is out of our hands."

Daniel allowed her words to seep into his soul.

"I'm not telling you to give up," she said. "I won't give up. Everything I do will be to prevent Hope from taking her last breath, but I will not be held to the standard you hold yourself to. We're not gods. We're people with extraordinary skill, learned from men, that allows us to be used by a higher power. When you remember that, the lives we help to save will come into perspective. Short of true malpractice, we do not write the story of those under our care. Another is in charge of that."

Daniel pushed the emotion back. Somehow, he found it easier to believe he had control of life and death. Yet, Hope's precarious situation shined a new light on his misconception. "Thank you. I'm going to go check on her."

Mara nodded. "She's still asleep. We're trying to keep her off the respirator. I plan to bring her out of it and get some breathing therapy, hoping to break up the infection."

He pushed open the curtain to Hope's cubicle and stepped inside.

Hope's breathing continued to be labored. Pneumonia at this stage of her treatment could be deadly.

Daniel squeezed Hope's limp hand. "I'm here," he whispered. "But I'm not going to baby you. Here's a promise to you. I'll never run away again. I won't give up on you or on God. I'll have faith in Him, but I need to know that you're not giving up, that you love me enough to fight for a life together." He leaned and kissed her forehead. "I will be undone without you. Totally undone. Don't leave me here alone." A single tear slipped down his cheek and fell onto her face. With a tender hand, Daniel wiped it away. "Hope, you know that picture on the Riviera and the one on the carousel. I want to commission you, for our wedding anniversary, to paint us into those pictures. You and me. Together. Okay?"

He couldn't be sure, but he thought that she flexed her fingers.

"I'll take that as a yes, baby, and here's my promise to you ..." He brushed his lips against hers. "I shouldn't have done that. I won't do it again until I release you from the practice's care. And I won't release you until we move on together to seek the options in your recovery. So..." He wiped his eyes. "Don't let that be our last kiss."

The room they'd taken her to slipped away from Hope, almost as if she'd been sucked from it down a long dark tunnel. She tried her best to scream, to ask them to bring her back, but the tunnel continued to pull her deep inside a place she didn't want to go. "Danny," she cried out. "Please let me go back."

Her movement stopped, and she stared around her. Darkness.

This wasn't what heaven was supposed to be like. She imagined God's glory shining around her, angels along with the saints who went before her, singing praises.

A loud click and color burst forth.

Hope stepped onto the worn grass of the Central Florida Fairgrounds. Around her, the rides and concessions began to appear. The noisy calls of carney barkers and the ringing of their games sounded. Then the music—blaring carnival tunes mixed with pop songs she no longer knew the name to, filled the air.

Hope moved forward.

"It's not supposed to be like this, Lord," she cried. "I'm frightened."

She closed her eyes tight and opened them again. In the distance, something familiar caught her attention. Her heart released its fear.

Tiffany.

She had to be there.

Hope practically hop-skipped to the carousel. She hadn't been this strong for many months now. "Tiff ..." she called. "Are you here?"

The carousel turned, it's calliope music loud. A figure moved forward, grasping the poles of the horses as it moved. "Hey, you." Tiffany held out her hand.

Hope laughed and grabbed hold, jumping up and holding on to a pole with one hand and holding Tiffany with the other.

As the carousel turned, Hope imagined herself floating on air. She leaned back. Her hair—long and silky, the way she'd always kept it before the chemo—caught in the breeze. "I'm free."

"You've been free for a long while now, Hope. We

both are." Tiffany leaned back, copying Hope. "But you're not coming with me. You can't. You need to go back." She pointed in the direction Hope had traveled.

Hope drew her attention there. The long, dark tunnel lay just beyond the edge of the grass where she had entered. The darkness there frightened her. "I don't want to go back. I'm sick there. I want …" She motioned down the front of her. "I want this."

Tiffany smiled. "Don't you know, silly? This will always be here waiting for you."

"Am I dreaming?" Hope asked.

"What do you think?"

"Why?"

"You've never forgiven yourself for my death. Let it go. What you're feeling now, the reason you don't want to leave, I'm already there. Free from pain. I don't want to go back."

"Don't you miss your parents? What about Daniel?"

Tiffany's warm smile spoke loudly of the peace she had. "They're doing just fine, and so are you."

"Are you kidding?" Hope chided. "Look at me."

"Look at you." Tiffany made a motion like wavy hands. "You're gorgeous. All put together."

Hope stared down. Her hair wasn't the only thing that changed. Her breasts were back to normal and her skin was creamy soft. She tried to speak but stopped.

"This is the way you'll be."

"When? When I get to heaven."

Tiffany shook her head. "This is you as God sees you." She leaned forward. "As Daniel sees you."

"Danny can't—he's seen the mess I am."

"He only sees the beauty in you. He wants you to come back. Others are looking for you to pull through. Do you even have to wonder if they're praying for you? And someone has something very important to say to you. You need to give that person a chance because you're the only one that has ever shown Christ to that individual."

"Danny?"

Tiffany shook her head. "Go back and find out. She needs you."

She? Mother?

"Let's take a ride." Tiffany climbed onto the horse on the inside of the carousel. Hope, in no hurry to leave her friend, climbed onto the one beside her.

She closed her eyes and, again, leaned back, holding tightly to the pole. "I miss you, Tiffany."

No answer came. Hope opened her eyes. Tiffany was gone.

"Hope ..." the voice was off in the distance, toward the tunnel. She held tightly to the pole, her body shaking.

She didn't want to go back through that tunnel and to the pain and sickness that awaited her.

"Hope, please wake up."

The voice was soft but insistent, but who?

"Honey, I know you can hear me. I see your eyes moving. Come back. I have something to say to you."

Recognition caused her to flutter her eyes. The tunnel's suction began to pull at her, and she held tightly.

Finally, the wind shook her hold free, and Hope tumbled back into darkness.

She gasped and coughed.

Someone pushed her up and stuck a small plastic container near her lips. "Here," the nurse said. "Spit it out."

Gross.

"Spit it out," the nurse insisted. "This is good. It's breaking up."

Hope did as directed, coughing even more. When the urge to hack diminished, she laid back in her up-raised bed. The nurse put the oxygen mask over Hope's face again.

"Well, we can be glad, can't we," the familiar voice said.

Hope turned her head. "Ms. Anne?"

21

Hope reached up to take the oxygen mask away. Ms. Anne stilled Hope's hands. "You don't want your doctor to kick me out, do you?"

Hope shook her head and laid back. "Thank you for praying for me."

"Hope, you shouldn't talk," the nurse said.

Hope looked from the nurse to Ms. Anne, whose smiling face brought such peace.

"I was in the chapel, and I heard some nice folks talking about someone who needed prayer. How surprised I was to see it was you."

Hope nodded. The dear lady had remembered her.

Ms. Anne placed her hands on each side of Hope's. "I don't often listen to gossip, unless it's good news. You're a lucky little girl, I hear."

Hope raised her brows.

"Four doctors and one's in love with you." Ms. Anne

winked. "I put two plus two together and realized that you're the one who's the talk of this hospital. Seems no one has been able to break down the barriers that Dr. Duvall has placed around him. You have apparently bulldozed them to the ground—much to the chagrin of a lot of eligible nurses in this hospital."

"Ain't that the truth," Hope's nurse murmured and smiled. "The man is a looker. You have to admit."

Didn't she know it.

"So, we have to pray that God brings you through this little set back."

Hope again nodded. "Please," she mouthed though she didn't know if Ms. Anne could see it.

The older woman bowed her head. "Heavenly Father, we come before You today, and we ask that You strengthen Hope for this journey. You are her strength, and we pray she rests in You. Though we pray all things in Your will, we do request that You let her live. Hope has been a shining example to those she loves. We pray that she be allowed to continue, but whatever Your will, Lord, we pray that Your glory will be declared. Guide Hope's physicians. We pray in Jesus' Name, Amen."

How a short, simple prayer would infuse such hope and a surge of determination—only God could do that for her.

Ms. Anne stood, and Hope reached for her. The older lady leaned forward. "I'll be praying for you, darling. They only let me back here outside of visiting hours because I promise to keep my visits short."

"Are you an angel?" The rush of words flowed.

"I think not." Ms. Anne giggled.

"Oh, she's going to tell you that. Everyone in this hospital calls Ms. Anne our visiting angel," the nurse corrected.

"Oh, posh." Ms. Anne waved as she walked toward the door.

Hope's gaze followed her until the tears slipped down, curving over the edge of the mask and running down into her hair.

"Oh, honey." The nurse pulled out three Kleenex from the box and thrust them into Hope's hands. "Are you okay?"

Hope nodded. "I'm going to live."

The nurse's lips didn't quite make it into a smile, and a little tither of fear seeped back into Hope. *Lord, I want to live. Someone needs to keep Daniel's barriers down so he can find You. I think You've already seen that it's me. Please let me continue to be there for him.* Her eyes closed against her will. She forced them open.

The nurse straightened Hope's covers. "Dr. Ramesh has ordered a breathing treatment. The therapist will be here soon. Rest, Hope. I'm praying, too."

Daniel eased the chapel door open and stepped inside.

Evan prayed while the others sat, heads bowed in agreement with his petitions. Whispered "amens" peppered Evan's words. Daniel eased into the seat closest to the door and bowed his head.

"Lord, we leave Hope to Your will, but we pray You guide the doctors who are treating her and the doctor we know loves her. Hope's light needs to shine for him."

Daniel closed his eyes and listened as one by one Hope's friends prayed on her behalf. Last to pray was Delilah, and he touched her hand to let her know he had something to say to God. She turned her head, smiled, and nodded.

Daniel cleared his throat. "Put life back into Hope, Lord. She has been a light to me. I can see the light she has been for her friends. Don't let Hope die without reconciliation. Others need to see her light and to know that she has changed. Help her to find the forgiveness she seeks."

Delilah patted his hand now, and he nodded. "In Jesus' holy and precious name, we seek Your favor, dear Father." Dee ended the prayer.

Libby took off her glasses and wiped her eyes. She leaned against Charisse, who put her arm around the sweet woman. Gideon stretched, but beside him, Evan remained deep in prayer.

Charisse pointed toward the door, and they filed out, leaving Evan with the Lord.

Gideon shook Daniel's hand, but he didn't ask him

about the prayer. Daniel breathed a sigh of relief. How could he tell these good people that he still had a foot in unbelief, and he was waiting—for what he didn't know?

"How is she?" Dee asked.

"I looked in on her before coming in here. She was still asleep. Her breathing was a bit labored." If only he had better news for them.

"Do you think we'll be able to slip in so she knows we're here?" Dee wrung her hands. Her eyes filled with tears, and she swatted them away as she would an annoying mosquito.

Daniel nodded. He'd see that at least two of them could visit with Hope. She'd moved her hand in his. She had to be hearing those who talked with her, and if she realized the worry that her friends had for her, maybe she'd fight harder. "I'll go make arrangements."

Evan opened the chapel door and stepped out. His face was drawn. He looked as if he hadn't slept for a month.

Libby held out her hand, and Evan clasped it in his, bringing her closed fingers to his lips and offering his wife a tight smile. "Would you mind if I visit Hope with Dee?" he asked Libby.

"Not at all." She reached and smoothed his hair. "You two have known her for so long. Maybe Charisse and I can see her in the next hour. Right now, we'll go get something to eat and bring it back."

Evan nodded his agreement. "We'll meet you back in the waiting room then."

Gideon followed the girls down the corridor, and Evan and Delilah walked with Daniel from the first-floor chapel to the ICU waiting room. Daniel held open the door. "You have a very understanding wife," he said to Evan.

Evan stopped in the doorway. "I should have asked if you minded. I'm sorry, Danny. I didn't think."

"Nothing to think about. I don't have any hold on Hope."

Evan smiled. "You and I know that's not true, and you need to start acting as if you do. Hope puts on a brave front, but she's very insecure. She needs you to spell it out for her."

Daniel motioned him inside. "And what should I spell out."

"For goodness' sake, Danny." Delilah punched him in the arm. "You love her. Let her know. Stop using this 'I'm your doctor' stuff as a barrier and start showing her that love."

Daniel pursed his lips. They had him there. He had built a wall to keep Hope at a distance. He had to change that. What Hope thought was important. He gave Delilah a curt nod and turned to Evan. "She's your friend. I'd never have a problem with that."

"Thank you." Evan said.

Daniel pulled open the door and motioned Dee and Evan into the ICU.

A nurse pulled Daniel to the side. "She woke while you were away, Dr. Duvall. She's sleeping now. I asked the respiratory nurse to give her at least thirty minutes. Good news, I think."

"Very good news." Daniel followed the two visitors into Hope's cubicle.

Hope slept. Her breathing, while a little raspy, was not as labored as before. She still had a way to go to get out of the deep woods of congestion she found herself in now. They were monitoring her condition very closely.

Dee stood over Hope and looked down at her as if Hope were a corpse in a funeral home. Daniel couldn't have that.

"She's improved. I'm still guarded, but let's not give up hope for Hope. We all know that she can be a tenacious foe. Let's pray she battles her cancer with that same determination.

"That she is." Evan picked up on Daniel's rah-rah speech. "She certainly gave Libby and me a run for our money."

Dee nodded, but she swatted at a renegade tear. "Hope, you don't give up. Do you hear me? I'll go into a funk like you've never seen, and then I'd have to deal with Ms. Libby running intervention. Besides, you still have that man to fix me up with—whoever he might be."

Evan stepped closer to the bed and touched Hope's hand. "You're tougher than you're acting. You're almost to the end of this trial. You've made it this far. Don't let a little pneumonia win the battle."

Hope's eyes fluttered open and threatened to close

again. Her lips curved into a smile. "I'm going to win."

Delilah's laugh filled the room. She clasped her right hand to her chest and leaned over Hope. "Good. So, get out of the bed already."

Daniel's own laugh, loud and without reservation surprised him. All eyes turned to him. He winked at Hope. "You heard her. Get out of bed."

Hope studied him for a long moment. Then she raised her hand, pointing a finger at him. "You kissed me," she managed before coughing and removing the oxygen mask from her face.

"And I'll do it again—when you're not coughing all over the place."

22

Hope had never been so glad to leave one location for another. So, what if it was from ICU to a regular hospital room? The respiratory therapy had been going well. Her cough was a little croupy but drying up, and she'd soon be able to take her last radiation treatment.

After that, they would hold their breaths and pray like crazy for this ordeal to be behind her.

The orderly giving her the ride from one place to another, turned the bed and headed down the hall and into a room. He helped her to shift from the ICU bed to a clean, freshly made one. Hope scooted up and got comfortable under the covers.

She leaned back and closed her eyes. A cough wracked her. Daniel and Dr. Ramesh had pulled strings to lengthen her stay for a day or two of intravenous antibiotics.

Upon hearing of her imminent removal from ICU, her friends had sent word that they were going out to celebrate with some real food and not fast food and would return to visit.

She was thankful for the alone time. The ICU was a busy place, and being parked on the other side of a curtain from the nurses' station had been no picnic, not that she was complaining.

Hope curled up on her side and let her gaze wander up the IV tube to the bag dripping medication into her veins. The cloak of illness had been lifted, and anticipation of a renewed life bubbled within her. She closed her eyes even as the *squeak, squeak* of a nurse's shoes sounded by the door. For once, the future seemed bright enough for her to dream beyond the cancer's ravishes.

She was going to survive.

"Excuse me," a familiar voice sounded.

"Yes, ma'am," another answered.

"Is this Hope Astor's room?"

Hope cringed. Well, this would stop her dreaming of Danny, she was sure.

"Yes, ma'am. She was just brought up from ICU. If you want to visit, I can come back in a few minutes."

"Thank you."

The *clip-clop* of designer heels strummed Hope's nerves. She sat up and turned toward her visitor.

Elsa Duvall stood, hands on her hips, a scowl on her face. Hope could only imagine the blistering lecture she would get from Daniel's mom today. "Hope Astor," the woman said her name as she had done to all three of the children in her care—Daniel, Tiffany, and Hope—when they had done something wrong.

Hope had perpetrated the biggest evil against this woman.

Elsa's pinched lips and narrowed brow spoke volumes. Hope was in trouble now. But what could she say? She'd already apologized for Tiffany's death. She'd accepted Elsa's decree, but Hope wasn't in charge of her dying breath any more than this woman who stood before her.

Elsa moved to Hope's side and peered down at her.

"Elsa ... I ..."

Elsa turned from her and pulled a chair up to the bed. Then she flopped into it. "Hope ..." Her shoulder slumped, and she seemed to wilt.

Tears filled Hope's eyes. "I know I said I was sorry, but it isn't enough. I wish I could bring her back."

"Well, you can't." Elsa plopped her expensive purse on her lap and leaned over it. "And we're not going to talk about that one more day. When we talk about Tiffany in our household, it will be only with fondest memories. We're not ever going back to that awful night."

"But ..."

"We're never going back to that awful night."

Hope bit her lower lip to keep the trembling at bay. She could barely see Daniel's mother through the gathering of tears.

Elsa stood and thrust her purse on the chair. She sat

beside Hope and wrapped her arms around her, cradling Hope like a child, rocking her. "I love you," the words rang from the woman, washing over Hope.

Hope sobbed against her.

Elsa continued to rock. "I had two daughters, you know. Always two. You and Tiffany were like twins to me. Tiffany may have wanted you to go everywhere with us, but I wouldn't have had it any other way. Daniel's right. I spoiled you girls. I'd do it over again, too, and I'm not going to apologize for it."

How hungry had Hope been for a mother's love? She'd never missed her mother's touch because Elsa always delivered. "I love you, too," she mumbled. "So much. So much."

Elsa pulled Hope away and held her at arms' length. She wiped the tears away with her well-manicured fingers and reached for a Kleenex in a box on the bedside table. Then she wiped Hope's face some more. "Daniel said something ludicrous to me."

Hope stared, not wanting to break this renewed bond.

"He said you wanted Jacob and me to bless a union between the two of you."

Here it came. The Lord gave, and the Lord took away. Elsa was only being wonderful to make it hurt worse when she took it away.

Elsa tipped Hope's chin. "Take what you want, young lady. Make that boy yours. No need to ask us."

"I needed your blessing. I couldn't take Danny away

from you and put a wedge in your relationship."

Elsa waved her hands as if swatting at something annoying. "Jacob will visit you later, he said, but he sent me here to offer you that blessing and to say to you that we can't wait to call you our daughter—our real daughter."

Hope stared for a long moment, words not coming forth.

Elsa smiled. "You have always made that boy of mine happy. You've always made us happy. I'm sorry for the words I said to you. When Daniel told me what you were going through, the truth shook me to the core. I uttered words I didn't truly feel only because I knew they would hurt you. I wanted you to fight back. I wanted to tear into you, but you accepted what I said and simply walked away. What could I do with that? Perhaps if you'd fought with me, we would have had a nice battle and come away friends in the end.

"Instead, your actions proved much more powerful to this old woman. Daniel's revelation left me utterly undone. I couldn't imagine the pain I caused you, and when I thought about that, I thought about Tiffany and how I would have never said such a thing to her—and I shouldn't have said it to you either … my daughter."

Hope lowered her head and stared at her fingers. Words had failed her, but the truth built deep inside and pushed forward. Elsa was her mother, though she'd never betray Connie Astor like that. She'd tried to connect with her mother and father, but even her father hadn't returned after buying her painting. Hope suspected his guilt had been assuaged with his money. Even while she was in the ICU, they never came to see her.

She could have died, and they might not have found out until Delilah called them. If Delilah called them.

Elsa wasn't a consolation prize for Hope. She had always been there, except through this trial Hope had caused.

Hope wrapped Elsa in a hug. Her eyes closed, she clung to the woman who'd cast her a lifeline of optimism. "I love your son, and I am proud to be your daughter."

When she pulled back and opened her eyes, Daniel stood beside his mother, his hand cupped to his chin and his eyes wide.

"So, Daniel, when are you going to put a ring on this one's finger?" Elsa stood.

"There are a few things we need to get through first, and something I have to do. Then you can bet I'll get her down the aisle as fast as I can.

Out in the hallway, Daniel hugged his mother. "You amaze me."

"Oh, how so?" she teased.

"You just do."

A crowd of people walked toward them. His mother made to leave, but Daniel reached for her arm. "I'd like you to meet some friends of mine."

Delilah approached first, her eyes like steel.

"Mom, you remember Delilah James and Evan Carter. I'd like you to also meet Evan's wife, Libby, and Charisse and Gideon Tabor. Gideon is also a judge. Charisse is his wife. She's finishing law school soon."

Mom beamed. "I'm so pleased to meet you. Delilah," she stepped toward the judge, who still glared, "I owe you an apology for the way I treated you after Tiffany's death. Hope and I have just had a long talk about it, and we've cleared the air. I hope we can do the same."

Delilah swallowed. "That's wonderful. I know there was nothing Hope wanted more."

"Is that so?" Daniel joked.

"Yeah, it's so," Delilah bantered. "Elsa first and then her son."

Mom excused herself, and Daniel offered to walk her downstairs. Before he left, he turned to Evan and Gideon. "Can we talk in the waiting room?"

"Sure." Gideon shrugged. "We'll meet you there after we get our Hope fix."

When Daniel returned, he found Evan and Gideon waiting in the empty room. Running his hand through his hair, he sighed. "I'm beginning to realize that God exists. He looks after us. I'm new at this religious thing. Is there something I need to do in order to know God."

Evan smiled at Gideon before turning to Daniel. "I think you're getting to know Him already. First off, it's not a religious thing we have. We have a relationship with Him, which can only occur because of His Son. Jesus died on the cross for our sins. Knowing God comes with a knowledge that we aren't all that perfect or in control."

"I'm beginning to understand that." Daniel nodded, listening intently. He wanted that relationship that Hope had exhibited throughout her sickness.

"Sin keeps us from a right relationship with God. We all have it. It's in our DNA. We're born sinners."

"So how do we get close to Him?" Daniel pressed.

"You're asking the right questions," Gideon said. "Jesus tells us that He is the Way, the Truth, and the Life. The only way to get close to His Father is through Him, which is pretty amazing when you realize that Jesus and the Father are one."

Daniel scratched his head.

"Too much information, Gid." Evan laughed. "Danny, if you realize you're a sinner and you have no other way to shed that sin except by asking Jesus to forgive you, then you pray and ask for that forgiveness. The Bible tells us that Jesus is faithful to answer that heartfelt prayer."

"It's that simple."

"Oh, for some it is the hardest thing they can do. Pride gets in their way, or they think they balance the scales with their own righteousness. Doesn't work that way."

Daniel shook his head. "I've had a lot of pride. Hope all but said it outright. I thought I was the savior of people, when I really haven't been."

Gideon's smile told him he was getting close to understanding. "So, I put that pride aside, and I ask him, and what happens. What do I have to do next?"

"For what we call salvation, nothing. It's freely given by the Lord. Now, for your relationship to grow, you'll need to do some things. A relationship with God is a lot like our friendship. We grow apart without the effort," Evan offered.

Daniel had seen the effort his friends had put into their family. Their relationships with one another had showed him how alone he had been. He never wanted to feel that way again. He wanted what they had—friendship and a relationship with God.

"To have a close relationship with God, attending church is a good thing, so is prayer, and Bible reading," Gideon said. "God will direct your life as you begin to do those things."

Daniel cleared his throat. "Okay, help me out here. I really want to pray."

Hope

23

Hope couldn't keep her hands still as she sat in Dr. Bambridge's exam room with Danny beside her. He'd rearranged his appointments to be with her.

He reached and took her hand in his. "We've prayed about this, and we've made God-led decisions."

She leaned into him and closed her eyes. *Thank You, Lord, for giving me the desires of my heart. I'd do this all over again to get to this very point.*

A short rap sounded on the door, and Dr. Bambridge entered. "Dr. Duvall, good to see you." He shook Danny's hand. "Fraternizing with the patient, I see."

"Your patient. I closed my files on her last day of radiation with Sullivan."

Danny stood quietly as his associate conducted Hope's examination and then looked through the files. He pulled out a report. "Hope, may I?" He motioned the report toward Danny.

Hope nodded and bit her lip as Danny studied the report, his stoic face giving nothing away. "Should I tell her, or do you want to?"

"I will," Dr. Bambridge sighed and turned toward Hope.

Hope trembled with anticipation. Was she or was she not cancer free? "Tell me. I can take it."

Dr. Bambridge smiled. "The tests show that the cancer is gone. You opted out of hormonal therapy, which I think was prudent based upon examination of the cells. All that's left is to decide if you, as a young woman getting ready to enter into marriage, would like to schedule the reconstruction surgery."

Hope waited for Danny to speak, but he shook his head. "That's your decision. We talked it over, and you can change your mind. I'll be with you whatever you decide."

"Well," Hope scooted forward, excitement building in her. "As far as reconstruction surgery, Danny said he doesn't care, but I want to talk to Dr. Palleto. Danny says he's the best. I wasn't going to have reconstruction because—well—I've learned that my breasts aren't the best part of me, but a little part of me misses the gals."

Dr. Bambridge laughed. "I'll get the referral off to him. Perhaps the girls can be back prior to your wedding, which is …?"

"Four months from today," Daniel announced. "You'll be getting your invitation."

"I wouldn't miss that one for the world."

Hope stood from the table. "Thank you so much for seeing me through this."

"It's been my absolute pleasure." Dr. Bambridge hugged Hope. "I know you two will be happy and blessed in your marriage."

Hope

24

Two months later

Daniel pulled his car into the parking lot of Stephen Astor Interiors. He turned off the car and reached over to the seat for the wedding invitation his mother suggested he hand deliver after Elsa had knocked on Connie's door without being asked to enter. She'd left the invitation with the maid.

The receptionist greeted him with a smile and a "May I help you?"

"Yes, I'm here to see Mr. Astor."

She cast a look toward the closed door beside her desk.

"May I tell him who's calling?" She picked up her phone and waited for Daniel to relay the information.

"Daniel Duvall."

"And this regards …?"

None of her business. Daniel shook the errant thought away. "I'm here with an invitation to his daughter's wedding."

She pressed two numbers on the phone and waited. "Yes, Mr. Astor, there's a Daniel Duvall here. He says he has an invitation to your daughter's wedding to give you." As she spoke, she looked up at him, a crunch to her forehead.

A moment ticked by.

She put the phone down. "He'll be right with you."

After a few more moments, Stephen opened his office door. "Daniel, come in."

Daniel followed him inside.

"Sit down," Stephen offered. "I saw the announcement in the paper and the article on your medical group in the local business magazine. Seems life is looking rather rosy for you and Hope."

"I can't deny that. God has been good."

Stephen sat but seemed to pause at the mention of God. "How is she?"

"I would think you wouldn't have to ask if you'd picked up the phone and called her or visited her the way she said you promised. Hope's a woman now, but her heart is broken because every woman is a little girl who longs for her father's attention."

"I didn't want to burden her with what's going on with Connie and me."

Daniel leaned forward. "What is going on?"

Stephen sighed. "For all her bluster throughout the years about my worthlessness, seems that my business's net worth is more than hers. She wants a piece of the pie."

"So, you're quarreling over the assets."

"The woman is quarreling. I've offered her everything: the house and all that's in it, the stocks. I just want to start over and be shed of her."

Sadness fell over Daniel. The marriage of Hope's parents had come to an expected end, but Daniel prayed that God would give them the unexpected: a desire for each other that passed understanding.

"I can't understand it. All she ever did was complain about me and my choices. I was never good enough, and now she won't let me go in peace."

"Perhaps your leaving isn't what Connie wants at all."

Stephen laughed. "No. She hasn't been happy since Hope was born. Until then, she never chastised me about my business or my art. After Hope arrived, she seemed to think I didn't love her as much as I did Hope. Looking back, I see that she'd perverted that relationship—at least in her own mind. I doted on Hope because Connie wouldn't."

Daniel held out the invitation. "Well, Hope would love for you to dote on her one more time."

Stephen took the proffered card. "You'll make her understand. I don't feel as if I deserve to be at her wedding."

"Whether you feel you deserve to or not, would you have Hope miss out on the father she has always adored giving her away?"

"I don't know …"

Daniel stood. "I'm sorry about you and Connie. I do pray that you can find a way to love one another again."

Stephen half-laughed. "That's impossible, I think. I don't know that I'd ever want to go back to that type of environment. I don't want to live under her control for another minute."

"And you shouldn't. Perhaps if you meet with a marriage counselor, you'd come away with a deeper love for each other. Hope and I just finished counseling with our pastor. I'll be happy to recommend you."

Stephen laughed outright, and Daniel's face flamed with the heat of embarrassment. He was learning to trust God, but he hadn't gotten used to the naysayers.

"Connie and a pastor. Now, that's something I'd love to see. Not going to happen, Daniel."

"Then perhaps you could meet with him."

Stephen stayed silent for a long moment. Then he sighed. "I'll think about it."

"I'm meeting Hope and her friends for lunch at the nursery in about an hour. Would you like to join us then?"

Stephen reached out to shake Daniel's hand. "No. I think not."

"I'll tell Hope you said hello."

"I'd rather you not. I don't want her to get her hopes up that I'll be at the wedding."

Daniel thought about rescinding the invitation, leaving this place, and never uttering a word to Hope about it.

Daniel's mother had been working so hard with Hope on the wedding plans. Every time they left his parents' home, Daniel's heart broke for his bride-to-be as she looked with such longing to the house where she'd lived.

Lived? That's about all she'd done there. She'd been a tug-o-war rope between the two adults who'd given her life. The Duvall home had been the place she thrived, and she was thriving there again. Connie and Stephen Astor had made conscious decisions to leave their daughter out of their lives. He had hoped Stephen would come around, but the man disappointed him.

Hope had successfully talked Daniel's parents into attending church, and his mother and father were making friends there. Mom seemed happier than he'd ever seen her before, and her devotion to Hope was breathtaking.

"I'm sorry, Daniel," Stephen said. "I just have to do what I have to do."

Daniel blinked and nodded. "I am sorry for your losses, Mr. Astor, especially that of knowing a daughter's love."

He would have to pray for Hope's parents, leave them in the Lord's hands. Right now, he had an important appointment to keep. Then on to a family lunch at Happily Ever After.

And that's what he planned in life for him and for Hope … Happily Ever After.

Hope

25

Another two months later

Hope stood alone in the reception/bridal room to the right of the church's foyer. A lot of time had passed since she'd stood and primped in front of a mirror, if only because the ghastly image staring back at her made her flinch.

Today, though, the image was one she could never have imagined. Her silk off-white tulle and lace wedding gown flowed from the intricate collar over her newly constructed breasts and down her thin figure, accenting the curves she would never have developed short of the cancer. She turned to get a look at the open back. The trumpet-train was the perfect length. She ran her hand over the beaded sequence and took a deep breath.

She smiled at the image and touched her short red hair encircled by a tiara—her something borrowed given to her by Elsa, who said it would one day be hers to give to the daughter or daughter-in-law they were all trusting in God to provide—either by birth or by adoption. Hope smiled as the tiara gleamed, certain that its beauty would outshine the fact that her hair was a simple style due to its short length. The old Hope would have postponed a wedding for the hairstyle she'd always dreamed of for her wedding when she'd had the long flowing tresses. Not this Hope. She'd waited long enough for Dr. Duvall.

A rap at the door made her turn. Elsa entered. "I've got the men all straightened out."

"I bet you did," Hope said. "Where are the girls?"

"They're in the fellowship hall marveling at your wedding gifts for Daniel."

"Do you think he'll like them?"

"As much as the bridesmaids and groomsmen loved the paintings you gifted them with."

"But Danny's are special."

Elsa waved her off. "Honey, even if they were the ugliest things I'd ever seen, he'd see only beauty. Since I think they're beautiful, he's going love them."

Giggles sounded at the door and Libby, Charisse, and Delilah entered, dressed in their elegant pearl pink chiffon bride's maid dresses. All three wore their hair up with braids entwining, the same way Hope had always dreamed of wearing hers.

"Okay, line up," Delilah ordered. "Something old, something new, something borrowed—you already have that to-die-for tiara from Elsa—and I'm something blue."

Charisse stepped forward first. "Hope," she held out a pair of ivory cameo earrings, "I found these in an antique store years ago, and when we were trying on dresses, and I saw you in yours, they came to mind. They're my gift to you."

Hope hugged her. "I'll treasure them always."

Libby stepped up next. She brushed Hope's face with her hand. "You are so special to Evan and to me." She reached down into her purse and pulled out a small New Testament. She opened the book to the place marked by a simple pink ribbon. 1 Corinthians 13 is marked so that you can always return here when you need a refresher on what love is all about." She kissed Hope's cheek. "And you are loved Hope. Not only by Snarky Dr. Duvall, but by all of us."

Hope looked to the ceiling to keep the tears at bay. It wouldn't do to ruin her makeup. Libby's gentle reminder that even though her parents had not indicated they would come, Hope was still wrapped in the loves of her eclectic little family. "Thank you," she half-laughed and half-cried. "Now go away. I don't have time to do my makeup again."

Delilah smiled at her, hand behind her back. "Something blue. I'm it. Because you're leaving me. I never thought a roommate could survive living with me, but you and me, we just fit, didn't we?"

"We sure did," Hope agreed.

Delilah brought her clasped hand forward. A blue

tatted ribbon dangled from her fist. "I didn't expect Stephen or Connie to show today, but I know that despite their actions, you want them to be with you on your special day." She held out her hand and Hope gasped.

A small photo of her mother and father on their wedding day was framed in a simple plastic covering. Delilah had glued on a soft blue, tatted frame. Hope glanced to the only one among them who tatted. Libby blushed and turned away. "All right. Libby made the lace," Delilah admitted.

"Where did you get the picture?" Hope asked.

"I remembered you'd posted it on social media a few years ago, to wish them a happy anniversary. I took it off your page."

Hope hugged Delilah. "This is special, Dee. You are special to me."

Delilah waved her off and turned away. Charisse started to engulf their friend in a hug, but Dee pushed away. "I'm good. It's all good."

Hope had always loved the brash judge, but she'd seen so many facets of Delilah's personality throughout her illness, that she doubted she and Dee would ever drift apart.

Another knock sounded on the door. Charisse opened it and spoke. Then she turned to them. "In my husband's words, we need to get a move on."

Elsa was the first to leave so that an usher could walk her down the aisle.

Hope lingered in the room. Important people were

missing, but given all that she'd gone through without so much as a note of concern, she wasn't sure how she'd react if her parents did show.

She took in a trembling breath and picked up her bouquet of small pink and white roses. Her parents might never admit it, but they were going to be lost without one another.

"Hey, sweetheart," Jacob stood in the doorway. "How's my favorite gal doing?"

Hope offered him a genuine smile. "She's doing wonderful."

"Then let's get that scoundrel standing at the front of the church married off. What do you say?"

"I say, I love you and Elsa both so dearly. Thank you for being here for me." She slipped her arm in his.

"And we love the both of you. Thank you for not giving up on us while we grieved."

Hope squeezed his arm to let him know that she'd never held it against him and stepped to the door. She took a deep breath and thanked God once again for bringing her to this day.

A light touch on her shoulder caused her to turn.

Her father, eyes red and wet with tears, stood behind her.

Hope took a stuttering breath, willing the tears not to fall. "Daddy."

Her father looked from her to Jacob. "I know I don't deserve this honor, but I'd like to walk my little girl down the aisle."

Hope cast a glance to Jacob, but she didn't need to worry. Her soon-to-be father-in-law lifted her hand from his arm and tucked it in her father's. "As it should be, right, Hope?"

Hope kissed Jacob's cheek. "Thank you."

Jacob patted Stephen on the back. "I'm glad you're here." He stepped into the sanctuary.

"I'm glad I am, too." Her father wiggled shoulders that probably held a ton of guilt and shame.

Hope wouldn't add to it. She opened her hand and held out the picture Dee had so lovely given. "I was carrying you with me anyway."

Her father squeezed her arm. "Danny told me I was missing out on a daughter's love. Forgive me. This time I will keep my promise. You'll be seeing me so often, you both will be sick of me."

"Never, Daddy," Hope kissed his cheek.

The music sounded inside the sanctuary. Charisse smiled bright as she took the first step, followed by Libby and then Delilah.

"I'm sorry, Hope," her father whispered. "I should have been there for you."

"Just be there for me and for Daniel, Daddy. And let's continue to pray for Mother."

Her father let out a deep breath. "She will hate herself for missing this day. She often regrets her cast-iron decisions."

"Let's focus on the people here today and worry about Mother tomorrow." The music stopped, and Hope's wedding march began. Dresses and suits rustled as the wedding guest stood. "Today is too perfect for regret."

Daniel had peered at his father as he walked into the sanctuary without Daniel's bride. His father had motioned him to relax, as if he could.

He gave the sanctuary door his full attention as Charisse was the first one in the processional followed by Libby and then by Hope's maid-of-honor, Delilah. Then, with the music playing, Hope walked the aisle on the arm of her father. Daniel closed his eyes and thanked God for the answer to his fervent prayer.

His bride beamed at her father before turning her gaze to Daniel.

His breath caught. They'd gone through so much to get to this one moment that would give them a lifetime together. The mischievous girl he'd always loved had grown into a woman he admired, a woman he wanted more than life itself.

Daniel met his bride and her father as they stepped to the center of the aisle. "Who gives this woman to be married?" the pastor asked.

"I do." Stephen stepped back and shook Daniel's hand. Then he placed Hope's hand in Daniel's before taking a seat on the opposite aisle from Daniel's parents.

Daniel and Hope stepped before the pastor—their pastor. Never had Daniel imagined that he'd be in a church that was so dear to him, wedding the only woman he'd ever loved, seriously taking his vow before the God he'd grown to realize had always been there for him.

He clasped Hope's hands in his. *Thank You, Father, for this oh, so precious gift You have bestowed upon me. This gift of being Hope's husband. I'll treasure her always.*

The vows, now so much more meaningful to him because they had both promised to keep God in the center of their marriage, were spoken and rings exchanged.

"Daniel, you may kiss your lovely bride."

Daniel didn't need coaxing. He brushed Hope's face with a tender caress and leaned to brush his lips against hers. She put her arms around his neck, and he kissed her deeper, leaving her with a promise of more to come. "I love you, Mrs. Duvall."

"And I love you, Dr. Duvall."

The pastor held up his hands. "I present to you Dr. and Mrs. Daniel Duvall. May you go with God's love surrounding you."

With the formal wedding pictures taken at Libby's nursery next to the church, Daniel and Hope entered the decorated fellowship hall. He greeted their guests with

Hope by his side, conscious that Hope was leading him forward.

The crowd had hushed as they neared the front of the hall where Gideon and Evan stood next to two covered easels. "What have you done?" He eyed his wife.

"Surprise!" she clapped as the two men lifted the cloths.

Danny's eyes widened. How had he forgotten he'd asked her to do this? How had she remembered? She'd been sedated—sleeping in ICU when he'd made the request.

Hope had painted the two scenes he'd commissioned. He took in the first, a picture similar to the Riviera she'd painted, which had been removed from the office and was now in his home—their home. Only, in this new rendering, a young girl with red flowing tresses leaned back in the embrace of a dark haired young man. They were locked in a kiss for the ages. Daniel blushed at the memory and the realization that the woman in his arms in the painting would never again feel as he'd made her feel that night long ago. Looking at the painting he could almost imagine they'd never lost time.

"I'm so—"

Hope must have anticipated his apology. She put her finger to his lips. "God is in the details," she whispered and led him to the second portrait.

The carousel was alive with color. Hope had captured the colorful spectacle, the horses, and the three individuals.

She'd depicted Tiffany on one horse and her on the other. Daniel stood between them, smiling as if posing for a camera. He reached out and touched his sister's face on the canvas. "She'd be so happy for us."

"I have a feeling she is happy for us." Hope slipped her hand in his. "I hope to paint more pictures of us as we grow old together. If God allows us to have children, I will paint them at every stage."

Daniel kissed her and held her tight. "I can't wait to see our future unfold."

Daniel had asked Hope where she wanted to honeymoon. She'd thought of the Riviera or some of the other places they'd visited with his family. Memories would linger there, and she wanted her new life to be special just for them. Cheesy as it was, she'd asked him to take her to Niagara Falls, but the flight out wasn't until the next day. They would spend the night in his home—her home now that the family had helped her move in the day before.

She closed her eyes and leaned back, tired from the day's activities as the light faded into dusk.

"Hope." Danny's voice broke through her sleep.

She startled awake. "Goodness. I can't believe I went to sleep." She blinked and looked around her. They were not in the garage or in the driveway of their home. "Where are we?"

Daniel opened her door and helped her out.

"You've got to be kidding." She laughed, her eyes wide. Night was falling, and the fairgrounds were alive with the laughter and call of people, the screams from the midway, and with the roar of the carnival rides. "Danny, we're still in our wedding clothes."

"Exactly as I planned it." He wiggled his hands.

"There are people. They'll stare."

Again, he wiggled his hands. "Where's that adventurous spirit?"

She grabbed hold of his hand and let him pull her onto the Central Florida Fairgrounds. The crowd parted as they passed. People whistled and hooted calls. Hope waved and laughed as they rushed forward.

Then Danny stopped.

Hope's heart fell when she saw their destination. The carousel was dark, not moving.

Danny held up his hand. "You have to say the magic words."

"I don't know them."

"Yes, you do. Tiffany wrote them on the picture."

"I've got you?" she asked.

"No, say it like you mean it. Look me in the eyes, and we'll repeat them together."

Hope's throat clogged with emotion. "I've got you."

"I've got you," Daniel repeated. "Say it with me."

Their voices rang the three words out in harmony, and

Hope

Daniel lowered his hand.

The carousel lit up and began to turn. The music, slow at first, began to sound. Danny pulled her along. He waited for her to jump aboard and then he followed.

He lifted Hope up onto the horse.

Hope leaned back, feeling the slight breeze in the air. People gathered around the carousel, but Hope didn't care.

"Hope," Danny raised up.

She leaned down.

His lips touched hers, light at first, and then deeper, claiming possession she never wanted him to relinquish.

The crowd looking on cheered.

Daniel kissed her neck and then his lips brushed her cheek. "Now and always, whatever may come, I've got you," he whispered. "Always."

We're confident hope you enjoyed *HOPE*.
Please consider returning to the Amazon page and
leaving a short review and hopefully 5 stars.

Study Questions

1. Before Hope came to know the Lord, she would have said that she had hope. Afterward, when all that is familiar and secure to her, her family, her home, even her well-being, is stripped from her, how is true hope manifested? Was her hope now in life or in whatever God desired for her?

> Psalm 22:9: "But thou art He that took me out of the womb: thou didst make me hope when I was upon my mother's breasts."
>
> Psalm 71:5: "Thou art my hope, O Lord God: Thou art my trust from my youth."
>
> Psalm 71:14: "But I will hope continually and will yet praise Thee more and more."
>
> Proverbs 14:26: "In the fear of the Lord is strong confidence: and his children shall have a place of refuge."

2. Hope's heart seems to rest on Tiffany so much so that she dreams about her often, and those dreams always take her to one particular place that holds a special place in Hope's heart. Why do you think Hope's dreams take her to that place? What is Hope truly seeking there? Can she find it in that location?

3. Psalm 103 declares,

"Bless the Lord, O my soul: and all that is within me, bless His holy name. Bless the Lord, O my soul, and forget not all His benefits: Who forgiveth all thine iniquities; Who healeth all thy diseases; Who redeemeth thy life from destruction; Who crowneth thee with lovingkindness and tender mercies; Who satisfieth thy mouth with good things; so that thy youth is renewed like the eagle's. The Lord executeth righteousness and judgment for all that are oppressed ... The Lord is merciful and gracious, slow to anger, and plenteous in mercy. He hath not dealt with us after our sins; nor rewarded us according to our iniquities. For as the heaven is high above the earth, so great is His mercy toward them that fear Him. As far as the east is from the west, so far hath He removed our transgressions from us. Like as a father pitieth his children, so the Lord pitieth them that fear Him. For He knoweth our frame ... But the mercy of the Lord is from everlasting to everlasting upon them that fear Him ..."

As an author, I want to be clear that I do not seek dreams or visions for answers from God. Nor do I look for a dream or a vision to provide answers from God. I believe that God's answers are always found in His word. I do believe, though, that God can use a dream to speak to His beloveds, but that dream should always align with Scripture if it is to be considered an answer from God.

In light of the Psalmists declaration, though, what could Hope have learned about God's redemption and His love for her from the progression of the dreams she had?

4. Ephesians 6:1-4 says,

> "Children, obey your parents in the Lord: for this is right. Honour thy father and mother; which is the first commandment with promise; That it may be well with thee, and thou mayest live long on the earth. And, ye fathers, provoke not your children to wrath: but bring them up in the nurture and admonition of the Lord."

Hope and Daniel both have lessons to learn about honoring one's parents, and the question is raised about honoring and obeying a parent, especially in light of an adult child. How did both Daniel and Hope honor their parents in the story? Did their parents always deserve honor (careful, that's a trick question)?

About the Author

Fay Lamb writes emotionally charged stories that remind the reader that God is always in the details. Three of the four books in the Amazing Grace romantic suspense series are available: *Stalking Willow*, *Better than Revenge*, and *Everybody's Broken*. *Hope* is the third book in The Ties that Bind Series, which also includes *Charisse* and *Libby*. Fay's adventurous spirit has also taken her into the realm of non-fiction with The Art of Characterization: How to Use the Elements of Storytelling to Connect Readers to an Unforgettable Cast.

Future releases from Fay will be: *Frozen Notes*, Book 4 of the Amazing Grace series, and *Delilah*, Book 4 from The Ties that Bind.

Fay loves to meet readers, and you can find her on her personal Facebook page, her Facebook Author page, and at The Tactical Editor on Facebook. She's also active on Twitter. Then there are her blogs: On the Ledge, Inner Source, and the Tactical Editor, and Goodreads

Note to My Readers

Today, when I was asked by my editor if I had a word for my readers, I realized that I had been pondering words for several days. I had not known, though, that the words were for you—those who read my books and give me such encouragement. I thought God was urging me to sort out some deep emotion that has caused me to sit and cry, seemingly for no reason—at least not one that had surfaced enough that I could grasp the meaning.

Recently, I saw a post from someone on Facebook. Sadly, or maybe by design, I do not remember the writer's name, but oh how I remember the depth of her question, which went something like this: "As a writer do you ever feel so lonesome yet you do not desire the company of others?"

I had an answer, which fell from my lips very quickly and without much thought. "Yes."

For me, this had nothing to do with being an introvert or an extrovert. I am at times both and neither. My makeup is such that I do require lengthy times of solitude. Being alone does not bother me. What does bother me is that often in my solitude I do not think of others ... or maybe I think so much that I fear.

"What do you fear?" You might ask. "Is it what they will say? What they will think of you?"

After pondering the question of my fellow writer, whose name is still unknown to me but for whose heart I do sorrow, I concluded that for me the answer is, "I'm afraid of loss. I am afraid of losing someone I love. I am afraid, then, when I have lost the person I love, and I have not shown the love I truly felt for that person, that I have failed that person. I am afraid that at some time, at some place in my life, that I may have hurt the person I have now lost and that I will never be able to make things right with that person who holds such an intimate piece of my heart, whether that person be family or friend or even an acquaintance.

With the astute author's question coming so soon upon the writing of Hope and several months after the loss of several very dear people to me, and the impending and daily loss of someone I love like a mother, the question hit me like a load of bricks being dropped from heaven above. (I'm so glad that God uses Acme products. *Beep beep.*)

Just like that, Hope's story and God allowing me to see into the precious heart of someone I do not know, who hurts in a way possibly similar to mine, gave me hope—not for those who have already left me but for me to offer hope to those who remain. There are those in Hope's life she can never apologize to or again have the opportunity to declare her love. There are those in the story, though, that Hope can hold to for dear life and pour her love into with a kind word or a hug or Scripture to ease their way.

So, to you, dear reader, I pray that God, through a story that He has allowed me to write, gives you a gentle reminder that there are those who need your love, and in your love, they might find hope to carry on day by day.

Also by Fay Lamb

You've enjoyed Hope's story. Now see how the friendships began ...

Read about Charisse and Libby and keep a lookout for

Delilah - coming soon!

Delilah debuted as the antagonist that all the readers learned to love, and she describes herself best, "Being a lying deceiver wasn't too much fun. I thought I'd try the honest, direct route. I like it much better." But now, her friend, Hope, has a man in mind for her, and the once lying deceiver finds the honest, direct route might just get in the way of happily-ever-after.

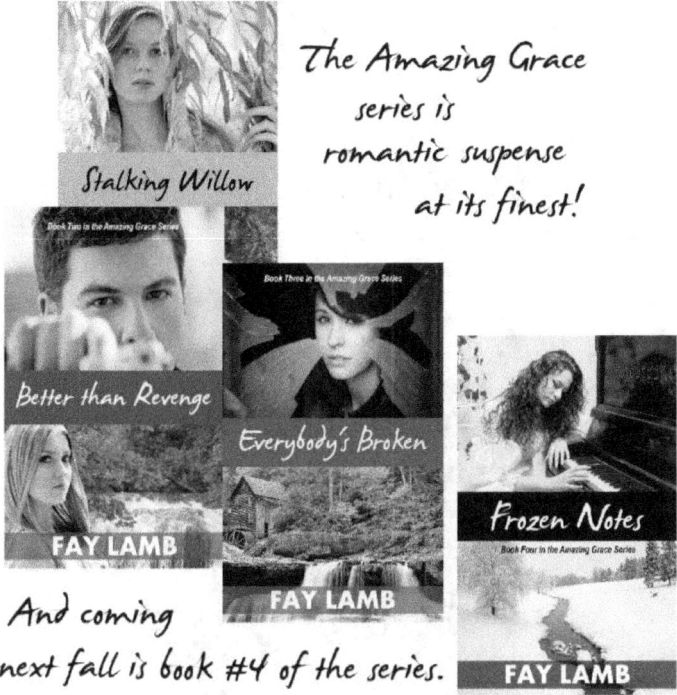

The Amazing Grace series is romantic suspense at its finest!

Stalking Willow

Better than Revenge

Everybody's Broken

Frozen Notes

And coming next fall is book #4 of the series.

Lyric Moxley had dreams of being the keyboardist for her boyfriend, Balaam Carter's band. Instead, Balaam leaves her pregnant and alone to revel in life as a rock star. Desperate to believe Balaam's brother's promise of love and protection, Lyric marries Braedon, but he fails to keep his promise to raise Balaam's child as his own, and Braedon's demons, make Lyric's life a nightmare.

After an dangerous overdose, Balaam gives his life to God. News arrives that Braedon has murdered a friend and committed suicide, leaving Lyric a pawn between rival drug lords and making her an FBI suspect. With rehab on hold, will Balaam remain sober, resolve the problems his selfish dreams caused, regain Lyric's trust, and earn his son's love?

Recently Released from Write Integrity Press

Political scandal surrounds the whirlwind romance of beautiful Shawna Moore and Tennessee governor, Hunter Wilson. If the wrong people begin asking questions about Shawna's baby, Hunter's chances for reelection, as well as Shawn's reputation, will be ruined.

But the secret they're guarding is destroying their marriage.

Coming Soon from
Write Integrity Press

Strange people and mysterious events at a wilderness therapy camp trigger an avalanche of deception, landing Haven Ellingsen in a hidden mountain cabin, prisoner of a dangerous and delusional captor.

**Thank you
for reading our books!**

**Look for other books
published by**

Write Integrity Press

www.WriteIntegrity.com

www.ingramcontent.com/pod-product-compliance
Lightning Source LLC
Chambersburg PA
CBHW070552260626
47161CB00002B/577